The Pecan Trees

a novel

KRISTINA MOORE

The
Pecan
Trees

a novel

Kristina Moore

For the family I came from and the family to come.

1

THE MY LITTLE Pony poster was still above her bed. Her mom had put it there when she was four. The tape was now yellowing and peeling at the edges. Her eyes fluttered, heavy with exhaustion while she twisted her diamond ring around her finger, clasping her hand when it was in her palm and stretching her hand when it was on the outside of her finger. It was loose. Loose enough for her to wonder why her fiancé was so off the mark. They had been together for long enough. Surely he had known her fingers were smaller than a bratwurst.

Her head sunk into the stack of stuffed animals guarding her pillow, fluffy feet and arms poking her in the face as she tried to ignore the scratching of the dog outside the master bedroom door. She could hear him whining, which he'd been doing all week. She didn't care for dogs, but this one was her dad's and she had some obligation now.

This moment was the first peace and quiet she'd had in two days. Her father's funeral was hard enough without her mother or fiancé beside her, but the wake was exhausting. She was filled with gratitude for the abundance of people who had come to say a final goodbye to her father and in the same breath welcomed her back to town. They bombarded her with, "Look at how grown you are . . . Your dad would have been so proud . . . How long has it been?" She'd answered so many times that she wasn't sure how it wasn't small town gossip by now. When people said, "I remember when you were born," or, "You look so grown", she'd smile and nod, doing her best not to reveal that she did not, in fact, know who they were.

She lay in her bed, pressing her fingers to her eyes, making swirls of purple and orange on the backs of her eyelids, desperately trying to remember the last few days she had spent in this house. If she had known it was going to be the last time, maybe she would have tried a little harder to hold on to the memory. She knew it was right before her fifteenth birthday, but the memories of the house were like a passing train: they came and went, leaving some little passengers or flickers of information here and there. Her mind started to get foggy and she knew she was drifting off. She quickly rubbed her face and shook her legs.

The sound of little clicks pacing the hallway startled her for a minute until she remembered the dog, Rusty. *A fitting name,* she thought, given his wiry, yellow-orange hair that resembled a two-year-old dish brush with two beady, black eyes..

"Come here, Rusty," she called. The clicks stopped for a moment and she called again. She heard him coming toward her door and then he nosed his way into her room and jumped up on her bed, straight onto her chest. Lucky for her he was only about the size of a bigger-than-normal rat. She scratched him on his head and he licked her face, sticking his slimy tongue in between her lips. "Ugh." She wiped off her mouth. He tried again. *Persistent little thing,* she thought. His collar and tags looked new. She gently grabbed the tags and Rusty resisted, trying to gnaw her hand. *The rabies is up to date,* she noticed. When she grabbed the bone-shaped tag that said "Rusty" on it, she turned it over to reveal a phone number she imagined to be her father's. Curious, she grabbed her phone and dialed the number. It went straight to voicemail.

"Hi, you've reached Peter Webber with Webber Furniture. Um, leave a message and I'll call you back." She clicked off the phone before the beep.

"Dad," she whispered. She stretched her legs long and arms up high, stretching and waking her body. She rolled to her left, swung her legs off the side of the bed, and made herself get up; she had too much to do. This house was hers now, along with the few acres that came with it. That meant a lot of work going through the packed closets and overflowing shed, dealing with whatever neglect to the property that her father had left for her, and then heading to his furniture shop, pretending to know what was supposed to happen next.

The shop had twelve employees—eleven now that her dad was gone—but most of them had been there for more than fifteen years, and some of them as long as her dad, Peter, who had taken it over from his father thirty-one years ago.

When she walked out of her room and headed to the stairway, Rusty went to the master bedroom door and looked at her.

She sighed. "Not yet, I'm not ready." He whined and followed her to the stairway.

Step by step, her hand passed over the wooden railing, which was smooth from years of passing hands. Just then, a memory landed in her mind: her mother always waiting for her at the bottom of the steps, arms stretched out, and a smile like she hadn't seen her in days. Jayne sighed.

The kitchen smelled of grease and cardboard from the few days of takeout containers sitting on the counter. She looked at the dishes piled in the sink, opened up the cupboard underneath, and pulled out a trash bag, haphazardly throwing out plastic plates and empty pizza boxes. Quickly the counters became less cluttered and she noticed something she hadn't seen before. On the kitchen table sat a quiche with a note written on her father's furniture shop stationary.

It read,

> *Jayne,*
>   *I figured you might be too busy to cook with everything going on . . . and evidently I was right. I made a quiche Lorraine for you. Sorry I let myself in – I got here before you. We wanted to drop off the spare key too.*
>   *X Liz*

Jayne picked up the key, feeling the cold metal in her palm, as if it would hold some clue as to who Liz could be. She did remember a shorter lady with cropped blond hair and a sweet face. She'd been with her husband, Joe Martin, Peter's partner and best friend, and their son, Luke. Joe was the opposite of Liz: tall and sturdy with a dark complexion. *Built like a tree,* Jayne had thought. *They mentioned they would stop by to give back the key later.*

Jayne studied the quiche. She smelled the crust and the scent of baked egg filled her nose. She mentally probed her stomach for its level of hunger. There was a half-clean fork on the counter and she pressed it into the crust, causing flakes to break off onto the table. The first bite was so good she took a seat and didn't stop until she was over a quarter of the way through. She would have kept going if her phone hadn't started to ring.

"Hey Mom." She shoved a small lingering piece of crust into her mouth, chewing slowly.

"Hey honey, how are you?"

"I'm okay. Just tired. Trying to clean up a bit." Jayne looked around at the kitchen, ashamed of how messy it was.

"Oh, don't worry about that, honey. You've been dealing with a lot." Jayne could hear her mom smiling on the other end.

"I wish you could have been here with me. You should have seen all the people who came out today." Jayne pressed her finger into the flaked crust on the table and nibbled it off her fingertip.

"I know. I wish I could have too. You know your grandmother, though. She's not doing well. But the good news is that I will be flying out tomorrow. I'll send you the flight info. Uncle Anthony is going to stay with your grandma."

"That's great news. She's okay with that?"

"Yes, *she* demanded I come out and be with you—her 'last dying wish' she said. I told her that wasn't funny. When is Blake coming out?" Dani changed the subject.

"He's supposed to be arriving tomorrow at—" Jayne looked at her phone. "Hey, can I call you back? He's calling right now."

"Someone's ears are burning. Talk to you soon, love you."

"Love you." Jayne switched calls. "Hey, hon."

"Hey baby, how are you holdin' up?" Blake's deep southern accent was like a hot bath on Jayne's tired body.

"I'm better now that everything is over. Just wish

you were here." Jayne pushed her chair back and picked up the quiche and placed it along the other clutter taking up counter space. She searched for a new piece of plastic wrap, but with no avail, stretched and tucked the old one over the top the best she could. Rusty was behind her licking up any stray pieces of crust that fell to the ground.

"About that, um, I have some bad news." Jayne didn't say anything. "Hello? Jayne?"

"What now, Blake?" she said with ice in her voice.

"Well" — he cleared his throat — "Ralph took on a new client and he wants me to head the meeting and you know how this — "

"Could be great for your career. Yeah, I know." Jayne's stomach felt tight as her face flushed. *I should be happy for him,* she thought. "I'm sorry, that's great. I could just really use someone here, you know?"

"Did Natasha or Claire call you?"

"No, why?"

"They said they would call to see how you were."

"Oh," Jayne replied, not surprised they hadn't called. All her city friends were superficial and only really friends of convenience, thanks to Blake. Her friends from school texted her almost every day though. "I still wish I had someone here to deal with all of this. It's been a lot harder than I thought it was going to be."

"I thought you weren't that close with your dad?"

Jayne nearly gasped and choked on her breath. "He was my *dad,* Blake. You may have never met him, but he was my dad. I know you're not close with your family at all, so you wouldn't understand."

"You're right. I'm really sorry. When's your mom coming out?" he diverted.

"Tomorrow. Grandma's not doing well, I guess." She leaned on the sink, looking out the window, scanning the land at the back of the house. It was long but not wide, surrounded by trees and divided by a small creek close to the house.

"I'm sorry to hear that. I should be coming out the day after her then and I can help. Thank you for understanding."

"Mm-hmm. I'll talk to you later, I've got a lot to do around here."

"Okay, babe, I love you."

"Love you too." Jayne hung up the phone and stuck it in her back pocket. She took a deep breath and walked to the sliding glass doors leading to the deck. A sawed-off broomstick sat in the sliding doorframe acting as a back-up security feature. She popped it out and the door slid open. The October air around her was cool and dry, providing some relief from the Texas humidity. The air smelled fresh, like brand new air, with some old grass and the smell of someone burning wood nearby.

With her shoes still on, she pulled her cardigan off the back of the kitchen chair and stepped outside. Rusty tried to follow her, but she shooed him back inside with the promise of a treat later. She was unsure if he would take off or stay beside her.

Across the creek stood the old house she was never allowed to go to. To her right she could see the little bridge her grandfather had made to cross the creek and she started toward it. The beaten path to the house was long gone. It was the first house on this property, built by who she believed was her three-times great-grandfather. She had always wanted to play in the house, but her parents never allowed it.

She crossed the bridge and waded through the tall grass, careful not to get her pants dirty. From the big house, it looked like a black and white photo placed in the yellow grass, but once she got closer more details became apparent. The chipping paint and rotting wood stood out; it made her feel sad to think something could be so neglected. The roof was starting to droop like a wet sheet hung over two chairs, the pillars framing up the porch were leaning toward the south from the years of the dominant wind coming from the northwest. The leftover memories seemed to be the only thing holding the building upright; it stood as a reminder of what once was and now was just left to be forgotten. *If walls could talk,* Jayne thought.

She stood in front of the porch and looked down at the old walkway, smelling the scent of old wood, wet plaster, and moist grass. The stones laid as a make-shift sidewalk were broken, allowing the shoots of grass and small weedy flowers to push through the cracks. She approached the house silently. The energy drawing her had not ceased — if anything, it got stronger. A few steps more and she found herself on the porch where two wooden rocking chairs sat next to each other promising someone's return. The front door was missing as if to say, "Welcome home, come on in." Jayne took cautious steps to peek inside. It opened into a small living area with two dividing walls at the back, leaving an opening into the kitchen. She stepped over the threshold, pushing each board with her foot before letting her weight fall. Each step sounded like an old toad squeaking beneath her feet. Other than the two rocking chairs on the porch, there was no more furniture inside the house. Wallpaper was peeling off from years of humidity and heat. Termites had gotten a good feast out of this place and she didn't need an inspection to tell her that; the floorboards looked like Swiss cheese and if it wasn't for the sheetrock, the beams would look the same. On paper, the house should have been falling apart, but it felt almost as strong as if it was just built.

Jayne walked through the living room into the kitchen. The sunlight came in from both sides of the kitchen, allowing for brightness that no light bulb would be able to match. The appliances, if there had been any, were all removed and the cabinets seemed to be in good shape, so she peeked in a couple. Nothing was left but a few dead bugs. Texas heat and humidity mingling with old carpentry left a smell like an old antique store that had been left in a rain forest. It smelled of damp wood and old, sun-heated linoleum. She pulled on a drawer, but it wouldn't budge. A couple more yanks and the swollen wood squeaked open in protest. She peered in and to her surprise there were a few scattered utensils. Another drawer revealed an old bottle with no label and two small glasses. Jayne grabbed the bottle. It felt cold and heavy in her hand and was filled with a golden liquid, slightly amber in color. She held it up to the window, letting the afternoon sun stream through. *Whiskey?* she thought. *This has to be at least forty years old.* She unscrewed the cap and took a small sniff. *Yup, whiskey — or something like it.* She coughed and contemplated taking a swig. Instead she closed the drawer and turned to more cupboards on the back wall. A few more drawers turned up empty and when she got to the hallway leading to the rooms, something caught her eye: legs. Legs attached to someone sitting in the hall. Her heart started to race and her own legs started to feel wobbly. She searched the countertops for anything that could be used as a weapon.

The bottle of whiskey. She took it out of the drawer again. Holding it up, ready to knock someone over the head, she shouted, "You can't be in here!" giving the vagrant space to escape if need be. "This is my family's home."

"*You* can't be in here. This is *my* family's home," he retorted.

It's just a boy. She lowered the bottle and peeked around the corner. It *was* a teenager, about seventeen.

But he was not dressed modernly; he was wearing a plain, cream-colored shirt tucked into dark brown pants, his shoes were old and worn but leather and looked like they were from about the 1920s or earlier. *What in the world is this?* she asked herself. The boy's legs were drawn to his chest and his head was resting on his crossed arms.

"Who are you? What are you doing here?" she asked.

"I told you, this is—" He looked up and stared at Jayne, mouth open. His hands fell to the floor beside him. "Bunny?"

Jayne paused for a second. She was about to tell him he had the wrong person, but as the words rose to her throat, a childhood memory came rushing into her mind and almost caused her knees to collapse. She grasped for the counter, missed, and settled for the edge of the wall. Billy.

1997

Four-year-old Jayne lay awake in her bed, watching the moonlight play off the dream catcher she had hung in the corner.

"Billy?" Jayne's small hands brushed her hair out of her face.

"Yes, Bunny?"

"What are you?"

"Darling, I've told you: I'm a spirit."

"Mama says people are afraid of spirits."

"Well, yes, sometimes. People are usually afraid of what they can't explain. You don't have to be afraid of me though."

"I'm not." Jayne paused. "Billy?"

"Yes?"

"Why do you call me Bunny? You know my name is Jayne." She drew out the "e" at the end and slipped her hands into the Little Mermaid pillowcase right below her cheek. This was a sure sign she was about to fall sleep. Her heavy eyes blinked heavily and flickered open when there was a crash downstairs.

They are at it again, Billy thought. He lay on the floor next to Jayne's bed, staring at the wooden beams in the ceiling and rocking the empty wooden chair with his foot. Twelve loud thumps made their way up the stairs and passed the door.

"Because it's short for 'honey-bunny' and you used to hate when I called you honey," he whispered.

"When I was a baby you mean?" Twelve softer thumps followed but stopped outside her door.

"Shhhh. Yes, something like that. Go to sleep now," Billy said.

The doorknob squeaked as it turned, the mechanism clicked and the door opened with ease. Billy stopped the chair from rocking just as Dani opened the door. She peeked her head in and looked straight at the slowing chair. She couldn't see Billy, but he froze in place anyway. Dani squeezed her body through the small opening, knowing the door would creak if it opened any farther. She made a mental note to put some WD-40 on it tomorrow. Jayne's sleepy eyes were peeking out from her comforter.

"Who are you talking to?" she asked. She looked toward the chair. "Were you playing in the chair again?"

"No, Mama," Jayne said. Billy smiled and nodded at her.

Dani assumed Jayne was telling a fib. She walked

over to the bed and knelt down in front of her, barely missing Billy's arm.

"Okay, well it's time to go to sleep my love, so please shut your eyes and try. You have an appointment tomorrow and then it's your birthday in a couple days. You're going to be five. But what happens to little girls who don't behave before their birthday?" Dani asked teasingly as she brushed a stray blond ringlet from Jayne's face. Jayne could smell the sweet scent of Dani's patchouli and vanilla body spray. It made her eyelids feel heavy with comfort.

As if it had been drilled into her, Jayne replied, "They don't get all the toys they asked for."

"That's right. Now close your eyes." Jayne squeezed her eyes shut so tightly her little nose scrunched and her lips pursed. Dani turned her head toward the sound of boots in the hall and pushed off her knees to head toward the door. "Goodnight, my love."

"Night Mama."

Billy and Jayne could hear the voices outside the door arguing about something in a lowered tone. Billy started singing "Twinkle Twinkle Little Star" and didn't stop until he heard Peter and Dani go back downstairs.

2017

"Jayne?" Billy asked again "You okay?"

Jayne blinked really hard and opened her eyes. He was still sitting there. *I'm losing it,* she thought. "Are you real? I mean, you can't be *real,* but are you really here?"

"Very much," Billy replied, standing up for more presence. "Well, as much as a ghost can be, I suppose.

And you're not losing it."

"You can read my . . ." *Well of course he can.* Jayne felt a conflicting sense of comfort and relief but also worry for her mental health. He looked real, he wasn't see-through like a stereotypical ghost and he looked exactly the same as he did when she was here last.

"Don't tell me you've forgotten about me already," Billy said, a corner of his mouth turning up in a half smile that only showed one dimple.

"Well, I guess . . . I don't know. I was fifteen last time I was here and ten years coupled with therapy can do a lot to convince someone that they have a strong imagination."

"Has it really been that long? Wow," Billy exclaimed. He scratched his head, which wiggled his hat out of place. He straightened it. "I guess being dead really does affect one's perception of time." He shook his head and patted down the back of his hair. "And, you're almost right—that bottle of whiskey is from around 1972."

"How'd you—" Jayne cut herself off. "If you can read my thoughts, why didn't you say anything when I was in the house, before I found you? Or why didn't you come to the house when I got here a week ago? Surely you heard or felt me?" She watched him walk toward the front door and followed him out to the porch where he gestured for her to sit. She hesitated, testing the strength of the porch boards with her foot.

"I guess I've been in a bit of a breeze since your dad . . . it's not going to fall to pieces, trust me. I know who built it." He smirked.

Jayne sat down and he sat in the other chair. Neither of them spoke for a few moments and just looked out toward the big house. "How long have you been here?" she asked.

"Oh, boy." Billy blew some air out of his puffed

cheeks and looked up thoughtfully. "Depends what year it is, but I'd say at least ninety-five years."

"No, I mean, here in this house, where you were sitting."

"Oh. Well, I'm not entirely sure." Billy looked at her. "I guess since your dad died. After Joe and the paramedics came and left, I came out here and sat myself in that corner. I'm sorry Jayne. I really am. Is that why you're here?"

Jayne nodded and took a deep breath. "I'm the only survivor of the Webber family now." Billy nodded slowly and cleared his throat — a habit from his physical years. Jayne shifted and looked at Billy. "Is my dad here too?" she asked excitedly.

"No, I'm afraid not, Bunny." Billy felt weird calling her that after all these years apart, and now, as she was a grown woman. "Not all deceased choose to come back into the spiritual life. He might eventually, but for now, it's just me."

Jayne nodded again, as if she understood. "Did you see he got a dog? Crazy-haired little thing. I've never seen something like it before. I don't know what I think of him yet. I think he misses Dad."

"Yes, Rusty. That little devil hates me. Whenever I would come by, he would just bark and stare at me. Or he'd run after me until I left the house. I think your dad thought he was going crazy and would shout at him, threatening to give him away, but of course he never did. He loved that little thing."

"What's funny is that Dad said he would never get another pet after the cat fiasco." Jayne laughed, remembering when her parents brought her home a cat. It relieved itself all over the house and Jayne was allergic, so they had to get rid of it.

"Please, tell me what you've been up to in all these

years. You're obviously a lot older. What have you done?"

Jayne smiled, feeling a little more comfortable. She relaxed into the chair and started to gently rock. "Well, you know that Mom and I moved to North Carolina after the divorce. I stayed there after I graduated high school and went to college and got my degree in fine arts with a minor in history. I worked in a library and helped the genealogists while I went to school. I would paint in my free time and started with a few showings at small galleries, then started selling to corporations and businesses. I got quite a following of prestigious clients and that's how I met Blake, my fiancé." She showed him her ring. "He worked at the law firm of one of the first businesses that purchased one of my pieces."

"He's a lawyer there?"

"He is." Jayne said proudly. "He had just graduated when I met him."

"That's wonderful. How are your mom and your grandmother? I always liked both of them very much."

Jayne's smile disappeared. "Grandma isn't doing well, she has lung cancer and doesn't seem to be getting any better. Mom is good. She's been taking care of Grandma since she got sick, but she's coming out tomorrow, actually."

"I'm sorry to hear that about your grandmother. She was a wonderful lady. How long have you been with Blake?"

"For a few years now. Took him awhile, but he just proposed a few weeks ago." Jayne paused to chuckle through her nose. "Dad would have hated him, he was too perfect, not relaxed or blue-collar enough. Actually, I'm sure Dad wouldn't have approved of much of the way I live now." She laughed.

"That's great, Jayne." Billy's said. "Marriage can be a

wonderful thing once you've found the right person."
He smiled at her.

"You were married, right? I remember you telling
me you had a wife."

"Evelyn Rose Carter. That was her name when I met
her. She was something else."

"What was she like?" Jayne smiled, encouraging
him to continue.

Billy was taken slightly off guard; Jayne had never
asked about Evelyn before. He eyed her suspiciously
for a moment and started tentatively. "She was the
most beautiful woman you would ever meet, inside
and out. Very much like you and your mother; she
always put everyone else first."

"Were you married for a long time? How did you
meet her?"

"Well, we were married many years in life and even
longer after death. Evelyn had stayed with me as a
spirit too, which is rare. We were very young when
we got married, much younger than people who get
married now. We met because I worked for her father
in the lumberyard. I was seventeen—the same age I
chose for my spiritual body—what you see now. Her
dad wanted us to meet. But see, Mr. Carter wasn't much
of a looker and had quite a few extra pounds to carry
around, so I wasn't in a hurry to meet his daughter."
Billy and Jayne both laughed.

"I also didn't think I was in the right class to be with
someone like her. My dad owned the furniture shop at
that point, but we weren't wealthy by any means. But
one day Mr. Carter had forgotten his lunch at home, so
Evelyn was beckoned to bring it to him. I was outside
cleaning the windows when she walked up. I can still
picture her wearing her light-blue dress with short
sleeves, a tiny bit of white lace around the collar and
sleeves. She looked like—what's that girl in that movie

you used to like? Oh, Sleeping Beauty. Her blond hair was in curls flowing over her shoulders. I must have been staring because she stopped and waved. I thought she was waving at someone behind me so I turned around to look and she laughed. Just then Mr. Carter came out and was quick to introduce us. I can still remember when she took hold of my fingers in greeting — the vision of a lady.

"That wasn't the end for us though, no ma'am. I knew where Mr. Carter lived, and on weekends I would ride my bike around her neighborhood in hopes she would come out."

"Did she?" Jayne asked.

"She did. And you know what? She chased *me* down on her bike." Billy laughed at the memory, which made Jayne chuckle too. "She must have saw me and before I knew it, she was peddling like a mad woman to catch up to me, shouting, 'Billy, Billy!' " He waved his arms like a monkey and raised his voice an octave for dramatic effect.

Jayne laughed. "What did you do?"

"I did what any sensible boy would do when a lady is chasing him: I slammed on my breaks and waited for her to catch up." Billy shifted in his chair. "Listen, if a man doesn't wait for you Bunny, you always let him go." Billy rocked his chair, making the porch groan and whine. "When she caught up, I asked if she wanted to go to Sammy's Soda Shoppe with me. I had just enough money for one ice cream for me, but I had hopes we could share."

"Wait, Sammy's? Like the old soda shop in town on Main Street?"

"Well, it wasn't that old when I went there, but yes, I assume it's the same one. We went to Sammy's and lucky for me, he was having a sale on his banana splits. We shared a dish with chocolate, vanilla and strawberry ice cream. Mr. Sammy liked me and I think he was trying to help me with Evelyn, so he gave us extra chocolate sauce that dripped over the edges of the bowl — you couldn't even see the banana. He even threw some extra cherries, sprinkles, and nuts on top. It was delicious and we ate until we were sick." Billy smiled at the nostalgic memory. "We talked about school; I went to the local school here but Evelyn was homeschooled. We talked about friends, places we'd been, and hobbies. She told me about her art — she was good at art, like you. And I told her about my new interest in baseball. When it was time for her to get back home, I rode my bike to drop her off and then I went and sat by the river until my stomach didn't hurt anymore."

Jayne laughed. "I love that story." He smiled and they sat staring toward the big house, listening to the birds and the trees moving with the breeze. "I should get back to going through Dad's things. Are you going to be here tomorrow?"

"I should be here, around somewhere, I suppose." Billy smiled at her and they both stood up. Jayne stepped off the porch and started back to the house. She turned around, checking if Billy was still there. He was, looking right back. He raised a hand and shouted, "Thank you for coming back, Jayne!" Then he walked back into the old house.

I'm still not convinced I'm not just having delusions. I need to get some sleep, Jayne said to herself.

2

JAYNE WOKE TO the sound of Rusty whining and scratching at the master bedroom door again. She moaned, wishing he would stop and she wouldn't have to use her voice just yet. The light from the rising sun was starting to peek over the edge of her east-facing window frame. The backs of her eyelids were turning the shade of a tropical sunrise, slowly bringing her out from her sleep. She blindly reached for the phone under her pillow and looked at the time.

7:28, *just in time to have some coffee, get ready, and head to the shop.* She'd put it off long enough, and even though Joe said to take her time, four days was more than enough.

She rolled to her left side and noticed someone sitting in the rocking chair. "Jesus, Joseph, and Mary! Billy, you scared the living shit out of me." She thought she might still be sleeping, but judging by the grasp she had on her phone, she was definitely awake. She quickly sat up. "What are you doing in here?"

Billy chuckled. "Sorry to startle you. I used to always sit by your bed while you slept. When you were younger, you couldn't go to sleep without me being here."

Jayne rubbed her face, the memories floating back in. She and Billy had some of their best talks in the morning when she first woke up. "You're right. I remember now. You were always sitting in that chair, or over by the window. I remember looking for you when I first woke up." Jayne stretched her arms up and her legs straight out. "What are you going to do today while I go to the shop?"

"Well, I'm not sure."

Jayne stood up and grabbed her thin cotton cover from the bedpost. She forgotten how cold the house was during the fall and winter months. "I see. Well, I have to get some coffee, take a shower, and get ready to go to the shop. I'll see you later?" She wrapped the fabric around herself tightly. The cool fall air seeping through the windows and walls made it the perfect, crisp temperature for a hot coffee and a warm shower.

"Of course." Billy smiled and nodded. Jayne smiled back and left the room. Rusty was curled up against the master bedroom door. His scratching had ceased for now.

"Come on, dog," she called. He jumped up and followed her downstairs.

She opened cabinet doors, looking for coffee and filters. Her mom or dad couldn't start the day without it, so there were multiple varieties. She opened up the pantry and despite the array of random cans and boxes, she spotted a box of filters and three different kinds of coffee. She grabbed the Caramel Texas Turtle, smelled the contents, and decided they smelled fresh enough.

While she waited for it to brew, the light coming in over her father's land caught her attention. *It sure is beautiful here.* She remembered being in the backyard with both her parents. Jayne didn't know the real reason of her parents' divorce—all Dani would tell her is that sometimes two people aren't meant to be together forever and it was time for her to leave. Jayne never asked more questions knowing her mom didn't want to talk about it.

Rusty barked at her from the corner and pawed at his food dish.

"Shit, sorry Rusty. I'm crap at being a dog mom." She grabbed his food from the pantry and poured some into the bowl. "Is that enough?" she asked. He didn't respond, but instead dug in. She filled his water bowl and the coffee beeped. She smelled the cream for freshness and poured some in, then took her mug upstairs to get ready.

Jayne opened the front door and Rusty went running out. She called after him but he refused to budge. He ran straight up to her dad's old 1969 Ford truck in front of the shed at the side of the house. Old Blue, he called it. It was the color of a clear blue sky with hardly any scratches or rust. Her dad took very good care of it and Jayne had loved it as long as she could remember. After a minute's thought, she grabbed Rusty, tossed him back inside the house, and grabbed the keys off the hook by the door. When she sat inside the truck, she noticed papers and take-out coffee cups stashed in almost every crevice. He'd recently had the bench seat redone with leather, but it still smelled like wood shavings and coffee; just like her dad. She put the key in the ignition and turned it, but instead of an engine coming to life, she only heard short little clicks. *The battery,* she thought. Defeated, she sighed and got out, hopping back into her little compact car and set her GPS to Webber Furniture.

The shop was less than a fifteen minute drive from the house. Joe's truck was already there and she could hear the cacophony of saws and nail guns in the back. She walked around the storefront to the shop office. At the front desk sat a man on the phone, about her age with wavy dark hair, styled in the trendy, more modern version of a greaser. She could see he was good-looking and well-built. He had on a clean, beige Webber's T-shirt that fit perfectly to show off the tone of his body. The bell on the door had announced her arrival but it was a few seconds before he looked up to see who was there. When he did, their eyes locked and he placed his hand to his mouth, in awe. She looked around and scrunched her eyebrows in a confused reply.

"Mrs. Jackson, I'm going to talk to my dad about your chairs and I will give you a call back right away . . . Yes I have your number, it's in your file. You're welcome, thank you." He hung up the phone and stood. Jayne's stomach did a little flip. "Hi, welcome back," he said.

Jayne was still confused but assumed she just caught him off guard. "Hi, I'm here to see Joe. I'm Jayne—"

"Webber, I know. I'm Luke Martin, Joe's son. It's been awhile. I think the last time I saw you we were about eight, or maybe a bit older. I really can't remember." He shook his head and held out his hand. "It's nice to see you again."

Jayne remembered him, but not like this. She remembered him as a thin boy with very crooked teeth and long, unkempt hair. She'd played with him a few times as a kid when their parents were working, but it was a friendship of convenience. She shook his hand and said, "It's nice to see you again. How have you been?"

"Good, thank you," he replied. "Let me just get my dad for you." He walked around the desk to the shop door and shouted in for Joe. "He's coming," he assured her.

Jayne examined the framed black-and-white aerial photo of the town from the 1960s in front of her. She was trying to figure out where the shop was in the picture when Joe stepped into the office.

"Jayne, how are you?" He came over and without acknowledgement for her personal space, wrapped his arms around her and squeezed tight. She could smell the dried sweat, wood, and paint thinner on him.

"I'm good, thank you. Just adjusting, you know."

"I'm sure. I see you met Luke again. It's probably been awhile since you've seen each other though." He attempted to brush some of the sawdust off the front of his belly. "Well, you want to get reintroduced to the shop and the store? Your dad has built something great here. Of course your great-, great- . . ." He paused to think. " . . . great-grandfather really is the one who started it, but your dad turned it into something else."

"When was it first built?" Jayne asked, a little ashamed she didn't already know.

"Oh, I'd say around the 1900s." Jayne raised her eyebrows and glanced at Luke. He raised a corner of his mouth into a half smile.

"Well, I guess give me the tour and then if we can sit down and chat about some things, that would be great." She felt calm but her mind was whirring with decisions and emotions. She cracked her knuckled and rubbed her palms together.

"Sure thing, kiddo." He tapped his forehead with his fingers. "Sorry, it's been awhile, and 'kiddo' was probably the last thing I called you."

Jayne chuckled. "It's fine, my grandma still uses all those names too. I have a feeling I'll be thirty-five and still be called 'baby' by my mom."

"Probably" Joe laughed and held open the door to the shop. "Let's start here and then I'll take you through the store and we'll come back to the office." Jayne nodded and walked through.

The shop was just as wide as the building and divided into three major sections. She could see where they processed the wood and made it into smaller pieces like table or chair legs. In the middle was an area dedicated to larger pieces like the tabletops, chair seats and even some chests and drawers. The far wall was for assembly and any decorative adornments. Joe took her past everyone working, introducing her to some of the guys. They all gave their condolences for her loss and she thanked them for being loyal employees. Once they got to the far wall, they went through a door leading to the storefront.

Inside was a store with all the items made in the shop. Joe explained that many of the items they made were custom orders, but in their free time, they would make pieces to show in the store, which were also available for purchase. It helped the customers to figure out what they were looking at for their custom orders as well.

"Each guy has a unique set of skills," Joe explained, "so one might be better at leather embellishments, one might only be good with wood and metal. It's kind of like a tattoo shop: people can come in and if they don't see anything in here they want, they can pick and choose ideas from each."

"These are beautiful," Jayne exclaimed. She ran her hands over a tabletop, a solid section from a tree that must have been three and a half feet wide. The edges were the raw outside of the tree, showing the roughness of the bark. The whole thing had been stained and varnished — preserved forever.

Joe pointed to some silver streaks laced throughout. "That was one of your dad's signature traits." Jayne leaned over the table and saw the little strands of silver in crevices and openings in the wood. "He would paint any little flaws in silver or gold to highlight the raw mistakes or natural occurrences of nature. In the case of this table, a huge crevice created by something like disease or just stunted growth." Joe showed her a side table that had been eaten by worms and the holes had been filled with a gold-dusted resin.

"It's stunning," Jayne said. "I knew my dad had skills, but I really had no idea how creative and talented he was." Her throat caught and she cleared it.

"He was something else, your father—despite his shortcomings." Joe peeked at her through the corner of his eye. They wandered around the store a bit more, Joe introduced her to the salesperson, Linda, and they made their way back to the office.

When they entered, Luke asked, "So what do you think?"

"I think it's fantastic," Jayne said. "Y'all do some wonderful things here, it's no wonder it's been a success." Joe and Luke smiled at each other and Joe motioned for Jayne to follow him into his office. She noticed a closed door across from Joe's that read "Peter Webber."

"Has anyone gone through there yet?" She nodded toward her dad's office.

"No." Joe cleared his throat "Not yet. We weren't sure if that's something you wanted to do or wanted us to do. Either way, you just let us know." Jayne nodded and sat down in the chair across from Joe's desk. Joe scooted around his desk, his larger-than-average belly making it hard to navigate in such a small space. "So, what do you think about taking over this place?"

Let's just get right to it, Jayne thought. "I'm going to

be honest with you Joe. I don't have the first clue about building furniture or running a business like this. I was five when I left here with my mom and I was fifteen when I left for good, so any learning I would have had from Dad was non-existent. I can't even decorate a townhouse, so my eye for detail isn't going to be much help either. I'm more of an artist than anything." Joe smiled with one side of his mouth. "But with that said, I think I would like to be a part of this company. I'd like to see it continue to grow. I may have been an art major, but I tend to be business savvy when it comes to online marketing. Maybe we can explore a partnership or something. I know you've been here longer than me and my dad trusted you and Liz with his life. I just have to talk to the bank and find out my options first, if it's going to be feasible and also, I don't even know if I'm going to be staying here, to be honest."

Joe nodded and smiled sincerely with a look of understanding on his face. "I think that's something that we could work out. We can teach you many things; you'd be surprised. As for the partnership, your dad and I spoke of this also, so I'm pleased to hear you mention that. As you can see, I'm no spring chicken." He ran the tips of his fingers down the sides of his stomach, modeling his figure, making Jayne laugh. "It's going to get harder for me to continue in the back, building the pieces. That's where Luke comes in. He's been around this shop since he was born. He's been working here for about five or six years and has been making his own pieces for over three now. He would be an excellent replacement for me."

Jayne nodded. "This all sounds great, Joe. I'm so grateful for your help and honesty. My mom is coming into town tomorrow and hopefully we can talk about it and our best options. Me keeping the shop will be awfully hard if I don't live here."

"You're right," Joe said with a pang of disappointment in his voice. "But, if we're going to be *completely* honest . . ." He pulled his desk drawer open and took out three business cards. "I hate to do this, but since your dad's passing, investors have been sniffing around this place and they say they're willing to pay a lot." He handed the cards to Jayne and she flipped through them. "One of them is Frederick Manns. He owns a few properties around here and has been developing the town. I just ask that you really think about it, Jayne. This company is over a hundred years old and was started by your own ancestors. It would be a shame to lose it to some minor technicalities we could work out. It just wouldn't be the same without a Webber. Not to mention, some of these guys would lose jobs they've had for over a decade if one of those guys gets in here." He pointed to the cards in her hands. "They'd most likely just come in and turn it into a big chain furniture store, if they don't tear it apart. But I understand you have to do what you have to do."

"Thanks Joe. It sounds like I have a lot of thinking to do." Jayne stood up and Joe followed her into the main office.

"Hey, Luke is about to take a break for lunch, why don't I get him to take you to Sammy's Soda Shoppe to grab something to eat?"

"Oh, that would be great, I'm starving. Only if you don't mind." She looked at Luke who stared at his dad in confusion.

"All I've got is a ham sandwich, so that would actually be great. I'd be happy to."

3

LUKE AND JAYNE walked through the door of Sammy's. It smelled of sugar cones and fresh bread. Memories of the place drifted in and out of her mind. They still had their ten standard rotating flavors of ice cream and soda fountains behind the counters, only now they had sandwiches on their menu. Jayne browsed the mounted chalkboard menu and quickly picked out the turkey and cranberry on a roll.

As she waited for Luke to decide, she took a moment to look around the small shop. Little cars and toys from all the years lined the shelves, some of which she remembered as toys from cereal boxes when she was little. Old road signs from the area hung on the walls and antique oilcans or jars were displayed on shelves, some of them for sale. She imagined Billy coming here with his wife, Evelyn. Maybe even bringing their kids. She pictured them at the table by the window, eating the banana split.

"Jayne?" She snapped out of her vision and turned to Luke. "Do you know what you want?"

"Oh, yes. Can I please get the turkey and cranberry?

I'll get a peach Italian soda as well, please." Luke placed his order and reached for his wallet. "No, no, I got this. We're here on work business." Jayne was the only person she knew who couldn't wink no matter how she tried, so she wiggled her eyebrows to indicate her innocent yet mischievous intentions.

"Okay then," Luke said to the teenage boy taking their order. "About the only time I'd let a lady pay for my meal."

Jayne waited for their drinks while Luke went and chose the seat by the window. *He sure is cute,* Jayne caught herself saying. *Stop that, I'm engaged to be married.* Her inner dialogue continued. She reached her thumb to her ring finger to reinforce her betrothal, but the ring wasn't there. She panicked slightly, trying to remember the last time she saw it and a memory of it sitting on the bathroom sink that morning came to mind. She exhaled audibly and the soda jerk gave her a funny look. She just smiled, grabbed the sodas, and headed to the table.

"How long are you in town for?" Luke asked, placing a napkin in front of her.

"I'm not actually sure," Jayne replied. "I was only planning on coming in for a little while. But I quit my part-time job to come take care of my dad's estate, that way I could stay as long as needed. I can do my art from anywhere and ship it, if needed."

"But not live here?"

"I don't know. It wasn't in my plan, but everything happens for a reason."

They each took a sip from their sodas as the sandwiches arrived at the table.

"What *was* in your plan?" Luke asked.

"Well, I guess to maybe work on my art, get some more gallery space, possibly become an art professor, get married, have kids, and live in North Carolina."

They both talked in between bites of their sandwiches and Jayne became at ease with Luke. She noticed he asked a lot of questions about her and found it relaxing. She didn't have to try and think of things to say with him — the conversation was like a fluid match of tennis with the banter back and forth.

"Your dad was a great person," he said, stabbing the toothpick into the bun. "I'm sorry you have to deal with all of this alone, it's a lot." Jayne smiled at him. "If you need anything, please let me know."

"Thank you," she said sincerely, wiping her mouth with the paper napkin. "There is one thing: maybe you might know someone who can come take a look at my dad's truck?"

"The battery dead?" Luke grinned.

"Yes, how did you know?" she asked, surprised.

"Old Blue's battery is always dying." Luke laughed. "Especially after a long weekend if he just stayed at home. He would call my dad on Monday and my dad or one of the other shop employees would have to come out and give him a boost. My dad tried to get him to replace the battery many times, but your dad would just say, 'Not in this lifetime; this is a Ford, it doesn't need a new battery, it just needs a pat on the butt.' "

Both Jayne and Luke laughed. "Sounds like my dad," Jayne said. "He's not in this lifetime anymore, though, so do you think you can you give me a boost to take it to a shop?"

"I can do better than that, I can replace it for you. We can stop by the auto shop after this and pick up a battery. I'll come by later this week to install it."

"You would do that? That would be amazing, Luke. Thank you so much. I owe you big."

"It's really no problem. Will only take a few minutes."

"Thank you." Jayne thought about the differences

between Luke and Blake. She thought of one time her mom needed a boost. They were already at her house, but Blake was still annoyed, saying she should've been more careful and not let her mom run the lights so long. And here was Luke, offering to do maintenance on her vehicle without so much as a frown.

"You know, you haven't changed much," Luke said. "Your hair is still the same, just like Shirley Temple."

Jayne ran her fingers over a section of hair by her face. The curls straightened out and then bounced back into place. "Yes, well, it's more of a curse than a blessing. But I suppose people with straight hair say the same thing."

"You always want what you can't have, right?" Luke's face changed. His eyebrows becoming slightly furrowed as his smile disappeared.

It wasn't lost on Jayne. "Is something wrong?"

"Oh, no. I'm sorry. Because my dad was your dad's best friend, your dad and I became close. He used to say that all the time; we would be talking about you or family in general and that's what he would say."

Jayne nodded. After a moment, she asked, "Did Dad say anything about me?"

Luke looked up at her, slightly surprised. "Oh, always. He said lots of good things about you. When you graduated high school and were accepted to college, he showed us the pictures that your mom would send to him. He missed you a lot. He always said he wished he could have been different and he could have seen you grow into a young woman."

"My mom sent him pictures of me?" Jayne struggled to hold back her tears. She pressed a paper napkin into the corner of her eyes to soak up the tears before they breached her eyelashes. "Sorry," she said, half laughing, embarrassed.

"Don't be. I shouldn't have brought it up. I'm sorry."

Luke placed his hand on hers and the warmth of his touch made Jayne realize that with everything she'd been through the past few days, she really needed a hug. "Do you want to go get that battery?" he asked. Jayne nodded and stood up. Luke took the dishes back to the counter and they walked across the street to the auto parts store.

4

ONCE JAYNE GOT back home, she turned on the local radio station and set to work going through her dad's stuff. She decided to start at the front of the house, in the living area. She grabbed a couple of boxes and sat down on the floor. Rusty hopped off the couch and curled up against her leg.

Against the far wall was a large shelving unit lined with drawers on the bottom. Starting at the left, she pulled open the first drawer and looked inside. Usually she'd be excited to rummage through someone's belongings, finding new things, but now it was uncomfortable and a little bit nerve-racking because it was her father's. She felt like she should know what would be in these drawers, but instead she had no idea what to expect and that scared her.

The first drawer was just filled with cassette tapes from the eighties. "Really Dad?" she whispered to herself. Slowly she started taking the tapes out and placing them in the box. There was an overwhelming amount of Madonna, Prince, and U2, sprinkled in with some Michael Jackson and The Beach Boys.

After a few minutes, Rusty stood up, the hair along

his spine raised. He sniffed the air and let a low growl vibrate from his throat. Billy came around the corner from the kitchen.

"How was your trip into town?"

Jayne nearly jumped out of her skin and whipped around to face him. "You have to stop scaring the shit out of me like that," she exclaimed. Rusty let out one last growl and Jayne patted him until he settled back by her leg.

"I'm sorry, I can't exactly make footstep noises." He pointed to his feet, which were barely hovering off the ground.

"Ghosts make footstep noises all the time," Jayne replied.

"That's what they're focusing their energy on. If I did that, you wouldn't be able to see me." Jayne nodded in understanding. "Do you remember that time before your last birthday here when I convinced you to make your bed with the promise of flicking some Cheerios at your mom at breakfast?" Jayne smiled. "It took me a long time to get my energy back after that." Billy remembered that day for different reasons than Jayne would have.

1997

"Don't forget to make your bed, Bunny," Billy said.

She slumped. "Do I have to?" she whined. Billy raised his eyebrows at her in answer. "Can't *you* make it Billy?"

"You know I can't, darling. But if you make your bed, I'll do something special for you when we get downstairs."

Jayne ran around her bed and pulled the covers up, tugging on the corners and throwing the pillows against the headboard before propping her favorite teddy bear in the middle to stand guard over the room while she was gone.

The banister railing was about as tall as she was, but she reached up to wrap her little fingers around it before she started down the wooden steps; both feet landing on each step before starting on to the next one. Dani came around the corner to meet her at the bottom. Just like every morning, she smiled at her like she hadn't seen her in years.

"Good morning, my love. Are you hungry?"

"Mm-hmm." Jayne nodded and reached for Dani to pick her up. "Just one more day until my birthday, Mommy!"

Dani lifted her with ease and propped Jayne on her hip. "That's right, honey. Are you excited?"

Jayne nodded, wrapping her small arms around Dani's neck, tucking her little face perfectly into the arch from Dani's ear to her shoulder as if it was molded for her.

Dani walked her into the kitchen and sat her at the table. She brought over a cup of milk as she prepared Jayne's favorite mix of Raisin Bran and Cheerios.

When Dani set the bowl in front of her, Jayne grabbed her spoon and shoveled cereal into her mouth, letting milk drip down her chin onto the table. Dani turned to make her own breakfast and Billy looked at the Cheerios in the bowl and nodded to the table in front of him. Jayne grabbed a Cheerio and placed it on the table in front of Billy. He took a few mock deep breaths, touched his middle finger to thumb, and flicked the Cheerio toward Dani. It missed and landed on the floor behind her. Without hesitation, Jayne placed another Cheerio on the table. This time he concentrated more, focused it on the Cheerio, and tried again. It hit the back of Dani's calf. She didn't feel it through her flannel pajama pants but that didn't stop an eruption of giggles from Jayne. Dani was busy preparing her coffee and didn't turn around, so Jayne set Billy up again and he flicked another. This one hit her again, nearly in the same spot, sending Jayne into a fit of rolling laughter. Billy couldn't help but chuckle at her little laugh—it reminded him of when his kids were small. This time Dani turned around to look at Jayne.

"What's so funny, Missy?" She caught Jayne's gaze to the floor and spotted the rogue Cheerios. "Oh, you think that's funny, huh?" She bent down, picked up the Cheerios, and tossed them back at her. Jayne bounced with laughter.

Peter walked in and the natural smile left Dani's face, replaced with a generic version. He walked over to Jayne and kissed her on the head.

"Hi Daddy!"

"Hey kiddo." He messed her blond curls before walking over to Dani, where he placed a hand on her waist and kissed her cheek. He gave her butt a squeeze and walked to the coffee maker. "Is this done?" he asked, pointing to the coffee,

"Should be," she replied shortly.

"Can I pour you a cup?" he asked.

"Sure."

He grabbed her favorite cup, poured the perfect amount of cream in, and handed it to her. "Go sit down with Jayne. I'll make your breakfast." He smiled at her and she smiled back as she reached for the cup.

Dani was a mix of hot and cold thinking about the fight they had the night before. Peter had made an appointment without Dani's permission to take Jayne to a specialist to see about her "imaginary friend." He also wanted to speak to the doctor about her possibly having a socialization problem.

"She doesn't have any friends," he'd said, "except for this imaginary friend she's always talking to."

"It's nothing, Peter," she'd retorted. "She's four. Four-year-olds have imaginary friends and play by themselves. She only has six kids in her class and we live in the middle of nowhere. She can't just pop down the street to see them."

"Well what if she's got a developmental issue or something—" Dani had made a grunting noise and took her wine glass to the sink. "I saw it on the TV. She's really good at art already and keeps to herself."

"Jesus, Peter." Dani had rubbed the bridge of her nose. She was too tired to have this sprung on her. It was late and the darkness was making her more tired. "She's not autistic. And look at the paintings around this house, all done by your grandmothers. It runs in the family. She's not going. Cancel the appointment."

The expression on Peter's face was always fixed, which made it difficult for strangers to understand his mood, but Dani was a self-taught expert at knowing how he felt by just a twitch of his eyebrow or clench of his teeth. If his hair was parted and slightly combed, it would be a good day; if it had gone awry, he was not in the mood for anything. That night he was wearing a hat: a force not to be reckoned with.

He'd used his toe to pick at a tiny tear in the yellowing linoleum. Then with a quick rap of his knuckles on the wood counter, he announced that he'd still be taking her.

"I've already made the appointment."

Dani had stared at the Texans logo on his hat but didn't say anything. A few minutes later, Peter said he was going to the pub for a couple hours. He "needed a drink." *You always need a drink*, Dani thought, but knew better than to say. She didn't fight him because she could use the alone time as well.

This particular after-fight morning, Peter was now breaking down her wall with thoughtfulness, making the energy in the kitchen mix like whiskey and soda, creating little sparks that only Billy could see and feel like pins and needles all over his body. *This is what happens when people say they "could cut the tension with a knife,"* he thought. The feeling was overwhelming and he had to leave.

Billy went through the kitchen door to the back of the house. The sun wasn't fully up yet, and the dew on the green grass looked as if a fairy came the night before and sprinkled silver over all the land. He passed the hanging laundry.

Dani will be disappointed she forgot to bring it in last night, he thought, and he walked straight toward the creek to sit down on the bank. He reminisced about the feeling of fresh dew on his feet and hands, the grass tickling between his toes, and the morning humidity kissing his skin with pecks of warm and cold. But it was August, which meant it was probably already hot. Billy disliked Texas summers and he hated winters too. One was too hot, the other too cold, and when you're in Texas, you don't get much of a middle ground. But now, as a spirit, he could enjoy both since he was always the same temperature as the air around him.

Wintertime meant he could lie in the snow under the stars. While alive, he never realized how different the sky looked in the winter, because he'd always been worried about staying warm. The sky was more crisp, if only he could touch it, it would shatter into a million pieces like sugarglass. The stars twinkled brighter and sharper and the air had electricity about it. If it snowed, it was like a star had exploded, sending tiny star particles down to the earth, floating and dancing around one another until they left the ground covered in stardust that kept sparkling until it melted. The land around the house looked particularly beautiful in winter if it snowed — which it didn't very often. The creek in the back appeared to be the only thing living; the trees empty of their leaves dotted the ten acres like little landmarks, a reminder that nothing can live forever, but can always leave a memory. Summer was just as pleasant and beautiful in its own right: the trees were lush, the grass was green, and if the spring provided enough rain, the creek in the back flowed strong.

Billy looked over to the edge of the property at the small, run-down building. It used to be a beautiful house, the first property on the land, nothing too big or fancy but special to the people who had lived there. Jayne's third great-grandfather, William Webber Sr., had worked hard to buy the supplies to build that house. Each beam of wood and dab of paint meant hard work and dreams coming true. They had made it their home over the years. The two boys would chase each other around the house, laughing while their parents sat on the small porch. Now all that was left were frames of memories.

Billy was roused from this memory by Jayne's excited voice. She pointed to the box of cassettes.

5

2017

"LOOK AT THIS," she said. "Cassette tapes! I haven't seen a cassette tape . . . well, probably since I lived here."

Billy laughed and knelt beside her next to the box. "Your dad used those in his truck a lot. He would always be rifling through them, taking them back and forth between the house and the truck. People don't seem to use them anymore though."

"No, we use CDs now, or our phones can stream the music."

"Are CDs the little discs that look like miniature records?" he asked.

"Yes, that's it."

"What do you mean by 'streaming' though? How can you play music from your phone?"

Jayne paused for a second, figuring out how to describe it. "Here, look," she said, grabbing her smartphone. "I'm sure you're familiar with a cell phone, since you've been around. Some people have figured out how to load music onto a phone so you can listen with headphones, or you can open an app." Jayne tapped the phone in demonstration. "Then pick your song. It's like a computer." Jayne paused, tapping through some screens on the phone while Billy watched intently. "What's your favorite song?"

"I have a few," Billy said. "I guess one that comes to mind would be 'Body and Soul' by Paul Whiteman."

Jayne stared at him for a moment, unsure. She forgot his favorite song would probably be from the early 1900s. Her fingers moved over the phone quickly and Billy sat cross-legged, trying to peek over her phone until finally an upbeat piano tune came through the phone. It was clear, but had the tinny sound of 1930s music played through a gramophone. A man's nasally voice dripped through and Billy smiled at her with his eyebrows raised and an open mouthed grin.

"I haven't heard this song since the fifties, probably."

Jayne smiled and let the song play until the end. "Billy, can I ask you something?"

"Of course."

"When I went to the shop today, I met Joe's son, Luke. We went for lunch at Sammy's and he mentioned that Mom had been sending pictures of me to Dad. Do you know about this?"

"Oh, sure. Most of them are in his room. He took some to the office and carried some around with him and even made copies of a couple to keep all over, like your graduation photos." Billy smiled at her.

"Luke said that Dad was sad with the way things ended up, and wished things could've been different." Jayne could feel the prickle of tears rising to her eyes like bubbles of soda in a carelessly poured glass. She ran her hand over Rusty to move her mind to something else momentarily.

Billy nodded. "Well yes, I suppose he did. I don't think anyone plans for their marriage to dissolve and to only be able to see their child a couple times a year, then not being able to see them but every two or three years after that. He wanted more for himself and felt bad that he did that to you."

Jayne picked at the toe of her sock but didn't say anything. She just nodded. She wanted to ask about how he was after she left, but the effort of trying not to cry prevented her throat from working. Billy sat closer to her and Jayne could feel the sensation of static electricity on her skin, followed by a serene sense of comfort and love washing over her.

"You know he cared about you, right Bunny?" Jayne nodded and two small tears spilled over her eyelids and ran down her cheeks. She wiped them away quickly, but the dam was broken now and more overflowed. "Oh, honey. Your mom did the right thing. Your dad loved you more than anything, but this wasn't a good place for a teenager. You know he had a problem with alcohol and he couldn't control it. It was an unpredictable habit and it overtook his life, his emotions, and eventually his health. Who knows if you would have developed the same habit in his wake. In my time, alcoholism was very much passed down to one's adult children."

Jayne nodded. "I should have come back though, when I was older, I mean. It might not have been a good place for a teenager, but I'm not a teenager and I haven't been for a while. I could have helped—I could have made him feel better." Jayne sniffed. She implanted thoughts of her taking care of her dad, of him becoming healthier because she came back. "I could have made more of an effort, but instead I was selfishly saying 'maybe in a couple months.' " She dabbed at her nose with the cuff of her shirt.

"Maybe," Billy said, "but what if it didn't? What if you came back and the habits stayed: the drinking all night and sleeping late into the morning, going to work smelling like day-old alcohol, coming home and doing it all over again." Billy thought of his own father's struggle with alcohol. "He was a smart man and he knew how to run a business, but he couldn't give up that habit. Maybe you could've helped him, but more likely, it would have ruined you in trying. He would have picked fights. He never liked to be told what to do. You can't feel guilty about that."

Jayne stopped crying and looked at him. She wiped her tears with her hands and sighed. "You're probably right. I just wish I'd made more of an effort to see him in the past ten years. You know he came to North Carolina once to see me when I was in school. We spent a couple of days together. It was nice. It must have been when he was sober—or not drinking as much, at least. That's the dad I remember, but I can't imagine that's who he was or Mom wouldn't have made the effort to keep me from him. I have to believe that." She straightened a little.

"You're right—that wasn't the type of person your dad was most of the time and your mom did the best she could. You know, your dad tried to quit drinking once—it nearly killed him." Jayne lifted her chin and looked with surprise at Billy. "It was after your mom cut back the amount of time that he was allowed to see you. I imagine she brought up his lifestyle as a contributing factor. He ended it with the girl he was going steady with and stayed home for a week from work. Any alcohol he had in the house, or stashed in the garage, was put in the trash and set out to the curb for pick up three days later.

"The first day he was fine; the alcohol wasn't completely out of his system. The next day he started to get shaky and was wobbly on his feet. It didn't help that he didn't want to eat. He spent most of the time on the couch, watching TV, trying not to think of what he was going through, but it was hard come the third day when the delirium tremens started. He had to put towels and blankets down to cover the couch because he was sweating so much. Then he had to change them every few hours." Billy saw Jayne's eyes harden, then soften into regret. "Bunny, I'm not telling you this to make you feel bad about not being here; I'm telling you because this is what you would have had to deal with. This is only one of a handful of times he went through this and there was nothing you could do. Joe and Liz came over every day to check on him — sometimes more. They would straighten up the things your dad had thrown around the room in his delirium, or clean up the messes from knocked over cups or vomit that hadn't made its way into the designated bucket. Liz would wash and replace the sheets he had soaked through. It was terrible to watch and would have not been any place for you. He begged them for just an ounce of liquor to make the hallucinations, vomiting, and tremors stop. He cried that his stomach felt like it was being torn from his body and his head was splitting open. Once they left, he ran out to the trash, digging through, looking for any bit of alcohol he had thrown out, but the garbage men had already come. He kicked the can into the road and then picked it up and threw it back toward the house in a rage.

"Throughout his sleep he would sweat and moan, sometimes yelling, 'No, don't touch me!' The D.T.'s were giving him terrible nightmares. He was very lucky he didn't have seizures. My own father was not so lucky through his withdrawal periods." Jayne pressed her fingertips to her mouth and let the points of her eyebrows raise. She would have grabbed Billy's hand if she could have.

"After a few days, the symptoms started to subside

and your dad would get up, walking or tinkering around the house. He'd tell people he was a new man and couldn't believe he'd gone so long without sobriety. But, like most alcoholics, he would get an invite to a bar or there would be some party and he would come stumbling back up the porch, drunk as a skunk, and it would all start over again."

Jayne hung her head low. A single last tear dropped. She wiped the wetness from her eye.

"I'm sorry Bunny."

"It's okay," Jayne said. "I'm just glad my mom is coming tomorrow."

6

JAYNE STAYED UP late into the evening boxing up old, useless things from the living room. She talked to her mom and Blake, giving them an update on the day before going to bed.

Now the sun was just starting to turn the sky a light shade of pinkish gray, like the belly of a newborn puppy. Before she even opened her eyes, she could feel the aches in her body: a combination of sitting so long and lifting boxes.

"Billy?" she asked, eyes closed, assuming he was there.

"Yes, Bunny?"

"What time is it?"

He looked at the alarm clock on the nightstand "It's about seven thirty."

"Okay. Mom gets in this afternoon. I might just sleep a bit more." She reached for her phone under her pillow and with one eye open checked for any notifications. There was a generic text from her mom and one from Blake that read:

"Call me."

She groaned and sat up. Billy looked curiously at her. "Don't ask," she said and then dialed Blake's number. He picked up after two rings.

"Hey, babe. Did I wake you?"

"I didn't hear your text. I just woke up."

"Oh, okay, good. I sent that over an hour ago. How are things at the house?"

"They're fine," Jayne said. "What's going on Blake? You said to call, has something—"

"Yeah, so listen," he interrupted. Jayne felt her stomach drop and put her face into her hands. "I don't think I'm going to be able to come out for a couple more days now."

"Blake, no. What now?"

"That client I was telling you about the other day, he's having a bit of a meltdown and needs us here. There's just no way I can get out of it. I'm really sorry babe."

"Is this how it's going to be, Blake? We can never take a family vacation or weekend holiday because your clients throw a tantrum and then you can't go out of town?" There was a silent pause on the phone. Jayne looked over at Billy who shrugged and gave his best "I'm sorry" look.

"You knew it was going to be like this for a bit. It just comes with the territory. It won't always be like this, but for a while, yes, it will."

"We're supposed to be getting married in Key West—will you even be able to make it to the wedding, or do I have to do that alone too? Or maybe they can just FaceTime you in," she said with mock enthusiasm.

"I'm sorry babe."

"Blake, my dad *died*. I'm here, going through his belongings, taking care of his house and business by *myself*. You don't think that I could use somebody? Somebody that can find time to be with their fiancée whose dad just *died*?" She tugged on a loose piece of hair, twirling it around her fingers.

"I know, Jayne, and I'm sorry. You know I'm new to the firm. I'm trying to grow some roots here, not just take off in the middle of an important case. Besides, isn't your mom coming today?"

"That's beside the point. I'm happy my mom is coming, but she's not a replacement for my fiancé. Just, never mind. Come when you can, if you're still coming at all. I don't care." Jayne hung up and instantly regretted saying she didn't care; the burn in her heart said it was obvious.

"Are you okay?" Billy asked.

"I'll be fine," Jayne said briskly. "Eventually. This is just going to get *really* old, Billy. He's supposed to be there for me when I need him. I can see what his priorities are now, and I understand it's his job and he's trying to make a name for himself, but I'm just not feeling supported in any way."

Billy nodded. "I'm sorry Bunny."

"I better just get up." Jayne made the bed and walked over to the little vanity where she took a long look at her face and smoothed her hair back, tucking some of the loose curls into the elastic band holding her hair in a messy bun. Without saying anything to Billy, she left the room. He knew better than to follow her. Rusty was lying outside the master bedroom door. He peeked at her but didn't move. When she got downstairs, she put on a pot of coffee. Rusty soon left his perch beside the master bedroom door and followed her, eager for a morning meal.

She walked over to the box of folders she'd found in the closet under the stairs the previous night. After a quick assessment of her mood, she wasn't awake or keen enough to dig through them. *Maybe after coffee*, she thought. Instead she walked into the living room, opened the bolted door, and gazed out the screen door. The sun was up, but the west-facing porch was still shaded along with the garden in the front. She could feel her heart still racing from Blake's call, but she couldn't tell if it was anger or just disappointment she was feeling. She spied the overgrown bushes lining the porch and the jasmine plant vines twirling their way up the railings and column.

She swung open the screen door, letting it slam shut behind her, and headed for the shed in her flip-flops. Inside the shed was a disaster: tools, more boxes, furniture pieces, and a small riding mower. She went over to the workbench looking for a small pair of plant shears but found a large pair of what looked like oversized scissors instead.

That will do. She stormed back to the bushes and started snapping the shears at the big bushes like Edward Scissorhands. When she got to the vines, she lopped off the tops and sides, pulling the vines from their grasp around the house and flinging them into the yard like an Olympic discus thrower. She stood back to see her progress; one of the bushes was shorter than the other. She started again, snapping at each bush.

"You should probably stop before there's nothing left," a voice said behind her. Jayne swung around, shears in hand. With all her commotion she hadn't heard Luke pull up. "Whoa." Luke stepped back with his hands up like he was about to be arrested.

"What are you doing here?" she said as nicely as she could, instantly regretting her choice of pajamas and lack of bra.

"I came to change your battery, like promised." He smiled. "I'm glad I got here when I did. For the bushes' sake, can you put down the trimmers?" Luke reached one hand out for the shears. Jayne handed them over and crossed her arms in front of her chest. They both stood back and took a look at what was left of the greenery. "We can take care of that later," Luke said and Jayne covered her face with her hands, groaning. "So, Dad also sent me because there's this commission that the owner is picking up in a couple hours. It's a big one: entire bedroom, including shelves, dresser and chest, everything you can think of. Anyway, it was the last set of pieces your dad worked on and we thought you might want to see it before it goes to the new owner."

Jayne was touched they would think of her before giving it away. "I would love to, but you have to give me a minute to get dressed."

"Please," Luke motioned to the front door. "I'll just put these back in the shed where they can't do any more damage. I'll get started on your battery too" He glanced back at the bushes.

"Okay. I just put on a pot of coffee, can I get you a cup while I straighten up?"

"That would be great."

When Jayne came back out with the coffee, Rusty appeared from nowhere and ran out front. She chased after him shouting his name, but he jumped straight into Luke's waiting arms. Jayne slowed her pace and watched as Rusty licked every inch of Luke's face. She hadn't noticed before, but he had on a nicely fitted T-shirt with the logo of some surfing company on the front. It showed off the definition of his arms and shape of his stomach. His dark hair was styled in his same 1960s wave with the modern fade on the side. His blue jeans fit so perfect they could have been tailored to him. Jayne was blindsided by the flipping of her stomach when she saw him. *Where's this coming from?* She thought. She stumbled over her words, forgetting what she was doing for a moment, distracted by her sudden attraction for him. She tried to force any thoughts away but as she got closer, he smiled and whatever hadn't flipped now melted to a pool in her feet. There was an immediate longing for him to scoop her into his arms, pressing her body into his, like silly putty against a washboard. Instead, she smiled.

"Thanks for coming to do this today. You've been a crazy amount of help in just a couple of days.

"It's no problem." There was a long pause then finally Luke knocked on the driver's side window with his knuckle and said, "The door is locked."

"Oh, of course it is. I'll just get the key." She handed him the coffee and took Rusty's squirming body from Luke, her hand grazing his chest and stomach. She peeked at his face to see if he noticed and quickly turned around, heading toward the house before remembering she'd left the key in the rental car from the other day. She turned back around and announced, "It's in the rental." The car was parked at the bottom of the porch stairs. She jumped off the last step and realized that car would be locked too. She again shouted, "I'll just get the key for that one." Luke laughed and shook his head. Once inside, Jayne chided herself. *Get it together. What's my problem?* She was engaged, but she didn't know what to do with these feelings for Luke, it was like she was just handed a puppy with no owner; she didn't necessarily want it, but she was curious about the possibilities and it was so cute that she wasn't quite ready to give it up yet. She dashed to the kitchen where the keys were on the countertop and ran back outside.

Jayne opened the truck door, then Luke popped the hood and took a look. "The connections are pretty dirty and rusty. Do you have a wet cloth?"

"Yeah, I'll grab one." She came back out with the rag and Luke smiled. "Is there anything else you need?" she asked

"No, I think everything I need is in the shed. I should

only be about thirty minutes."

Jayne took this as her cue to leave. She told Luke just to come in the house when he was finished. Unwanted thoughts of him coming into the house and finding her intentionally sprawled out on the couch in her nicest underwear set, like in some cheesy romance novel, flooded her mind. *Fifty Shades of Not Happening,* she thought to herself. When she closed the door Billy sat up from the couch.

"What's going on there, Bunny?" he asked, nodding toward the window where evidently he had been watching the two of them.

Jayne rolled her eyes. "It's nothing—just some stupid girl hormones or something." She crossed her arms and sat down in the chair by the front door. "I can't help it. What's wrong with me?"

"Nothing," Billy assured her. "It happens. Don't worry. Keep yourself busy. Everything is meant to be, so let it. Maybe these emotions are trying to tell you something, or maybe they're just trying to challenge you. Either way, just let them happen; they'll either go away or they'll tell you what you need to know."

Jayne nodded. "You're right. Keep myself busy. Okay." She balled her fists, released and looked around the room, settling on the box with the newspaper clippings. There were a few papers already stacked neatly on top of the rest. Jayne picked up the first paper on top, dated 1964. The title read, "Son of White Business Owner Willfully Employs Black Men at Same Pay Rate as Other White Employees." Jayne scanned the article, her eyes caught on one paragraph.

> "'I voted for JFK and I fully plan to uphold and defend the Civil Rights Act being put in place. These [black] men deserve to live the same life any

one of us do. I hired them because they are some of the best furniture builders we've ever hired. They are creative, hardworking, and well-behaved. I would encourage any business owner to hire these young black men whose families have taught them what real suffering felt like; not like the privileged, white families who think the world owes them something.'

When asked if he thought this would hurt his business, owner of Webber Furniture, Gerry Webber, replied that he didn't think his clients, who were of decent upbringing and good family values, would care who made their furniture as long as it was done to their liking."

Jayne looked at the picture above the article. She could see her father's furniture store in the background with an old, tin "Webber Furniture" sign nailed to the front. A man, noted to be her grandfather, Steve, was standing in front of the store to the left of the sign with an older gentleman, Gerry, her great-grandfather, beside him. Both of them were squinting at the camera with a blank look on their face as if this picture was taken in the middle of answering questions. For a moment Jayne thought back to her history classes, the Civil Rights Act of 1964 and the political climate in the south during that time.

Hell, it's still going on to this day. She thought about how her grandfather and great-grandfather were putting a lot on the line and how risky it would have been to be a white activist for the black people in the sixties. She felt an overwhelming amount of compassion and pride for them.

She placed the paper facedown on the floor near the box. The next paper she picked up was another article about Webber Furniture. This article was titled "Arson Suspected in the Case of Webber Furniture Burning." The photo attached to the article showed a broken window that the Molotov cocktail had been thrown through. The door to the building was painted with foul words and quick scribbled drawings of monkeys. Steve was standing in front of the building, facing away from the camera this time, the back of his hand on his forehead, shading his eyes from the sun, and the other hand on his hip, a dirty rag hanging out of his fist. The caption under the photo read, "Fire broke out at two o'clock Wednesday morning. No one was injured and Steve Webber assures us that business will be open as usual while he cleans up the graffiti and repairs the minor fire damages."

Jayne looked up to Billy, but he was gone. She had a tornado of emotions: respect for her grandfather who just wanted to do the right thing, and hatred for the people who violated his business in the name of racism. She flipped over the article to rest on the first. A Polaroid photo fell into her lap. The face staring back at her was dirty and tired, but someone she now recognized as her grandfather. He looked much more mature than the previous photos, a few years older and more experienced at life. Even though she didn't know him, he had a sense of familiarity. He was wearing a green uniform, faded and smeared with dirt and other stains. His shirt was unbuttoned halfway, revealing a muscular chest. He was sitting on a pile of sandbags with a gun in one hand and a finger-gun pointed at the camera with the other. His nails were dirty and he had a cut on the back of his hand. His helmet was on, crooked to the side, and his sleeves were rolled up to his elbows. He had a genuine smile, like he had just been laughing. Jayne imagined the cameraman telling him to say "cheese", or something else inappropriate. *He would have been a handsome man,* Jayne thought. He looked a lot like her dad: same thin face, long pointed nose, and stalky build. She turned it over and there was a note on the back.

It read,

> June 30,1968.
> To my love, Mary-Anne. Here's your pinup. Give that boy a kiss and a hug for me. Miss you both more than the world. I can't wait to have a piece of your warm apple pie.

Jayne wasn't sure if the apple pie was an innuendo for something naughty, but something else caught her attention. *He has a son,* she thought. *Of course he does — Dad was born in 1964, so he would have been four when Grandpa Steve went off to war.* She imagined her grandfather's age to be about thirty-two in the photo and pictured her grandmother raising a baby boy alongside the other women in the community whose husbands were also off at war.

Before she picked up the next piece of paper, dated 1980, she already knew it was not good. A small photo in the corner depicted a headshot of a kid who looked like he had been through the wringer; his long, dark hair was disheveled, he had bags under his eyes, and had a cut on his cheek. The larger photo showed the scene of a horrific car crash with a small car, the driver's side completely smashed in, the windshield in pieces scattered across the dash, and the tires all flat. The car was partially submerged in a river while four policemen stood on the shoreline examining the scene, one pointing to the driver's side door. Jayne scanned the article and felt a knot in her stomach when she read the caption. "Mary-Anne Webber (40 years), named victim in crash involving drunk driver, Alonso Sanchez (depicted in inset)."

"Oh my god," Jayne said out loud. Her dad had never mentioned exactly how his mother died. He would give her vague details about "an accident", and if she pressed on, he would say it was something he didn't want to talk about. She read more of the article to better understand what happened.

> "Mrs. Webber, wife of furniture store owner Steve Webber, was driving westbound on TX-80 Saturday evening, returning from a trip to Houston. Forty minutes from home, at approximately 9:30 p.m., a drunken Alfonso fell asleep at the wheel, swerving into her lane and colliding with the driver's side door. Mrs. Webber's vehicle lost control and careened through the barrier into the Blanco River, just outside of San Marcos. Mrs. Webber was deceased when officials arrived and Mr. Sanchez was passed out from injuries sustained to his head. He was arrested and taken to the Hays County Jail. Our deepest sympathies go out to the Webber family and fellow business owner. Mary-Anne Webber leaves behind her husband, Steve, and sixteen-year-old son, Peter Webber. She would have been forty-one on Tuesday."

The rest of the article was details on the funeral and where donations could be made in her memory. Jayne felt an overwhelming sadness for the grandparents she never met and even more so for her father. She thought of how her grandfather and father didn't get along most of her dad's life—not until Peter came to live in this house and take care of Steve when he was sick with cirrhosis of the liver; the same thing Peter suffered from. She wondered if her grandmother's death was the catalyst on which their relationship started to falter.

I did the same thing to him as he did to his father. He wanted to be different from his father, he wanted to have a relationship with his child, and I took that from him. A single tear slid down her cheek into the corner of her mouth, then another, and another, each exploring the curves of her face. Before she knew it, she was crying into her hands, the feeling of guilt overwhelming, wishing she could take back the past ten years and have put more of an effort into their relationship instead of being selfish. There was nothing she could do about it now—she had to move on.

She realized Luke must be close to finishing and she hadn't gotten ready yet. She dried her face and ran upstairs to quickly change.

7

LUKE WAS SITTING at the table playing on his phone, Rusty in his lap, when Jayne came back down fifteen minutes later. Her hair was a more organized version of the messy bun it was before. She'd put on her usual go-to mascara, blush, and tinted lip-gloss. She wore a comfortable pair of dark jeans Blake bought for her and a thin cream-colored cashmere sweater that hung comfortably off her shoulders. She loved that sweater; it cost a fortune but it felt like wearing a cloud. She added cream to her coffee and poured it in a to-go cup. Out the window, she could see Billy heading toward the old house. She felt bad for how she acted toward him when she woke up. She grabbed her purse off the chair.

"Shall we go?"

Luke tried to hide his smile by looking down. "We shall. We can take my truck, I'll give you a ride home when we're done."

"Okay, thanks." Rusty followed them to the front door and whined when she held him back with her foot as she closed the door.

"You know, your dad used to bring Rusty a lot of places with him."

She hopped in the passenger's seat. "We're not there in our relationship," she said.

"You don't like animals?"

"It's not that. I'm just used to having a hair-free, noise-free, dependent-free life."

"Do you want kids?" He glanced at her quickly as he put the truck in reverse.

"Maybe, eventually, I think. Right now I enjoy spending my money on myself, though." She laughed. "I'm not high-maintenance, but I like nice things without bite marks. It's pretty clean in here for a guy's truck." She changed the subject.

"Yeah, I get that a lot. So what was the assault on the bushes about?"

"Oh. It was nothing."

Luke gave her an "I'm-not-buying-that-for-a-moment" glance.

She took a deep breath. "It's just that my fiancé was supposed to be here with me for everything, including my dad's funeral, but he keeps putting it off. Work stuff. He's a lawyer and has new clients. He was supposed to be coming tomorrow, until I talked to him this morning."

"And he's postponed again?"

"Yep, indefinitely. Well, maybe not indefinitely, but I hung up on him, so I didn't get to hear if he's still coming out."

"I'm sorry. It may not be the same, but I'm here to help however I can."

"Thanks. I appreciate it. Your mom already left me an amazing quiche." The thought of it made Jayne's stomach grumble.

"Oh, the quiche Lorraine? That's my favorite. It's a best seller at The Café."

"Yeah, it was delicious. I ate almost all of it in one sitting," she confessed.

"So, I have to say: I didn't realize you were engaged."

Back to this, Jayne thought, but maybe she heard a hint of disappointment in his voice this time. She looked at her bare hand. "Oh, I forgot to put my ring back on yesterday when I got out of the shower," she said. "Still getting used to it, I guess."

"So it's a new engagement?"

"Yes, fairly. It's only been a couple of months."

"Oh, well, congrats. I thought women wanted to show off their rings usually."

"Well, I suppose they do. This one is . . . well, it's big. And I'm not trying to sound pretentious, but I'm an artist and it gets in the way a lot. I'm not used to having jewelry on."

"I see."

"And it doesn't fit."

Luke laughed harder than he should have and Jayne actually smiled. He glanced at her for a moment "It doesn't *fit*?" He laughed again.

"What?"

"Nothing." He shook his head. "I always thought that was just some cliché thing that happened in movies."

"Nope, I guess not." She rubbed where the ring should have been.

They got into town within a few minutes and Jayne asked if they had time to stop at The Café so she could grab a muffin. Her stomach was audibly rumbling now so Luke didn't refuse.

"Let's park at the shop and The Café is right around the corner. We can walk right over."

"Perfect."

When they got to The Café, it was fairly busy for nine thirty in the morning. Luke's mom, Liz, was behind the counter pouring coffee. The smell of freshly baked goods and brewed coffee filled Jayne's nose.

"Hey you two, what are you doing here? Aren't you supposed to be at work, Luke?" Liz asked, straightening out the apron around her neck.

"Dad sent me to get Jayne before the Hill Country set was sold. She was starving though, so we're just going to grab something."

"Oh, great. What can I get you Jayne?"

"Well first off," Jayne said, "thank you so much for the quiche, it was exactly what I needed and it was delicious!"

"You're very welcome." Liz smiled big and genuine.

Jayne peered into the glass case at the side of the register. "Everything looks so good. Any recommendations?"

"The peach cheesecake muffin is Luke's favorite, but the dark chocolate cherry is our best seller." Liz pointed each out.

"I think I'll try the peach. I can't do chocolate first thing in the morning."

"You got it," Liz said. Jayne reached for her wallet.

"I got this," said another voice. Jayne turned to see a tall, thin, middle-aged man wearing a button-up shirt and slacks. His thick-rimmed glasses made his eyes look smaller than they were and his graying hair was partly disheveled as if it had been styled that way. "You're Jane, Peter's daughter, right?"

"Jay-nee," she corrected. "But yes, I am." She posed more of a question than a statement with her tone.

"My name is Frederick Manns." He reached out his hand. "I've bought many of your father's pieces — even some of your grandfather's. The Webber quality has definitely been passed down throughout the generations." Frederick pulled a five-dollar bill from his wallet and waved his hand when Liz tried to pass him the change.

"Oh, thank you," Jayne replied. "That's very nice to hear. I unfortunately haven't had the pleasure of seeing my grandfather's work."

"I'm a bit of a collector. Of course, you're more than welcome to stop by and see some of it if you have the time. I run the old Carter house up on Ember Street. I've used a lot of his pieces in there. Luke can bring you by sometime."

"That's very kind of you." She took the paper-wrapped muffin from Liz, nodding her thanks.

"Of course. You can reach me at any of these outlets." He reached into his chest pocket and handed her a business card. "Liz, it was a pleasure seeing you as always. Luke, good to see you." Frederick shook Luke's hand.

"Good to see you too Mr. Manns. Come by the shop sometime and we'll show you some new pieces." Jayne looked at the card and recognized it as one of the cards Joe had in his stack of possible buyers.

"You know I will." He turned and nodded to Jayne. "Miss Webber, it's great to see you have grown into a nice young lady. I hope to see you around town some more. Come by the house, it was your family's a few generations ago after all."

"Oh?" Jayne said, surprised. She didn't know of another house her family had ties to. "You never know. Thank you for the muffin Mr. Manns."

"Call me Frederick, and you're very welcome."

They watched him leave.

"Am I *supposed* to feel creeped out by him?" Jayne whispered.

Luke shook his head.

"He's pretty much harmless, just a little odd at times."

"Okay." Jayne sighed. "We should probably get going."

Busy with a customer, Liz just waved goodbye.

On the way back to the shop, the air was brisk, but the sun was out, warming where it touched. Jayne asked, "So what's this Frederick guy's story anyway?" She ripped off a piece of her muffin and popped it in her mouth.

"He either owns or runs the Carter house on Ember Street. I'm not entirely sure."

"And that was my family's somehow?" she asked.

"I guess so. It's a big house that's been here for over a hundred years. There aren't many of them around anymore, but the big ones stayed because the businessmen in the area could afford to keep them maintained. The Carter house has been turned into a tea room and they do tours once a week, so it gets a bit of foot traffic, but mostly businessmen go there to make their business deals. It's quieter than The Café or Sammy's and has a homely feel. I could take you there sometime."

"That would be amazing," Jayne said around a mouthful of muffin, a spray of chewed crumbs exploding out. She clapped a hand over her mouth

Luke smiled.

8

WHEN THEY GOT to the shop, Luke bypassed the office and walked them to the back. An alluring combination of fresh cut wood and stain was thick in the air. Jayne breathed a big lungful of it. Joe and three other guys were in a pile of foam and cardboard, wrapping up the legs and corners on a side table.

"Just in time," Joe boomed. He finished taping his piece and walked over to Jayne and Luke. "We're just wrapping the pieces for pick up. The new owner is going to meet us this morning to pay the remaining balance and take a look to make sure everything is satisfactory. Let me show you some of the pieces." Joe motioned for Jayne to follow a few steps to the side where there was a six-foot-tall headboard covered by a blanket. Luke helped him pull the headboard out and carefully remove the blanket. "Your dad made this one and used it as a centerpiece for the rest."

Jayne was stunned by the detail. "It's amazing. I . . . I don't have words." The headboard was one massive cut from a tree. It must have been six feet wide. She ran her fingers over the top two feet of raw bark, which had an intricate pattern of wild longhorns, cattle, and horses carved along the top. A Texas star ended the pattern back in to the raw wood. Peter's signature mark of poured silver was laced through the cracks and fissures. It made the animals seem connected in a mystical way. The entire thing was varnished and it looked like a piece of art behind glass. Jayne reached out and touched the face on one of the horses. "I didn't know he could carve such complex pictures. Did he do it often?"

"He didn't really realize he could do it either until recently. This was his first major piece," Joe said.

"Wow," Jayne said, barely audible. "When is the owner supposed to be here?"

"Looks like he's right there," Luke said. He and Joe covered the headboard back up and carefully leaned it against the padded wall.

They walked over and Joe introduced Jayne to Mr. Johannas. He apologized for Jayne's loss and she thanked him, tucking her hands in her back pockets.

"I'm honored to have one of his last pieces." He turned to Luke. "Thank you for finishing the pieces to match and doing them justice at that. You can barely tell where Peter left off and you picked up."

"You did these?" Jayne asked, pointing to an end table. Luke nodded.

"When your dad got sick and was admitted to the hospital a few days before he passed, Luke stepped up and finished the detail and varnish on these two end tables." Joe patted Luke on the back. "He's been up all night for the past week."

Jayne bent down to take a better look. The same pattern on the headboard was wrapped around the drawer and sides of the table. In the middle of one drawer stood a longhorn, and on the other table, a horse. Mr. Johannas was right—she couldn't tell that two different people had carved and finished the pieces.

"It's remarkable, Luke," she said. He nodded at her, too modest to say anything. "Thank you for your business, Mr. Johannas. I hope you'll come back for more pieces or recommend us to your acquaintances." Jayne stuck out her hand.

Mr. Johannas took her hand and gave it a shake. "As long as you're still here, I'll be a loyal customer. Are you taking it over?"

Jayne felt her cheeks flush. "We're working out the details right now." She glanced at Joe.

"Good. This is a fine shop with quality artists. I don't think I could commission work from anyone else."

Artists. She'd never thought of any of the employees like that before, but that's exactly what they were. They created beautiful collector pieces from nothing but their bare hands and raw materials.

"Well, I'll let you guys finish up," she said. "I should get back to the house. I have a lot to do there still, but is there anything I can help with before I go?" she asked Joe.

"I don't think so Jayne. We're just working on a few more things and the paperwork has already been done for the weekend. Luke can give you a ride home."

"Okay, thanks. Well, it was nice to meet you Mr. Johannas. I hope you'll send us some pictures when the pieces are in place. I'd love to put them up on our social media."

"It was my pleasure. I'll send some over as soon as everything is set up."

Jayne nodded and they headed out to Luke's truck.

"Um, Jayne?" Luke said, opening the door for her. She turned to him, pulling a stray piece of hair from her mouth.

"Hmm?"

"We don't have any social media accounts."

"What? Really?" She wasn't surprised since the shop had no millennial influence other than Luke, but that was how she'd made her own art business so successful. "Okay, I'll set something up. Do you mind sending me some pictures? Anything that you have, especially of finished pieces. It would be a great way to advertise to people who don't live here."

9

BACK AT THE house, Jayne was getting ready for her mom to arrive. Rusty left his spot by the master bedroom to follow her around. She received a text that Dani was on the plane coming from North Carolina to Texas. It would be a two-and-a-half-hour flight and then an hour drive from San Antonio. Her mom insisted on renting a car instead of Jayne coming to pick her up. That meant another hour, at least, until Dani arrived. Jayne was fine with that—she had things she needed to get done.

She gathered the blankets from the spare room and took them out to the laundry in the garage. The rooms needed a good dusting and a vacuum in the meantime. She wondered if it was going to be weird for her mom to be back in the house she'd left twenty years ago.

Jayne went to the store to pick up something for dinner and get her mom's favorite chocolate and coffee. Luckily she didn't run into anyone who knew her. She wasn't in the mood for more condolences. She thought about Luke. He hadn't offered any condolences, but instead of feeling offended, she felt a surge of gratitude and appreciation toward him for that. She didn't like being reminded at every turn that she was the MIA daughter of the beloved furniture-maker in town. *Maybe that's why I feel so comfortable around him; he doesn't treat me with a bunch of formalities,* she thought.

When she got back to the house, she put the groceries away and went out to the garage to get the blankets out of the drier. *I haven't seen Billy all morning. I wonder where he is.* As if being beckoned, Billy sauntered into the garage.

"I was just thinking about you," Jayne said, folding the bed sheet.

"I know." He smiled. "You were asking for me?"

"I was?" Jayne paused. "Oh, I was just thinking about how I hadn't seen you since this morning."

"I see." Billy hopped up onto the washer. "Whenever you want me to come, all you have to do is ask. I'm connected to you, I guess."

"You are? Why?"

"Well, for one, you're the only one I know of that can really see me, and I've known you since you were a baby."

"I never thought of that," Jayne said, surprised. "Were you there when my mom had me? I know she had me in the house."

Billy nodded with wide, excited eyes.

"Tell me about it." Jayne folded some more linen and leaned on the warm pile of clothes.

"Oh, well, I was the first thing you saw when you broke through the surface of the water. You may not have *seen* me, but you kept looking in my direction. It had seemed like hours that the midwife paced back and forth from the kitchen to the mini pool in the living room. Your dad spent his time awkwardly massaging whatever part of your mom he could get his hands on and finally, after about five hours of her making weird sounds and humming, he gave up. But within two more hours the midwife announced that you were coming. It was the moment I had been waiting for. I couldn't wait to see you and the soul of a precious new life — a life I felt I already knew.

"I desperately wanted to have my turn at holding you, but I never could. My most precious thing and I could only look at you." Billy looked somber. "I would have given anything to hold you that day. You smelled so nice. I remember the smell from my own kids: a mix of sweet almonds, fresh vanilla cream, and clean laundry."

Jayne silently wondered what Billy would have looked like as a grown man. It was odd listening to a teenager talk about his wife and children.

"The following days I spent staring at you, jumping at every sound you made and trying to comfort you when you cried. Your mom didn't get much sleep and like some new dads, yours wasn't much help. It wasn't for a lack of trying, he just couldn't and he felt hopeless about it. He made up for it in different ways, like letting your mom take a shower, or eat her lunch without having you attached like a little monkey.

"When they finally got into a routine a few days later, your mom would put you down in your cradle or chair and you would just stare into space. I tried to talk to you while your mom tried to sleep or clean.

"Finally, three weeks later, it was a warm afternoon and your mom had already finished all the housework. She sat in her favorite chair with you and her book. I admired you over her shoulder and said, 'Hello there, Honey Bunny.' A smile spread over your face and your eyes locked on mine. I couldn't believe it; you *saw* me. 'What are you smiling at?' your mom asked and I just kept repeating, 'Hello, hello, hello,' in a high-pitched voice, shaking my head."

Jayne was smiling at these recollections that were making Billy so happy.

"Your mom became suspicious and looked in my direction. Of course she didn't see anything, so she poked you on the nose and said, 'Whatever you're looking at sure is making you happy.' If I had a heart, it would have melted straight onto the floor. From then I was hooked."

Jayne waited to see if there was more but a few seconds pause told her he was finished talking. "That's really sweet Billy. Thank you for sharing that with me."

Billy smiled but didn't make eye contact. "It's one of the things I got when I . . . you know . . . died. I'm able to remember anything that happened in my human life and my spirit life."

"That has to be wonderful and hard at the same time." Jayne smiled and looked at her watch. "Half-past four. Mom should be here soon."

"You know, I haven't seen her in a very long time. Has she changed much?"

Jayne grabbed the pile of clothes and headed toward the house. Billy followed behind. "Hard to say, since I've grown with her, but when I look at the pictures she seems the same. She looks very young for her age; just a few gray hairs." Jayne peeked around the pile of clothes and almost ran into a round woman with puffy hair, probably once a shade of red but now orange from fading. "Oh!" Jayne exclaimed and almost dropped the laundry.

"I'm sorry to startle you, dear," the woman said. "You probably don't remember me: Patty Brockett. We met briefly at the funeral. I'm so sorry again."

"Thank you. Yes, hi." She walked past the woman onto the porch and set the laundered blankets on the wicker rocking chair. She turned to shake her hand before she noticed a casserole dish cradled in Patty's arms.

Patty looked around to the garage. "I'm sorry, I heard you talking to someone. Do you have company?"

Jayne looked over at Billy, who had stopped in between the garage and the house. "Oh, no." Jayne laughed awkwardly. "I sometimes get caught up in thoughts and they come out of my mouth."

"Happens to the best of us. Gets worse when you get older." Patty chuckled.

"Can I help you with something? Do you want to come in?" Jayne wasn't in the mood for company, but southern politeness always surpassed mood.

"No, no, of course I don't mean to bother you." The woman giggled like an English duchess hosting a tea party. "I just wanted to drop off this chicken-and-potato casserole. I know you probably don't have time to cook much with everything you've got going on. I can drop it inside since you've got a handful of clean washing there." She nodded to the pile on the chair.

"Yes, thank you." Jayne opened the door and let Patty enter. "Please don't mind the mess, I'm just starting to go through things now. You can set that anywhere in the kitchen."

"Okay dear." Patty stepped over a rogue sofa cushion and walked into the kitchen, setting the casserole on the table. "Is it just you here?"

"My mom is going to be here soon and my fiancé is coming in a couple of days." Jayne set the laundry on the bottom step of the stairway.

"Oh, great. It would be terribly sad if you had to deal with this all alone. I'm very sorry about your loss. Your father was a great help to the town. He would always be helping everyone when something broke. No matter what time of day, we knew we could call Peter Webber to fix our things. He always knew the right thing to say as well. I was going through a terrible time with the death of my Frank and it seemed that everything went wrong after that. Your father came to check on me almost every morning to see I was getting out of bed and not letting the sorrow envelop me. He's actually the one who got me my job; negotiated my wage and everything so that I could still live without my Frank."

Jayne smiled. "Where did you say you worked?"

"Oh, I guess I didn't. I'm the chef at the Carter house. I just work a few days a week when they have business luncheons or tours." She smiled.

"Oh! I actually want to come down there to see the place. I didn't realize it was in my family relations until this morning when I ran into Mr. Manns."

"Oh, yes, he mentioned he ran into you at The Café. He said I should stop by and . . ." Patty trailed off, then smiled and said, "Well, I just wanted to drop this off and see that you're doing okay. You seem to be just fine." She stepped over the same cushion and walked to the door. "Please let me know if you need anything at all, dear."

"Thank you Patty, I will." Jayne opened the door for her. "And thank you so much for the casserole. I think that will do just the trick. It's much appreciated."

"You're welcome, dear. Stop by the Carter house sometime for breakfast."

"You can count on that. Nothing like a good southern breakfast, and from the smell of that casserole, it's bound to be delicious." Jayne plastered on a big, toothy grin.

Patty smiled and giggled again. "Okay sweetie, well you take care and we'll see you soon."

"You too Patty, thank you." Jayne waved at her as she drove off and glanced at the garage where Billy had been standing. He was gone.

10

JAYNE FINISHED MAKING the bed, cleaning up what she could, and tidying the kitchen. Billy had disappeared after Patty visited, giving Jayne some much needed space.

Her mom was destined to pull up at any minute, so she opened a chilled bottle of locally-made white wine she had picked up, poured two glasses, and went out to the porch. She let Rusty follow her out this time and sat in one of the wicker chairs overlooking the gravel driveway and front yard with all the pecan trees randomly placed throughout. Rusty hopped up and snuggled beside her, propping his baseball-sized head on her thigh. His beady eyes were looking up at her.

"I know, I need to go picking the pecans in the next couple of days," she said to him. He wedged his head into the crook of her knee and she laid a hand on him.

If she could get someone to shell them for her she could make pecan pie or Blake's favorite: pecan bars. At the thought of Blake, she grabbed her phone, imagining there might be a text. The screen of her smartphone only revealed a picture of her and Blake when they were in Key West on two separate bachelor and bachelorette parties. Both of them were smiling at the camera. Blake was towering over her, holding her tight against his chest.

Jayne's heartstrings fluttered thinking about the days when he wanted to spend every day he could with her. Now, in an ironic twist, he wanted to provide for her and their future family by working all day, every day. She knew she needed to be there for him and support him, not bash him for wanting a better life for them. She opened the messages on the phone and typed: "Hi my love, I hope you're having a good day and able to take a break to eat something. I love you and I'm sorry for being a bitch lately." Jayne knew she had a reason to be upset, but she also recognized where Blake was coming from.

Almost immediately, a text came through from Blake:

"Babe, you're going through a lot, I'm sorry I can't be there. I love you and I'll see you soon. I just had some pho at our favorite place on the corner."

Jayne smiled.

Dani pulled up a few seconds later and Jayne took a sip of her wine as she watched the car come down the long driveway, rocks popping and crunching beneath the tires. Rusty's ears perked up and he watched Dani park near the garage before he let out a small, informative bark. Jayne got up and met her to give her a big hug.

"I'm so glad you're here," she said into her shoulder, squeezing her, a hug was everything she'd needed for the past week.

"Me too, baby girl." Dani hugged her tight and gave her a kiss on the side of the head. Rusty sauntered over, stretched, and then reached up Dani's leg. She laughed and asked, "And who's this little guy?"

"That's Rusty. He's my new little companion, came with the house. I'm still unsure about him."

"Funny, your dad was against pets of any kind." She scratched his head, instantly making a new friend out of him.

Jayne shrugged. "How's Grandma doing?" She grabbed Dani's suitcase from the back seat while Dani grabbed her carry-on and purse.

Dani sighed and pushed her dark, curly hair out of her face. "She's okay right now. Uncle Anthony is staying at the house while I'm gone. He always takes good care of her and she likes having him around; it's a good change from me and the nurses."

"That's good," Jayne said. She stepped onto the porch and put her bag down by the door. "Do you want to go straight inside or have a glass of wine first?"

Dani paused, thinking. "Let me have a quick swig of that wine and then we'll go inside." Jayne handed her the cold, sweating glass and Dani took a deep gulp. "Okay, I'm ready."

Jayne opened the door and walked in first, holding the screen door open. She watched Dani's reaction when she came through.

"Oh my gosh." Her eyes circled the room. "It's exactly the same. Weird." She set down her bag while Jayne dragged the suitcase in. "It's as if no one had lived here since I moved out. It even *smells* the same." There were still decorations hung that Peter's parents had put up in the seventies.

"I don't suspect Dad was doing much living since we left. You wouldn't believe some of the stuff I've been boxing up." Jayne pointed to a box near the kitchen. "That one is full of cassettes and some VHS tapes."

"They were in that drawer over there, weren't they?"

Dani motioned to the middle drawer of the shelving unit. Jayne nodded and Dani laughed. "Somehow that doesn't surprise me. Your father wasn't one for change. I see he still has Ol' Blue, from his dad."

"Yeah, the battery died though, so I got a new one. Luke, Joe and Liz's son, helped me put it in."

"Your dad would hate that; he didn't want to change that battery for anything." She laughed. "How are Joe and Liz? And Luke, he's about your age, isn't he?"

"Yeah, he is. They're good. Liz owns The Café just off Main Street still. She actually brought over an amazing quiche after Dad's wake. Joe is keeping things together at the shop. He's a bit . . . rounder than I remember."

Dani laughed. "He was destined to be a chubby man. You could see it in his bones, even twenty years ago." She looked over the living room and kitchen and said, "Well, should we take this up?"

"Sure." Jayne led the way. "Since I'm staying in my old room and the only rooms available are the master and the spare, I figured you would choose the spare."

"You would be correct." Rusty followed them up the stairs where they paused and Dani fixed her gaze on the master bedroom. "Have you been in there yet?"

"No. I'm not ready. It's like I'll find him just lying there or something."

"We can do it together when you are ready."

Jayne nodded and walked into the spare room. "I don't think this room had been touched since we left. I did wash the sheets today, at least."

Dani shook her head and chuckled. "I have to see something." She walked over to the armoire across from the bed and opened up the front doors. The TV was big and from the eighties. Underneath was a small drawer Dani pulled open, and inside was a phone book. "Yep." Dani grabbed it and held it out to Jayne.

"That's the year before we left. This has been here for over twenty years."

Jayne held the phone book to her chest. "Well, I guess this doesn't need to be in here anymore, then. Let's go downstairs. I grabbed a couple things for dinner."

Dani dropped her bags, took one last look at the room, and followed Jayne out.

After dinner, Jayne helped her mom clean the dishes while Rusty moved around their feet, cleaning up crumbs.

"So, tell me about this Luke. I remember him as a quiet kid. What's he like now?" Dani asked.

Caught off guard, Jayne replied, "He's still quiet. And he's tall, with a nice, dark complexion, which he probably got from Joe. He works out, I'm sure."

"You're *sure*?" Dani hummed, passing her a wet plate.

"Well, I mean, he's built. His body is . . . never mind." Jayne felt the blood rushing to her cheeks. She dried the plate with vigor.

"Oh boy," Dani replied.

11

THE NEXT MORNING, Jayne got up, said a quick "hello" to Billy, and went downstairs. She was too excited to see her mom to make small chat with Billy. He sat with his hands rested on his belly and smiled.

Dani was already making coffee and pancakes and the smell of them frying in the skillet made Jayne's stomach growl. The aroma of coffee drew her instinctually to the coffee pot. She stumbled into the kitchen, readjusting her ponytail and smoothing the baby curls off her forehead. Rusty was digging into the bowl of food her mom had poured for him. He paid no attention to her.

"Morning honey. I'm making pancakes, but I can't guarantee how they'll turn out. I'm pretty sure that's twenty-year-old flour." She shrugged and flipped the pancake. "I went through the pantry and most of that can be thrown out." She waived the spatula at the table. The kitchen table was full of cereal boxes, tins of soup, cartons of oatmeal, iced tea, packages of hot chocolate mix, bags of rock-hard sugar, and other baking goods.

"Thanks. Worst case, we can just dig into the casserole if that doesn't work out."

"True. Grab a plate and your coffee, and we can eat outside on the deck. I'll be right out."

Jayne grabbed her plate, covered the pancakes in a maple-flavored syrup, and headed out the sliding back door. Billy was already out there. Jayne sat in a chair a few down from his. Rusty came out and ran down the deck stairs to relieve himself before coming back up to join them.

"Your mom looks exactly the same. A few gray hairs, but same long, brown curls and soft face," he said.

Jayne smiled with a puffy, pancake-filled cheek.

Dani came out and started to squat into Billy's chair.

"No! Don't sit—" Dani jumped up, causing her fork to fall to the deck.

"What is it?" she exclaimed.

Billy had hopped up quickly and moved to the railing, sitting with his feet up, leaning against the column. "Nothing, never mind, sorry. I thought I saw a bug."

"Nothing my ass won't get rid of quick." Dani bent to pick up the fork and sat back into the chair. Billy chuckled and Jayne gave him a quick glance. "I was thinking we could stop by the shop today, check to see if Joe needs any help with anything. I wouldn't mind seeing him again. Then we could pop over to the supermarket real quick and I'll grab a couple more things."

"That sounds good. I'll get showered and ready after breakfast."

"Okay." Dani took a couple bites of her pancake. "You know, if I'd have known your dad was living like this—"

"Mom, there's nothing you could have done. You can't blame yourself. You did what you knew was best for us." She decided not to share what Luke had told her about Peter's regrets. After talking to Billy, she agreed that her mom had done the right thing. "At least he was clean and tidy."

"He probably had a maid," Dani said.

Jayne chuckled. "Then he got ripped off, leaving twenty-year-old phone books in drawers." Billy smiled and hopped off the railing and walked around the side of the house.

Jayne finished getting ready before Dani and then headed out to the back deck again. Billy was there, watching the shadows from the banisters crawl around the deck as the sun rose higher.

"Hi Billy," Jayne said. He turned to her, looking like he had just woken up from a nap, and patted the seat beside him. "What were you just thinking about?"

"I was actually just reminiscing about your fifth birthday party you had here. Do you remember? There was a bit of a fiasco when you told the other kids about me."

"I remember," Jayne said with a tinge of regret in her voice.

"Yeah, that was quite the day." Billy recalled the memory. It was only the start of the day that would end their time together.

1997

Billy was just as excited as Jayne was for her birthday. He whizzed around the house, following Dani and making sure everything was perfect. Peter had already picked up the bounce house and was outside setting it up. He insisted that he didn't need anyone to come help him and that he would be just fine to do it on his own. But judging by the "god dammits" and the "stupid things", it wasn't going as well as Peter had hoped.

Dani was still in her pajamas and had already put together the party favors, supplies, food, and everything else. While she sat and connected with a few people who hadn't RSVP'd yet, Billy headed up to Jayne's room. She had just woken up and was playing with her teddy bears. She smiled when she saw him come in.

"Hi Billy! It's my birthday!" She bounced up and down, making the stuffed animals fly around the bed.

"Hi Bunny." He rubbed his hair. "Can we talk a little before your party?

"Yeah." She bounced one more time, landing on her butt, and then gathered up her stuffed animals, squishing them to her chest. She rested her chin on the head of a dog stuffed animal.

"So, you know how I said you couldn't talk about me to your parents?"

"Uh-huh."

"Well, what I meant was that you can't talk about me to *anyone*."

"You mean, not even my friends or the kids coming?"

"Definitely not them."

Jayne was quiet for a moment, then shrugged. "Okay."

That was easy, Billy thought, skeptical, but he didn't want to push the issue more.

Jayne got up and examined a dress Dani had laid out for her birthday. It was a pink, faux satin with no sleeves to accommodate the summer heat but compromised by three layers of tulle underneath. Jayne made a scrunched face and looked at Billy.

"You don't like that one?" he asked. She shook her head and went over to her closet to find something else.

"That one is too itchy." Instead she pulled out a well-worn cotton dress with pink polka dots and a teal bow on the front.

When Jayne came down the stairs she got to the last step and Dani was still in the kitchen.

"Mama?" she yelled.

Dani put down the stack of plates and walked to the stairs. "Good morning, baby."

"I don't want to wear that dress, Mommy. It's itchy."

"Okay, come on, let's go back up and see what's so itchy about it." Dani patted her butt up the stairs.

It took a small argument, but Jayne managed to convince Dani — like she always did — that it would be better if she just let her wear a more casual outfit. That way she could play and get dirty. They came to a compromise on the dress Jayne had chosen with an added pair of shorts underneath.

By two o'clock, Dani was putting the finishing touches on the food. Peter had just finished getting dressed and Jayne was still sleeping from a nap she demanded she needed before the guests arrived. Peter grabbed a beer out of the adult cooler on the back deck and sat down to admire his handiwork on the bounce house.

"Why don't you come sit down and have a beer before everyone gets here?" he yelled through the screen door to Dani. "I can help you finish when people start arriving."

Judging by Dani's eye roll, Billy knew she didn't believe he would help one bit. She couldn't deny that she did want to sit down a minute. Plus, anything left to do could be done with guests around and her mom and brother would be there to help.

She felt the heat body-slam her when she opened

the door and wondered if it would be too hot for the kids to play in the bounce house. *Make some Kool-Aid*, she added to her very long mental checklist. She had checked the weather again and it didn't waver from a sunny ninety-eight degrees.

With a sigh, she grabbed a beer from the cooler and sat down.

At two thirty there was a quick rap at the door like a woodpecker on a piece of lumber. It was Anthony, Dani's brother. He looked like a well-dressed Sherpa: his glasses were askew, his dark hair was disheveled and in need of a cut, and he had two duffle bags making an "X" across his chest with their straps. A small suitcase adorned each hand and an overnight bag was squished under his arm. Dani's mom, Reina, walked in like Elizabeth Taylor at the premier to her one-woman show. Billy watched silently by the stairs, always amused by her.

"Where's my grandbaby?" she called out, searching the living room with her eyes. "Thank you, Anthony," she added.

Dani walked into the living room, which was now filled with the familiar scent of Chanel perfume. "She's sleeping right now, but she should be up any minute."

Reina took off her sunglasses, folded them up, and hung them on the front of her blouse.

Billy had always liked Reina. She was the type of lady that fit her name: different, but elegant and slightly edgy. Her hair was done in a Jane Fonda 1980s style and had been that way since he could remember. The only difference this time was the color, which seemed to be a mix of dark brown and red, depending on the way the light hit it.

They hugged each other long enough for Dani to gaze at her brother and quickly realized he really needed help. She watched him shrug off one of the bags and place the others on the floor by the stairs before pushing his glasses back up

Peter poked his head around the corner with a cheeky smile. "I thought I heard trouble."

"There's my favorite son-in-law." Reina walked over to Peter and grabbed his face for a kiss on each side, then pulled him in for a hug.

"I bet you say that to all your sons-in-law," he jested.

"Well, considering I only have one, yes."

Peter noticed all the bags and started taking them to the spare room. "Looks like you brought everything but the kitchen sink, Reina."

"I'm insulted!" she said in her North Carolina accent. "How do you know that most of those aren't Anthony's?"

"Ma'am, please," Peter said with a knowing tone. He was already halfway up the stairs.

"Okay, you got me." Reina giggled and shrugged. Her eyes followed Peter all the way up the stairs then turned to Dani. "Mm-hmm, you've got to appreciate a man with strength."

"Mom!" Dani and Anthony whispered loudly in unison.

"Sorry. It's been awhile."

"Mom!" Dani said more firmly and Reina winked in reply.

Anthony shook his head and announced he was going to go help Peter upstairs.

"Come on Mom, I've got some sangria in the fridge that's been screaming your name since yesterday."

Reina followed her into the kitchen. "I've already

had two margaritas, but what's a little sangria going to hurt?"

Upstairs, Billy was sitting in the chair. He could tell Jayne was on the verge of waking up. Her toes stretched and pointed like a ballerina and her eyes opened briefly then closed before blinking open and staring at Billy blankly.

"Guess who's here, Bunny?" he said softly. She didn't say anything, but stared at him as if she'd just come out of a coma. "Grandma and Uncle Anthony!"

"What?" She pushed herself up and rubbed her eyes with the tips of her fingers. Billy nodded and smiled. She threw the blankets off and ran through the door and down the stairs.

Billy slowly got up and followed her. When she got down the stairs, she didn't wait for Dani before she ran into the kitchen and into Reina's arms.

"Hello, darling." Reina scooped her up and hugged her.

Jayne giggled and snuggled into the embrace. "Where's Uncle Anthony?"

Reina let her grasp loosen and Jayne slid to the floor. "He'll be right down, my baby. He's just putting our stuff in the spare room. My goodness, how tall *are* you now? Last time I saw you, you were knee-high to a grasshopper and now you're huge."

"Yup, I'm big and strong," Jayne said matter-of-factly. She flexed her muscles to prove it. "I eat most of my vegetables Mama gives me. Even the okra and I don't like it." She stuck out her tongue and shook her head.

"But look at you now, baby girl." Reina squeezed one of Jayne's little arms. Jayne beamed. "Can I help with anything?" Reina asked Dani.

"Both of us know you're not sincerely asking," Dani said, refilling her sangria.

Condensation quickly formed on the glass again and Reina wiped a falling drop with her finger. "You know me too well, darling, but I know your husband and he is exactly like your father, which means what he makes up for in some areas, he lacks in others. And that means helping with things around the house."

Dani met Reina's eyes but dropped before they told a story she wasn't ready to talk about. "I'm okay, I think. Nothing I can't handle when people start arriving."

Reina smiled and pointed to the door with her wine glass.

Dani walked to the door, wiping some barbeque sauce off her hands with a dish towel. She opened the screen door before Melody and her five-year old son, Frankie, got to the threshold.

Melody had been divorced twice. Her son was from the first marriage, but the second marriage was what brought her to Texas. She'd been single for about a year and in the same time span been through at least three boyfriends and a couple one-night-stands that the town knew about. Some of the school moms called her the Man-Snatcher. Dani paid no mind to town gossip.

"Hi Melody, " Dani smiled. "Hey Frankie, how are you?" She patted his red-haired head.

"Good." Frankie shrugged as he ducked under his mom's arm. He had expensive, oversized earphones around his neck, plugged into his new Gameboy. Dani couldn't help but assume they were from Frankie's dad.

"Jayne is in the back playing in the bounce house." Dani motioned to the back door.

"'Kay," Frankie said without looking up. Melody didn't move from her spot in the doorway, nor did she move her hand from Frankie's shoulder.

Dani's eyes grazed over Melody's long nails, decorated with blue tips and silver zebra stripes across each nail. "Can I get you a glass of wine or sangria? Or we have some beer in the cooler out back," she added.

"Beer is great. I can grab it. Thanks." She smiled and visibly relaxed.

"Frankie, we have some soda or juice in the kid's cooler too."

"'Kay," Frankie said again, pulling away from Melody's grip and heading toward the back door.

Dani led Melody through the kitchen, introducing her to Reina. Reina held out her hand, awkwardly trying to figure out how to shake it through the painted claws. Once she was able to grab ahold of her fingers in a floppy, grandmother-like grasp, she said, "How do you do?" in her most Northern Carolina accent.

"Just fine, thank you," Melody replied in her equally strong New Jersey accent.

"The beer is on the deck." Dani pointed to the cooler by Peter and Anthony.

Reina didn't move from her leaning position in the curved hallway arch, but turned to raise her eyebrows at Dani. Dani shrugged in reply and made herself busy in the kitchen.

Billy made himself comfortable on the kitchen counter next to the sink. He watched as Melody inched her way to a comfortable spot near Peter while he introduced her to Anthony, who was making some random hand gestures to the bounce house, politely smiling and nodding at Melody. Finally, after a few minutes, Anthony came back in through the door.

"Phew, it's hot out there."

The only reply he got was a glance in his direction from Dani and Reina. He sat at the pale, wooden table, grabbed a stone coaster, and gently set his beer down. He gazed in the direction of Dani chopping vegetables for the salad. Billy noticed Dani glancing out the patio door every few seconds. She'd expected Melody to get her beer and come back inside with the other ladies but she still hadn't gotten her beer and looked like she was in a serious conversation with Peter.

Eventually Peter took out a beer, twisted off the top, and handed it to Melody before leaving her outside. Melody turned toward Frankie and leaned down to speak into his ear. From behind, Billy could see Frankie's shoulders rise and fall with a deep breath before he made his way down toward the bounce house. Everyone turned to watch Melody come through the door.

Just as Dani was searching for some nonspecific topic of conversation, the knob to the front door turned. Everyone, including Billy, breathed a silent sigh of relief.

"The party has arrived!" Suzanne, Dani's best friend, exclaimed as she burst through the front door, sauntering straight into the kitchen. "Hi Mama Bear. How are you?" She was tall enough she had to lean down to give five-foot-six Reina a hug. With her platform bamboo wedges and Reina sitting at the table, it looked like a flamingo trying to hug a rabbit.

Reina squeezed her hard but let go quickly. "I'm just fine, darling. I'm so happy you could make it."

Suzanne smiled at her and turned to Dani. They didn't say anything, but embraced for a long time. "Where's that stud-muffin of yours?" Suzanne asked.

"Which one?" Dani asked jokingly.

Suzanne winked and tousled her short, bleached pixie cut. She heard someone coming down the steps and leaned sideways to peek through the archway and the banister, catching sight of Peter's signature khaki shorts and Jimmy Buffet flip-flops. "There he is."

"Is that Her Majesty of Mischief I hear?" Peter asked.

Billy never noticed how many nicknames could be used in one group of people and he struggled to keep up with who was "snuggle-butt", "waffle-face", "pie-mouth", and so on.

He liked Suzanne though. She was one of Dani's oldest friends; a free spirit, massage therapist, and self-proclaimed Reiki healer. Suzanne was nothing like anyone Billy had ever met, and definitely not from his time. Every time someone asked Suzanne how she was doing, "just living the vibe" was her reply. Her place of residence changed almost as often as her hairstyle and she never had fewer than four rings on at a time. She was the yin to Dani's yang.

Over the period of an hour, three more couples and a combined four kids showed up. Suzanne helped Dani in the kitchen while everyone else was outside getting to know each other and laughing at the kids tirelessly and fearlessly playing on the bounce house.

Billy stayed in the kitchen with Dani and Suzanne.

"So," Suzanne started, looking around. "Give me the lowdown on everyone."

"Well, Joe and Liz, the couple with the matching beer cozies and the little longhaired boy, Luke, work in town. Joe works at the furniture shop and Liz owns The Café.

"David and Consuela are also from the shop, or at least David is. They have the adopted son, Jesus. Then there's Barb and Ed Stalton. They have the twin girls, Heidi and Hannah. Ed helps at the shop sometimes and Barb works at Jayne's school. You met Melody."

"And what *about* Jersey? What's her story?"

"What do you mean?"

"Well, she didn't say one word when I came in and she seems to be more comfortable standing with the men than with the ladies." She nodded toward the patio where Melody stood in the men's circle while the other wives stood to themselves a few feet away.

"Oh, yeah, I'm not sure. Apparently Peter knows

her from Jayne's drop-off. The only reason I invited her was because she showed up when I was inviting Barb and Ed."

Suzanne didn't say anything right away, but she watched Melody through the glass. "I'm going to keep my eye on that one. You should too. I'm getting a weird energy from her."

The party was going smoothly, so Billy was confused when he heard Jayne calling for him. He peeked around the doorway into her room, and she was searching around for him, opening and closing the closet door. She quickly ran down the stairs and out to the bounce house. He followed her out and just before she flung herself through the bounce house door, she yelled, "Billy, come out!"

Oh no, he thought. *She told them about me.* He sat down outside the bounce house and listened.

Frankie started egging her on. "How come he's not coming out, Jayne?"

"I don't know," she said, frustrated. "He always comes when I call him."

"What does he look like?" Frankie asked. "Is he see-through, or white? Or does he look like he has a sheet on his head?" Some of the other kids snickered at this.

"No, he just looks like a normal boy. He's tall and has dark hair and green eyes. He's older than *you!*" she exclaimed, pointing a finger at him.

"Yeah, but he's dead. I'm not afraid of any dead person," Frankie said back, practically spitting out the word "dead."

"Well you don't have to be. He's the nicest person I've ever met. He's my best friend."

"Your best friend is a dead person?" Frankie laughed.

Jayne was on the verge of tears. All she could get out was, "He's a better friend than you are."

"I'm not your friend," Frankie said matter-of-factly. Jayne got up with tears about to spill over her eyes. "Go cry with your fake, dead friend."

She tumbled out of the bounce house, rolling down the slide with a *thud* that made her cry even harder.

"That's not nice," Luke said and left the bounce house after Jayne.

"What?" Frankie shrugged.

No one else answered and soon the kids resumed bouncing and playing. Billy followed Jayne, who was now sprinting up the deck stairs toward the patio doors. The adults all turned and stopped talking when they heard the glass door slide open in a fury. It was noticeable that Jayne was sobbing at this point. She paid no attention and ran through the kitchen and living room, up the stairs, and into her bedroom.

While a couple of the parents made their way outside to investigate what the cause of the weeping girl was and who was to blame, Dani made her way up the stairs to Jayne's room.

Billy beat Dani up to Jayne's room where Jayne was lying on her bed facedown. Dani opened the door and walked over to the bed, putting a light hand on Jayne's back. She didn't have a chance to get a word out before Jayne flung herself up and against her chest, arms around her waist.

"Okay baby, okay. What happened?"

"It's that stupid boy, Frankie," she said with gulps of air in between each word. "He said that Billy was fake and he was making fun of him." She started to calm down as Dani stroked her back and her hair.

"Okay baby, shh. We've talked about Billy, remember?"

"I know, Mama, but he *is* real. He's right over there!" Jayne pointed right at Billy. Billy shook his head furiously. Dani looked in his direction. She tried to gather something to say but couldn't seem to come up with anything off the cuff. The hair on her arms stood on end.

"Does he want to hurt you, or any of the other kids?" Dani asked. Billy was still shaking his head.

"Never. He wouldn't hurt anybody, Mama. He loves me."

"Okay, baby. You're not scared of him, right?"

"Oh no, Mama, he's my best friend."

Dani squeezed Jayne tighter, glancing toward the rocking chair. Jayne was now exhausted and could barely keep her eyes open. Dani told Jayne to lie down and come down when she was ready, then went downstairs to explain to the adults what had happened.

By the time she got downstairs, Melody had all her belongings and Frankie ready to go. She saw Dani come down the stairs and without moving, asked, "Is she okay?"

"She'll be fine, thank you."

"Okay. I'm sorry Frankie doesn't have any manners," she said through gritted teeth, glaring at Frankie as his eyes were fixed on the floor. "What do you say, Frankie?"

"Sorry."

"You can apologize to Jayne later at school."

Dani didn't say anything. There was too much going on in her mind and she just wanted Melody to leave.

The party continued into the night with kids falling asleep on random pieces of furniture like lions in the wild. The adults drank and talked, laughing and reminiscing.

12

2017

TWENTY YEARS LATER, Jayne and Billy talked about that day until Dani came down and slid the door open. "You ready, darling?"

"You bet." Jayne called Rusty to get him to move from his comfy perch on the chair and they went inside.

"Were you talking to someone?" Dani asked.

"No, just myself." Jayne choked on a fake laugh. She reached down to get her purse by the front door. "I do need to call Blake though." They got into Dani's rental car.

Dani's memory led them through the country roads flawlessly; down Main Street to the corner of Main and Chapman. She laid eyes on the shop and hummed. Jayne looked over. "Everything looks almost exactly the same."

"I know, it's kind of eerie, but endearing at the same time," Jayne said.

Dani pulled into the back parking lot along some of the employee trucks. The big garage doors were up and the guys were working. A few of the guys glanced up at the car curiously. Ed Stalton, an old friend and part-time employee, came out to greet Jayne and Dani.

"As I live and breathe, Dani Webber."

"I'm back to Dani Harel now, but I'll let this one pass."

Jayne stayed a few paces behind and watched her mother reach up to wrap her arms around Ed's neck without regard for his dust-covered apron. "It's been awhile, hasn't it? Clearly we're not getting any younger." She tugged at a piece of Ed's white hair. "How are the twins?"

Ed whistled through his teeth. "Oh boy, they're a handful. I thought it would be easier when they got past twenty, but I feel like I just pay for more now." He pretended to flip his hair. "Dad, I totally need to get my nails done and rent is *so* extra high this month," he said in his best Valley girl accent, making Dani laugh. "I can't wait until they become someone else's responsibility." Ed chuckled.

"How is Barb?"

"Oh, Barb and I parted ways a few years ago. You know how it goes." Ed kicked a piece of wood with his boot. "Unfortunately, she passed soon after."

"Oh, I'm sorry Ed — about all of it. I enjoyed spending time with you both when I did."

"Oh, it's all right. We've all made our peace. Are you remarried?" he asked.

"I'm not," Dani said, matter-of-factly.

"Shame," Ed said. "You were always a keeper." He winked at Dani, pulling his mustache on one side. Giving Dani no time to reply, he looked at Jayne. "My gosh girl, last time I saw you, you were about this big." He gestured to his thigh. "You probably don't even remember me."

"Yes sir, I do. I remember the girls, too." Jayne came to stand by her mom.

"Well, what a fine lady you've turned into. I'm sorry about your dad; he was one of my best friends. I'm sorry I didn't get a chance to talk to you at the funeral." His face changed to a brief sadness. "Did you stop in to see Joe? He and Luke are in the office; they just came in to grab something."

"Oh, great. I didn't know if they would be here. I would love to see them and say hello."

"Okay, let me take you to the office. I've got some things to get back to." Ed walked them to the office door adjoining the shop. As far as Dani was concerned, the office looked empty. None of the lights were on and the front desk was clean and tidy from the weekend.

"They're probably in Joe's office." She led them past the reception desk to the hallway with the extra offices. Joe's office light was illuminating a patch of gray carpet in the hallway. They could hear the men's voices coming from inside. "Hello? Joe? Luke?"

"Come on in Jayne, we're just having a chat," Joe's voice boomed. She stepped through the doorway, followed quickly by Dani. "No way." Joe laughed and started to get up. Luke's southern manners got him out of his chair, too. "I knew you were coming, but it didn't feel real until just now." He walked over to Dani, who wore a genuine smile. They embraced quickly and Dani shook Luke's hand. "What can we help you with?" Joe asked

"Nothing in particular, we just wanted to see if there was anything we could help with today," Jayne said.

"No ma'am, we're still good and ready. I sure do like the social media page you made last night. Luke showed me some of the pictures you put up. I think it's going to be great. We already have a few likes and even a share." Joe sat back down in his worn office chair.

"Yeah, and did you see we already have over fifty followers and at least eight of them are from San

Antonio and a couple in Houston? I checked the stats this morning and the reach is in the hundreds. Luke's going to get me some more pictures and I'll post them later today. I'll get a few of the guys working before we leave, too." Jayne's voice was laced with excitement.

Dani rubbed Jayne's back and looked at Luke. "Luke, Jayne mentioned that you've been helping out a lot. Do you think you would be able to stop by sometime this weekend, or early next week, to help with a few things around the house? There are a couple handyman things we need someone with a bit of strength for, including mowing the yard and some of the land. We'll pay you, of course. It would just be nice to have someone who knows the property."

Luke waved his hand as if to erase the comment about paying. "I'll come by later today if that's okay?" He glanced at Jayne. "I can meet you at the house around two?"

"That would be great, thank you so much," Dani replied.

"Anytime. I did tell Jayne I'm happy to help however I can." He smiled at Jayne. She smiled back, feeling a whoosh of warmth travel from her middle through her arms and neck.

"Thanks Luke. Well, we better be off. I told Jayne I'd pick up a couple things for dinner, so we're headed to the supermarket. I'm so glad to see you Joe — all of you. We'll need to have you over soon for dinner before I leave."

"That would be great. I know Liz would love to see you. I'll bring some of Granddaddy's infamous moonshine."

Dani laughed. "Oh gosh, the last time I remember you bringing some of your grandfather's moonshine, we got into a world of trouble. Are you still making it over in that spot you do?" Dani asked with a wink.

"Just smaller batches these days. For friends and whatnot. It's a piece of history, that little still. I can't let his recipe fade away."

"That's right. Well, that sounds great, Joe. Luke, we'll see you later? Do you have Jayne's number so you can just give us a heads-up when you're going to stop by?"

"I don't." Luke pulled out his phone and Jayne dictated her phone number.

"Well, it was so nice to see y'all," Dani said. "We'll see you soon."

Jayne and Dani headed out through the back so Jayne could snap a few photos before they left. Dani said goodbye to Ed, giving him a hug before leaving.

A couple minutes later they pulled up to the supermarket; a small shop that had been run by a family for generations. Prices were a little higher than the local chain supermarkets, but Dani loved supporting local, family-owned businesses.

Dani turned off the car and waited while Jayne finished sending a text to Blake. Her fingers moved around the phone screen as furiously as a spider making a web.

"Still no word when he's coming?" Dani asked.

"No. I haven't been asking, either. There's no point; I don't want to get my hopes up." The calmness in her voice surprised her, as it betrayed her true feelings.

When they got inside, Dani instructed Jayne to find a corn bread mix, some cream, eggs, rice, and vegetable oil. She was going to get the okra, sausage, and shrimp for a not-so-Louisiana take on jambalaya. Jayne went straight to the middle isles while Dani went to the meat counter and then in search of the okra. She finally found it and was filling a produce bag when, through the corner of her eye, she spotted a woman awkwardly stop in her tracks about fifteen feet away. Feeling a sense of unease, Dani glanced quickly and felt as if warm honey had been poured over her shoulders, then dripped down her arms and drained into her feet. She wanted to look away and pretend she didn't see her, pretend she was more interested in the okra on the table beside her; she *should* be more interested in the okra. Instead the woman started walking toward her. Dani glanced around to see if—hopefully—someone else was the intended target. She was the only one in what seemed like the entire grocery store.

As the woman got even closer, Dani could see the prominent, familiar curves shown off by just the right style of clothing; much more appropriate than what she wore twenty years ago. Dani took a quick glance at her nails: filed short and painted a nice shade of pink, no zigzagging pattern or sparkling tips. *It's her*, Dani thought.

Melody's face was a little more filled out, but it looked good, like someone who had been too skinny and gained a healthy amount of weight. Her hair was still dark brown, straight, and past her shoulders. She looked more like a real estate agent than a bar waitress now.

"Dani?" Melody asked.

Dani looked up to meet her gaze, pretending she didn't see her. "Melody," she said coldly.

"Hi," Melody squeaked. "Sorry to bug you. They told me you were back in town. Out of all the places, I didn't think you would be here."

Dani knew "they" were the town criers: a group of women who knew everything, it seemed. Patty Brockett was the main gossip and seemed to pass down the information to the women in her clubs.

"Yes, well, I've always shopped here," she said, as if her twenty years of absence made no difference. She said it with a bit of bark in her tone. Melody either didn't catch on, or didn't care.

"I was going to come talk to you. I never got a chance . . . you know, before . . . before you left."

"You mean twenty years ago when you were party to helping split my family?" Dani's heart started to race. She noticed a flare in Melody's eyes and decided to back down. Twenty years mellowed her patience and rounded the sharp edges of her voice.

Melody looked at the ground and switched her grocery basket from one hand to the other. "Yes. That." She looked up at Dani. "I never got a chance to say I was sorry about what happened." Dani didn't move or speak. "I didn't realize at the time how much I was hurting an entire family. He never —"

Dani held up her hand to cut Melody off.

"I just mean —"

"Melody," Dani said sternly. "I don't want to hear about what Peter may have thought or felt or what he said to get you into bed with him — and to date him after we left. It's been dead for twenty years now. And now *he's* dead." Melody made a sound like a hiccup and her eyes turned red. "It doesn't matter anymore. I'm only here for a few days, and then you won't have to worry about me. If this apology makes *you* feel better, then I'm glad, but for now —"

"Mom? Is everything okay?" Jayne rested her fingertips on Dani's arm and the energy flowing through Dani's body could have given Jayne a shock. Jayne felt it and glanced at Melody, wondering who this woman was and how she could get her mom so angry. She didn't recognize Melody, but Melody recognized her and was staring like she'd just seen a ghost.

"You look just like your father," Melody said. Dani flinched and looked away.

Jayne looked at Melody and then to her mother.

"Were you a friend of my dad's?"

Dani patted Jayne's hand, still on her arm, and said, "We have to go. Thank you for your condolences, Melody. I may or may not see you around. I hope your family is well." And with that, Dani led them to the checkout. Jayne turned to look back at Melody, who was standing awkwardly and confused.

They got to the register and Jayne said, "I got some chocolate and wine, too. Now do you want to tell me what that was about?"

"Nothing," Dani said. "Melody was just giving her condolences and it hit me a little harder than expected."

Jayne knew her mother better than that and her body language was saying more than her words were. Jayne had overheard the end of the conversation, but she decided not to press the issue just yet.

"Good thinking on the wine and chocolate," Dani said, with a smile so fake it was like a bad patch job on a leaky dingy.

13

DANI AND JAYNE put on some comfortable, ragged clothing and made their way to the shed. The sun was still up, and the humidity was low, though it provided little warmth.

The little building looked like no one had gone through it in years. The shed was large enough to hold the riding mower, the washer and dryer, and a few other things, but too small to be called a garage. It had a narrow, built-in workbench, useless for actually building anything on, and a few boxes on a shelving unit to the far side of the mower. It allowed just enough space for Jayne and Dani to squeeze through. Rusty circled the shed, eating random weeds.

"We'll have to take these boxes out if we want to go through them," Dani said.

"You're right. Let's just put them outside the door and we can carry them in once they're all out."

Dani shimmied a box off the top shelf, causing a cloud of dust to fall in her face.

"Oh god!" Dani shouted, quickly handing the box to Jayne.

"What?" Jayne shouted, jumping back from her mom.

Dani shook her head off, brown curls whipping around like a feather duster. "A dead spider just landed on my head, I think. At least I hope it was dead."

Jayne yelped and took another step back. "I think you just shook it onto my foot."

"That's just the first box; I can't imagine what's going to come out with the others."

Jayne plopped the box outside the shed door and saw Billy making his way over. Rusty barked at him and Jayne yelled at him to stop.

"What's he barking at?" Dani asked.

"Who knows? Maybe he saw a squirrel or something."

"You're going to find some treasures in there," Billy said. "Especially in those ones in the far back, second shelf. Those have been in here longer than your dad. I can't even remember what's in them."

Jayne went back in and said, "Why don't we just focus on those old boxes in the back—the ones that look like they haven't been touched at all." She pointed to the ones Billy indicated.

"Okay, I suppose we can get Luke to grab these other ones later."

Dani and Jayne got four more boxes from the back corner out of the shed. Billy looked like a kid at Christmas waiting for the go-ahead to open his presents. Jayne and Dani brushed off the loose dust with a towel before they brought them through the house.

Once all the boxes were on the table, they paused to look at each other, faces betraying their excitement. Billy stood at the end of the table, just as eager. Dani grabbed a knife from the knife block and set to slice open the packing tape. It was so old it almost disintegrated at the touch of metal. One push and the tape slid right between the flaps; the adhesive was completely gone. Dani peeled it all the way off and opened one flap and then the other. Inside was yellowed, crumpled magazine paper wrapped around Christmas decorations. Jayne pulled each decoration out, discarded the paper, and examined the ornaments. "These are gorgeous. They're in perfect condition."

Dani wasn't looking at what was in the paper. "Look at these pages. They're from the Christmas Sears catalog. If these are right, guess how old they are," Dani said.

Billy leaned in. "They're right, but go ahead and guess."

"1935?"

"Close," Dani said. "1942." She smoothed each one out on the table, moving her hands over the creases like she was afraid they might fall apart at her touch.

Jayne picked up another decoration and held it up to examine it. "Just look at these. They're stunning. I don't think I could find better vintage decorations at an antique store." Jayne wasn't just talking to her mom, but Billy too. "It's been almost eighty years since these were touched."

Dani brought over some current newspaper to wrap them in. "I'd love to look through this catalog. Wrap them in these instead." She handed the newspaper to Jayne and went for another box. The next box was loosely packed with toys. Jayne pulled out a freakish-looking teddy bear with wide eyes and a grin that would have frightened more than comforted a child. It was worn and stained and gave her the heebie-jeebies. She put it facedown in the box and pulled out a medium-weight cylinder tube that looked like a bean can. It had larger ends and a long stick for the handle.

"What do you suppose this is?" she asked, holding it up.

Before Dani could answer, Billy said, "Roll it on the

ground." When she did, it played a little musical song.

"Neat," Jayne said and placed it back in the box. Next Dani pulled out a small, disintegrating box with "Halsam American Log Set" written across the top. They lifted the worn top off to reveal what must have been all the pieces still intact, with small divots in each side and details that looked like little axe-chops. These toys were well played with. Jayne imaged all the houses built again and again with these. The last thing in the small box was a toy tank.

"These must have belonged to your grandfather, Steve, when he was younger. That would have been right around the war and he would have been about . . ." Dani paused to do some math in her head. "Five," Dani and Billy said simultaneously.

Billy sunk himself into the memory of when Steve got these gifts.

1943

Steve was sitting in the living room of the old house. He and his brother had just finished opening their Christmas gifts while Billy watched them in between glances of his day-old newspaper. Evelyn helped their daughter-in-law, Margaret, in the kitchen to get things ready for Christmas dinner.

Billy could see Evelyn and Margaret zooming back and forth, chopping, stuffing, and mixing. He smiled at them and observed the two boys, who were in a blissful unawareness of what was going on across the ocean where their father—his own son, Gerry— was fighting for their country and just trying to stay alive. He wondered if Gerry knew what day it was and whether he'd had a moment to think about his family. Billy hadn't stopped thinking about *him* since he'd left. He begged him not to enlist, to just wait for a draft, if it even came to that. Gerry was as stubborn as Evelyn though, and insisted he couldn't just sit back and hope others would protect him.

Billy pulled on his growing beard and watched Steve push the toy tank around the room, making *vroom* noises and *rat-a-tats* for the machine gun placed on the back. He smiled and looked back again to his newspaper. The warmth of the fireplace and the oven heated the house to a comfortable temperature against the chilled winter air. His thoughts again went to Gerry and if he was warm enough. Over the radio came the announcer's voice.

"He had the number-one Christmas hit last year with 'I'm Dreaming of a White Christmas', now he brings to you this year's number-one Christmas hit, "I'll be Home for Christmas', by the great Bing Crosby." Bing Crosby's baritone voice came over the radio and there was pause throughout the house.

"I'll be home for Christmas . . ."

The boys continued playing. Margaret's stirring slowed as thoughts of her husband flitted through her mind like snowflakes outside.

"You can plan on me . . ." The stirring stopped altogether and Evelyn's chopping slowed as she glanced at Margaret.

"Please have snow and mistletoe, and presents under the tree . . ." Margaret took a deep breath and held it in while she continued stirring mechanically. Evelyn kept one eye on Margaret, ready to console her.

"I'll be home for Christmas, if only in my dreams . . ." Margaret dropped the spoon and braced herself on the countertop. Her shoulders shook with each sob.

Evelyn walked over, giving Billy a look and nodding to the boys.

Billy folded the newspaper and said, "Come on boys, get your coats. Let's go outside and see if those slingshots work." The boys excitedly got their coats, barely getting them on properly before they were out the door, new slingshots in hand.

2017

Billy was jolted from his memory.

"Did you know these were in there when you lived here?" Jayne asked.

"No clue," Dani replied. "I knew there were a few boxes in the shed, but I didn't go in there that much; it was more your dad's place. This box looks kind of familiar, though." She reached for a brown-and-white file box and lifted off the lid. "Oh," she said excitedly. Both Jayne and Billy perked up but all Jayne could see was a bunch of papers and files.

"What is that?" she asked.

"It's my old research."

"Research?" Jayne asked.

"Well, I did a bit of a genealogy for your dad and some of the locals before I left. It kept me busy while I was at home. I was in the middle of tracing back some of your dad's history."

"I had no idea," Jayne said, genuinely surprised. "We should start that back up again. I bet we could find out a lot considering Dad's family goes way back."

"You're right. Let's keep this over there." She pointed to the corner by the front door. Through the glass they spotted someone making their way up the steps. Jayne had already started walking toward the door when the doorbell chimed.

"You're earlier than I thought you would be," Jayne said when she opened the door.

Rusty jumped at Luke's leg. He picked him up and scratched Rusty's head while he dodged licks to his face. "I didn't have much going on today, to be honest. When I got done with Dad, I decided to come straight over. Is that okay?"

"It's just fine. We appreciate you coming," Dani said, appearing over Jayne's shoulder.

"It's no problem." He smiled and set Rusty down before patting his head.

Jayne stepped aside to let him in. "What were you hoping to do with him, Mom?" Jayne regretted the string of words as soon as they exited her mouth. "I mean, what can he do for us?" She sighed and pinched the bridge of her nose. "Did you have some things lined up for him, I mean." Billy was sitting on the couch, laughing at Jayne's inability to put a sentence together that didn't imply sexual acts.

Dani looked at Luke, oblivious to Jayne's hidden innuendos. "Well, I was hoping the riding mower in the shed would be working and you could take it for a quick spin around the land. We have some more boxes in the shed that need brought in, if you don't mind. Then it would be great if you could check the gutters and air filters." Dani raised her eyebrows and clenched her teeth, wondering if that was too much.

"Not at all," said Luke. "I'll go check the filters and gutters first if that's okay?"

"Whatever you want to do is fine with us."

Jayne and Dani tidied and continued going through the boxes, all the while watching Luke doing large circles in the yard behind the house and across the creek. Three hours had passed and Luke finished with the chores he was enlisted to do. He came inside to announce his exit to the women. Both Jayne and Dani were sitting at the table looking over some of the torn Sears catalog pages.

"Where would you like me to put these extra boxes?" he asked.

Dani got up and motioned toward the other box in the corner. "Right there is fine," she said.

After he brought in four more boxes, he reached for the last piece, a wooden chest with metal clasps and leather straps. "This looks old, and it's definitely heavy," Luke said as he muscled it through the doorway, biceps and triceps flickering at Jayne like a diamond ring to a barracuda. She willed herself to snap out of it. *You've seen muscles before,* she told herself. *Blake has muscles too.*

"I thought your dad got rid of that," Billy said.

"I used to have my toys in this when I was younger," Jayne said. Luke set it down near the stairs.

Dani reached for her purse. "Thank you so much Luke, let me just —"

"Please, ma'am, I couldn't possibly. Peter was like a second father to me. I owe him more than he or anyone knows. It's the least I could do."

"Well, okay then," said Dani. "We still owe you."

"How about Jayne comes out with me and some friends tonight?" Luke asked and Jayne lifted her eyebrows in surprise. She looked at her mother like she was sixteen again, asking for permission to go out with her friends.

"I don't see why not," Dani said, not taking her eyes off Luke. "She's been very busy here. A night out might do her some good." She smiled.

"Sure." Jayne said. "That would be . . . good."

"Great, I can pick you up at eight?" Luke asked excitedly.

"I'll drop her off," Dani interrupted, sounding like an old, southern father.

"Great," Luke said and turned to his truck.

Dani closed the door behind him. "You feel comfortable going out with him and his friends?"

"Mom, he's Joe and Liz's son. If anything bad were to happen the whole town would declare a witch hunt on that family."

"Okay then." Dani smiled.

14

DANI PULLED UP in front of the pub — the same pub Peter would go to and stay all night, the same pub Melody used to work at, the same pub that would contribute to the crumbling of their marriage. She worried for her daughter, but only because it was a projection of her past. "Be careful. Call me if you need anything. Remember, you might know Luke, but you don't know his friends."

Jayne bent down to look back at Dani in the car and smiled softly. "How about *you* call me if you need me to come home?"

"Okay, get back in the car then," she joked.

"Bye Mom, love you." Jayne closed the door and Dani waved.

Jayne walked through the doors of the pub and was hit with a fragrant mix of spilled drinks and smoked tobacco. She already regretted that her hair and clothes would smell like an aged, watered-down version of it tomorrow. She wished she hadn't worn her Neiman's velour hoodie. The music was loud, but not deafening. She moved her eyes along the crowd, searching the barstools along the far wall. There were only a few couples and stray men; the booths along the walls were pretty much empty too. As she was looking at the tables, she heard her name called. A few people turned to look at her but her eyes settled on Luke. She smiled and waved and made her way over to the table where he sat with two other guys. They shuffled around a few of their things and shifted in their seats as if making way for a celebrity.

"How's it going?" Luke asked. He got up to give her an awkward, one-armed hug.

She reciprocated, wishing it could last a little longer without being weird or interpreted as affection; she just needed some comfort. "Good. It's nice to get out for a bit."

"I bet." He turned to his friends. "This is Jayne, Peter Webber's daughter." The other two guys made sympathetic noises and nods. One of them said a small "sorry."

"Jayne, these are some friends I've known since high school." He pointed to the guy to his immediate right, a decent-looking young man with sharp features, green eyes, and dark hair that was cut short but long enough you could see the curls starting to form. "This is Connor Walsh." Connor raised a hand and smiled. "And this is Jason Muller." The young man to her left was blond and blue-eyed, a little on the skinny side, and seemed shyer than Luke and Connor.

"Nice to meet y'all," Jayne said. "Did you grow up here too?"

Connor spoke first. "My family is from the Northeast, Boston area, but we moved down here when I was twelve. My dad got a job in oil and gas. He's a geologist." Jayne nodded and looked at Jason.

He cleared his throat. "My family has been in New Braunfels since the Germans came and settled in the area, but we moved *here* when I was about fourteen."

Jason took a swig of his beer, noticeably uncomfortable.

"Oh, cool," Jayne said. "My dad's side of the family is German too. They've been here for years as well. From what I'm told, they didn't want to stay right in New Braunfels or Fredericksburg, and definitely not in San Antonio or Austin, so they compromised by moving a little ways away, here. They were a bit rebellious, trying to get away from the rest of the Germans." Jayne laughed. "They even added an extra *b* in Webber."

Jason smiled. "Yeah, my family took off the umlaut above the *u*. Very risky." Jason visibly relaxed a bit more.

"Can I get you a drink?" Luke asked.

"I'll have a Shiner, draft if they've got it."

"Good choice," Connor said.

Luke flagged down the waitress, a short girl who looked only a day older than twenty-one. She had her boobs high and her shorts low, cut off just before it showed her underwear—if she was wearing any. Her hair was long and curled, pieces of the dark waves resting comfortably on the curves of her breasts. She put an arm along the back of Luke's chair. "What can I get for you, babes?" she asked, smiling and gnawing on her gum.

"Can we get Jayne a Shiner, draft?"

"Sure thing, babes," she said and turned and left without looking at Jayne.

"I didn't realize this was that kind of place," Jayne said.

"Amanda's harmless," Connor said. "It's all a show, really. I went to college with her and she's a sweet girl. She puts on the whole act for the tips."

"She does have a thing for Luke, though," Jason added.

Luke took an awkward sip of his beer, scrunched his face, and shook his head as if it was the beer, not the comment that tasted bad. "Nah, I don't . . ." The guys gave him a look. "Well, I mean, it's hard to say. Maybe a little, but she's not my type."

"What is your type?" The words tumbled out of Jayne's mouth like a drunk falling out of a taxi. When she saw Connor and Jason lift their eyebrows at Luke, she wished she could shove the words back into her mouth, chew them up, and swallow them down.

"Yes, Luke, what *is* your type?" Connor asked, using his beer mug to hide his grin. Jayne assumed they might have known more about her than Luke let on. Everyone waited for his response.

Luke got flustered and shifty in his chair. "Well, I suppose I like them a bit older and not so showy." He patted his chest in demonstration. "I prefer blondes, but I'm not picky."

"So, like Jayne then?" Jason asked, smiling. Luke's friends weren't about to let Luke get away scot-free.

Luke glared at his friends, then turned to Jayne. "Sure, you're a good-looking girl and you have a great head on your shoulders. But gentlemen, I'm sorry, she's spoken for." He glanced down at her bare hand. "Maybe. She says she has a fiancé and a ring, but I've yet to see either."

Amanda slid the Shiner in front of Jayne without saying anything and walked off. Jayne shook her head and covered her eyes. "I keep forgetting to put the dang thing back on. Besides, with all the work I've been doing in the house, I don't want to wreck it."

"I'm just teasing," Luke said sincerely.

"Where's your fiancé?" Connor asked.

"He's back in North Carolina. He's a lawyer and has some needy clients. He's supposed to be coming out soon."

"But he's cancelled twice already," Luke added.

"So, let me get this straight," Jason said. "Your father

passes away—I'm sorry about that—and then your fiancé lets you come to Texas to wrap up not only his estate, but also his business stuff, all by yourself, even though he's a lawyer that could be helping you with all the legal stuff?" Jason looked at the other two guys for confirmation, took a gulp of his beer, and looked back at Jayne.

"Well, it's kind of complicated," Jayne said, desperately wanting to stick up for Blake, but deep down she felt the same way. Regardless of Blake's commitment to the firm, she wanted to know that during the rest of their future, he would be there for her—no matter what.

"No offense, but I really don't see it as complicated," said Luke. "But as long as you are okay with it . . ."

"I'm not, but there's only so much I can do." Jayne shrugged.

"Hey, a pool table just cleared up," Jason announced. "Do you play?" he asked Jayne.

"I've played, if that's what you mean."

"Good, you can be on Luke's team then." The guys grabbed their beers and coasters and started toward the pool tables. Luke waited while Jayne grabbed her jacket, purse, and beer.

"I'm really not that good," Jayne repeated.

"It's okay. I'm pretty good—that's why they put you on my team. Connor is good, but Jason sucks," Luke reassured her.

"Okay," Jayne said.

Jayne and Luke joined the others. With the lack of fans, the cigarette smoke seemed to gather in the corner and blanket the pool tables. Amanda found them and offered another round.

The other pool table was taken by a couple of guys; one was so built, the pool cue looked like a pencil in his hands, just ready to be snapped in half without a second thought. The other guy caught Jayne's attention because he kept looking at her. Not in a flirty kind of way, but rather a "you're-invading-my-space, why-do-you-exist" kind of way. Jayne would have ignored it if he was just a stranger, but he looked *so* familiar. He was the opposite of his friend: tall and thin with fluffy red hair trying to escape from under his hat. His pants were too big and hung halfway down his butt, revealing his red boxer shorts every time he bent over to take a shot.

She let it go for a few minutes while they began their game. Luke *was* good. He made all the shots Jayne missed and insisted that she was good at blocking any shots Connor and Jason might have, which was a nice way of saying she wasn't doing anything strategic.

The familiar guy was holding his pool cue in front of him, smoking a cigarette and leaning on the bar table.

"What is it?" asked Luke, sensing a shift in her demeanor.

"Don't look now, but that guy over there, behind you — the less-muscly one — keeps staring at me. Not in a good way." Luke pivoted and reached his other hand to the bar on her left side, pinning her back against the bar. He grabbed his beer off the bar and turned back to stand beside her. He took a quick glance and waited a second before saying anything.

"Your shot, Jayne," Connor said. The guy at the other table whipped his head around at the sound of her name.

Jayne took her shot and sunk the cue ball as accurately as if it was intentional. She and Luke went to stand against the bar.

"So, that guy," he said, nodding to the one she spoke of. "You actually know him, sort of."

"I do?" Jayne asked, surprised.

"Yeah. That's Frankie." Luke waited for it to register

in Jayne's mind, but when he saw her face blank, he continued. "Do you remember at your birthday party when we were kids, you had the bounce house?"

Jayne's eyes moved like they were searching the archives in her mind. "I remember. He was the boy who made fun of me and said something about not being my friend." Jayne remembered him making fun of her for having an imaginary friend.

"Yeah, that's him," Luke confirmed.

Jayne turned to look again, he was taking his shot over the table and she instantly recognized the younger boy in him.

"No way," Jayne mouthed at Luke. She recalled the incident from the grocery store earlier and how her mom hoped Melody's son, Frankie, was okay.

"Yep." Luke moved to take his shot and she followed. "He's not the most stand-up human these days. He dropped out of school when he hit senior year. He's been in and out of jobs since then. He tried to get a job at the shop but when your dad said he would only hire him as a part-time receptionist he never came back. I think he works at a grocery store now."

"Do you think he knows who I am?" Jayne asked.

"Maybe. I don't know if he would remember you just from looking at you." Luke went and took his shot, sinking the eight ball to win them the game.

Jayne and Luke were celebrating when Frankie materialized beside her. Her stomach flipped and clenched.

"I think I know you," Frankie said bluntly.

"Do you?" Jayne replied, following Frankie's gaze to Luke, standing with his friends watching a few feet away.

"No, but by the way you've been looking at me, we either must know each other or you've been wanting me to come over." His smile made Jayne feel sick.

"I can assure you, it's not the latter," she said strongly.

"I think I would disagree." He took a step closer to her and the smell of vodka, Redbull, and cigarettes on his breath drifted over her face. She scrunched her nose and turned her head.

"You're not my type. Sorry to disappoint." She took a step back, her spine now pressing into the round, wooden bar shelf—a much different feeling from when Luke had her pinned. She grabbed her drink just to keep something between her and Frankie.

"I don't know if I believe that." His smile widened so Jayne could see the crooked top tooth and chipped bottom.

"Everything okay Jayne?" Luke was beside her now, shoulder-to-shoulder.

"Oh, sorry Luke, I didn't realize she was yours. She didn't seem all that interested."

"She's not *mine* Frankie; she's not *anybody's.* Jayne, you wanna go grab another drink?"

"Jayne? Why does that sound familiar?" Frankie took a step back and tapped his chin with his finger comically. She felt the heat of his body go with him. "What's your last name?" he asked.

"Webber," Jayne replied.

"Ah, that's it. We probably shouldn't get together anyway. That would be a little ironic, now wouldn't it?"

"Ironic?"

"Well, you know: your dad, my mom." He made a clicking sound with his tongue. Jayne's parents had been separated for twenty years. Frankie's mom must have been one of his girlfriends.

She didn't respond, but Frankie read the ignorance in her expression. "Oh shit, you didn't know." He laughed, so boisterous some people a few feet away looked over. Jayne could feel Luke tense. "Oh yeah, your dad and my mom were hooking up for a long time—before you left *and* after. In fact, I'm pretty sure that's why your mom left. At least that's what my mom told me."

"Wha—what's your mom's name?" Jayne mumbled.

"Melody."

She felt like she'd just been hit by lightning. Heat spread through her body, radiating from her chest. Frankie laughed one big laugh again and walked away, nodding for his friend to follow behind him.

Jayne's mind was reeling. *An affair? Frankie's mom, my dad? That's why we left?* Her mind was flipping through things her mom had said, searching for some hint that this could've been the cause of their divorce. An image of the woman at the grocery store flickered into her mind. *That was the other woman,* she thought.

"Jayne, you okay?" Luke had one hand on her shoulder and one on her arm.

When did he put them there? she thought absently. Connor and Jason started toward them.

Jayne smiled at him. "I'm fine. I think I just need to sit for a moment." She motioned toward the table.

15

AS THE NIGHT got later, people filed out of the bar. Connor and Jason left shortly after the game of pool, saying they had to work early.

By eleven, Jayne texted her mom and told her she would just take a cab home, not to wait up. She and Luke stayed at the table, talking and sipping on their drinks.

"I have an idea," Luke said.

"What?" Jayne was suspicious.

"Have you been to the river yet? The rivers around here have a limestone bottom. That's why they're so green and clear. There's one not too far from here. We could go if you like."

Jayne looked at the time on her phone. "It's getting pretty late. Maybe just for a little bit."

They walked out the front door and around the back of the building. With the sun gone, the temperature had dropped significantly. Jayne pulled her sleeves down over her hands and crossed her jacket over her body, tucking her hands into her armpits.

"There's something so lovely about a night where the air is crisp and cool. It's like it cleans the atmosphere for the next day, so sharp, like breathing in mint." Jayne said.

Luke looked back at her at smiled. "I love the cold. This is my favorite time of year. You're not too cold, are you?" He noticed her shoulders up to her ears and her arms pressed tightly to her chest.

"No. Well, yes, but I'll get used to it in a moment."

"Once we get through the trees, they'll block the wind and you should warm up a bit."

It was dark and Jayne thought about how uneasy she'd feel under any other circumstances. The path was dimly lit and Luke seemed to be leading her straight into some trees where no one would see them. *This is how women end up on Dateline*, she thought. Regardless, she continued to follow him. Luke led the way, holding branches out of the way for her, telling her to watch for little steps she might miss and reaching back to help her along.

It wasn't long before the trees cleared to a rocky shoreline. The river was shallow and flowing. It was emerald green in the moonlight. The crunch of Jayne's shoes on the rocks turned to the light grinding sound of walking on coarse sand.

"This is it," Luke said.

"It's beautiful." The water was moving almost silently. The stars and the moon rippled on the surface.

Luke smiled and led her to a large rock, just big enough for the two of them to sit on. He sat down first and held out a hand to help her across the rocks. When she sat next to him, she could feel the heat coming off his body. *If it was a few degrees colder I'd be able to see steam come off of him,* she thought.

"I come here sometimes when I just need to think, to get away from the madness."

"Is there a lot of madness in this small town?" Jayne asked.

"Not really. It's mostly the craziness in my brain. I tend to think a lot—overthink, really. It puts me in a mood, so I come out here to get back to simplicity."

Jayne didn't want to pry, so she let him have his silence. After what seemed like a minute she asked, "When was the last time you came out here?"

Luke glanced at her and tossed a rock into the river, listening for the crisp *plop*. Unsure whether to answer truthfully, he took a breath and let it out with resolution. "When I found out about your dad."

Jayne looked at him, seeing the profile of his face in the moonlight; his triangular nose and full lips, his high cheekbones which gave his face and jaw a more chiseled appearance. "When my dad died?" she questioned him.

Luke nodded. "I haven't mentioned how much he meant to me. He was there for me. Something about the way he listened and helped. Everyone tried, but your dad just knew what to say." Jayne let him speak without interrupting. "You probably didn't know, but I was in the navy. I had just signed up and gone through my training. I was *loving* it. I wasn't the best kid growing up. I'd get into some minor trouble here and there—nothing crazy or illegal, but I'm sure I almost gave my parents a few mental breakdowns. Anyway, a couple years out of high school, I thought the navy was what I wanted to do. I was good at it, too. I took to the training with ease, I enjoyed being out on the boats; I liked everything about it—even though I got seasick every time we went out." Luke chuckled, then his attitude changed. He looked at his hands and squeezed a rock in his fist. "I was so stupid," he seemed to say to himself. Jayne turned her body toward him, listening intently. "We were getting ready to leave. It was a week before I was supposed to head out to the Carolinas for some final training and Connor, Jason, and I decided to have one last night to live it up. We met up with some friends in downtown Austin on a Friday night. We were walking down the road, barhopping. I'd probably had too much to drink and wasn't paying attention when I went to cross the street. All I remember is hearing Connor and Jason screaming 'No!' and 'Luke!' But it was too late—I got hit by a truck. Next thing I know, I'm waking up in the ER and I can't feel my left leg or arm. I couldn't move them, either. I'd broken my back and my hip. I was going to need surgery and the doctors didn't know if I would ever walk again."

"Oh, Luke." Instinctually, Jayne put a hand on his back, feeling the warmth through his jacket.

"Long story short, I was in a wheelchair for weeks. The navy decided to discharge me because the doctors had no idea if I'd be returned to full capacity. My life— as I thought it was going to play out—was now no more than me sitting in a chair, day in and out, trying to learn how to do everything with my right hand. I was miserable.

"A few months later your dad called and told me to come to the shop. I'd been through physical therapy and was starting to regain feeling. I could walk, but only with the help of a crutch. I had surgery on my back and hip already and they were optimistic but told me, with the nature of my injuries, that I had a 60 percent chance of recovering fully—fully being with a cane or crutch to help the drop foot.

"So, I went down to the shop and your dad was waiting for me with some scrap slabs of wood and a few chisels. That day, and every day for a month, we worked on carving wood. He showed me how and we worked around the weakness in my hand and arm. He'd listen to what I had to say, how I felt about everything, and he'd give me advice or just listen. Every once in a while he'd talk about how he wished his life had gone differently, or the relationship with his parents was different. But mostly, it was about me. Peter — your dad — helped me through those times after the accident. If it wasn't for him, I don't know where I'd be or if I'd even be recovered to the capacity I am. My parents tried, but sometimes it takes an outside perspective to make a change. We resist our parents for some reason. We act like the people who know us best don't know us at all.

"Your dad meant a lot to me. When I thought I wouldn't get a job, or didn't know what I wanted to do, he gave me a job at the shop and promised to train me."

"Is that how you got so good at the carving and woodworking? My dad?"

"One hundred percent. Your dad gave me the life I know now. But it was also when your dad realized he could carve, too. In trying to help me, he found his talent."

Jayne sat with the story, unspeaking. Luke let her have the peace. They spent a few minutes watching the water rippling down the riverbed. Then Jayne said, "Thank you for sharing that with me."

"Sure."

"Are you all better?" Jayne asked.

"I still have some numbness in my hand and my leg hurts when the weather changes, but I wouldn't change a thing." He smiled but Jayne was looking at the water. "Well, shall we get going? I promised your mom you wouldn't be too late, but here we are, almost midnight."

Jayne groaned. "Yeah, I suppose we should go. I've

had enough to drink to know I'll probably feel like shit tomorrow."

Luke laughed and held out a hand to help her up. "You want to go for a swim?"

Jayne laughed and brushed the seat of her pants off. "You might be a living furnace right now, but I'm a step away from being an icicle, so unless that water is a hot spring, my answer is no."

"Worth a shot." Luke shrugged.

16

JAYNE WOKE UP with dry mouth and a splitting headache. She groaned and reached up to rub her eyes, which were crusted together with sleep. She groaned again. As she recalled the events of the night before, Frankie came crashing back into her mind. She pressed her palms into her eyes, which didn't help the pain in her head.

He told her that his mom and her dad had been having an affair, and that's what caused her mom to leave. But not only that, they continued their relationship afterward. It was a weird thought; she always remembered her dad as the single guy ladies flirted with everywhere they went, but not one to be attached to anyone. With every fiber of her being, she didn't want to believe her dad would have an ongoing affair behind her mom's back, but it wasn't so far-fetched as to be unbelievable. These kinds of things happened to the best of people.

She pushed up onto one elbow to look for a glass of water, hoping she'd been smart enough to leave one by the bedside the night before.

Nothing.

She squinted in the bright light and sighed. She spotted Billy in his usual spot in the chair beside her bed. He smiled at her.

"You probably think this is hilarious," Jayne croaked.

"Of course I do," Billy said. "Your mom put a glass of water over on your dresser, along with a piece of peanut butter toast." He nodded toward the plate.

Jayne lay back down for a minute to let her stomach settle; it was rolling like a pot of boiling water. Once she was able to gain some control of her gag reflexes, she got up, grabbed the plate and water as quickly as she could, and lay down halfway to eat and drink. Two little Advil pills rolled to the center of the plate when she picked up the toast. She smiled, feeling grateful for her mom.

Billy mentioned something about a doozy of a night, but Jayne ignored him and continued taking tiny bites of the bread. It was still warm and the peanut butter melted over her tongue but stuck to the roof of her dry mouth like plaster on drywall. She heard her mom downstairs: the sound of pans and dishes being used. She thought she heard bacon cooking and eggs being whisked, but it could've just been her imagination. At this point, she didn't know if eating would make her feel better or worse, but she decided if she was going to throw up, she would have had something in her stomach.

"How was your night?" Billy asked.

Jayne looked at him through the corner of her eye and swallowed, taking a moment to gather her thoughts. "Do you remember, at my birthday party here, the one with the bounce house, there was a kid named Frankie?" Billy nodded, unsure and a little uncomfortable with where this was going.

"Well, I ran into him last night and he told me that his mom and my dad were having an affair that turned into a relationship after mom and I left. He told me that this woman was the *reason* mom took me with her to North Carolina." Billy didn't say anything. "Did you know about this?" Jayne asked meekly.

"Well, yes, I suppose I did." He took a deep breath and then let it out slowly.

"And you didn't tell me?" Jayne felt a stab of betrayal.

"Well, there wasn't really a good time to say it. And if your mom hasn't told you already, how would you explain that *you* knew? Or worse, how would you feel about that? It's never been my intent to change the view you have of your father, and I couldn't guarantee that it wouldn't." Jayne didn't say anything and Billy took this silence as an invitation to continue. "I was there when your mom found out about her. In fact, it was the day after that same party and your uncle Anthony, grandmother, and your mom's friend Suzanne were all here as well. I can tell you about it, if you'd like? But I think it would be better if your mom told you."

She nodded. "Tell me. I'll get my mom's side later."

1997

The evening of Jayne's fifth birthday party was crisp and clear but warm like an open oven door. Despite her excitement, she fell asleep almost as soon as her head hit the pillow.

Peter went upstairs to bed. It had been a long day and he'd had quite a few drinks. Anthony followed not long after, going into the spare room. Billy got up to make the rounds, mostly just curious what everyone was up to. Anthony had turned on the lamp next to the bed and took out a book and pen. He picked up the phone and his instinct was to put it back down when he heard someone talking. He stopped himself and lifted it back to his ear to apologize. A woman's voice stopped him. Someone else was on the line. Anthony's emotions went from confusion and regret to anger.

Billy moved toward him to try and hear who Peter was talking to. He could hear the voice was female, but couldn't make out any words. Without thinking, he went through the walls, through the hall, over the staircase, and into the master bedroom. Peter was sitting on the bench near the window, looking out over the back of the house, speaking in almost a whisper.

"I understand and I appreciate that," he said to the woman, "but you can't call me anymore. It was a onetime thing. I can't have Dani finding out." He was agitated and nervous, looking over his shoulder and tapping his fingers on his knee. "I know it was more than once and yes, I did like it, but it's not going to happen again. Whatever you thought it was, you need to get that out of your head. I'm married and I don't plan on changing that."

Billy stared, stunned. If he'd not already been dead, he surely would've died of shock. He remembered Anthony listening on the line and thought of ways he could stop him from hearing: he could jam the line, which would end both calls. No, it was too late, he'd heard enough.

There was no way Anthony would keep this from Dani. Dani was his older sister and she protected him growing up. When Dani and Anthony's parents would fight, or their dad would get physical, Dani would be the one to take him out of the house, into the playhouse in their backyard. They wouldn't come back until the yelling had stopped. Sometimes, if it was warm enough, they'd sleep out there.

Peter continued. "I'll see you at the school and I'll be civil, but I'll talk to you as little as possible — let that be clear. And if you dare try and tell anyone about this — especially Dani — I swear to god Melody . . ."

Billy had enough and made the floorboards creak outside the door.

"I have to go," he whispered. "Melody, take care of yourself. Find a nice, single man." He lightly pressed the phone to the receiver and then pressed his fingers into his eyes. He took a deep breath, stripped down, crawled into bed, and grabbed his book, but his thoughts stopped him from opening it. He lay there thinking until the thoughts consumed his mind, bouncing back and forth like a racquetball. He gave up and turned the bedside light off.

Anthony was shocked. He'd just found out that his brother-in-law, who he liked more than most of the people in his family, was cheating on his sister. What was he supposed to do with that information? He knew he had to tell her, but when?

Now? It's late though, he thought. *Maybe once we've left?* He sat there for a few more minutes before getting up to change into his pajamas. *Tomorrow, I'll tell her tomorrow when her mind is clear*, he thought.

The next morning, Anthony was downstairs quietly making a pot of coffee. Billy left Jayne still sleeping and headed downstairs. Reina was coming down the steps in her silk robe and Suzanne was asleep on the couch.

"Good morning," she said softly.

Anthony jumped and turned, his hand at his chest with a fistful of his shirt. "Jesus." He let out a troubled breath. "Morning," he replied quietly and turned back to scooping coffee into the percolator.

"Why is everyone so jumpy around here?" Reina asked as she pulled out a chair at the table.

"I don't think it's everyone else, Ma." Anthony said. "I think you're as sneaky as a mouse and . . ." Anthony trailed off. He grabbed two mugs from the cupboard. "Well, this house has always given me a bit of a creepy feeling, like there's always someone watching."

Reina agreed. "This land has been passed down a few generations." Her eyes passed over the ceiling, through the archways and windows, and out to the old house. "I wouldn't doubt if there are a couple lingering tenants."

Anthony sat down beside her, handing her a cup of coffee. She peered into the mug. The coffee was the color of maple wood; just the way she liked it.

"I have to tell you something," he said.

"Now? I haven't even had my coffee yet."

"Peter is cheating on Dani — or was, rather."

Reina let out a heavy sigh and seemed to deflate in her chair. "How do you know?" she asked, leaning over the table.

"When I went to make my work calls last night, I heard Peter on the phone talking to *her*," he said.

"What was said?" an angry voice asked from the doorway.

Reina and Anthony turned around to see a very disheveled and sobering-up Suzanne leaning against the archway.

Anthony took a deep breath. "It was Melody fr—"

"That *cow!* I knew it!" Suzanne growled in a low voice through her gritted teeth.

Reina rolled her eyes. "Shush. Now go on," she urged Anthony.

"He was telling her that he couldn't see her anymore

and that he would ruin her if she tried to jeopardize his marriage." Reina scoffed. "He said he didn't want to leave Dani, so Melody was to leave him alone from now on."

"Right, well, we have to tell her," Reina said matter-of-factly.

"I know, but how? When?" Anthony asked.

At this point Suzanne had moved to a sit on the counter where she poured herself a cup of black coffee and ate cereal straight from the box. "The minute we get her alone."

"What's she going to do?" Anthony asked.

"She and Jayne can come stay with me in North Carolina until they figure it out."

Billy shifted uncomfortably at this. He was attached to the house and there was no way for him to leave. If Jayne left, he may never see her again.

Anthony asked, "What if she wants to stay?"

"With *him*?" Suzanne said, disgusted.

Reina wasn't convinced either. "If she truly wants to stay then we'll do nothing, but if I know my daughter, she won't stay."

At that, they all stopped when they heard footsteps coming down the stairs. They knew it was Dani; Peter was more than likely still sleeping off his hangover.

It *was* Dani, and she started speaking before she even came around the bannister. "So I've been sitting on the stairs listening from the part where Mom said you have to tell me something. Care to indulge?" She came into the kitchen and stood tall with her arms crossed and her lips pressed into a stern line.

Anthony, Reina, and Suzanne all exchanged glances. Billy examined their expressions. Reina looked firm, yet consoling, ready to comfort Dani or bash someone's head in — depending what Dani decided.

Suzanne was shoving cereal in her mouth and

Anthony was staring into his hands, as if he was about to be get a lashing.

"Honey," Reina started, "we *do* have something to tell you."

"I've gathered that much," Dani snapped back. Billy didn't know why she was so angry.

Reina cleared her throat and glanced at Anthony, who was still staring at his hands. She moved her gaze to Suzanne, still sitting on the counter, now waiting in suspense with her cheeks filled like a chipmunk caught red-handed, not chewing or moving.

"Well, get on with it!" Reina snapped at them, impatiently throwing her arms in to the air.

"What the hell is going on? Ya'll are in here like you're planning someone's murder," Dani said. Suzanne shifted her eyes to Reina and Anthony at the table.

"Peter has been cheating on you!" Anthony shouted. Everyone, including Billy, was visibly surprised. "Well?" Anthony looked at Reina and shrugged.

Dani stared at Anthony. *"What?"* she said very slowly. Her whole body started to tingle. Her nerves were on fire and her heart was starting to pick up speed.

"Peter has been having—" Anthony started to repeat.

"I heard you," she said softly. Those three words seemed to use up all the air in her lungs and she started to feel dizzy. She reached for a chair to sit. Reina grabbed her hand and helped her down to the chair at the head of the table. "How do you know?" She was gripping her necklace—a gift from Peter—with such force she could have ripped it off her neck.

"I overheard him on the phone last night talking to her," Anthony said.

"Her," Dani repeated, feeling the word in her

mouth. So heavy, like a big rock, making her tongue numb with meaning. "Who is she?"

"Well, it seems it's—"

"That New Jersey bitch that was here at the party yesterday with that little bratty kid," Suzanne blurted out.

Reina rolled her eyes. Usually she liked Suzanne's humor, but now wasn't the right time. Anthony slowly turned in his chair to give her a look that suggested he felt the same as his mom.

"What?" Suzanne asked, surprised.

Dani didn't look anywhere but at a small dent in the table. She reached toward it and pressed the tip of her finger into the small crevice. Her mind was bouncing like a Ping-Pong ball from thought to thought. It would have been impossible to catch just one.

"What are you thinking about honey?" Reina asked.

Dani looked over at Reina and then back at her finger rubbing the sharp edges of dent. "I'm thinking about how one day, after day care, Jayne came home and sat here at the table. I wasn't watching and she'd grabbed a steak knife Peter had left out and started banging the handle on the table. She hit it just right and it made this dent. I got so mad, I wasn't mad at her but she thought I was. I was taking my anger for Peter leaving the knife out on her. But really it was my fault; I was neglectful. I didn't look what was on the table before I set her down. Of course Peter and I went back and forth about whose fault it was." She looked at Reina with tears brimming in her eyes. "Peter was so mad. He couldn't understand how that happened with me sitting right there. The table was something him and his grandfather had made and now there's this dent. He could fill it, but it wouldn't be the same—it wouldn't be the original material, so he would rather just let it be a hole—a reminder."

"Oh, darling," Reina said softly. "This isn't your fault. Please don't think that." She grabbed Dani in a tight hug and the others chimed in little notes of agreement. Anthony came around the side of the table to join the hug. Suzanne jumped off the counter and came around the back to complete the group hug. Dani burst into tears.

"What am I going to do?" she whispered.

Instinctively, Billy came over. He wanted to comfort Dani with his energy—something he had learned to do early on after his passing. Everyone seemed to relax like they had just been given some kind of opium.

"Don't you worry about that, we'll help you figure it out," Reina said.

"Can someone get me a cup of coffee?"

"Got it!" Suzanne exclaimed, jumping up and heading to the cupboard to get Dani's favorite Minnie Mouse mug.

"Don't mention anything to Peter until I figure everything out," she said. Reina started to protest but Dani cut her off. "No, I don't need there to be any drama until I figure it out. I want everything to be cut and dry. That's best for Jayne."

Reina nodded. "Anthony has to go back to work," she said, "but I'll extend my trip as long as you need."

Dani smiled for the first time that morning.

2017

"Wow," Jayne said. "I had no idea Mom was put through that. And my dad did that to her. Do people in town know that's why we left?"

"Well, yes, I suppose they do. It was hard to ignore

that your dad was seeing someone right after you and your mom left."

"Did he love her? The other woman?" Jayne asked abruptly.

Billy thought for a moment, collecting his words carefully. "I don't think so. I think he messed up; he made a big, terrible mistake — a few times, apparently — and he didn't want your mom to leave, and he didn't want to be alone. He knew that Melody was infatuated with him, so he just ran with it for a couple years. It never became anything serious."

"Melody." Jayne ran the name through her teeth. "I nearly forgot — we ran into her in the supermarket."

"You did?" Billy asked, surprised.

Jayne rolled onto her back. "Yeah. She was talking to Mom and I walked up on them. Mom didn't seem happy to see her, but when I asked her about it, she just brushed it off. That explains so much now. Tell me more about what happened after. Were you there when Mom and Grandma talked about leaving?"

"Yes, I was. I — " Billy was interrupted by a knock on the door and the squeak of the knob turning.

"Darling? Are you awake? I thought I heard you talking to someone," Dani said, poking her head through the door.

"Yeah, I'm awake. I was just dictating a text to Blake," she lied. As the words were coming out, she realized she hadn't talked to Blake in a whole day. She made a mental note to text him when she had a second.

"I made some breakfast if you want. Eggs, bacon, and pancakes."

The piece of toast was sitting heavy in Jayne's stomach, but she felt her stomach growl. Unsure if it was from hunger or the alcohol, she replied, "Sounds delicious. I'm just going to wash my face and I'll be right down."

"Okay, honey." Dani closed the door.

"We can talk about it later," Billy said and then left right through the bedroom door without opening it.

Jayne got out of bed and pulled on the burnt orange Texans hoodie she found in the dryer. It was three sizes too big, but it belonged to her dad and despite the washing, she could still smell the Giorgio Armani cologne he wore. Today it was mixed with the smell of the stale smoke in her hair, making her stomach bubble with the reminder of last night. In the bathroom she splashed her face with water, letting the excess water drip down her forearms into the hoodie. It felt cool and refreshing on her skin, but no amount of refreshment would get rid of the knowledge she had now.

Downstairs, she met her mom at the table. Dani was already eating but had a plate made and a cup of coffee poured for Jayne. "How are you feeling?" Dani asked.

"I've been better," Jayne replied. Rusty jumped at her leg until she picked him up.

"I bet. I don't think I've ever seen you like that, not even when you turned twenty-one. Was it a good time at least?"

"It was. I don't feel like I drank a lot. We paced ourselves, but I haven't taken shots in a while." Jayne smiled. Shifted uncomfortably in her seat and cleared her throat. She didn't know how her mom would react if she brought it up and she wasn't up to that right now. The only thing she had on her mind was the plate in front of her and getting rid of her headache. "What do we have to do today?"

"I think you said Luke is coming over to look at the truck again—something about the oil—and I'm going to run out and do a few things. Last night I was looking at some of those papers from the genealogy stuff I was doing years ago and I would love to do some more on the house and the family. It's amazing what Google and the last twenty years have provided for us."

"So you've found out some stuff?" Jayne asked excitedly.

"Not necessarily. I found a lot of information about your dad and how the company grew, but there's still so much for me to go through. If you're interested, the library would probably have some old records about the Webber family." Dani finished and placed her knife and fork upside down on her plate, waiting for Jayne to finish.

"That would be great. When can we go?" Jayne asked. She scratched Rusty's head and set him down on the floor with a piece of pancake. He wagged his tail, snatched it from her fingers, and took it to his bed by the back door.

"Well, anytime you like. Maybe tomorrow? We still have a few papers here we should go through too."

"That's great. I'm excited — it's like finding a treasure map."

Dani grabbed their plates and put them in the sink while Jayne pulled out her phone and texted Blake: "Hey babe, how are you?"

17

DANI LEFT SHORTLY after breakfast and Jayne got a text from Luke saying he would be over in a couple of hours. Jayne decided that smelling like a washed-up bar rat wasn't a good look regardless of who she was or wasn't trying to impress.

She went upstairs and took a long shower, soaping off all of the residue from the night before. Her engagement ring was still sitting on the shelf under the medicine cabinet. She looked at it and the diamond sparkled like glitter in the sun shining through the transom window above the bathtub. Faced with the choice to put it on or leave it, she let it sit on the cold, glass shelf. *I still haven't even heard from Blake,* she told herself, almost an excuse.

After thinking about the conversation with Billy earlier, Jayne decided to go over to the old house and see if Billy would tell her more. Rusty followed beside her, hopping a few feet ahead every couple seconds and then waiting for her to catch up. *Well, if anything, you're well behaved,* she thought. She stopped on the bridge over the creek and watched the water flowing. It had rained last night and the water was high and rushing. *It's amazing how one little storm can add so much chaos to something so normal and mundane.*

Jayne picked Rusty up, but his paws and short legs were damp from the rain-soaked grass. She put him back down when it became too hard to keep his dirty little paws off her Ralph Lauren shirt.

The house seemed more empty than normal. What is it about abandoned houses that seemed more desolate and lonesome than any other empty house? Once inside, she called for Billy.

"I'm in here!" he shouted. Rusty let out a small bark and Jayne walked through the kitchen into the hallway and peeked into the room on the right, but it was empty. In the room to the left, she found Billy lying on the floor facing the window with his legs up against the wall and his hands under his head. "You saw the creek?" he asked.

"I did. It's nice and full. Something about it looks so beautiful and tempting."

"You're right. It's fresh and new and it fills all your senses." He smiled.

"Will you tell me more about what happened after the party?" Jayne wasted no time.

Billy swung his legs down and sat up. He smiled at her and said, "Sure, Bunny. What do you want to know?" They sat across from one another while Rusty sniffed the corners of the room.

"I guess, what else did Mom do when she found out about Melody?"

"Well, I went into your room to check on you and you were already awake, lying in bed. You had your new doll you got for your birthday. You were bouncing it around on the side of your bed, wiggling its arms back and forth. I asked what you were doing and you said, 'Playing with Tisha. That's her name.' I asked how you came up with that name because my brother's wife's name was Trisha, with an R. 'It just popped into my mind.' You said. I was stunned at the coincidence.

"You didn't want to get out of bed once I told you that Grandma Reina, Suzanne, and Uncle Anthony were downstairs, you slowly got yourself out of bed and started toward the stairs, rubbing your eyes. Your dad had just gotten up and he waited for you halfway down the steps before carrying you down the rest of the way.

"Things were obviously tense and your dad felt it the minute he walked into the room."

Jayne interrupted Billy's story. "How come you wanted to wake me up if you knew what was going on downstairs?"

"I think part of me thought that things would be civil if you were there. You would keep things calm."

Jayne nodded and let Billy continue.

"Anyway, your grandma tested the water. 'We were just talking about that Melody girl,' she said. This made your mom spin toward her with a pleading look on her face. Everyone else stared at your grandma. 'We were talking about how her son is a little prick and she's probably a . . .' She broke off, remembering you were in the room. 'A promiscuous woman,' she finished.

"Your dad seemed satisfied with this answer and grabbed his coffee mug and handed you off to your mom. 'Yeah, maybe. There are rumors about her *promiscuity*,' he said. 'I think she's been with a couple of the guys at the shop,' he said nonchalantly, and that was it.

"Over the next week, Anthony left and most things remained the same. With Grandma there, your mom was able to pretend she was just spending quality time with her and not actually avoiding him. It helped that your dad had a commissioned set of a kitchen table and chairs due the following week, so he spent most of his time at the shop. Things remained calm at home, but I knew the waves were coming; not little waves, but a tsunami that was going to tear your family apart.

"Almost a week after the party, Dani and Grandma Reina were sitting out on the porch, having a glass of wine and sharing a cigarette. Your dad had gone to the bar after work and surprisingly this didn't bother your mom at all. I sat on the porch railing, leaning against the column, listening to the ladies talk. It reminded me of when my mom and grandma sat together, gossiping and laughing into the night. I had always wanted a glimpse into those conversations.

"Grandma Reina said, 'It's a shame you'll have to move out of this house when you leave. Are you sure you can't keep it? I could come stay.'

"Your mom replied, 'I'll miss it. It's been in Peter's family for years, though. I wouldn't feel right taking it, even if I could. I'd rather just come back to North Carolina. I can do some ancestry stuff in my spare time, until I can find something more permanent.'

"I didn't like the sound of that. If you left, I thought I'd never see you again, and if I did, it might be just a couple times a year. I was supposed to be there while you grew up and then the house was to be passed on to you.

"Anyway, Grandma took a long pull on her cigarette and passed it to your mom. 'You can't let this drag out any longer. Have you thought of what you're going to do and when?' She asked.

"'Yes,' your mom said. 'I'll tell him tomorrow. It'll be Sunday and he won't be at work, so he can think about it.' Dani blew the remaining smoke from her lungs and passed the cigarette to Reina. No one spoke while the cicadas started to chirp, filling the space with a sound like rushing water, getting louder and louder until slowly, it started to subside. Your grandma was worried about your mom being able to take you across state lines.'

"'He won't have much of a choice,' your mom said and paused to look out on the front lawn. 'I'll come to an agreement with him before we leave. I don't want anything from him. That has to count for something. I'm not going to keep her from him. He's a good father and I'll cooperate with him so he can see her as much as he wants.' It was almost ninety degrees out, but your mom pulled her thin throw blanket across her lap, twisting the tassels. You could tell she was uncomfortable. When Grandma tried to pass the cigarette back to her, Dani shook her head.

"Grandma Reina said, 'You know it's over a sixteen-hour drive from here to North Carolina, right? You can't just meet him halfway on a whim. Do you think he would even drive eight hours to pick her up?'

"We all knew he wouldn't – at least not sober. Like the flicker from a flame, annoyance passed over your mom's face. 'I did think of that,' she said. 'But to be honest, I think I pushed it to the back of my mind.' She thought for a moment. 'Or maybe I thought I could convince him that it would be a good plan, knowing he wouldn't follow through and I wouldn't have to worry about it.' "

Billy lay back down on the floor, resting his head in his hands, staring at the ceiling. "At this point, I was starting to worry more than before. I wondered if there was anything I could do to fix it. I thought of all the ways I could help your mom to overcome your dad cheating, and try to prevent him from cheating again, but I realized there was nothing I could do. If you left, I would remain here, in the house, with your dad for years. Eventually you would get the house, but not until your dad passed away – if he didn't sell it first. I didn't know how many years that would be. I wouldn't see your school projects, or hear about your first crush. I wouldn't get to see you get ready for prom or warn you about you first boyfriend and scare away your first love." Jayne laughed and Billy smiled shyly. "All the firsts I'd had with you up until that point would be all that I'd have to remember you by."

He sighed, then continued his story. "Your grandma looked at her watch and back out to the long driveway. 'What time does Peter usually get home from the bar?' she asked.

"Your mom told her the truth. 'I don't know. Sometimes a couple hours, sometimes not until it closes.'

"Grandma nodded. Her silence was response enough. Finally, very carefully, she said, 'I'm glad you're leaving him.'

"I sat up straight at this and your mom turned to face her. 'What? I thought you liked him?' she asked

" 'I do,' Grandma replied. 'I think he's a great guy. He was good to you for many years, but y'all lost your way. When do you think that was?'

"Your mom thought for a second and said, 'It started before Jayne was born. When we couldn't get pregnant, it caused a lot of stress between us. A lot of it was my fault, some of it his. I think it built a divide between us, and the wider it got, the more we thought a baby would close it. But instead, it stayed there. Sometimes we would meet halfway but mostly we just kept to ourselves.' Your grandma put her hand on your mom's knee in consolation. 'It's okay,' your mom said. 'I didn't want to tell you. I didn't want to tell anyone. Not even myself.' "

Billy didn't know if he was oversharing with Jayne or if she'd want to hear this, but she asked, "Did you know my parents were having these kind of problems?"

"I knew of the problems they faced. I didn't need

to be a therapist to diagnose their marriage as failing when I lived with them full-time. Evelyn and I went through a few rough patches, but there were only two that tested our relationship and weren't long-lasting like the ones your parents went through."

"What were they like? What was the difference?"

"Well, the first one was when I lost my job at my father-in-law's factory. The second was when our first son, Ted, was born. Losing my job with her father was hard. It created a lot of resentment toward Mr. Carter, which I then took out on her. I didn't hold back when I spoke ill of him and it started to change Evelyn's perception of me. Luckily, with Evelyn being a no-nonsense type woman, she straightened me out real quick. Your mom is like that as well, but your dad was very stubborn. The hardest, though, was dealing with new fatherhood. Some men can step into fatherhood as easy as stepping into a new pair of shoes. That wasn't the case for me. I had to go through the blisters and sore feet.

"I loved being a new father; the idea of bringing life into this world that was part of me was extraordinary. What I struggled with was the balance of home life and work life. By the time Ted was born, I had already been fully established at my dad's shop, which was starting to become more popular. People were coming all the way from Tennessee and Louisiana. They had money, too, and they were paying extra to have it done in half the time it would normally take. This made us extra busy, but Dad didn't want to hire more people. He said, 'It's just a rush that will end soon.' It didn't end at all, and when I spent most my day at the shop I was exhausted when I came home. I just wanted to relax. Evelyn was notably and understandably irritated and just wanted some alone time for a few minutes. She would hold the baby and say things like, 'Just thought you'd want to spend some time with him since you've been gone all day!'

"This would get me fired up because of course I wanted to see him, but every day felt like I had run a marathon. Instead of yelling back, I would shut down and lock myself in the office before I said something I'd regret. This happened on almost a nightly basis and finally, like a kettle building pressure, Evelyn couldn't take it anymore and burst into my office one day, baby on her hip and told me, 'Billy, you listen to me. I know you work and I know you're working hard. You provide for this family better than any man I know between my friends. But you're killing me, you hear? I may not have a job like you, but I have a job raising this baby, cleaning this house, doing your laundry, making sure you have every meal ready for you at your beck and call. I am the face of this house and look at this face.' She pointed to her face and for the first time in months, I really *saw* her. She was my Evelyn, but she looked different, something that had gradually changed since Ted was born, but in such small increments, it was like snow melting — there's no change minute by minute, but day by day, month by month, you can see it. She looked worn and tired with bags under her eyes and her unbrushed hair was pinned back with little strands falling over her forehead. Suddenly, I noticed little things, like how she didn't wear makeup anymore except for church and she almost always had spit-up on her clothes. Ted was a colicky baby, which also had her up many nights. Not once did I offer to watch the baby as she got ready — not unless she asked. Nor did I tell her to go have some time to herself. I just assumed she had everything under control, because she really did. Now I saw her; I saw her pleading with her eyes. I could see that if she asked for help from me so she could take

146

care of herself, she would feel like a failed mother and wife.

"I told her to sit down and we would figure this out. From that day forward we built a routine that helped her and we were both on parent duty. The simple conversation between us that night was the profound change in our marriage and the rest of our lives. This is the difference between your parents and us. Your dad was unwilling to give up the remainder of his freedom, he was unwilling to see your mom for the person she was, and instead held on to any resentment he had, letting it burn in him like a wildfire during a drought. In no time, there was nothing left to hold on to, no memory of what was before, and therefore, nothing to love about each other after. They were at that point. The fire was so far gone, it practically extinguished itself, and just as there might have been any room for improvement, Melody took that away. I don't know if there's anything I *could* have done."

"Can you tell me a bit about how it ended?" Jayne asked and readjusted her position on the floor, stretching her legs out in front of her and reaching for her toes. She settled back with her forearms on her thighs.

"I really don't think it's my place to tell you all these things, Bunny."

"Please. My mom won't tell me, and now you're the only person who can."

Billy swung his legs off the wall and sighed. "Okay then."

1997

The day after Dani and her mom talked, Peter slept in as usual while everyone else ate pancakes downstairs and cartoons played on the TV.

When Peter finally came downstairs, he went straight to the cupboard and grabbed the bottle of Ibuprofen and a coffee mug. Dani mentioned he might have to make another pot and her body clenched up, anticipating the reaction she expected: he slammed the pot down onto the counter. Without saying anything, he dumped the coffee filter into the garbage, grabbed a new one, and scooped three tablespoons of The Café Du Monde in. He filled his coffee mug with a little water from the sink and popped the pills in his mouth, washing it down like taking a shot of tequila. He turned toward the ladies as the coffee percolated.

"Anything on the agenda today for you ladies?" he asked through a tight mouth. Without looking at him, Dani shook her head. "I guess there's not much left to do when you've already been here a week. Eh, Reina?" Without waiting for a response he turned to get the cream out of the refrigerator. Dani and Reina exchanged glances but when Dani opened her mouth to talk, Reina stopped her with a firm hand on her arm.

"There's a lot to see when I only get to see my family twice a year." She gave Dani's arm a soft squeeze. "I'd be happy to leave if I'm a bother," she said, staring at the back of Peter's head.

He turned around to look at her, his demeanor changing. "No, no, of course not. I'm sure Dani and Jayne are happy for your company and it's always nice to see you." Then out of nowhere, he blurted, "Dani, you guys should go on a girls' trip to the wineries. They're not that far and I bet your mom would love it."

Dani was confused, taken aback, but not bothered

by this comment. "I bet she would. I would too. Maybe one day we will."

The coffee pot beeped four times, letting everyone know it was done. Reina squeezed Dani's arm twice and nodded toward Peter, as if it was a secret code between them. Dani nodded once and Reina removed her hand before walking out to the living room to get Jayne. She bribed Jayne from her cartoons and pancakes by saying, "Hey, sugar, I really wanted to see the river in the morning and your daddy says you're the best tour guide for it. How about you come show me and I'll watch cartoons with you later in my room?"

Peter sat down at the table. "What was that about?" he asked

"Listen, we need to talk."

"Okay."

Judging by Peter's body language, he had no knowledge of what was about to happen. Dani's hands were shaking, her heart was like a jackhammer in her chest and her voice was starting to waver. She wished she'd given some thought to how she was going to do this. Instead, maybe still in denial, she thought planning it out would set everything in stone. Her feelings were like a volcano about to erupt; there was no dancing around the subject, it just spewed out.

"I think that we should separate." It felt like a weight coming off her shoulders as she said it, but it was like dropping the weight on her toe.

"What?" he asked with a chuckle, as if she just told a joke.

"I want to separate. I'm telling you now because I want you to think about it, but I've already made up my mind."

"Where is this coming from? What the hell, Dani?". He leaned back in his chair and pinched the bridge of his nose. "Why? Where is this coming from?" he asked again, crossing his arms.

"You had to know this was coming, Peter. You don't want to be with me. All you do is try *not* to be with me; staying late at work, going to the bar. When's the last time we went on a date, or you spent the night with your family having a nice dinner?"

"It wasn't for a lack of wanting to be with you guys," Peter said. "I love spending time with Jayne and you. But, Jayne would usually be in bed by the time I got home anyway."

Dani took a deep breath and watched the look on his face. His eyebrows were raised as if it should erase away everything she just said. Then the subconscious twitch of a frown said he was taking her seriously. When she didn't speak, he started, "So, let me get this straight. You want a divor—"

"Separation," she corrected.

"You want a *separation*," he said, making air quotes, "because I haven't taken you on a date in a few months and I go out a couple times a week to be alone?"

"No, that's not all."

"Oh, that's not all, she has more. Well, enlighten me." He smirked and nodded for her to continue.

She sat there for a moment taking it in and realized she was making a good decision. Billy was there, quietly listening.

He's not even upset, Dani thought.

"I know about you and Melody," she said finally. "I know everything—or at least enough that you can't deny it." There was a long pause as the words settled around them. Dani was shaking uncontrollably at this point—vibrating even. The only thing she could do was to sit on her hands to hide it. It didn't seem like Peter noticed, but Billy did.

"How?" he asked. She told him about Anthony

overhearing him on the phone.

"He heard you say that it's happened more than once. He heard you say that you didn't want to continue — you want to end it and focus on your family."

As if he was just thrown a life ring, he clung on. "I do!" he replied, leaning forward, toward her. "She means nothing. It was just a few, random times."

It wasn't until now that her thoughts of him and Melody together flooded her mind, drowning out his words. She was imagining them together, in the full sense of the word. *Where was Frankie?* she wondered.

"Oh, give it a rest, Peter," Dani snapped. "You're making yourself sound worse with each word that comes out of your mouth. This wasn't just a onetime thing."

"It was just a . . . a handful of times, not a weekly thing," he said desperately.

"Oh, *just* a handful? Perfect. Thank goodness, I thought it was two handfuls." She pushed her chair back and walked over to the kitchen sink. The blood rushed to her head and she leaned on the counter, waiting for the spots to clear. Peter swiveled in his chair to face her, his feet dragging on the linoleum.

"Please," he pleaded, "tell me what I can do to make this better."

"*Sorry* would have been a good start." He hadn't said anything resembling an apology up until this point.

"I *am* sorry," he finally said and dropped his hand palm up on his worn jeans.

"Have there been others?"

"No!"

Something about his response sounded like a lie, but not one she would get him to admit to, given the circumstances. And really, it didn't matter much. She'd made up her mind. She wished Suzanne hadn't left;

she'd have wrung him like a towel and gotten every last drop of confession out of him.

"Okay," she said. She told him that she'd made up her mind. Peter tried to plead with her, asking about Jayne, saying no one in his family has ever been divorced. He didn't know what a tumultuous relationship looked like.

Dani explained that nothing would change between him and Jayne; she wasn't going to take her from him, which, years later, ended up not being the case when his drinking got out of control. Dani's parents had a bad marriage that ended poorly and she didn't want to go through all those years like her mom, pretending she was happy. She could see the problems between them, no matter how well hidden they kept them. She told him that. He must have understood, because he asked what the next steps were. Dani looked outside to Jayne and Reina walking hand-in-hand along the creek. Jayne would stop and point at something then continue to pull at Grandma's arm.

"I'm going to North Carolina for a bit with my mom, until we can figure out something."

Peter didn't like that. He tried to tell her she couldn't. She told him to relax, she was just going for a couple of weeks. She told him she didn't want to be here and they needed to figure things out separately. They came up with a plan to meet halfway in a couple of weeks and Jayne would come home with him.

"I can't talk about this anymore," Peter said, pushing back from the table. "I'm going to the shop."

Dani nodded. For a moment that felt longer than it was, like a pause in time before a hug or a kiss, they looked at each other, memories of their courtship and first couple years of their marriage flashing through both their minds. Billy could see it play through.

Dani crossed her arms over her chest and walked to

the sliding doors. She watched Jayne and Reina, still by the river. She waited a moment — she *needed* a minute.

Her marriage was over in as many syllables as it took to start it.

2017

Billy stopped for a moment; he could see Jayne was affected by the story. "You okay?" he asked.

Jayne nodded and swallowed down the lump caught in her throat. "It's just a lot, you know. But I'm glad to hear it. I wish my mom had told me, but I understand why she didn't; she was trying to protect my dad."

"Yes," Billy said. "But let me tell you, your dad was not a bad person, he just had a couple bad problems that affected his life deeply. He was a generous man who was always there for the people who needed him."

"Except for Mom," Jayne said.

"Well, yes, at that time. When people get complacent in their relationships, they tend to assume their other half is just happy with how things are, that they don't need looking after. When it gets to that point, *if* it can't be fixed, it gets worse and then the person takes a back seat in the other's life."

Jayne briefly thought of Blake and how he wasn't there right now.

"What about Dad? Jayne asked. "That was it? He didn't care or try and fight?"

"No, he didn't try and fight, but he certainly cared. After your mom went outside to see you and your Grandma, I went upstairs to their room, but your dad wasn't there. After a small search, I found him in your room. There he was, his massive form sitting on the bed facing the window, hunched over the teddy bear you were given when you were born. He rubbed one finger over each plastic eye and nose. I came around and sat beside him on the bed and put an arm around him. He couldn't feel me, but the intention of love swept over him and he started to cry. He put the teddy bear aside and dropped his face into his hands, sobbing even harder. I told him it would be okay, I would be here, and we would get through this. He heard you girls come into the house and he quickly stood up, placing the teddy bear back. Then he wiped his face with his shirt and quietly walked out of your room."

"Do you know how I felt about it?" Jayne was concerned.

"You were excited; you were going to Grandma's for some time and your mom promised you beaches and parks. You didn't quite grasp what it meant for the family."

"I remember now," she said, staring out the dirty window of the old house. "I remember I so desperately wanted you to come, but you said you had to stay here to keep Dad company." Billy nodded.

Jayne's phone rang. Luke's name appeared on the screen and she hit "Answer."

"Hello?"

"Hi, Jayne? It's Luke. How you doing?"

"I'm good, Luke. How are you?" She glanced at Billy and stood up, brushing off the butt of her pants.

"Good, good. I'm just outside of your house, I'm here to check the oil in your dad's truck. I don't know if you're home but I can—"

"I'm home, I was just . . . uh . . . I'm at the old house in the back. I'll come to the big house, just give me a minute to get up there.

"No problem."

Jayne clicked the phone off.

"I'll talk to you later," she told Billy, then picked Rusty up and headed for the main house.

18

LUKE WAS WAITING outside by the truck when Jayne came up to the house. He smiled when he saw her and she waved. Rusty wiggled in her arms, asking to be let go.

"You doing okay?" Luke asked.

"Hurting a little from last night, but nothing a hot shower and some bread and bacon couldn't fix."

Luke laughed. "I used that recovery method this morning as well." He opened the unlocked truck door and popped the hood. "It shouldn't take me very long. I just want to check your fluid levels."

"Okay," Jayne said. "I'll just be inside when you're done."

A few minutes later Luke knocked on the door a couple times before entering. Rusty barked once then wagged his tail when he saw Luke.

"I'm in the kitchen!" Jayne yelled and grabbed two glasses to fill with ice. "I made some lemonade, if you're thirsty? It's not the best, but it's fresh and it has ginger for your stomach." She handed him a glass.

"Thanks, sounds great."

"Want to sit on the back porch?"

"Sure." He motioned for her to go first.

"Everything go okay with the fluids?" She sat down on the loveseat and Luke sat beside her, inviting Rusty into his lap.

"Yep, everything looks great. Your coolant may need a change in a few months and it looks like the filter is new."

"Okay. Thank you so much for doing that. I really appreciate it. I don't know the first thing about cars."

"You're welcome. It's no trouble for me." He smiled. "This is really good." He held up his glass of lemonade. "I wouldn't have thought ginger and maple syrup would make a difference."

Jayne smiled and they sat for a few moments, listening to the birds singing and swooping from tree to tree. Jayne looked over at Luke staring off in the distance at the old house. "What is it?" she asked.

"Oh, it's nothing. I just thought I saw someone over there by the old house. It's gone now, whatever I saw."

"Like a person?" she asked, her voice tight.

"Yeah, well, like a teenager or something, going into the house, but I'm sure I sound like a crazy person." Luke took a gulp of his lemonade.

"You don't," Jayne assured him. "That's an old house, it's been here for over a hundred years. Who knows what's going on over there?" she said in a joking tone. At the same time, she wanted to confide in him all about Billy. If he could see Billy—if that was who he saw—then she wasn't crazy and Billy wasn't just a figment of her imagination. But the last thing she needed was to be considered insane by someone who was technically one of her employees. She hadn't thought of Luke being her employee until now and she wondered if she should be backing off the friendship a bit so no one would be getting the wrong idea. She looked over at Luke and he looked back. The sun brought out the copper in his dark hair. "So, do you like working at the shop? Is that what you want to do or is it just a stepping-stone for something else?" she asked.

"I'd love to continue working there and growing a client base." He paused and stretched his shirt out to wipe the condensation off his glass. "Maybe one day, when I'm much older, I could open my own shop, but that's in the far future."

"That would be great," Jayne said sincerely. She thought she heard a car pull up out front and assumed it was just her mom. The air was cool on the skin, but the sun was warm between clouds. The wind brought smells of mowed grass and damp trees.

Luke shifted in his chair, angling himself so he was propped in the corner, his ankle resting on top of his knee. Rusty readjusted too, sticking his nose into the crook of his leg. "I love that these houses have been in your family for generations. It gives them so much history and character."

"Yeah, I really don't want to leave this house. My grandfather and his father built it. And I think my great-great-grandfather and his father built that small house, but I'm not entirely sure. I never really asked."

"I think you're right. At least from passing comments your dad made about it. That's just so neat. My family has a lot of history in this town, but nothing to really tie us to one place like this. My relatives from generations ago were mostly just workers from Mexico. They were paid small wages to do tasks around the houses and farms, not to leave any kind of legacy."

The door to the patio slid open and Rusty jerked his head up. Luke peeked back over his shoulder to see Dani step out and Jayne smiled until she saw the look of surprise on her mom's face.

"Hey Mom. What's up?"

"Oh . . . um . . . well," Dani stuttered. She glanced back into the house, not removing her hand from the doorway. Luke and Jayne both sat up, concerned. "I just wasn't expecting Luke to be here still."

Jayne felt embarrassed for Luke, like he was suddenly an unwelcome guest in their home when just a day ago Dani was inviting him over.

"I thought I told you he was coming over to help with the truck. He just finished and I figured the least I could do was offer him some lemonade." Dani stared blankly and looked in the house again. "Mom, what the hell is going on?" Jayne demanded.

"Well, I sort of have a surprise for you."

19

DANI REMOVED HER hand from the doorway and a tall man wearing a tan, long-sleeve polo and jeans stepped out onto the patio. Rusty growled, the hair on his back standing on end.

"Blake! What are you doing here?" Jayne didn't move until he started walking toward her. She got up and wrapped her arms around his neck and he bent down and lifted her off her feet. Luke stood up at the same time. He tried to force a smile, but it couldn't have been more fake if someone had taped the corners of his mouth up.

"Well, I called your mom and told her I was coming down and to keep it secret from you, so it would be a surprise. Are you surprised, babe?"

"I am, I just . . . I can't believe you're here. You didn't return any of my texts this morning. What about your clients?" She was gripping his arms so tight, Blake removed her hands and held them in front of him. His hands were warm against Jayne's.

"I mentioned to Ralph what was going on with you and he berated me for not telling him sooner and leaving you here alone. He even paid for my flight here to get me on the next flight out. I should have listened to you in the first place." He pulled her in for another hug.

Jayne felt an odd sensation of guilt. Now she had the awkward task of introducing Blake and Luke. She pulled away quickly and made the introduction. "This is Luke, the son of one of Dad's best friends and long-time employees. He works at the shop now. I've technically known him since I was born."

"Well, it's nice to meet you, bud." Jayne cringed. She hated that word, "bud." Those three little letters left so much room for interpretation when used on an adult.

Luke wasn't bothered, or pretended not to be. He stretched out the hand that wasn't clutching a struggling, gnawing Rusty and said, "Nice to meet you. I've heard a lot about you."

Blake shook his hand, then wrapped his arm around Jayne and smiled. "That's nice to hear. Nothing but good things, I'm sure." Jayne looked from Luke to her mom, who was wearing a terrific poker face.

"Of course." Luke said and smiled at Jayne. "Well, I better get going. Let me know if the truck has anything else to be looked at."

"I will. Thank you again for coming over to fix that. We owe you."

"The lemonade was more than enough." He raised his glass to them, still half-full, and walked into the house followed by Dani.

Blake turned back to Jayne and placed a hand in the curve between her head and neck. He bent down and gave her a kiss that said he'd been waiting for them to leave.

Jayne reciprocated but couldn't help feeling a little uneasy. She pulled back a bit, wrapped her arms under his, and pressed her hands into the familiar muscles covering his shoulder blades. He smelled of his normal fruity cologne and the musk of an airplane. "I'm so happy you're here. I can't believe you didn't tell me you were coming. I was worried you forgot about me already."

Blake smiled, chipping away at the new brick wall Jayne had built for him. "Never, babe. In fact, I have something for you." He reached into his back pocket.

"You do?" Jayne felt another brick fall off.

"Yes. I felt really bad about how I acted and regretted not being here for you. I thought I was doing the right thing, but now I know I wasn't." Blake handed Jayne a small, rectangular box and she smiled so big, she felt silly. She slowly lifted the lid and revealed a circular rose gold pendant, about the size of a quarter with beveled edges. The middle was engraved with a "J." The other side read, "My heart, my soul, my life." She picked up the long chain and pulled it over her head. The pendant rested on the roundness of her chest. Blake pinched the pendant.

"Perfect length," he said, grazing her breast as he removed his hand.

"Thank you, Blake. It's beautiful. I love it." She reached up to grab his neck for a kiss then wrapped her arms around his shoulders.

"You're welcome, my love. Now, I do have a question for you."

"What is it?"

"Where's your engagement ring? Should I be worried?"

Jayne looked at her bare hand as if she'd forgotten again. But she hadn't this time. "No, no. I've been doing a lot of work in the house, going through old boxes and cleaning. I didn't want to get it all dinged up or dirty. It's in a safe spot." She wasn't completely lying. She also made a mental note to get it off the bathroom mantel before Blake saw. That was about as safe as keeping it on the toilet seat.

"Okay, babe."

"You want to see the house?" She changed the subject. Blake motioned for her to lead the way.

Inside the kitchen, Dani was scrolling on her phone with Rusty on her lap. Jayne announced she was going to show Blake around. When they got upstairs, Jayne went through the spare room and then into hers. She anticipated Blake trying to make a move once in her room, but she didn't anticipate the aggressiveness. As he groped at her and led her to the bed, she had to push him off and whisper sternly, "Not now."

"Come on, babe. It's been so long."

"My mom is right downstairs and probably expecting this to happen. It's not." She pushed him off again and stood up, leaving him lying on the bed, looking upset. "You just got here—it would be nice to relax and hang out for a bit."

"This *is* hanging out," Blake argued back. "We're going to have plenty of time for *your* hanging out later."

"And we'll have plenty of time for *that* later, also. Just let me show you the rest of the property."

Jayne started for the door and heard Blake sigh in disappointment as he rolled off the bed. "This place smells old," he said, "like an antique store." Jayne felt the jab in her stomach, taking the comment personally. "Like, a combination of dust, mildew, and aging belongings. Oh, and mothballs," he added, trying to be funny.

"Well, it is old," Jayne said, without turning to him. He asked about the room at the end of the hall with the closed door. "That was my dad's room." She paused. "I haven't been in there yet."

"Why not?" Blake asked sincerely but with a jerk back of his head.

"Because there are just too many memories in there. A lot of disappointment, too. Plus, I don't know what kind of state it's going to be in."

"I'll go with you babe, whenever you want. I'm here for you now." He ran his hand over her ponytail.

"Okay. Thank you. I'm not ready now, but soon."

When they got to the bottom of the stairs, Rusty barked once and Dani turned in to her chair and asked if they were hungry. "I'm making this recipe for tacos I found on Pinterest."

Jayne looked at Blake. "Sure, that would be great. I was just going to show Blake the creek and old house. Do you want some help?"

"No, you guys catch up, I'll let you know when it's ready."

"Thanks, Mom," Jayne said, giving her shoulder a squeeze as she passed by.

Blake and Jayne walked out into the backyard. He started talking about work and his clients. She tried to seem interested, but the truth was, she never could convince herself that the small cases Ralph had been teasing him with were all that exciting. She nodded and mumbled "mm-hmm" when needed, but didn't really understand. She was an artist for a reason: she understood brush strokes, lighting, movement, and life. She couldn't wrap her head around the legal mumbo jumbo that Blake knew.

She led him down the porch and over to the bridge. "This bridge has been here for a long time. When they built the big house, they built this bridge. Before that, they used to take a road that was over there to get to the old house." Jayne pointed through the trees, a few hundred feet from the old house. There was still barely an opening where the road would have turned off to a small gravel road. But over the many years of abandonment, the trees and plants had taken back what was rightfully theirs.

"I don't think I wore the right shoes for trekking through farmland," Blake said, brushing off his leather loafers every few steps.

"Yeah, I probably should have told you to change them. It's just grass though, so they should be fine." Blake didn't say anything and Jayne heard the disagreement in his silence. "Did you bring any other shoes?"

"Not really. I have my not-as-nice loafers. No tennis shoes."

"You didn't bring any casual clothing?" she asked.

"Well, no. I thought we were going to be in a civilized place with sidewalks and roads."

Jayne took a deep breath through her nose. Her tennis shoes, which had a comfortable spot in the back of her closet in North Carolina, were getting their wear and tear in Texas. "We're almost there." She pointed to the small house a short distance away.

"What's so special about this little house?" Blake asked, slapping away a weed and rubbing a scuff off his shoe.

Jayne didn't know if it was irritation with his shoes, annoyance with her not wanting to fool around, or the inconvenience he had to be here at all. She felt hurt by his question. "It was the first house built on this property, before the big house was built." Blake didn't say anything. "My *family* built both houses, Blake." All she got in reply was a grunt as Blake made his way to the overgrown pathway and assessed his shoes. She felt a stab of regret for bringing him here to this place that meant so much to her.

Without this house, there wouldn't be as strong of a connection to the land they still lived on. That thought made her feel a welcoming energy, expanding throughout the land around the houses. *How can I leave this place and go back with Blake? Would he stay here?* She knew the answer was no. She thought she could convince him, but as they approached the old, weathered house, she saw it through his eyes. It wasn't the family house that she knew and loved, but a disgusting old house that should be torn down, not left to rot. She saw the problems: the peeling paint and the rusty nails popping out of the joists, the sway of the deck from years of rain, the wooden shingles that were gray and turning up at their fraying edges. The house was truly an eyesore. Regardless, she started to walk up the stairs.

"Babe," Blake said quickly. "What are you doing? Don't go in there."

"What? Why not? I've been in here many times already." She stood at the top of the steps, looking down at him on the sidewalk. "Come on Blake, it's fine. I want to show you the inside." They had a stare off for a moment while Blake contemplated whether or not he wanted to risk it. Eventually he made his way onto the porch, stepping over the stairs. It groaned in protest. He slowly made his way into the house, ducking through the doorframe.

"It smells in here," he said, scrunching his nose.

"Well, it's over a hundred years old and it's been abandoned for many." They walked through to the kitchen. Jayne was really hoping to run into Billy.

"Why hasn't anyone torn it down?"

Truthfully, Jayne had wondered the same thing, but in defense asked, "Why would they? Other than the weathering on the outside, and probably some structural damage from termites, it's mostly fine." The minute she said it, she almost laughed at how silly it sounded. Even if she wanted to, there would be no rebuilding this house without starting over. "Go look in that small drawer, on the left side, in the corner." She pointed in the kitchen.

Blake walked over and wrenched the drawer open. He saw the bottle of whiskey Jayne had left there. "Whoa, this must be almost eighty years old."

"Something like that." She smiled. Blake started looking through more drawers. "There's nothing else, I checked." Jayne made her way into the smaller room she found Billy in earlier. He wasn't there, nor was he in the room opposite of that. She looked in the master but he wasn't there. *Where is he?* she asked herself.

"Babe, this place is creeping me out. Can we go?" Blake asked, a nervous vibration in his voice.

"What do you mean?" Jayne called back from the master room. She started toward the kitchen.

"This place, it gives me the creeps. Like someone still lives here—a homeless person or something" He looked around cautiously.

Jayne stared through the kitchen window. The light was falling on the wooden floor, making squares from the sun. "I can assure you, no homeless person lives in here."

"Babe." Blake was by the front door. "Let's go. Maybe your mom will have the food ready."

Jayne had forgotten about the food and the thought of tacos woke up her stomach with a grumble. She started toward the door.

Bye Billy, she thought.

20

"**WHY WAS LUKE** in the house?" Blake asked as they headed back.

"I told you—he's looking at Dad's truck. For *free*," she added. "I wasn't just going to shoo him off without at least offering him something to drink."

"How long was he here for after he finished?" Blake asked

Jayne stepped back, realizing where this was going. "Not long. That was his first lemonade and it was still half-full when he left." Jayne's voice softened. "Why?"

"I was just wondering," Blake said. "Normally people don't invite their mechanics in for a lemonade."

Jayne wasn't anticipating the added remark and the softness in her voice hardened. "Well, he's not just my mechanic. He works at the shop, he's my dad's best friend's son, and I've known him for years." She paused. "Nothing is going on, if that's what you're getting at."

"Okay," Blake said, short. He slid the patio door open and they walked into the kitchen. The coolness of the house wrapped around them, giving Jayne small goose bumps from being in the warm fall sun. Rusty barked at Blake and then resumed dancing around Dani's feet, licking up fallen shreds of cheese and tomatoes she was plating to go with the tacos.

"Have a seat. I'll be done in just a few minutes," she said.

Blake sat down and Jayne got them both some lemonade. Dani brought everything they needed over to the table.

"Thank you, Dani," Blake said. "This looks wonderful and I'm famished."

Dani smiled.

After lunch, letting their full bellies rest, Blake went out to the living room to watch football. Jayne passed the plastic wrap to Dani and asked about the box of articles she'd found. Dani nodded and took a deep breath through her nose.

"So you saw the article about your grandmother then?" Dani asked.

"Yes. And now Dad's relationship with Grandpa and why he never wanted to talk about Grandma makes complete sense."

"Good."

"I didn't realize Grandpa was such an advocate for black rights." Jayne rubbed her full belly and stretched like a pregnant woman trying to make some more room.

"Yeah, he was a bit of an activist and hero in this town. Especially when he went off to war. Of course your great-grandfather had the same values, but Gerry wasn't as vocal as Steve—he liked to just keep the peace."

"Are there more articles in there about them?"

"Sure." Dani got up and went to get the box. Jayne cleared a few more dishes while Dani brought the box into the kitchen. Dani pulled out a fistful of papers, some worn and old, some new copies. "When I was living here and looking into your dad's family history, I found a lot." She waved the papers as proof. "There was a lot more to be found though. His family has been here for over a hundred years; they would have been some of the founding members of this town. That's one of the reasons your father's business gets so much credit. When businesses open here — especially on Main Street — they usually shut down within a couple years because they're not getting the foot traffic. Webber Furniture has the credibility but also the quality behind it. It's like one of the old oak trees of the town.

"One time, a furniture store opened down the road from your dad's. It was cheaper but the price reflected the quality. Your dad didn't have to lift a finger to put that store out of business. The reputation of Webber Furniture succeeded it and in a couple of years that store closed down. That's why a lot of the stores you still see on Main Street — Sammy's, The Café, Stan's old pub — have a hundred-year-old reputation and people have been going there for just as long. That's not about to change." Dani put the papers on the table. She flipped through a few and found a copy of a newspaper article with a young man, about ten, dressed in what looked like a tweed suit and a bow tie. Next to him was an older gentleman — still young in his own right — wearing a similar suit and sporting a combed and styled mustache. His right hand rested on the young man's shoulder. The caption read, "William Webber Jr. and his son, Theodore Webber." The article was for a relief function for the hurricane that hit Texas and flooded San Antonio in 1921.

William and Theodore had been raising money to help the less fortunate, lower-class, and colored areas of San Antonio and surrounding areas that were affected by the floodwaters.

Jayne scoffed as she read the article and Dani looked at her quizzically. Jayne shook her head. "It says they weren't well received because they were helping the colored people in the area; that they were almost run out of town and harassed because of it. It's just so hard for me to wrap my head around how things used to be." Dani gave her a sincere smile and Jayne flipped through some more pages. She could hear the low hum of the football game in the other room, accentuated by some shouts and derogatory comments by Blake. He would be busy for a few hours. Even though he was focused on the game, she was just happy to have him here. She caught herself peeking over at him every few minutes as if he would disappear.

Dani and Jayne spent the rest of the afternoon and evening flipping through more articles and papers. They stayed scattered on the table like playing cards. Jayne promised to put them away in the morning, when her tired eyes would be refreshed again.

Blake and Jayne made their way up to bed early. He insisted on taking a shower after the long day, so Jayne got him some towels and explained the old bathtub taps to him. They were finicky and after a few wrong twists and curse words, she finally figured it out. Rusty stayed with Dani for the night while she read in the living room.

Jayne put on an old t-shirt and sweatpants before crawling into bed. Billy came in through the closed door and sat in the rocking chair. "Hey, Bunny."

"Hey."

"How was your day? Are you happy to see Blake?"

"I am." She smiled. "Mom and I found some old

newspaper articles she'd been keeping downstairs. Did you see them? I think some of them are from your time."

"I saw on my way in, but I didn't look at them."

"They were about the San Antonio flooding in 1921. Do you remember what that was like?"

Billy nodded slowly. "I remember," he said with a somber tone.

"How old were you?"

"I was twenty-nine."

"And you went there to help too?"

"I did. I couldn't just stand by without doing anything. The rain came through and dumped twenty-three inches on the area. By the time it was done, people were getting from place to place in boats. There was so much water you could see someone a few feet away and not be able to help them. Over fifty people died by the time it was done and many were displaced from their homes. The less fortunate neighborhoods were affected hard because the housing wasn't sound to begin with and the landlords weren't up for the job of rebuilding; it was easier to just cut their losses, or if they would rebuild, it would take months or years, leaving many people without homes or even trying to live in a home with mold. If they were lucky enough to find a place to live, all of their belongings had been damaged by water.

"A bunch of us went to San Antonio to help. The power and telephone lines were washed out and we got there not knowing what the state of the place would be. It was like nothing I'd ever seen. By the time we arrived, people had already started tearing out their carpets and plaster. Some people would just be wandering the streets, almost lost, as if in a trance. Evelyn stayed home with our youngest but I took our older son with me so he could see what it looked like when the so-called 'bad neighborhoods' were affected by something so destructive."

"What did you guys do?"

"We helped rebuild for about a week. More fortunate families let us stay with them. We started by clearing out homes, then we got some supplies, we brought our tools, and we got to work helping as much as we could. We woke up when the sun rose and didn't stop working until we couldn't see what we were doing anymore. Some of the homes we tore up looked like the flooding had done them a favor. As we went, we learned how to work with plaster, lay wood flooring, and install sinks and bathtubs. I knew a little bit of everything when I built my house with my father, but I was young when he built our house. Luckily, some of the workers that came with us had experience.

"By the time we left, we'd helped many families, built about four homes to a livable standard, and gathered supplies and money for the rest. It wasn't a huge impact, but I think it helped a few." Billy smiled, remembering.

Jayne's eyes were heavy from the storytelling. She smiled and said, "That's incredibly selfless of you Billy. I hope one day I can be like that." She blinked her eyes and let them close for a second.

"You will, I know it."

The doorknob turned, making Jayne's eyes shoot open, alert. Billy left while the door was still open.

"You're not falling asleep on me, are you babe?"

"Never," Jayne whispered, reaching her arms out to him.

21

THE NEXT DAY Jayne woke up next to Blake, who at some point during the night had squished her against the wall in the corner of the bed. The twin bed was not an easy fit for two people, especially not for someone as tall as Blake. She thought about the conversation they had the night before: he had protested, asking why they couldn't just sleep in the master bedroom or switch rooms with Dani. She reminded him that there was no mattress in the master — it was removed since her father had passed on it. That ended the conversation immediately. She convinced herself that she had to go into that room — even if it was just to throw away some of the things that hadn't been cleaned.

She crawled over Blake, trying not to disturb his sleep, partially surprised to see the empty chair across from her bed. She figured Billy must be somewhere else because of Blake.

Dani was stepping out onto the back deck with Rusty when Jayne came into the kitchen. The freshly brewed coffee smelled delicious and she poured herself a cup. She leaned on the counter to feel the warmth in her palms. She glanced at her mom, sitting peacefully outside. Dani looked deep in thought as she looked out toward the old house.

"That was her favorite thing to do in the morning," said Billy, who was suddenly sitting at the table. "She always had her coffee on the back porch. That's where she does some of her best thinking."

Jayne smiled at Billy and took a moment to be thankful for her mom and the relationship they had. She had a little understanding of why things went the way they did, and of the mental shelter Dani had tried to provide for her. When she opened the glass door, Dani glanced toward Jayne and smiled. Rusty popped up from his spot on the seat and ran over to her, tail wagging. The air was crisp and although a bit chilly, it was bearable with the sweats and long-sleeve shirt she was wearing. Dani patted the seat beside her.

"What are you guys going to do today?" Dani asked.

"Well, Blake will probably sleep at least a couple more hours since he sleeps in until about ten or eleven on days he doesn't have to set an alarm. I might go hit up the library and see what I can find. What are you going to do?" she asked, blowing on the hot coffee.

"I think I'll do some tidying around here, mostly dusting, and then I might go for a walk around town, see if I can run into anyone. Ed—you remember Ed Stalton, with the twins—he wanted to catch up, so we might meet for a coffee."

"That's a good idea," Jayne said. They listened to the birds singing their morning song and watched the sun flickering between the leaves. "Well, I'm going to get a move on things and get out of here."

"Sounds good honey," Dani said, smiling.

Jayne got ready in the bathroom, wearing the same clothes from the day before so she wouldn't wake Blake. She slipped her engagement ring—which was now in a box in the medicine cabinet—back on her finger and went downstairs to say goodbye to her mom. She took her dad's truck, leaving Blake the rental. It started like a charm and with a few clicks from the cassette deck some music started playing. She ejected it to see who it was: Tom Petty. She pushed the cassette back in and imagined her dad listening to "Listen to Her Heart" as he drove to and from the shop.

On the way into town, she noticed a large billboard for Manns Enterprises and remembered that she needed to contact Frederick Manns about seeing the old Carter house and furniture made by her grandfathers. She also wanted to speak with him regarding what he had to offer when it came to their property.

The library was at the end of Main Street. Jayne read the plaque by the door that said the building used to be a large church. In the 1800s a priest started collecting books, which he bought himself or were donated to the church. After piles and piles of books took over the corners of the church, a man offered to build the priest shelves. The priest continued to collect books and hold services among them until his passing in 1901.

Unable to keep the building open as a church, the town took it over as a public library. Along the way, with nowhere else to keep them, they kept public records as best they could, documenting the citizens and events of the town for years to come.

Jayne had only been in the library a couple of times when she was little. She liked it—she felt a sense of ease being surrounded by books. It was quiet and cool and if she listened hard enough she could focus on the soft sounds of people breathing and pages rustling. The murmur of people whispering to each other reverberated around the pillars and high ceiling of the old nave.

As she walked in, the mix of brick, cement, and

old paper scented the air around her. She approached the front desk and asked where she could find public records from the 1900s. A young girl with long, wispy hair the color of a roasted chestnut pointed her to an area behind the desk that read "Public Records".

Jayne laughed, embarrassed. The girl didn't react and looked back down at the book she had been reading. As Jayne walked over, the heels of her boots clicked on the wood floor and a couple people looked up at her. She desperately wished she had chosen to wear her tennis shoes instead.

She wasn't sure how to use the microfiche, but the rows of cabinets were dated and sorted alphabetically. After some careful choosing, she walked to the table with a few in hand. The microfiche machine had clear instructions taped to it and after a few flips to make sure it wasn't backward or upside down, she got it.

Many of the ones she'd chosen were newspaper articles with nothing of interest in them. She briefly regretted choosing this as an activity to do "quickly", as this seemed to be a tedious process. But then she stopped on one dated August 24, 1907.

It had a picture with a group of boys, some wearing baseball caps and casual t-shirts with jeans rolled up. Three of the boys without hats were shading their eyes and squinting at the camera. They looked like they had been interrupted while playing a game of baseball in an open field. The caption read.

"Hottest day on record in the Hill
Country. Yet, these boys continue
to play ball in hundred-degree
temperatures."

Jayne skimmed over the article to see if there were any familiar family names.

"When asked why these boys wouldn't stay inside during this scorcher of a day, Billy Webber (Pictured far left) replied, 'No use staying inside. The air is almost as hot. We might as well play ball.' John Schmitt (middle) added, 'We got plenty of water to keep us hydrated. Mr. Jones at the corner store brings us bottles of Coke sometimes too. Real nice of him.' All the boys nodded in agreement. . . "

Jayne couldn't read anymore without looking at the photo. Could it be Billy? *Her* Billy? He had the same last name. *Of course it is,* she thought. *It's so obvious. It was blurry but it looks just like him.* She could barely contain her excitement.

She took out her notebook and began writing notes and questions. The first was to ask her mom for any resemblance of a family tree she had. She could ask Billy to fill in the gaps. *How am I going to explain this to Mom? I'm going to have to tell her this boy is the one I've been seeing forever — and I still see.* Jayne dropped her head into her hands and exhaled deeply with a slight moan. She printed the article. As the printer started to whir and click her phone rang. Blake.

"No cell phones!" the girl at the front snapped. Jayne quickly clicked off the volume and answered.

"Hang on one sec," she whispered. She gathered up her things, put the microfilm into a basket marked "For Returns," and grabbed her print, still warm, off the printer. She folded it neatly and wedged it in the cover of her notebook. After a quick check to make sure she didn't have to pay, she left the library saying a quick goodbye to the front desk girl on her way out.

Once out the doors she held the phone up to her ear. "Hey babe, sorry — "

"Where the hell are you? I've been sitting around waiting for two hours." Blake's voice tore through the phone, making Jayne pull the phone away for a second, feeling her whole body clench in regret.

"I'm at the library," she said. "I thought Mom would have told you. I thought you were going to sleep in since it's technically your day off. I'm sorry. I'm on my way home now."

"Well, I'm in town," he said bluntly.

Jayne came to a dead stop. Natural instinct made her look around the streets for the rental car. "What? Where?"

"Your mom told me you were at the library, so I'm looking for that now. I'm beside some coffee shop called The Café. How original." She could almost hear his eyes roll in his head.

"Park and I'll meet you there. I'm only a minute away. We can grab a coffee and something to eat. Love you." She waited to hear Blake return the endearment, but he said nothing back before he hung up.

Great, I'm walking on eggshells again, she thought.

22

WHEN SHE GOT to The Café, Blake was waiting outside for her. "Sorry babe, I really am," she said, wondering if she was just sorry he was mad at her.

"It's okay, I just didn't know why you had just left me there."

"You were sleeping and I didn't want to wake you. I really wanted to get to the library and check out some of the old records. I figured I would do that while you were unconscious since consciously you wouldn't want anything to do with it." She smiled.

He returned the smile and said, "You're right." He opened the door for her.

She couldn't see Liz behind the bar but didn't think anything of it. They each got a breakfast sandwich and a coffee. While Blake paid she sat down at a table beside the window. Jayne placed her hands flat on the table, warm from the sun coming in the window, feeling her fingers suck up the warmth.

"I see you've decided to wear your ring." Blake smiled wryly at her.

"Ah, yes, well . . ." She twisted it around her finger.

"So do you want to know what I found?"

"Sure," Blake answered in obvious obligation.

Jayne reached into her bag and pulled out her blue moleskin notebook. Inside the cover was the carefully folded paper. "I found a few neat articles and some advertising for my dad's—well my great-great-grandfather's—shop, but the biggest piece I've found is this." She unfolded the paper for him and placed it on the table. He studied it and read the caption.

"Cool. You found a relative that played sandlot ball?"

She looked at him, not sure what else to say. "Yes, well, it's my great-great-grandfather, who owned the shop second to his father. His name was William Webber Jr. He goes by Billy. When I was younger I could actually—" Jayne stopped herself from finishing. She had a sudden fear of telling Blake the truth. What would he think if he knew she could see Billy? He would say she was crazy and brush it off. He would call her weird and make fun of her. *Just like Frankie*, she thought. But he was blatantly uninterested, watching the sandwiches being walked over to their table.

"Thank you," he said to the young boy dropping them off. "Oh, can you get us some hot sauce and silverware please?"

"Blake, you go get it yourself up there." Jayne pointed to the cart by the counter with napkins, silverware, and condiments.

"It's no problem," the boy said and smiled.

"See babe? It's no problem." Blake smiled at her.

Jayne folded up the paper, sliding it back into her notebook, wishing she had just kept it private from Blake. He obviously didn't care. "Thank you so much, I'm sorry," Jayne said to the boy when he dropped off the silverware and hot sauce. The boy nodded.

"You shouldn't have to be sorry. That's their job.

If he didn't want to help customers, he shouldn't work here," Blake said around a mouthful of egg and croissant.

This wasn't the first time Blake had acted in such a way toward customer service staff, but being in her hometown with people she knew who had lines to her past, as well as direct connections to the shop, made her look at him in a different light. It felt like she needed to protect her family from an outside rebel. She was embarrassed to be spoken to the way he did.

"There's no reason *not* to offer an apology to someone if you have the remotest idea they might have been affected by something you said or did." She didn't know if Blake heard her or was ignoring her.

He swallowed and cleared his throat. "So, it sounds like you're getting attached to this place. Have you looked into selling the house yet? Contacted any realtors? Checked comps in the area or looked at an estate person to sell the stuff in the house?" He wiped his mouth with a napkin and ran his tongue along his teeth, picking food out of the corners.

"Oh, um, no." Jayne was taken by surprise with this. "I just got here, really. There's still so much to do, with the business especially."

"You've been here almost a month, Jayne. You have to come home at some point. What are you going to do with the business? Sell to Jesus, or whatever his name is?"

What's going on here? Jayne wondered. "I . . . I don't know Blake. I need time. I can't just come in and start clearing out his stuff, selling everything. He has no other family that can help take care of this."

"We can hire someone who takes care of estates. They can do all the work and you can be in the comfort of *our* home." He took another bite of his sandwich and wiped a drop of hot sauce from his lip.

"We have generations of history here. My family has lived in this town for over a hundred years. They lived on that property for over a hundred years too. I'm not going to just hand it over to someone who doesn't care." She was slowly losing her appetite.

"Are you thinking of living here? You have to come home," he repeated. "I can't live in a small town like this, Jayne. What would I do?"

Jayne watched him for a second, studying his expression. "Oh. Well, I haven't really thought about it, to be honest."

Blake rubbed a hand over his face and pinched his mouth like he was trying to keep words in. He inhaled and let his hand drop to the table. Jayne moved her gaze out the window to the people passing by. She saw Luke walking up the sidewalk toward them. Without a thought, she smiled and knocked on the window. When he looked, she waved dramatically at him. He laughed and waved back before coming in.

"Hey, guys," Luke said, approaching the table.

"Hey, Luke. You making a coffee run for the shop?" Jayne asked.

"Something like that. Y'all having a little breakfast?"

"Something like that," Blake said.

Jayne shot Blake a look. *What is wrong with him?* she wondered before glancing back toward Luke. "That's great," she said. "I'm going to try and be over there in a bit to see if there's anything I can help with. Mom and I are going to be cleaning out some more stuff from the house today."

"Sounds good," Luke said. "I'll let you guys enjoy your breakfast. See you later, Jayne." He held up one hand to wave and turned toward the counter.

She held up a hand in reply. *Luke would have loved to find out information like I did.* She thought about how he'd thought he saw someone walking into the old house when they were having lemonade the day before. *Did he see Billy?* she wondered.

"You done babe?" Blake asked, glancing at the remainder of Jayne's sandwich.

She picked it up and took a bite. "Just about. Do you want to go walk around or anything? I can show you the town, some of the historic buildings?"

"No thanks. I actually have some work to do. I brought my laptop." He reached for his bag.

She felt like a third wheel all of a sudden. "Oh, okay. Well I can go run by the shop and I'll head home." She stood up and grabbed her bag, popped the last bit of egg croissant in a napkin to go, and leaned over to give Blake a kiss on the cheek before heading out.

She left the truck at The Café and walked to the shop. It was getting chilly and she held her sweater tight, scrunching her shoulders up to her neck in an effort to stay warm.

From a distance she saw Luke enter the office before her. She stepped through the doorway soon after. The office was extra warm against the chilly October air. It felt like someone had wrapped her with a warm blanket straight from the dryer. She heard the door from the shop to the office open and Luke walked through followed by a cold gust of air. He didn't see her until she said, "They don't have a heater in there?"

He looked up, startled. "Oh, hi. Um, no. They have a few space heaters but the concentrated heat usually messes with the varnish, so only a few of the guys use them. It stays warm enough when the doors are closed and you layer up, though. What are you doing here?"

"Nice to see you too," Jayne replied with a smile.

Luke shook his head and laughed. "No, I just mean, Blake isn't with you?"

"Oh, no." Jayne looked around as if she had forgotten him. She paused, looking for the words. "He had some work stuff to do so he's still at The Café."

"I see."

"Can I help with anything? I'd like to start contributing more around here."

"Well, we have some finished orders that need to be filed, but that's about it. I was going to actually do a bit of work in the shop today."

"Okay!" Jayne said excitedly and walked behind the desk.

Luke showed her the orders and how they were filed. She separated out the complete orders from the requests and orders with deposits, then got to work on the smaller pile.

After a few minutes she remembered the article she had in her purse. "Oh, I went to the library today," she said. "I was looking through some old articles and found this." She pulled the folded copy from her book and handed it to Luke. He opened it and examined it, his eyes moving over the caption.

"Whoa, is that your great-grandfather?"

"Great-great-grandfather actually. Isn't that crazy?"

"That is so cool! Look at their clothes, and their baseball gloves." He handed the paper back. "That's really neat, Jayne. Are you going to go back and look for more?"

"Yeah, as soon as I can. I have some stuff to go through at the house first. And Blake isn't entirely into this stuff," she added. "He thinks I'm getting too attached." She looked up at him quickly and dropped her eyes back to the paper.

"Is that a bad thing?" Luke asked.

"He doesn't want to live here."

"Ah. That's too bad. This is a great place to live and grow up."

Jayne finished the filing while she and Luke chitchatted. She showed him some of the posts she'd made to their social media and the reach they'd gotten over the past few days and she wrote down the login information to all the accounts for him and Joe.

Jayne wanted to take some more pictures for their profile. She grabbed a vacuum and duster and they went around cleaning together throughout the office and the shop while she took a few pictures on her phone. When they were done, Luke said he was going to work on a piece he had started.

"I'd like to see it," Jayne said.

"It's just a blank slate at this point," he assured her. "So maybe some other time."

He walked her out through the office doors. She forgot she'd parked at The Café and the cold air struck her, almost making her gasp. *It's getting colder, and more humid*, she thought. *What an odd combination.*

"Oh hey," Luke called. She turned around. "I was going to get tickets to a tour they're holding at the Carter house tomorrow. They only do it a once a week and have limited tickets. I thought you might like to go, with it being your family and all."

"I would love that, Luke."

"Great. There's only one problem: they only have two spots left, so Blake couldn't come—unless you wanted to take him and the two of you could go."

"Oh, I see. Well, I don't think he would appreciate it as much as you would, so why don't we just go?"

"Okay, great. I can pick you up around ten."

"Why don't I meet you there," Jayne said, knowing Blake would be about as happy with her going with Luke as he would be stabbing himself in the leg with a rusty knife.

"Or that," Luke said. "I'll see you then."

Quickly she walked back to The Café to get her truck. Blake was still at the table, laptop open. It took her a minute to notice the person sitting across from him. She recognized him as Frederick Manns. They looked very deep in conversation; Blake had his laptop pushed to the side and he was looking over some papers Mr. Manns was showing him. *What in the world?* Jayne thought. *What would he be doing talking to Blake for?* The hairs on the back of her neck rose—and not from the cold. She had a bad feeling looking at them.

Instead of trying to get his attention, she found the truck and hurried home.

23

WHEN JAYNE PULLED in, Dani was working in the front yard. She had on an old sweatshirt covered in paint and her curly brown hair was pinned back with a long nail from the shed. *Interesting choice*, Jayne thought. She was wielding a spade and gardening fork, tearing out the intrusive weeds that Jayne had been tackling just a few days before. The car tires on the gravel crunched and Dani looked up. When she saw it was Jayne, she stood up and waited for her to get out of the car.

"How was the library? Did Blake not find you?" She pushed some hair off her face with the back of her gloved hand.

Rusty got up from his spot on the porch and bolted toward Jayne. She scooped him up. "Yeah, he did. We had some breakfast together and then he had some work to do, so I went to the shop and helped out there a bit."

"Oh good. Is Blake coming home now too?"

"I don't know." Jayne shrugged.

Dani stood up straight. "You don't *know?*"

"No. I saw him at The Café when I picked up my car,

but I didn't ask. He was busy." Jayne evaded Dani's gaze by going to pick at the bushes.

Dani's eyes followed her and she said "I see," and turned back to her gardening. "I'll just be a little longer out here."

"Okay. I'm going to go inside and look through some more articles. I found an old article about William Webber Jr. playing baseball in a heat wave of 1907."

Dani looked up but didn't rise. "What? Really? Show me later, okay?"

"Okay." Jayne headed for the door. She looked back at her mom: head down, prodding the garden with one hand and pinching up weeds with another.

Inside, the crisp smell of fall gave way to the smell of lingering coffee and bacon. Jayne grabbed the box of clippings from the corner and poured herself a cup of the lukewarm coffee left over in the pot. When she sat down at the table, she welcomed Rusty onto her lap and he curled in, pushing off her thighs to get a spot squished up against her stomach. Jayne covered him with her sweater to keep him warm.

Billy came in through the glass door and sat in the chair closest to the door. "Hey, Bunny. How was the library?"

"Hi. It was a bit overwhelming at first, but I found something you might be interested in." She pulled the picture from her purse and laid it flat on the table. Billy examined it, reading and rereading the article.

"Wow." The word came out like it was his last breath. "I remember this like it was yesterday."

"Billy, how come you've never talked about how we're related?" she asked casually.

"Well, I didn't *not* tell you, Bunny. I just didn't tell you that I was your great-great-grandfather specifically. I figured you knew." He smiled.

"No. I should have, but I never knew which relative

you were. I'd made up a story in my head, I guess. It all makes sense now. When I saw this article, my heart jumped, like I'd seen you a million times before — like I knew you *then*." She poked the photograph. His smile widened. "Of course I can't tell anyone or they'll think I'm crazy." She paused. "Do you know what's wrong with Mom? She was a bit short with me when I came home and doesn't seem too happy."

"I don't, I'm sorry. It could have something to do with a visitor that came by while you were gone."

"A visitor?"

"Yes, a rather tall woman. I think she was the owner of one of the shops downtown. I would ask her about that. Your mother's mood seemed to change after the woman left."

Jayne nodded. "Can you tell me more about this photo? About this day; it says there was a heat wave."

"There sure was." Billy slid into an empty chair beside her. "It was one of the hottest days on record. We had all been cooped up inside because of the advisories. They said to stay out of the sun for fear of dehydration and overheating. It was hotter inside though because we didn't have air conditioning back then.

"People who could went down to the river to take a dunk, but it was crowded and many people feared the water moccasins and other creatures. Mom and Dad sat on the porch in the shade, holding their fans, trying to catch a breeze, but there was none to be had that day. Dad stripped down to his drawers and Mother hiked her skirt up to her knees and took off her stockings. Very risky during that time." Billy laughed. "Anyway, Mom and Dad were getting sick of seeing us, so I decided to go round up some of my friends and see if any of them wanted to play ball. We'd just got into baseball and that's how we spent our free time. How we could stand the heat, I don't know, but we would do just about anything to get out.

"Luckily no one was using the field that day when we got there. We all spread out and started tossing the ball back and forth. The sun was blazing in our eyes and sweat was dripping down the backs of our legs. Sweat droplets seemed to form out of nowhere, just rising on our skin like blisters before they fell away.

"When people saw us playing, they brought us water and even ice, which, at the time, was very generous of them because ice wasn't as easy to be had as it is now. One man even offered us a bottle of beer. We split it between the few of us, getting a couple sips each." Billy looked off to the right and smiled at the memory.

"With sweat continuing to well up on our necks and backs, even our elbow and knee creases, we continued on. We got a lot of attention that day and a man came down to see us. He was a baseball player for the Detroit Tigers on his way to Georgia. He just happened to be visiting some friends in Texas and stopped by the field when the shop owner mentioned us. His name was Ty Cobb. He would come to be known as the Georgia Peach." Billy pointed to a man standing behind the group of boys. Jayne hadn't noticed him listed in the caption in her frantic excitement of finding the article. "He was newer to major league baseball, but he was good. All of us were over the moon to meet him. Luckily his manager — or whoever the man was with him — had brought a pen for autographs. Ty signed every one of our gloves, balls, or whatever we could get our hands on. Later in the years to come, we would find out he wasn't the nicest man in baseball, but he sure was to us. We played better than ever that day and went home sweaty, tired and happy."

Jayne sat listening to Billy and thought, *I should really write all these things down. It would help me match them to the articles I find.*

Jayne went to grab the box of clippings. "Was everyone okay during the heat wave?" she asked.

"Oh yes," Billy replied. "It wasn't anything serious like the dust bowl to come, but just a couple of hot days that kept people from their usual business." He smiled.

"Oh, that's good." She rummaged through the papers in the box, only finding articles about new store openings.

"Oh, looks like Blake is home," Billy said.

Jayne looked up and could see him talking to her mom through the front window. After a few seconds, he still hadn't come in and Dani looked more distressed. Jayne got up and went outside. Rusty followed behind her.

They were talking in low, serious voices. "What's going on?" Jayne asked.

"Nothing, darling," Dani replied. "I'm just asking Blake for some casual legal advice."

"Casual legal advice?" She looked at Blake.

Blake shrugged and held out his hand, motioning for her to come to him. She wasn't inclined to go to him after seeing him alone with Frederick Manns, but now wasn't the right time to interrogate him. He gave her a quick hug and leaned down to plant a kiss on her temple.

"It sounds like there's some gossip around town that Melody has a lawyer and is going to try to get the house from you."

"What?" Jayne shouted, pulling away from Blake and scaring a couple birds from their perch in the tree overhead. "Can they even do that?" The air was crisp and smelled like damp earth. The air felt colder with this knowledge and Jayne wrapped her arms around herself.

Blake squeezed her tighter. "Don't worry, ladybug,

it's just a rumor for now. Until we find out more information—"

"But how can they? They're not family. It's not possible."

"Well technically," Blake interjected, "it could be, but it's highly unlikely. I guess she lived with your dad for a while, so they may have filed as common-law married. It's possible that she's in the will too."

"I guess I should have started on that a while ago," Jayne perked the left side of her mouth and pressed her fingertips to her temple.

"I need to do some more digging into what kind of documents they have to think they can do such a thing. Plus, I'll take a look at your dad's will and make sure there aren't any loopholes." He gave her shoulder a squeeze. "Don't worry too much right now, babe. It's very unlikely."

Jayne looked at her mom and Dani smiled. "We'll get it figured out. We've got the best lawyer in the South." Dani winked at Blake.

"I could punch her right in the face," Jayne said calmly. Blake and Dani laughed.

Dani brushed the second step of the porch off and sat down. "There's only one problem," Dani admitted, without looking at Blake or Jayne.

"What is it?" Blake asked urgently.

Dani took in a deep breath. "I know Jayne was next in line, but I don't know if he actually filed the will. Or changed anything after I left."

"Shit," Blake exclaimed. He kicked a rock from the driveway and walked to the edge of the grass.

Jayne disregarded him. "What do you mean?" she asked. "How would you know anyway?"

"I came here two years ago to make him sign it to begin with."

"What?" Jayne asked again. She brought a balled

fist to her chest, feeling an anxious knot gather. She sat next to Dani.

"Do you remember when I said I was going on a retreat in Austin for work?" Jayne nodded, watching her mother's face. "I came here instead. I'd heard your father was having some health issues. I knew he'd been seeing Melody and I didn't want her to get the house or the shop."

"Oh, the shop," Blake moaned, pressing his palms into his eyes. Dani only briefly glanced at him.

Jayne let the birds fill the silence for a moment then asked, "You knew Dad was sick?" Dani nodded. "You knew," she said with a rumble in her voice, "and you didn't tell me?"

"I didn't know the extent of it," Dani said.

"But you knew?" Jayne asked and Dani nodded again. Jayne's heart was pounding so hard it felt like it was going to crack her rib cage. She thought of the guilt she'd felt not seeing him more often, not *knowing* he was sick, not getting to say goodbye. A single tear welled up and fell over her cheek, rolling into the corner of her mouth. She didn't bother to wipe it away.

"Oh, Jayne." Dani reached for her.

"No." Jayne jumped up as if the seat was on fire. "Please don't." She climbed the steps and scrunched her eyes. "You knew this whole time, and I've been living with this guilt. I could have been here for him, I could have said goodbye." Jayne's tears were overwhelming now and she pulled the door open, forcing it to slam against the outside wall. Rusty jumped from Dani's side and tried to follow her in.

"Jayne!" Blake shouted. Dani held up a hand to stop him. He followed Jayne into the house anyway, Rusty sneaking in past him. "Babe?" He could hear her footsteps in the upstairs hall followed by the small little pitter-patter of Rusty's paws and the slam of a door. For a second he hesitated on the first stair, but he knew it wouldn't do any good to go chasing after her just yet. She did better alone with her thoughts; she needed to think these things out, just like with her art — she had to see the bigger picture before worrying about the details. He went back out to join Dani on the steps. "This could be bad," he said.

"You really think Melody could get everything?"

"No. I don't, really. But if they were common-law married, she could. Not only would Jayne lose the house, but she'd also lose the money she could make on the house if she decided to sell it."

Dani nodded. "Well, we'll just have to find that will."

24

"**B**ILLY?" JAYNE ASKED quietly and desperately. She closed her eyes tight and lay back against the stuffed animals on the bed. "Please."

"I'm here, Bunny." Jayne opened her eyes to see him sitting in the rocking chair, a concerned look on his face. "What's the matter?"

"Mom . . . she knew . . ." she said between gulps of air. "This whole time she knew Dad was sick. She *came here* and she didn't tell me or even bring me; she could have brought me and I could have seen him again." Billy nodded. "You knew. You had to have known. You would have seen her."

Billy nodded again and Jayne turned over, burying her face in between two stuffed bears. "Yes, it was a few years ago. She came for just a couple of days. It seemed her main mission was to get your dad a will. I didn't realize she was keeping it from you." Billy rocked the chair back and forth, the tips of his toes pushing up and down on the floor. "You're upset she didn't tell you?"

Jayne wiped her eyes and sat up. "I'm upset because

she came here, found out how sick Dad was, and didn't tell me. I never knew and I could have been here, instead of living a guilt-free life gallivanting around and pretending like everything was okay."

"I see," Billy replied. "Well, in your mother's defense, your father wasn't as ill as you may have thought. He had an addiction, yes. Was it out of control? Yes. He did have some related health concerns, but it wasn't as serious as it became within the last year."

"She still should have told me," Jayne argued.

"Probably. Did you know your father was an alcoholic two years ago?"

"Yes."

"Well, not much else was different." Billy leaned forward, resting his elbows on his knees. "Look, Bunny, your mom was smart. She knew your dad had a problem and she knew how those problems could run in the family. It happened to Peter's father, and it also happened to my father." Jayne looked at Billy with a heartfelt furrow in her brows and a softened face. "I was about your age when my father died. But that's not the point. I was there when your father told your mother not to tell you she came, or about his illnesses. We were all sat down at the table. Your mother had just looked over his paperwork and handed it to him. He was quiet and steady as he adjusted his head and then signed everything without reading it. He still had a blind trust in your mother. After he was done, he looked up and apologized. There must have been more meaning behind it, because your mom's eyes welled up with tears."

Jayne pressed her lips together as she felt a prickle in her nose, trying to hold back tears herself.

"He told your mom, 'Don't you tell my baby girl.' Your mom protested fiercely on your behalf, but your father was a persuasive man. 'I'm going to kick this

Dani,' he told her. 'I might be signing this right now, but it's going to mean nothing because I'm going to stop. I have to, for her. Now, I don't want her to know because I don't want her to rush out here, feelin' all guilty about me. I want the next time she sees me to be free of worry. I don't want her to see me like this.' He slammed his hand on the table."

Jayne grabbed a tissue from the nightstand and pressed it to her face, feeling the tears soak into the tissue as they kept coming. "Did he? Stop drinking, I mean."

Billy looked uncomfortable and shifted in the chair. "He did for a couple months. Then one weekend he came home visibly drunk, stumbling around the kitchen before he passed out on the couch. It could have been just that one time, but he'd brought home a twenty-four pack of beer. The next day I watched him fight with himself as he stared at that beer, fidgeting in his seat, trying to convince himself not to touch it. He lost that day and never looked back." Jayne's frame slumped. She moaned and put her face into her hands. "Do you know why I tell you these things, Jayne? Why I don't just give you a 'Yes' or 'No' answer?" She shook her head. "Because I want you to know the truth. Your father was a good man; he did many good things and cared deeply for many people. He would give the shirt off his back to anyone. But he had a problem and it shouldn't be sugarcoated. It was no one else's fault it ended how it did. You being here would have changed nothing. Do you hear me?" She nodded. "You think that if he saw you he may have stopped — and maybe he might have for a little bit, but not forever. Okay?"

She nodded again. "Okay. I understand. I just feel so helpless."

"Most people do when it comes to a family member that's suffering from an addiction. But you can only lead the horse to water, Bunny, you can't get it to drink—or not drink, in this case." Jayne chuckled and sighed, wiping the tears away once more. "I saw what it did to my father and it tore my mother apart. She spent her entire life trying to shield us from it, trying to make sure we didn't think it was our fault. She died trying."

"I'm sorry, Billy," Jayne whispered.

He waved his hand as if swatting a fly. "I've come to terms with it, darling. He's been gone a long time."

"I guess I should go down and speak with Mom and Blake."

"Do you want me to come?" Billy asked.

"No, thank you. That's okay. I'll see you later, Billy."

25

B LAKE SAT ON the porch step sipping lemonade and watching Dani attack more weeds.

Jayne apologized to Dani, who pretended like there was nothing to be sorry for. Blake had made a couple calls in the time Jayne was upstairs and now they had a plan to go into town to see about probating the will and talking to the attorney, but it would have to wait until tomorrow.

"So, I was thinking of going to the Carter house tomorrow, if that's okay," Jayne said to Blake. Dani looked intrigued.

"What's there?" Blake asked.

"Well, it was the house my great-great-grandmother lived in. I'd like to see it, feel a part of that history."

"Ah, that's great. What time did you want to go?" Blake asked.

"Oh, well, um, it's by appointment," Jayne said awkwardly.

"Appointment?"

"Yes. It's a tour and they only let so many people in. There are no spots left," she added hastily.

"I see." Blake swatted at Rusty, who was trying to

paw at his pants. "So you want to go alone is what you're asking?"

"Well, yes, I suppose," she lied. She wanted to tell Blake that she was going with Luke. She didn't see the harm, but she knew he would blow it out of proportion.

"Okay. What shall your mom and I do?"

"The tour starts around ten, so after it's over, we could meet for lunch then go talk to Joe about the will. I saw a little Italian restaurant by the shop that looks delicious."

Blake was annoyed, Jayne could tell; his nostrils were flaring and his smile was pinned to his cheeks, but his eyes remained steady on her. He was acting nice in front of her mom.

"That sounds lovely, Jayne," Dani said. "You could learn so much. How did you know they did tours?"

"Frederick Manns," she lied and Blake flinched "He runs the place. He told me to come by and check it out." She waited for Blake to mention that he had run into him, that they had some kind of meeting, but nothing was said.

Dani nodded and resumed her gardening.

Later that night, Jayne was reading in bed while Blake showered. The room was warm and the dim light made it feel cozy against the wind and drizzle rattling against the old windows. Rusty was curled up beside her, his little chest rising and falling. She was grateful for him and happy he wasn't spending as much time whining outside her dad's door anymore. She could almost forget about that room.

"Hey, Bunny," Billy said as he walked through the door.

Jayne looked up over her book. "Why do you walk *through* the door when you could just walk *through* the wall?"

"Habit I suppose." He shrugged.

"I'm glad you came, actually." Billy looked inquisitive. "I'm going to the Carter house tomorrow. I wanted to let you know. You think you can come?"

"Bunny, if I could leave the property, I would be wandering all over this town. Unfortunately, I attached myself to the land."

"Ah." Jayne's shoulders sagged. "You can't go anywhere?"

Billy shook his head and his demeanor changed to a nervous excitement, almost twitchy. "But, I wonder if there's something you can do for me?"

"What are you thinking?" Jayne pushed herself up in the bed.

"There's a necklace—it's hidden in one of the floorboards of the room Evelyn stayed in. Given there haven't been any dramatic renovations, I would bet it's still there." His smile was enough to convince Jayne.

"You want me to *steal* from the Carter house?"

"Well, technically yes, but no. It's your necklace, or at least it was Evelyn's, but it's in our family."

"Okay. What are you going to do with this necklace?"

"I'm not going to do anything. *You're* going to wear it. If you find it, it's yours. I just don't want it in any other family."

"Are you going to tell me how this necklace came to live under the floorboards?"

"It's a necklace I gave her when we were nineteen. She hid it in her bedroom one night when her mother was in a particular state about our relationship." Jayne looked at him, confused. "Unlike her father,

her mother was very conservative about marriage, relationships, and status. When she found out that we were becoming more serious, she tried everything to stop it. First she wasn't allowed to see me after a certain time, then not at all. She was banned from talking to me and if I showed up at her house, their valet would usher me off, threatening the authorities when I started calling for her. They told me she didn't want to see me anymore; that she had found someone else. After a few weeks of trying and failing, I snuck into their yard through a space between the carriage house and the fence, creeping toward her bedroom window. I planned on climbing up to her window, but as I made my way along the carriage house, I heard voices inside. The carriage house was normally empty, but that night it was full of half a dozen girls laughing and talking. I tried peeking in the windows, but they were too high. I went and found a ladder in the shed and managed to carry it over without being caught. I got in through a window, tumbling onto the floor amidst a pile of blankets and pillows. The girls screamed, and it took some persuasion to get them to settle down before someone heard. Gave them quite a fright, I did.

"Finally, after calming them all, and with a joint effort between Evelyn and I to convince them I wasn't a murderer, I was able to take Evelyn aside and speak with her while the girls whispered in the other room. She told me that her mom produced a note in which I had declared I didn't want to be with her anymore, that I had moved on and also found someone else. I assured her I hadn't moved on or wrote that note. That's when she told me about Jeffery McNamara and the dinner parties her mother threw for him to court her under their roof. He was twenty-five and had a promising future working with his successful father." Jayne felt a deep pinch within her heart and looked at Billy. His face was somber.

"Once we finished talking, she helped me back out the window and promised me she wouldn't see Jeffery again, that her heart belonged to me. I took the necklace out of my pocket. It was a small diamond heart with a smaller ruby heart set on top. It was strung upon a long silver chain, which I placed over her neck. It had taken almost the three years of our courtship for me to be able to purchase it. She clutched it so hard, I thought she was going to break it. She gave me a kiss on the cheek and shooed me away. I found out later that she would wear the necklace every day, tucked beneath her clothing. At night time, when her maid would help her take down her hair and get ready for bed, she would keep it hidden away under a floorboard that not even her maid knew about.

"After months of doing this, her mother found out that we were still seeing each other and there was a large fight between them. She was told to leave the house if she wanted to remain with me, and she would have to leave immediately, leaving the necklace in that floorboard as her mother watched her pack. She was never able to retrieve it again.

"Eventually she and her mother reconciled enough for our children to get to know them, but there was always a divide and she was never allowed alone in her room. Her mother knew about the necklace, we're sure. I offered to steal it for her, but the risk of getting caught was too much. It would ruin our life. I would be forever grateful if you could get it for me. I can tell you where exactly it is."

Jayne nodded her head. "Yes, of course. I don't know how, but I will. I'll at least check that floorboard." Billy smiled and brought his hands to his chest. They heard the water in the bathroom turn off and the shower curtain sliding across the metal bar. He quickly told her exactly where she would be able to find it and she ripped a page from the back of her book to jot out which room would have been Evelyn's and where it would be.

26

BLAKE WAS SNORING when Jayne's alarm went off. She snuck around him and grabbed some clothes out of her suitcase she still hadn't unpacked. It was earlier than she needed it to be, but she was excited.

After showering, she found her mom in kitchen, reading the paper and having her coffee. It was raining out, which would explain why she wasn't outside on the patio.

"Good morning, darling," she said. "Looks like the hurricane is making its way toward the coast now."

"Is it supposed to be bad?"

"Well, it's a category two, but they're saying it could strengthen by the time it hits."

"I don't suppose the rain is going to stop any time soon?"

"I don't think so."

Jayne sighed and poured herself a cup of coffee. "I'm going to the Carter house this morning. I'll have to leave at around 9:30."

Dani looked at her watch. "So, you have an hour? I

really wish I could go with you. It was privately owned when I lived here."

"I wish you could come too. But we only have two tickets." Jayne froze when she realized she'd just incriminated herself.

"We?"

Jayne never lied to her mom; she never had to. Her mom never judged her and always had her best interest at heart. "I'm actually going with Luke," she admitted. "He got the tickets a while ago but I didn't want to tell Blake because — you know."

"Yes, I suppose I do." Dani peeked over the newspaper. Her glasses and messy hair made her look so little, Jayne wanted to just squeeze her in a hug.

"It's nothing. He just got the tickets after we ran into Mr. Manns and he heard that the house used to be in my family. It's just an innocent visit." Jayne sipped her coffee.

"I didn't say it wasn't." Dani was trying to suppress a smile. Lightning filled the house and thunder crackled outside.

"I better find a jacket and umbrella."

Dani nodded and resumed reading, hiding her smirk with the paper.

When Jayne got onto Main Street, she continued past the old buildings, taking in the vintage signs compared to the new ones, wondering what it would have been like to walk down these streets in the early 1900s. She got to the end where the road curved to the right and the trees got thicker, blocking any of the light that the clouds hadn't blotted out already. The squirrels were still out, playing amongst the fallen leaves and branches that scattered the roads. Jayne looked upon the houses, amused by their long yards and high, iron fences.

The gate to the house was already open with a few cars in the driveway. She spotted Luke's big truck and could see he was still inside fiddling with something. It had stopped raining briefly but the clouds and distant lightning suggested it might start again soon. She grabbed her umbrella, still damp, and tried to wipe some of the droplets off on her pants. Luke saw her walking up and got out of his truck.

"This house is amazing," she said, peering up to the curved windows and clay shingles.

Jayne admired the fountain in front with three cherubs, each back-to-back, holding an apple toward the sky. The brick road encircled the fountain like a roundabout before arching off, leading out of the property. She took in the enormity of the home.

The stone it was made with was beige, not weathered or darkened by time. There were two wings of the house that were met in the middle by a covered walkway, which led through to the gondola in the back end of the garden. It was a two-story home with four windows above softened by a half-circle transom window on each wing of the house. The property seemed to encircle the fountain with a cherub facing each wing and one over the front yard. *What a beautiful painting this would make,* Jayne thought. She took a picture.

There were strategically placed vines twirling and twisting their way around the windows, over the walkway, and through the balcony that looked over the front driveway. Jasmine bushes lined the house, spreading out underneath the windows. The floral scent made Jayne imagine running through a garden with a skirt brushing against her ankles. It was chilly outside, but warm where the sun touched her skin. In her imagination, she chased another girl, a sister, while the gardener's son looked on. She took a deep breath and opened her eyes.

Luke was waiting for her. "Shall we?" He held out his hand like a gentleman and she was grateful for it as she felt her heart race and dizziness creep up. She smiled at him and his dimples poked in when he smiled back. He squeezed her fingertips before he let go and they walked up the shallow stairs where a butler greeted them with a polished silver platter holding two glasses of champagne.

"Welcome to the Carter house," he said.

Luke took one of the glasses and handed it to Jayne. "Madam," he said, bowing slightly. The valet smiled and held out a hand to his right, showing them the way to the door where the next person waited.

"Hi there, I'm Linda," she said. She was wearing jeans that were a worn, light blue, and fitted perfectly. Her loose, beige sweater was draped so comfortably off her shoulders and arms, it made Jayne feel like she was wearing a wool parka in comparison. "Come on in. You can wait in the parlor and enjoy your beverage with the others. We're just waiting on four more people."

"Thank you, Linda," Luke said, tugging on Jayne's sleeve lightly, removing her from admiring the back garden through the walkway. The cool breeze filtered the smell of roses, lavender, and jasmine that had just been dampened by the musty rain.

Inside, there were two other couples waiting, each holding a glass of champagne and looking around the room at all the furniture, books, and knickknacks. Jayne took a sip of her champagne and made her way to the window looking out the front of the house. The bubbles sparkled in her cheeks. She held her tongue to the roof of her mouth, squashing them out.

"You're quiet," Luke said simply. "Everything okay?"

She turned to him, as if she had forgotten he was there. She shook her head, like shaking a memory from her brain. "Yes, sorry. I just got caught up in the house." She smiled. "It's beautiful, and hard to believe part of me was in it." Luke rubbed her shoulder and they continued looking out the window.

"Well, if it isn't Jayne Webber. I knew you would visit your ancestor's home soon. I was, in fact, wondering if that was you who was on the guest list for today."

Jayne and Luke turned toward the voice that had a hint of a German accent.

"Mr. Manns, hello." Jayne switched the champagne glass from her right fingertips to her left so she could shake his outstretched hand. "Nice to see you."

"You as well." He smiled. "Luke." His tone changed on Luke's name came out sharp and he nodded in his direction but didn't offer to shake his hand. Luke didn't either.

"Mr. Manns. Good to see you," he offered instead.

"Where's your betrothed, Ms. Webber?" Mr. Manns asked with an accusatory tone. "I ran into him at The Café yesterday—I'm sure he told you."

"Of course. He's at home. He had some work to do today and was unable to make it."

"I see. Well I'll be sure to tell him he was missed today."

Jayne felt a ball of panic rise up from her stomach and then settle. "He said you talked to him awhile then?" she lied.

"Yes, in The Café yesterday. We spoke about your father's shop and his home. I wasn't sure if they were going to be up for sale or not and I, being a developer, am very interested in those kinds of purchases. I was pleasantly surprised when he called me. I would have thought that would be something he mentioned, as I thought maybe you had convinced him to meet me."

"That's not the case," Jayne said, her voice wavering like flames while she tried to dampen the anger and betrayal she felt. Luke looked between them. "From now on, Mr. Manns, please refer to me when having such conversations about my father's properties and business. While Blake is my future husband, he has never been here, or even met my father. He may think he knows best, but we've not discussed what I want to do yet."

"I see," he said, standing tall, looking offended with his head high. He pushed his thick-rimmed glasses back up on his nose.

"Are you running the tour today?" Jayne changed the subject.

Mr. Manns threw his head back with a guffaw, practically flipping his spectacles off his face. "Oh dear, no. I just own and run the place. I like to check in on our guests, though. Which, it looks like we have some more." He nodded toward the window. Four people were getting out of a gray van with a local hotel name on the side. "Drink up and get a refill before the tour starts. I'll make sure Linda points out some of the pieces your family has made."

"Thank you," Jayne said. "I would love to know more about the artwork as well."

"That's right. Blake said you're an artist."

"I am. At least that's how I make my living back home."

"That's a tough career to make a living by."

"It is, but I've made my way and seem to do okay with it."

"Good to hear. Maybe I'll take a look at some of your pieces one day," he said, as empty of sincerity as an old tin can. He smiled and reached out his hand to a butler in the corner. "Please help yourselves."

Jayne smiled and tried not to squint as the champagne and the bubbles made their way up the back of her nose. "Thank you."

After Mr. Manns walked away, Jayne leaned in to whisper in Luke's ear. "He still gives me the creeps." A deep chuckle filled with satisfaction arose from Luke's chest. The butler handed them the new glasses of champagne and they turned back to the room.

Luke stood closer than before and lowered his voice. "I didn't tell you before, but I'm sure you've seen the billboards around town. Frederick Manns has been buying up properties around here for years. I'm not sure what his motive is, but he owns most of the houses here on Ember Street. These houses alone could keep him busy for years, but instead he's started offering to buy up the businesses around town and some of the properties on the outskirts. I found out recently that he's reached out to the neighbors around your dad's house and they seem interested. He's offered them a lot of money."

"What does he plan on doing with them all?"

"I'm not sure. That's what I can't seem to figure out. I don't think he plans on keeping them the same like he does with these old houses. I imagine he'll tear them down and use them for some kind of development. He owns a giant hotel with a water park outside of Austin, where he bought and built on the land out there. This area is turning into a bit of a hotspot for wineries and tourists." Jayne nodded. "I'm just telling you this because you saw his card in the stack of potential buyers at the shop and I'm almost certain he'll be coming to you about the house, if he hasn't already."

"Thank you," Jayne whispered. She had a lot to think about. Not only was Melody possibly coming after her home, but now him? And what if all her neighbors sold, how long could she hold out? *Billy,* she thought.

There were two cream-colored Victorian love seats facing each other in front of a lit fireplace. "That looks cozy," Jayne said, leading the way. She paused near the hearth of the limestone fireplace, letting the heat warm her up. "Thank you for bringing me here," she said, casually touching Luke's arm.

"Of course." Luke smiled, taking in the softness of her blond curls, perfectly messed around her face. "I hope I'm not out of place saying that you're a very special person. I feel like we've been friends for years already."

She could sense he might have wanted to kiss her and something about the place and the air, she might have let him. Linda cleared her throat, interrupting everyone. She was trying to get everyone's attention as the four newcomers made their way past her and stood next to Jayne and Luke.

"Hello again, everyone. We're running a couple minutes late," she said with a smile, looking accusingly at the family of four that just arrived. "Let's get this tour going, shall we? Obviously you're in the parlor. This is where the Carters would have sat with their morning paper or for a casual meeting. The guests would first come in here and then be taken to wherever their meeting would take place. As you can see, they had quite the collection of books." She waved her hand, gesturing to all the bookshelves filled with old, hardcover novels. "The Carters prided themselves on education and business, as the they owned one of the largest lumberyards in the South."

As Linda rambled on about the history, Jayne got distracted by the room. She admired the perfectly draped light-blue curtains, the sconces in the archway leading out of the room, the crown molding, and the lavender wallpaper.

What a beautiful room to sit in and have tea and read, Jayne thought and shook the thought from her mind. *I don't even like tea.* The group flowed through the archway into a main hall where Linda pointed out an entryway table made by William Webber Sr. *Billy's father.* She got excited and wanted to shout, "That's my third-great-grandfather!" Instead she took a picture for their social media page.

They made their way through the kitchen, the butler's pantry, and another sitting room with a few more Webber pieces. Old paintings hanging throughout the home caught Jayne's eye. They weren't by anyone famous that she knew, but she could tell they were all by the same artist; the color palette, scenes, and brushstrokes were the same.

"You're admiring the paintings, Ms. Webber?" Linda asked.

"I am."

"Well, those are actually painted by Evelyn, one of the daughters of Mr. Carter. She would be your relative."

"Wow. I didn't realize." Jayne stared at the scene with more questions than answers.

A beautiful staircase lead them upstairs where they moved from room to room, all filled with antique, Victorian furniture. while Linda described the people who used to occupy them. Jayne wasn't paying attention until, "Evelyn, the youngest of the three daughters, would have stayed in this room."

The necklace. Her eyes searched the hardwood floor. A massive Persian rug with royal blues and gold weaved throughout covered most of it. The tour guide ushered them all out of the room and Jayne knew now wasn't a good time to go poking about in the floorboards; Linda would notice if she went missing. She'd have to find a way to come back.

They finished with the bedrooms and were walking down the hall when the guide stopped in front of the portraits lining the staircase going down to the western wing of the house. Mr. Carter looked just as Jayne had imagined: round-faced, somewhat red complexion. *Like typical Santa Claus without the beard,* she thought. His wife was dark-haired and had it piled on top of her head in a bun. She looked like she was inconvenienced to be sitting for her portrait. The three daughters were to the right of her; the two older girls had dark hair, like their mother, styled in the same way. Evelyn, on the other hand, had curly blond hair just like Jayne.

"I believe *this* is your ancestor, Ms. Webber," Linda said pointedly.

There was no doubt; they looked exactly the same. Jayne squinted at the plaque underneath the portrait, which read "Evelyn Rose Carter."

"So it is." She smiled and took a step back. She noticed one of the guests looking between her and the portrait, mouth agape. There were whispers through the group, like cicadas at the first sight of movement. Luke quietly grabbed her hand to pull her to the back of the group.

"Quite a striking resemblance," Linda said. "There's rumor that the missus may have been led astray for a period of time. It was said that Evelyn might have been the outcome of a past love from her mother's younger days, which she reunited with later. Although, this is just a rumor since Mr. Carter was mostly blond haired."

Jayne smiled awkwardly. Green eyes—which seemed like her own—looked back at her. The voluminous, curly blond hair was so different from the flat brown hair of the sisters. Her high cheekbones and naturally pink lips, and even the one dimple she had.

Not two, like normal people, she thought. They could have been twins if born in the same generation.

Jayne didn't want to be the spectacle of the group anymore. "Shall we?" Arm stretched out, she led the way.

They continued through the rest of the house, the domestic worker's quarters, and the garden next to the carriage house. Just as Billy described it, next to the garden shed was a fence with a small space that he would have been able to fit through.

When they got back inside the library, which was neatly attached to the solarium at the back of the house, Mr. Manns greeted them and told them to enjoy themselves with some refreshments before the next group arrived in another hour.

Champagne glasses were filled and Jayne waved for Luke to follow her into the garden. They walked along the garden path, next to bushes that were now empty shells of what they would've been during peak bloom. She led them to the round gondola looking over the garden with a swinging chair inside. Luke followed, plopping himself in the chair, causing the seat to swing forward and strike Jayne, catching her off balance and pitching her forward.

"Sorry," he said abruptly, putting an arm out to stop her from falling forward. His palm landed perfectly on her right breast, as if he'd done it on purpose. She looked down and he swiftly removed his hand, appalled. "Sorry again," he said with a groan. "I didn't mean—"

"It's fine, I know." She laughed to ease his feelings. For a moment, the sound of birds in the trees and the smell of lavender filled the silence between them. Not sure if she felt drunk from the warm air and the scent of flowers or the alcohol, but she felt compelled to talk to Luke about the necklace, which also meant she had to tell him about Billy. She clasped her hands together in her lap and turned toward him. "Listen, I have to talk to you about something. I have to get something from this house."

Luke cocked his head to the side, his eyes narrowed. "Okay . . ."

"It's a necklace. It belonged to Evelyn, my great-great-grandmother. It's underneath the floorboards in her room." Jayne fumbled to get the paper from her back pocket, opening it to show Luke. "See, this is where it is," she said, stabbing her finger at the writing and scribbled map.

Luke took it from her. "I'm confused," he admitted. He scanned the paper, not really reading it. "Your great-great-grandmother left a necklace under the floorboards and you want to go get it? How do you even know about this? Up until a few days ago, you didn't know about this house, or your grandmother." He handed the paper back to her.

"Well, that's the harder part to explain," she said, jamming the paper back into her pocket. She felt a hard ball forming in her stomach and it manifested into a groan. "Have you seen anyone at my house, or around it, that you shouldn't be seeing?"

"What?" Luke said, even more confused than before. "Like vagrants?"

She laughed. "No. Not exactly." She could feel Luke pulling away and she relaxed. "More like people who you shouldn't be *seeing*." She let that sink in for a moment and watched Luke's face changing; eyes darting around the floor, searching for the answer she was implicating. "Like . . . oh, do you remember when you thought you saw someone at the old house the other day?" Luke's eyes widened.

"Like a ghost?" he whispered.

"Yes, like a ghost. A boy. He's always dressed in a

cap and brown pants with suspenders, high-top leather shoes, and a cream-colored shirt. He's about seventeen and looks as though he came straight out of the 1900s." Luke swallowed and nodded slowly. "Okay, because he's told me that you've seen him."

"He's *told* you?"

Jayne nodded and took a sip of her drink. There was no turning back now—might as well not be shy about it. "His name is Billy and he's my great-great-grandfather. He was married to Evelyn Carter."

"Oh, um, I see." Luke cleared his throat.

"I thought I was going crazy. I'm still not convinced that this time next year I won't be in an asylum—if Blake knew, I'd surely be."

Luke, still unsure what was happening, shook his head and then rubbed his face, pressing his fingers into his eyes.

"Do you believe in that kind of stuff?" *I probably should have started with that,* she thought.

"I suppose," Luke said, looking over the garden. "I never really thought about it too hard. I had some stuff happen as a child that I couldn't explain and it turned me off to anything paranormal." He stared into the distance. "You know, the first time I saw your ghost—"

"Billy."

"Billy, right. The first time I saw him was during your fifth birthday party. I'd seen him in the house and I asked my parents who the kid was that was wearing funny clothes. They told me that they couldn't see anyone. So, I figured it was the same situation as my parents' old house. I just kept my mouth shut. Then you came out, calling for him to show himself. We were so young. I didn't know . . . I . . . ." Luke couldn't finish his thought.

"It's okay," Jayne said. She grabbed his hand from his knee and gave it a squeeze. It was so much warmer than hers. She thought of Blake in that moment. Blake's hands were always cold and dry, but Luke's felt like a cashmere mitten that had been warmed in the dryer. She was surprised at how little she'd thought of Blake. Her stomach clenched and she forced herself to pull away.

"Anyway, Billy gave me the directions to get the necklace if we could. He gave me the specific directions to the floorboard. I don't know how I can get up there unseen, though. I can't just ask to go poking around because then not only will they wonder how I know about the necklace, but it'll belong to them."

Luke smirked.

"What?"

"I'll play defense," he said. He glanced at his watch. "The guests should be arriving soon, which means that the staff should be greeting them up front in the east wing of the house. Before they go on the tour, we'll sneak up the west wing stairs and if anyone comes, I'll misdirect them."

"How?" Jayne asked.

"I don't know, but I just will. Trust me." Luke smiled at her. "We'll wait for the first guests to arrive." He nodded toward the breezeway where the tour guide and a footman were waiting. "Then we go."

"Okay," Jayne said excitedly. Her heart picked up speed like a racing horse and her face felt warm.

After a few minutes of waiting, looking out over the garden, watching the birds come and go from the flowers, Luke stood up. "Go time," he said, holding out a hand to help her up. They made their way to the solarium door and just as they pulled it open, Mr. Manns was standing there speaking to a server.

"Shit," Jayne exclaimed and Mr. Manns turned around.

"Ah, Ms. Webber. You're still here. Can I help you

with something?" His suspicious eyes made her nervous.

"Yes, sorry. We were just about to leave but I thought I'd best use the restroom before we go, since I'm not going home right away."

"Of course. I can show you to it," he said, leaving the servant and making his way to the hallway.

"Oh, I'm sure that's not necessary. I'm quite capable, if you'll just point me in the direction—"

"Don't be silly, it's no trouble," Mr. Manns insisted.

The three of them made their way down the hall. *So much for defense,* Jayne thought as she glared at Luke.

Mr. Manns pointed to a wooden panel in the hall that had a handle sticking out. "Right there, Ms. Webber."

"Thank you," she said sharply, slowly making her way toward the door, eyeing Luke. Just as she was closing the door to the bathroom, she heard Luke shout.

"Argh, my knee!" he yelled, falling to the floor like a damsel in distress.

"Luke?" Mr. Manns exclaimed, bending down to help him up. "What on earth?"

"I've had a problem . . . with my knee . . . ever since the accident," Luke said in between gasps and grunts. "I need to sit down to stretch it out. Would you please help me?" He reached for Mr. Manns.

"Of course. Ms. Webber can find her way back. Come with me." He glanced back at the bathroom door as Jayne was shutting it. Through the open crack, she watched him lead Luke back into the sitting room.

She glanced around quickly and then booked it to the stairs, running on her tippy-toes. Her sneakers were slippery on the marble tile floors, but once she reached the stairs, she took two at a time. Her feet caused a couple of the stairs to creak, but not loud enough for anyone to notice. She smiled at Evelyn's portrait on the way up.

Jayne found the room quickly and as she entered,

simultaneously pulled the paper out of her pocket again. "About three steps straight from the window, one step left, and another forward," she read. Following these steps put her at the corner of the bed, right on top of the rug. She squatted down beside the bed so no passersby would be able to see her. She lifted up the corner of the rug. All the hardwood boards looked the same and were flush with one another, no gaps or holes. She looked at the instructions again. There was another window, in the opposite corner. She followed the steps from there. That put her at the other corner of the bed, in plain view if someone were to walk by. She thought about closing the door but decided that would take more time, create extra noise, and would catch the eye. She lifted the rug and right next to the bedpost she noticed one board just a little more worn and smaller than the rest. You wouldn't be able to tell at a glance, or without knowing what you were looking for, but she could see the perfect little scratches along the edges from past prying. She reached up to her hair and pulled out a bobby pin from under her ponytail. She wedged it in between the boards. After a few presses, she could see the board moving and she dug the nails of her free hand into the edge of the board, pulling it up. It popped right out into her hand and she peered into the hole. There was a small cardboard box with no lid. Inside was a handkerchief with the initials "ERC" monogrammed into the fabric. When she lifted it out, she heard something drop back into the box. When she looked inside again, she saw a delicate, tarnished chain and a folded note.

"Holy shit," she said. Wasting no time, she clutched the two items, placed the board back, and flipped down the rug. Still on her knees, she pulled the necklace over her head, quickly admiring the diamond and ruby flickering in the sunlight. As she was shoving the handkerchief and unread note into her pocket, she heard the steps of someone coming down the hall. Startled, someone said, "What you doing in here?"

A short Mexican woman wearing the uniform of a maid looked down on her. A long braid hung over her shoulder and her fists rested on her hips with a feather duster poking out the back of one. When Jayne didn't answer, but started getting to her feet, the woman stood tall and asked, "Can I help you?"

"Nope," Jayne said, matter-of-factly. "I found it." She held up the bobby pin. "I knew I had dropped something in this room and when my hair started falling all over the place, I knew it was this. Sure enough, here it is."

"You shouldn't be in here," the woman said in her accent.

"I'm sorry." Jayne moved to step past her. "I'm sorry," she said again. The woman watched her go.

Jayne power walked down the hall and touched the necklace, looking again at Evelyn as she descended the stairs.

"Oh, there you are," Mr. Manns said when Jayne entered the sitting room. "We were just about to come find you. Mr. Martin here hurt his knee and needed assistance. I figured you would be able to find your way back."

Jayne, somewhat disoriented from her excursion, looked at Luke. "What? Oh, yes. My contact, it slipped out when I was in there and I had some trouble getting it back in . . . anyway." She looked at Luke. "Do you think you can walk to your car? More guests are arriving and I'd hate for us to get blocked in."

"Yes, yes," Luke grunted. He pushed himself up off the armrest and reached out for Jayne. Playing along, she grabbed his bicep with one arm and his hand with the other, hoisting him off the chair. She gave his bicep a tentative squeeze and started to lead him out of the room.

"Oh, Ms. Webber." Jayne turned her head back to Mr. Manns. "I would like to come talk to you soon about your family's home and the shop. I may have an offer you can't refuse. And if I may say, that is a *beautiful* necklace. I didn't notice it before." He stood unmoving, hands clasped in front of him with a smile that made Jayne feel uncomfortable. Luke took a look at her neck and back up to her face.

"Thank you," she said quickly and helped Luke out the door into the breezeway. "Do you think you can drive in your *condition*?" she asked playfully.

"I think I can manage." He hopped into his truck and rolled down the window. "Well, that was fun. Do you think he knew about the necklace? The way he said that at the end . . ."

"I don't think so. I mean, he couldn't have, could he? Did he leave at all while I was gone?"

"I don't think so. He didn't leave me at all while you were gone, but I think he wondered what you were doing in there."

"It felt like I was gone forever. It took me a minute to find the right board," Jayne said. She told Luke about the maid who caught her. "As long as she doesn't say anything, we'll be fine."

"But you got it though," Luke said excitedly.

"I did." A smile spread across Jayne's face and she pinched the necklace in between her fingers. She lifted it up to examine it and felt a sense of comfort and familiarity. She leaned on Luke's door. "Well, I have to meet Blake and Mom for lunch. We're going to stop by the shop to find my dad's will, also. Thank you for inviting me to this. It really meant a lot."

"Of course. I thought of you immediately when I

saw it. Tell Billy I said 'Hi,' and hopefully I can meet him some day."

Jayne didn't know if Luke was being serious or taking a jest at her expense, so she just guffawed and said, "Okay."

27

BLAKE AND DANI were sitting at the table by the window at the Italian restaurant. She could see Blake's burgundy, knitted cardigan—the one she'd bought him for his birthday last month. She loved that sweater on him; it made him look like a male model in a high-end fashion magazine. He seemed less enthusiastic about it but wore it because he knew she liked it so much.

A bell above the door alerted them to her presence and Dani grinned. They exchanged hugs when she got to the table. Blake's cologne enveloped her before he did. It used to be her favorite smell—now, it seemed too much. It made her throat hurt.

"How was it?" Blake asked.

"Great! The house is spectacular and the artwork is fantastic. I hope to be half as talented as those artists one day. I was able to see a few of the pieces that William Webber Sr. made over a hundred years ago." Jayne showed them the pictures she took of the pieces and told them about the portraits and all the rooms throughout the house. Blake pretended to be interested while checking his phone, nodding agreeably at all the right times.

Jayne wrapped up her story and put her phone away. "So, what's the plan for getting the will?"

"Since your dad always kept his paperwork filed away at the shop, we'll have to stop there to find it," Dani said with a hunk of a biscuit in her cheek.

"Okay. Joe might have an idea of where it is," Jayne replied, pulling her sweater a little tighter. "It looks like that tropical storm is starting to hit land." Jayne nodded toward the edge of dark gray clouds coming in from the southeast. "They say it's not supposed to be too bad here, just lots of rain. Should we get supplies?"

"It probably wouldn't hurt to get a few things," Blake said.

"I don't know if your dad has any batteries and we should get some extra food in case we lose power."

"And wine and chocolate," Jayne added.

Dani smiled. "Of course. I'm sure that's on the top of the list of hurricane supplies."

The bell jingled as they walked into the shop. Joe shouted, "I'll be right there!" but Jayne and Dani walked straight back. He was sitting in his office, clicking on the computer. His big belly made the reach for the keyboard a valiant effort.

"Oh, hi there guys," he said, trying to push off the armrests. Dani noticed his struggle and quickly waved him to sit down. He complied. "What can I help y'all with?"

Jayne stepped forward and in one breath said, "We heard a rumor going around town that Melody wants to try and take the house and land from me.

She's claiming she was common-law married, so we need Dad's will. Do you know if he filed it here with his other stuff?"

Joe took a deep breath and shook his head. "That woman," he muttered. "I'm sure it's in there, if he had one. It would be where he always kept his paperwork." He looked at Dani and she understood.

"Okay, we'll take a quick peek. Do you know who he was using for a lawyer?"

"Yes, Randall, down the road a bit, in the old tax office. But he's on holiday for the next two days and his office is closed."

"Great," Dani said under her breath. "And how is *she* affording a lawyer? I heard she's working at the old hardware shop."

"Yeah, but she's dating the shady defense attorney that came in from Austin a few years ago."

"Aha," Dani said. "Okay. Thanks Joe."

"Sure." He smiled and scooted forward. "Oh, Jayne, whatever you've been doing with the social media, keep it up. We've had calls from people asking about the pieces they've seen online."

"Wow, that's great. I'll post some more and extend the reach and demographic as well. That should help." She grabbed her phone and started tapping.

Joe waived his hand. "I don't know what that means, but sounds good," He said. "If y'all need anything, let me know."

"Thank you, we will," Jayne and Dani said together.

They walked across the hall to Peter's office, where the door was shut and an ominous feeling radiated from it like the door was on fire.

"Blake," Jayne called, and he rounded the corner from the front room with a few steps. "Can you come here and help us find what we might be looking for? You know legal documents better than I do."

"Have you been in here yet?" Dani asked quietly, reading the hesitation on Jayne's body. Jayne shook her head. "Okay, take your time." She placed her hand over Jayne's on the knob and slowly helped her turn it, following her lead.

The door clicked open and easily swung inside. They were hit with a smell of wood, stale sweat, Giorgio Armani cologne, and mildew from the recent rain. It wasn't exactly a pleasant combination, but Jayne and Dani felt themselves inhaling deeply, trying to catch each individual smell, each igniting a memory within them.

Jayne remembered coming to the shop as a girl, smelling the fresh wood in the summertime as she watched her dad build. She recalled standing next to him while he wiped the sweat off his face with a handkerchief. The cologne made her think of times they all went out for dinner together as a family, or when her dad would get dressed up and how much he hated wearing anything but a worn-out T-shirt with jeans. As she took another breath and the musk of the mildew sunk in, she thought of his coffin being lowered into the wet earth and the dirt being shoveled over it. *Enough of that,* she scolded herself.

Dani, cherished the wood and the sweat. They were innocent and reminded her of the shop, but the cologne made her feel uneasy. It brought back nights upon nights he would splash some on his neck and go to the bar, not coming home until late hours in the evening.

After a few minutes of flipping through files, it wasn't hard to spot the one that said, "Will." It had presumably everything they needed in it and even had the lawyer's, Randall's, business card stapled to the front of the folder.

"Perfect. He must have filed," Jayne said and put the folder in her purse.

Blake took a look and said that everything was as it should be and Melody had no chance of getting the house. Everything had been made out to Jayne and there was no mention of Melody in anything.

They quickly and informally introduced Blake to Joe and let him know they got what they needed.

"Make sure you guys get that house ready for the storm tonight. They upgraded it from a tropical storm. It's supposed to get stronger and make its way up the gulf," Joe said. "It's going to hit the coast soon."

"Surely we won't get too affected up here, so far away from the coast?" Jayne asked.

"Well, no. The winds won't be as strong as they'll be down there, but we'll get some intense rain. Best be prepared to lose power and possibly have a few downed trees. I don't suppose you've picked those pecans off the trees in the front of the house?" Jayne pressed her lips together and shook her head. "Be ready for those to litter the ground. I'll send Luke over later to help with any preparations and make sure everything is taken care of."

Blake stiffened beside Jayne.

"Thank you, Joe," Jayne said. "You don't need to send Luke though, I'm sure we'll be fine."

"Have any of you been in a Texas hurricane before?" Joe asked. They all shook their heads simultaneously. Joe smiled. "I'll send Luke."

They stopped at the store on their way home to get some nonperishable food items along with vegetables, batteries, and water. Jayne felt like this was an overreaction—the news was always exaggerating—but the grocery store was cleared out. The only canned items they could find were things like split pea soup.

When they got home, Blake turned on the television to flip between the weather channel and local news stations. It seemed the storm was only gaining strength as it got closer to the coast.

"Looks like it's going to be a category four by the time the eye hits this afternoon!" Blake yelled into the kitchen where Jayne and Dani were putting the supplies away. "Just south of Houston is going to be impacted the hardest. It'll be devastating, I'm sure."

Jayne picked up Rusty, who was dancing circles around her feet, and walked into the living room to look out the front window. The front of the house faced west, but she could already see the clouds darkening with lighter bands streaked throughout, like brush strokes. She felt ominous, imagining all the people in Houston and the cities farther south. They barely made it out unscathed from the flooding of 2016. A chill rose up her back. Something buried in the gloom of the sky and the electricity in the air compelled her to walk outside. She wanted to feel the earth and the air before it was assaulted by the winds and the rain. Blake watched her walk out the front door, but didn't question her.

Jayne stood on the porch and took three deep breaths. The first was thick with static electricity, despite there not being any thunderstorms in the area. The next two breaths smelled of damp earth, as if the water was already rising from below. She thought she could smell the salt from the ocean. The slightly damp air coated her face in a chill.

Jayne put Rusty down and he ran out toward the pecan trees. She called after him, but he wouldn't listen. He stopped once he reached the biggest one closest to the house and Jayne remembered what Joe had said about checking how full the trees were. There were a *lot* of pecans. She stood there wondering if she could lay down some nets, like they do in Italy to catch the olives. Rusty picked up a small nut, tried to chew it, then let it fall out of his mouth. He tried two more before giving up on the idea of eating it and ran around the trees with the current one in his mouth. Jayne laughed at him. She'd never had a dog, or even a pet for that matter. When she was younger, living here, they'd had a dog briefly, but Jayne remembered her dad telling her she was allergic and all of a sudden there was no more dog. For years she believed she was allergic and avoided all dogs. Now, she wasn't so sure her father had been telling the truth.

"Hey, Bunny."

She smiled over at Billy. "Hey there."

"There's a storm coming."

"I've heard."

"Then why are you standing outside?"

Jayne chuckled. "I don't know. I just felt like I had to be outside while I still could—while the air was still. I wanted to feel what it was like before chaos hit, you know?" She walked toward the trees and Billy followed.

"Evelyn did the same thing," he said. Jayne looked at him and raised one blond eyebrow. "Every time it rained, she'd stand outside before the downpour, feeling the damp wind and the electric charge. Why are you standing under the trees though? You won't want to be standing here if one falls down."

Jayne smiled. "Joe, at the shop, was telling us that these pecans will probably fall down. I was just trying to assess how many we had to expect. Looks like a lot."

"Yes, it's been a good year; not too wet. You know, in order to have trees that yield the most nuts, you need two kinds of trees. Type one, protogynous and type two, protandrous. The trees have both the female and male parts, but rarely are they open at the same time. If you have the two different types, you have a better chance of pollination. I didn't know that when I planted

231

these trees. Your dad figured it out and planted some of those trees there." Billy pointed at a line of trees at the front of the property.

"Why did Dad care about the nuts? Did he ever do anything with them?"

Billy walked toward another tree with his hands in his pockets. "Sometimes he would gather them and take them into town. There's a store that's always paid a couple cents for each one. He would then give the money to your old school for teacher's supplies. Most times he would let the kids around here come collect them after they'd fallen and they could take them and make some pocket change." Billy chuckled. "Your dad would be out here trying to shake the trees or whacking the branches to get more off for them. He would shout, 'You missed one! Here's one!' and the kids would run around collecting them like Easter eggs." Jayne smiled and felt her heart expand just a little.

"I like those stories of my dad," she said. "It's hard to imagine he had the problems he did from all the nice things people say about him."

"Unfortunately, bad things can happen to good people, Bunny. Addiction discriminates against no one." There was a brief pause. "I see you got the necklace." Jayne reached up to touch it and Billy's eyes scrunched with a smile. "It looks just as good on you as it did on her. I hope you love it as much as she was able to for the short time she had it."

"I do already. It's beautiful. Thank you Billy."

"It's the least I can do." He smiled shyly.

Jayne told him about the events at the Carter house. Billy paid attention and laughed when she was done. She remembered the angel fountain at the front of the mansion and felt the urge to paint. Images flooded her mind. The need was strong; she wanted to feel her brush push into her oil paints, smearing the color onto the canvas, little methodical strokes coming together separately to make one big picture. She was already planning a painting in her mind, going over the brushes and colors she'd need.

"Jayne!" Blake called from the house. He stood in the doorway, holding the screen door open. Rusty barked and ran back to Jayne's side.

She looked up and only then did she realize it was starting to pour; her clothes were already wet through. She smiled at Billy and ran toward the house. *The wind is starting to pick up too,* she thought.

"What in god's name are you doing?" Blake asked. He grabbed a towel off the step, left from the laundry Dani had done earlier. "You're soaked and the mutt is drenched and muddy." Jayne pressed the towel to her face then scrunched her hair. "You looked like you were talking to someone out there."

Dani was watching dubiously from the kitchen.

"No, I wasn't. I was just looking at the pecan trees. I got caught up in a thought about Dad. I'm going to go change, I'll be right back." She ran upstairs, taking two steps at a time, leaving Rusty dripping at the bottom. Dani took the towel from Blake and started rubbing the water out of Rusty's hair and wiping the mud from his paws.

She finished drying off, changed into a loose sweatshirt and yoga pants, and went back downstairs to sit next to Blake on the couch. Dani announced she was going to run into town to grab Rusty some dog food. Jayne protested, but Dani insisted that this may be the last night in a day or two to be able to go and he didn't have enough food to last that long.

"The storm isn't supposed to get bad for a couple more hours, babe. She'll be fine." He smiled at her and rubbed her arm.

"Okay, do you want me or Blake to come with you?" Jayne asked.

"No, of course not. I wont be long. I already made a list of what I need so I'll be in and out."

"Okay," Jayne said tentatively.

28

OVER AN HOUR later Jayne paced around the living room, through the kitchen, and back. "How could she forget her phone?" she demanded to know, waving it in the air like a mad person. Rusty was following her around as if she was wielding a sausage stick.

"I don't know, babe. You keep asking. I'm sure she's fine. Give her a few more minutes before we start to worry, okay? There could have been a long line with people stocking up."

"Look out the window, Blake. It's pouring cats and mice out there."

"Dogs."

"What?" Jayne stopped and stared at him, her curly hair making her look wild in the dim lights.

"Dogs. The saying is, 'It's raining cats and dogs.'" Jayne glared at him with a look that Blake knew meant for him to shut up. He cleared his throat and looked back to the TV, which now had a reporter out in the streets of Port Aransas showing the flooding and devastation already happening.

"Should I go out and look for her? I could take Dad's truck."

"Absolutely not. Not right now. I said wait a few minutes. Sit down, you're making me anxious."

She sat next to him on the couch and tried to focus, unsuccessfully, on the TV. Her impatience made her speak, wanting to get to the bottom of something, even if it wasn't her mom. "I saw you with Frederick Manns," she blurted.

"Who?" Blake asked. He didn't look at her despite her staring holes in his temple. The inflection in his tone changed at the end, making him seem unsure of his own lie.

"Frederick Manns. He's a developer—the one who owns the Carter house and is trying to buy this one. He seemed to know exactly who you were when I was at the Carter house this morning. He mentioned you, said that you would 'talk later.' " She made air quotes.

"Oh, you mean the tall guy with a bit of a German accent? He saw me sitting with you at The Café. When you left, he came over and asked how I knew you. He told me he had a proposition for us on the house. He wants to *buy* it, Jayne. And he's willing to offer you a good amount of money to make sure you don't sell to anyone else. I don't know how you could turn that down."

"You're negotiating my property with a buyer without consulting me?" Jayne felt isolated, like she was an outsider in her own plans.

"No, it's not like that. I think he wanted to test the waters with me. He wanted to see if you'd be interested at all—if you had mentioned anything."

The hair on the back of her neck stood on end. "And you told him I was."

"Well, not in so many words." Blake closed his eyes and took a deep breath while smoothing the front of his sweater. "Look Jayne, it's something you need to start looking into. We can't live here. This is a tiny town with no promise for any kind of life that we want. How would you do your art here? You already have a gallery and buyers back home. You haven't even painted anything since you've been here." He pointed to the blank canvases that were propped up near the stairs. Jayne had put them there to remind herself to paint. "We have an apartment and a life *back home*. And what about our friends? We can't just leave our friends."

"*Your* friends, Blake. Not one of those friends has called me to see how I'm doing, or even to offer condolences. What kind of friends are those? I have friends here who've already helped more than those friends—or even my fiancé." She regretted the words the minute they came out.

He watched her face, watched as she fidgeted with her hair and the new necklace she had around her neck.

"I said I'm sorry. I can't live here, Jayne. I'd be a small lawyer with a small office and one secretary and small cases about land disputes or who took who's goat or something, like your dad's lawyer. This isn't a place for me."

Jayne didn't know what to say. She could have argued that bigger cities were only thirty minutes away, but she didn't want to; she didn't care. She felt her face get warm, and her eyes prickled while she tried not to show her emotions on her face.

"I see," she croaked. She now understood that she could choose either her new home or her fiancé. Both were as opposite as oil and water and while she might be able to mix parts of them for a short period of time, there was nothing that would emulsify them forever.

Blake was still waiting for a response when the sound of an engine and the crack and pop of tires on gravel could be heard above the ping of raindrops on the windows. They turned to look out the front window where they could see a truck coming down the driveway. Rusty barked and ran for the door.

"That's Luke's truck," Jayne exclaimed. "He has Mom. I wonder what happened." Blake got off the couch and followed Jayne out the door, letting the screen door slam closed.

Dani and Luke got out of the truck, each with a grocery bag, trying to cover their heads with their arms as they ran toward the house. Jayne held the door open while they rushed through, laughing as Rusty jumped at their legs. Blake handed another towel from the laundry pile to Dani.

"What the hell happened?" Jayne demanded to know.

As if just noticing her, Dani stopped tousling her damp hair, the dark curls settling around her face. She looked up at Jayne. "I was at the store, grabbed a few things, and ran into Luke in the parking lot. Apparently we had the same idea." She handed the towel to Luke. "Anyway, when I got to my car, it wouldn't start; wouldn't even turn over. Luke took a look in the pouring rain—poor guy—and couldn't see anything obvious, so he decided to give me a ride since the rain was coming down harder. It isn't draining as well as it should; the ditches on the side of the road are filling up and spilling over in some places."

"What about the shop?" Jayne asked.

"It should be fine," Luke said. "Main Street slopes quite a bit and the shop is on the top of the crest; same with the library. But do you have spare water?"

"I mean, a few bottles and a couple jugs."

"It may seem a little extreme, but I'd fill the bathtub if I were you. Just to have some extra for washing dishes and such, if you need. Chances are you won't need it, but this area isn't used to taking on as much water as we're going to get. With the storm, you could lose power, which is also going to mean no water. I'm not sure if your dad still has the hook-up to the well."

Jayne nodded. "We only have one bathroom. Does anyone need to shower first?"

"I do," Blake said. "I'll run up and do that now. I can clean the tub after and fill it up too."

"Thank you."

"There are two bathrooms," Dani said, and Jayne looked at her in confusion. "There's one in the master bedroom too. We just haven't been in there yet."

Blake paused.

"I'd rather just use the main bath," Jayne said. Dani nodded and Blake continued up the stairs. "What are we going to do about your car? Do you think it's going to flood in the parking lot?"

"We've already called a tow truck. They were right behind us." She pointed out the window and the tow truck turned into their driveway with Dani's rental. She grabbed an umbrella from the coatrack by the door and went out to direct them where to leave it.

Jayne went out to check the ditches on either side of the street. They were starting to collect water, but it didn't seem concerning yet.

"What are you thinking about?" Luke asked, giving her a fright.

"I was just trying to get an idea what the water is going to do; if it's going to sit or drain."

"It should be fine, I think. Let me show you." He placed a hand lightly on her mid back, his touch sparking a bolt of electricity up her spine. He directed her into the house, through the kitchen, and onto the deck where they pressed their backs against the house under the awning, sheltered from the rain. The air was damp and smelled of static and earth.

"The creek is filling up. That's most concerning right

now. You'll probably get some overflow there. But do you see how high up we are? We have to be about twenty feet above the creek. You should be fine. I'm afraid for that small house though," Luke said. "If the water crests over the creek walls and doesn't stop, it's going to have a straight path toward the little house, which is basically in the bottom of a bowl made by the land around it."

"Okay," Jayne said, tugging anxiously at a lock of hair. "I hope that doesn't happen but I'll keep watch on it."

Luke decided it would be in his best interest to leave before it was too late. Dani was outside with the tow truck and thanked him again before he left in his truck.

"Oh," Dani exclaimed when she came back in. "Let me put these groceries away." She grabbed the bags off the floor and went into the kitchen. Inside, the humidity penetrated the house and made the cool air tingle on their skin like sparklers.

Jayne tried to switch the channel to something else, but the hurricane had become nationwide breaking news, infiltrating every station. She dropped the remote on the couch beside her and spent the next few minutes listening to a press conference about shelters for the people who were expected to be flooded out of their homes in Houston. She was startled by a knock at the front door. Her mom came into the living room.

"Who's that?" Dani asked.

"I have no clue." Jayne rolled Rusty off her leg. "I couldn't hear anyone come down the driveway through the rain." When she opened the door, it was Luke again, soaking wet. "What's going on?" she asked, worried.

"The bridge that goes over the river has been shut down. It looks like the barrier has fallen off and some of it got swept away. I won't be able to get across and now I'm worried about flooding if I go around."

"Please, come in. You can stay here as long as you need. We'll let your parents know you're here," Jayne said quickly. "What is that?" She motioned to Luke's left hand.

"It's just a change of clothes. I always have some for after work. Do you mind if I change? I'm thoroughly soaked now."

Jayne looked him over. His wet shirt was clinging to his muscular chest and abs; the only dry place on him was in the crotch of his pants. "Of course."

"You can change in my room, hon. I'm in the spare," Dani interrupted.

Jayne turned toward Dani, worry in her brow. "What are all the people going to do that are still at work? They won't be able to get back. This is happening so fast. I know that bridge was old, but that's scary."

"I know, darling." Dani put an arm around Jayne. "They'll figure it out. This town is nothing if not resilient." Dani was about to head back to the kitchen when they heard an exchange of voices upstairs, brief and acute followed by two closing doors. Dani and Jayne exchanged a look.

29

AS THE LIGHT started to fade and the moon hid behind the clouds, the wind howled through the open doorway and the empty chairs rocked on their own. Billy sat in the old house listening to the ping of raindrops hitting the windows. He closed his eyes and listened to the cacophony of different sounds: the heavy rain sounded like wind, the wind sounded like someone was trying to knock the house over, and the thunder rolled through the valley like a derailed train.

He got up and walked to the front doorway to stare outside. The clouds were dark and he could see a blanket of rain falling like a waterfall from the sky. The creek was almost full and they weren't through the storm yet. This house was built a foot off the ground for this reason, but the cracks and uneven floors told him that years of erosion had most definitely brought it down a few inches. Not to mention how old and battered the cinder blocks would be.

It's been a while since a storm like this. He thought of the flood of 1921.

Billy had been thirty years old, married to Evelyn,

and they had two sons: Ted, who was nine at the time, and Gerry, who was eight. The creek overflowed, creeping like lava toward the house. The rain had come and didn't stop. The boys hadn't returned to school yet and luckily the storm kept them home. Evelyn did busywork throughout the house, cleaning cupboards and washing baseboards while they played in their rooms.

Despite Billy's efforts to go to the shop, Evelyn not only demanded that *he* remain at home, but his employees to do so as well. She had a feeling about this storm; she could smell it. It wasn't going to be the same as any rainstorm, like they were told.

As the water level rose, Evelyn and Billy became increasingly worried. Billy could see the shimmer of water through the grass, getting deeper and approaching the house, now only five feet away. One of the boys asked if they were going to be okay.

"Of course," Billy had replied automatically. A couple hours later the water reached the house and had swept underneath. Billy was thankful he'd left the car on the other side of the creek, up on the hill. He walked around to the back of the house and could see the water starting to come out the other side.

"Can we put our boots on and go play outside in the water? Please?" Gerry begged. Billy looked at Evelyn and they both looked outside. The sky was now a light gray instead of the dark charcoal it had been. Neither of them had a good rebuttal to this request, so Evelyn nodded.

"Make sure you put on your coats too. And pull up your hoods." The boys ran to their rooms to get the necessary jackets and footwear and burst out the front door like horses off to the race.

The rain continued for the rest of the day, but the shallow pond beneath their home had started to recede. When they woke the next morning there didn't seem to be any damage, so Billy decided to venture into the shop. This proved to be more difficult than he had imagined.

He came across many spots in the road that had been washed into the ditches. When he came to the bridge going over the river, there was a spectacle with a bunch of people, cars lined along the road and a medic waiting. As he pulled over, he could see the top of a vehicle peeking through the fast-moving water. The law enforcement eyed the car from the riverbank. They were trying to decide how to get to the car. *But, if no one is in there, where would they have gone?* Billy swallowed hard and walked across the bridge to join the group of onlookers. "Does anyone know what's going on?" he asked. A few people looked at him but said nothing.

"This car here was swept into the river last night during the hard rain," an older gentleman replied, his voice trembling slightly. "You can see where they busted through the guardrail." He pointed to where the wooden railing was now in broken pieces and jutted out with a missing section.

"Does anyone know how high these waters got last night?" Billy asked. Some of the onlookers glanced at him, but again said nothing.

The same old man pulled his long jacket tighter and tightened his cap to his head. "One of the women who lives nearby, she said her husband had to drive over last evening and the river had already crested over the bridge and was flowing up the banks. And that was before the worst of it. Poor bastards." He shook his head.

"Any word on who that might be?" Billy nodded toward the car in the river. The police had now tied themselves with rope and were slowly wading into the water.

"No idea as of yet. That woman over there seems to think it might be her nephew's family; they were coming back from Fredericksburg last night and she hasn't heard from them yet — says that looks like their car."

Billy looked at the woman. She was in her fifties, presumably. Her long dark hair, streaked with chunks of gray, was pulled up and pinned into a day-old bun on top of her head, still damp from the rain. Her face was still youthful but striped with life's thin wrinkles. Her clothes were rain soaked, but she didn't seem to notice; her thin, boney hands were what gave away her age. She clamped them over her mouth, staring at the car.

The police had formed a chain into the water and pried the driver's side door open. One of them peered into the car and shook his head. *No bodies.* There was an audible murmur through the small crowd. The policeman reached into the car again and pulled out a hat and pocketbook, along with a small pink sweater, made for a child no older than four. The dark-haired woman let out a choked scream followed by a sob and fell to her knees. A few people rushed over to the woman, wrapping their arms around her and trying to console her. The policemen looked up at the bridge and one of them started toward the crowd. Billy shifted his eyes from the woman to the car where the policemen were still retrieving some of the belongings: a kid's toys, a woman's scarf, and a little boy's cap. Billy couldn't help imagine what had happened to the family.

His heart skipped a beat at the thought that they might have tried to get out of the car in the rushing water. He turned back to the woman, collapsed on the ground with her skirt soaked heavy and draped around her legs. She sobbed and screamed while the others tried to console her. One man propped her up, like a baby, her head cradled in his elbow and his arm wrapped around her middle. A policeman had reached the small bundle of people and knelt down beside the woman. After a few whispered questions, the woman nodded and the policeman helped her up and took her toward his car. Without a word, Billy turned and walked back to his own car. He mindlessly turned the car around and headed to his home where his wife and kids were safe.

The city wasn't prepared for the storm. The news had said it would affect other parts of the state; counties near them, but not theirs. Fifty-one people lost their lives that day, a lot of them perishing in their vehicles trying to get away. *How scary that must have been,* Billy thought. *To not know one's death until it's looking them straight in the face, literally choking the life out of them.* He shook the idea from his mind, just thankful for his own family.

2017

In the big house, everyone was down in the main room. Rusty was curled up in his bed by the couch, shaking. Despite many efforts, he wouldn't come to sit with Jayne or Luke. Dani had grabbed the flashlights after the power went out. "This could be it for the rest of the night," she said.

The screen of a phone lit up Jayne's face. "Looks like we've got at least three more hours of this heavy stuff coming our way, then it should lighten up a bit." Blake groaned. Jayne got up and went to the kitchen, looking out the back porch to the old house. The thunder was crackling and hammering in their yard. The lightning lit up the sky like streaks of fireflies zooming through the curved clouds. Her hair stood on end and all at once a blinding flash filled the house and a boom that sounded like a plane crashing made the walls and the floors vibrate. Rusty yelped and Jayne rubbed her eyes to rid them of the temporary blob of white etched into her vision. She went over and picked up Rusty.

"That was close," Luke said.

"I think it hit the old house," Jayne called out. Everyone came into the kitchen to see. "Look." She pointed out back, across the creek. "You can see part of the porch is collapsed."

"Oh god," Dani exclaimed. There was another flash of light and crack of thunder. Not much farther away this time.

"We'll fix it," Luke assured Dani. Jayne couldn't help wondering if Billy was okay. Mentally she wished for him to join them in the big house.

They went back to the living room while Dani gathered some snacks.

"I really don't feel well," Blake proclaimed. "My stomach has been cramping and I'm getting waves of nausea."

"Is it something you ate?"

"I grabbed a gas station burrito earlier today. That could be it. I think I'm going to have to lie down for a bit." He started to get up.

"Okay," Jayne said. "I'll bring up some water, crackers, and Tums." Blake was already on his way up the stairs.

Jayne held a flashlight and took up a small plate of crackers and cheese, accompanied by a side of Tums and a glass of water. She could hear him in the bathroom emptying his stomach contents, so she left it on the nightstand in the bedroom. When she turned to go, Billy was sitting in the rocking chair.

"Jesus mother of Christ," Jayne said, clutching at her chest.

"You know, for someone who's aware that there's a ghost living on the residence, you sure are jumpy," Billy said with a crook in his smile.

Jayne gave him a look and whispered, "Right. I wanted to make sure you were okay. I saw that the house got hit and the porch is collapsing."

"It didn't get hit. The lightning hit a few feet away but the boom from the thunder caused it to fall," he said softly.

"We can fix it," Jayne said. "If you want."

Billy looked up at her and shrugged. He nodded toward the bathroom, where Blake was still getting sick. "Blake has some kind of stomach problem," Jayne explained. "We think food poisoning, maybe." Billy nodded. "Well, obviously the power's out, so we'll just be down in the living room."

"Okay. I might pop down in a little bit," Billy said.

Jayne headed back downstairs and found Luke and Dani in the living room. They had out the game UNO and were playing a somewhat heated match from the looks on their faces. Dani had lit some candles, lighting the living room like a 1920s séance.

"Oh good, you're back. This game is no fun with just two people," Dani said.

"Speak for yourself." Luke grinned.

Jayne joined them and they spent the next couple hours drinking wine and playing card games, shifting from UNO to Rummy and even Go Fish. By eleven, Dani took one more look at the radar and went to check outside.

"Looks like we'll be in the tail end of the storms until the morning at least. And that's a good thing because look at the cars."

Jayne and Luke got up and went to the door. Their flashlights reflected off the rippling water in front of the house. It was starting to pool around the tires, touching the rims of the smaller vehicles.

"Should we move them?" Jayne asked.

"If the rain is stopping we should be okay. Plus, I don't think we have anywhere else to move them. The highest point is that hill on the other side of the road, but at this point we wouldn't be able to get across the driveway."

Jayne didn't move her gaze from the water in front of their house. "Did anyone see if Dad had a boat anywhere?"

"I think I saw a blow-up pool mat in the shed. But max, it would fit two and maybe the dog. Y'all save yourselves," Luke joked.

Jayne suddenly thought of something and went and threw open the sliding door to the deck. Rusty heard the door and made a run for it.

"What are you—" Luke said behind her, then he saw—the water had crested the bank of the creek and was lapping over each side, moving like a slug, slowly pushing forward with each wave. It had already reached the old house, running through the gap between the ground and the floor. "It's only going to get higher and higher as the water starts soaking through the ground into the creeks and rivers. It'll get worse before it gets better," Luke said. "All we can do is keep an eye on it."

"I think I have to go to bed," Dani said. "I'm exhausted. Will you wake me if things get worse—or if you want me to take a watch while you sleep?"

Jayne nodded. "Okay. Get some sleep." She gave her mom a hug and followed her inside.

"Don't stay up too late," Dani said, and then she went up to bed, Rusty following close behind.

"One more glass of wine?" Jayne asked Luke.

"Sure."

"Well, I have to open a new bottle. Red or white?"

"Pourer's choice."

"Red it is. Can you see if that cheese and meat plate is in the fridge?"

Luke rummaged around in the fridge before pulling out a plate with diced cheeses and summer sausage. "Do you have any crackers?"

"In the pantry." Jayne refilled their glasses. "The rain has stopped. Do you want to sit out on the front porch and watch the water flood our cars?"

"Sounds riveting. After you."

The chair cushions were sopping wet. Jayne took them off but the wicker chairs underneath were mangled and jagged with age. She grabbed a towel off the bannister and wiped down the porch swing.

Billy came out and sat along the bannister, back against the column in his usual spot. Jayne saw him but when Luke didn't say anything about also seeing him, neither did she.

"You know how much I appreciate you and your dad, right?" Jayne said, putting down her glass in all seriousness.

Luke smiled and placed his glass down also, turning toward her, his knees touching hers. "I do. Where is this coming from?"

"Well, I'm always thinking it, but I suppose the wine helped me to express it," she said, grabbing her glass off the floor.

Luke laughed deep in his chest. "We know. We're here to help. You're going through a lot right now. I'll say something my dad won't, though: we can't keep these investors at bay much longer. They're raising their offers and even inquiring about the law."

"The law?" Jayne repeated.

"How long it can stay unowned, so to speak, before

it can be claimed publicly. Usually it's about five years, but you're going to have to decide what you want to do soon."

"I see." Jayne took a thoughtful sip and let it roll over her tongue into her cheeks before swallowing. Luke watched her. "What do *you* think I should do?" The warmth of the wine in her body was making her feel flirtatious.

"Hard to say." Luke looked away but Jayne could see the red flush in his cheeks. "Do you *want* to stay here and take over your family's legacy?"

"Well, when you put it that way." She laughed and met Luke's eyes, which had scarcely left her face since they sat down. She smiled. "I don't know. If I wasn't engaged, I would stay here in a heartbeat, keep this house and land, but, Blake."

"He doesn't want to live here?"

"No. The small-town life isn't for him. He likes the rush of living in a city, downtown, in the center of chaos. I try and tell him that eventually that won't work once we start a family. We'll need quiet and a yard. A place like this would be perfect. The house is perfect. I could turn the garage into my studio. The old house, if fixed up, could be a mother-in-law suite."

"You know what just happened there?" Luke asked. "Your face lit up when you were talking about being here. But when you mentioned home, it sounded like a chore."

Jayne didn't say anything and Luke was compelled to fill the silence. "I know *I* would like you to stay here."

Billy opened one eye, waiting for Jayne's reaction. She caught his gaze and became flustered more by his company than the comment itself.

"You would?" she whispered, feeling a flush creep up her cheeks.

"Sure. I mean, I've always kind of had a thing for you—the few times I've seen you—if you weren't engaged of course."

"You have?" she asked eagerly. "I mean, I never noticed," she lied. She'd noticed the way Luke acted around her and she was hoping he would say something.

Luke shrugged. "I couldn't help it. Look at you; you're beautiful. You always have been."

"Well, thank you." Jayne didn't like comments like that. She liked being humble and mostly introverted.

She met Luke's eyes and held his gaze as he leaned in. She felt his lips on hers and then his warm hand on her face, her lips moving with his. She quickly pulled away, not because she wanted to, but she knew it was wrong.

"I'm sorry, I didn't mean . . . I can't believe . . . the wine . . ." she stuttered. Luke's hand was still on her cheek.

"Sorry to interrupt whatever the hell you've got going on here," said Blake from the dark doorway.

"Blake!" Jayne jumped up, wobbly like she'd just been woken up from a dream. She looked toward Billy, but he was gone. She caught herself on the railing just as it felt like her legs were becoming as wobbly as licorice.

"Save it Jayne, I knew there'd been something going on here."

"There's nothing going on," Luke said. "Blame me, not her."

"Save it, bud," Blake said, moving toward Luke but not moving his gaze from Jayne. "Just sit back down." Blake put the tips of the fingers in the middle of Luke's chest but Luke didn't budge. He was nearly as tall as Blake, but a lot more sturdy.

"There's nothing going on, Blake. It just . . . happened."

"You're lucky I feel like shit and don't even care right now or I'd kick your ass off this porch." Luke still didn't move. "I just came down to see where you were and now I see. We'll talk about this tomorrow. Find somewhere else to sleep Jayne, maybe with him," Blake growled. "By all means, continue where you left off. I'm going to throw up, I'm so disgusted by you."

"Blake," Jayne said, but Blake ignored her and walked back inside. She contemplated going after him, but it would do no good to chase after him to have an argument in the middle of the night while she was still drunk.

Jayne groaned and crumpled back into the porch swing.

"Sorry," Luke said. "I shouldn't have—"

"Don't worry about it. I'm just as guilty. Now it's just awkward." She sighed.

"You got that right." He pulled his hands up to his face and took a deep breath. "Hopefully the water will be down by tomorrow and I can get out of here. What are you thinking?" Luke noticed her staring off into space.

Jayne pulled her knees to her chest and whispered, "I like you too, Luke. I know this is probably the wrong thing to say after you've just been caught by your fiancé kissing another guy, but I don't think things are the way they're supposed to be with Blake and me. I think I liked the idea of him and we had fun together, we look good on paper—the hometown dream of a little granola artist, painting her way through life, married to an up-and-coming lawyer. There will always be a stigma around me. I already see it. People think I'm just the lucky wife who gets to stay at home and paint all day—despite the name I've made for myself. The friends I have are superficial and so unattached, I doubt they've even noticed I'm gone.

"And our relationship—there's no substance, there's nothing that we bring to the table for each other. Do you know what I mean?"

"I think so," he replied.

"It's like meringue; the European kind. It's nice and fluffy and looks delicious, but without the berries it's just a hard, cooked bit of whipped-up sugar."

Luke laughed from his chest and covered his mouth to stifle the volume.

"What?"

"That has got to be the oddest comparison to a relationship I've ever heard, yet it makes so much sense. But you know what?" He smiled softly. "I think you have your answer." A long silence stretched between them as his words sunk in. "We should probably go to sleep. That's a profound thought to sleep on. I'll head out of here first thing in the morning."

Jayne smiled at him. She desperately wanted to give him a hug, but knew that would be too much. Luke followed her into the house. She got some blankets out of the ottoman for him while he made comments about how the couch would be just as fine a place as any to be murdered in his sleep by an axe-wielding, soon-to-be ex-fiancé. Jayne smacked him with a pillow but took note of his use of the word "ex."

"Are you sure you don't want me to sleep in my car?"

"Don't be silly. I'll see you in the morning. Good night."

"Good night."

She had some thinking to do. As she made her way upstairs to Dani's room, she already had her answer. One thing she knew for certain though—she had already been drinking more than normal and she had to stop to avoid following in her father's footsteps.

30

BIRDS WELCOMED THE new morning with song. The sun was trying vehemently to burn through the gray clouds, but instead it cast a dreary hue to the air around the land.

Jayne hadn't felt her mom get up but could hear her downstairs talking to someone. The events of the night before crept back into her mind like a wave coming over the sand. She groaned and sat up.

Blake was downstairs, not arguing, but speaking very intently with a loud voice, like he always did when he wanted to be heard.

"Got yourself in a bit of a pickle there, hey Bunny?"

Jayne turned to Billy sitting by the window. "I guess so. And you bailed on me last night."

"I was simply trying to give you some privacy." He turned back to look out the window. "What are you going to do?"

"I don't know," she lied.

"Well, you better make up your mind soon because Blake has booked two seats on the next flight out of Texas and I don't think one of those seats is for Luke."

"What? Are you kidding?"

"Serious as a heart attack, kiddo. You better get down there, he's got two suitcases about to be put into a cab."

Jayne jumped up and threw her cotton robe over her pajamas. "Billy? What would you do?"

He turned to her. "Follow your heart, my dear. Here, let's play a game. Without thinking, whose is the first face that comes to mind in sixty years?"

Jayne's eyes shot up to the ceiling in thought. Billy smiled, seeing the answer in her mind, and nodded at her.

Jayne smiled back. "Thanks." She turned and ran down the stairs amidst shouting in the living room.

Luke was standing behind Dani, holding the front screen door open. Jayne burst through the door and stood on the edge of the step.

Dani was shouting, "You can't do this, Blake!" Rusty ran outside also, then jumped off the porch and started barking at Blake, who stomped his foot in front of him, scaring the dog. Rusty retreated back to the porch and Luke scooped him up.

"What in the hell is going on here?" Jayne shouted. She was staring at Blake, who resumed shoving their suitcases into the back of a taxi.

"Blake has so kindly packed your bag and says you're going back with him," Dani said.

Jayne felt panic rise up and catch in her chest, but a sense of relief tickled the back of her mind as if the decision was made. "Blake, what the hell is wrong with you?" she said calmly. "Please remove my suitcase from the car. I'm sorry about last night but *I* can't leave right now." Dani looked at Luke but neither said anything. "Please remove my suitcase," Jayne repeated, annunciating every word. This time the cab driver looked from Blake to Jayne. Again, no one moved.

"For ever-loving sake," Dani said "Will somebody

get the goddamn suitcase out from the trunk?" Luke started toward the car, following the command, but changed his mind and stopped when Blake turned around to face him. By then Jayne was already walking toward the car.

"I'm not going," Jayne said.

"Oh, you're coming," Blake said, grabbing her arm. Jayne let out a small yelp. Not from pain, but from shock at his aggression. Dani came down off the porch. Luke passed the dog back to Dani and, in what seemed like two steps, he was beside Blake and grabbing his shoulder. Jayne started to pull away. Blake let go of her and reeled around with a closed fist, missing Luke by a hair. Luke looked surprised but didn't have time to think as Jayne lost her step and fell back into him. The taxi driver was still watching the scene unfold, stunned in his place. Blake was huffing and puffing like a bull about to charge.

"Don't do it Blake. Take a damn breath," Dani said.

"I'm sorry, sir," Jayne said to the driver. He shrugged. Jayne got right up to Blake, looked up into his brown eyes, and calmly said with her southern accent coming out, "Blake, I am not coming back with you. I'm staying here and I won't have you forcing me against my will to get on a plane and abandon my family and my father's estate—which I still haven't figured out what to do with. You know better than anyone that I can't leave until this situation is resolved." She reached up to her grandmother's necklace and pinched it between her fingers, rocking it back and forth on the chain.

"So you're choosing this place, and *him,* over me?"

Jayne took a deep breath to collect her thoughts. "Well, I don't know if I would interpret it that way, but if that's the only way you see it—"

"Fine." He took out her suitcase, tossing it on the ground beside her. The bag fell on the wet rocks and mud. He reached back into the trunk and pulled out two paintings Jayne had brought with her.

"Blake, no—"

He gave a small satisfactory smile and tossed them next to the suitcase, the corners digging into the wet dirt. Luke walked over to pick them up and handed them to Jayne.

"I guess you're happy," Blake said to Luke. Luke didn't say anything and headed back to the porch. When Blake looked back at Jayne, she was holding out the engagement ring. He looked at her and down at the ring. He took it from her and turned to get in the taxi. The driver, still stunned, took a moment before nodding and forcing a polite smile at Jayne and getting in the car.

When Jayne turned around, Billy was standing beside the porch. He smiled at her, gave a slight nod, and headed to the back of the house.

Back in her bedroom, Jayne tried to collect her thoughts. She could hardly believe what had just happened. The thoughts washed through her mind and she wondered if she'd made the right choice. Billy was sitting silently in the rocking chair, but just his presence was comforting.

"You know, Bunny, I told you about how Evelyn had the option to marry someone else too, but she chose me."

"Is that supposed to make me feel better?" Jayne asked, twirling a piece of her hair.

"Well, she could've had an abundant life, full of superficial things: a big house, fancy china, and air conditioning" Billy laughed. "But it would've come with a penniless divorce because of a cheating husband who ended up cheating on both his wives. Instead, she had two beautiful children with me, that house out there, memories with our kids, deep laughs, and love that never ended or strayed from her bedside." He smiled at the thought.

Jayne smiled. "I forgot to give back the necklace from Blake." She picked it up off her end table.

Billy shrugged. "Keep it."

She looked around the room until she saw her old jewelry box. It had a small ballet dancer who popped up when it was opened and spun to music when it was wound. She placed the necklace among a few plastic, grocery store rings her dad used to buy for her. The chain coiled on top of the pendant as she dropped it in.

"Billy?" Jayne asked.

"Mm-hmm," he muttered, eyes closed, head resting in the chair.

"If you're here, where's Evelyn?" He opened his eyes to look at her. "I know she can cross over because you said she came with you even into the afterlife. Where did she go?"

Billy smiled. "She's here, Bunny, in a sense. But that's a story for another time."

Jayne understood and left Billy where he was, looking as if comfortably asleep in the rocking chair.

"Where's Luke?" she asked when she got downstairs.

Dani was snuggled up with Rusty on the couch, reading an old newspaper. "Well, he figured since Blake was able find his way out of town, the roads must be okay. He went to check the old bridge and said he'd be back in a minute." She gave Jayne a quick peek through the corner of her eye.

"What?"

"What?" Dani repeated.

"I saw that look." She stared at her mom from across the room.

Dani folded the paper in her lap. "Well, I suppose I'm just curious about what's going to happen now.

Are you and Luke going to become a couple? What really happened to start this?"

Jayne sighed and dropped into the couch. "I don't know. The more time I spend here, the more I don't want to leave. And it has nothing to do with Luke. I didn't even realize I might like him until last night when he kissed me."

"Ah-ha," Dani sat up straighter, hitting her leg with the paper.

"Blake saw the whole thing and I didn't do anything to rectify it." Jayne looked over her shoulder to Luke's truck pulling up the driveway. "He's back. I'm going to go talk to him." Dani nodded.

Jayne met Luke at his truck. He put it in park and popped the door open. "Everything okay?" he asked.

"Fine. I just needed a minute."

"Of course." He closed the door behind him. "Do you want a hug?"

"Actually, that would be really nice." Before she knew it, she was wrapped in his arms, her chest pressed against his warm body. If it had been any colder outside, there would've been steam rising off them. He didn't let go until Jayne pulled away. "I was just going to take a look at how the pecan trees are doing after the storm. You want to come look with me?"

"Lead the way."

They silently walked across the driveway into the large front yard. She could already see the litter of pecan nuts splayed all over the ground like shell casings in a war zone. Luke picked one up, examined it, and tossed it back down. He violently stomped on it with the heel of his cowboy boot, making Jayne jump. He bent down to pick it up, peeled away the outer layers, and handed her the broken nut. She took it from him and then he repeated the process with another. "You got a good haul of nuts this year. It must be the alternate year.

Pecan trees only produce large amounts of nuts every two years, but they can live to be over two hundred years old, so you have a bit of time to go."

"Really? I had no idea." She looked at the pecan in her hand. "What should we do with them all?"

"Lots of things. You could make a pie, let the kids come get them and take them to town, or do it yourself. There's a lady down the road that'll shell them for you if you want. She charges a couple cents a nut."

"Hmm, maybe I'll let the kids get them this year."

He placed the nut in his mouth and tossed the rest of the shell. She put one in her mouth too, tasting the familiar nutty flavor with a slight chalky texture to it.

"So," Luke started. He continued walking, unsure of Jayne's intentions in the field of pecans. "What now, Curly Sue?" He smiled and nudged her with his shoulder.

"Funny, my mom asked me the same thing." She kept up pace with him, kicking some fallen nuts. "I don't know for sure, but I think I'll stay here."

"Is that so?" A smile forced its way onto his face and he focused ahead.

"It is," she said. "I can't fathom giving this place up, not to mention the shop and the history here. And Billy." She immediately regretted saying his name out loud. It was meant to stay inside her head. "I'm just not done finding out more about my family and this town. The Carter house was just a start." They circled around a tree.

"Well, I'm happy to hear it. I think you made a good choice." They got back to the driveway, to Luke's truck. "I'll leave you to it. I should probably head back to my parents' place. It sounds like they got a bit of water in their laundry room."

"Oh no. Do you need help with anything?" Jayne asked.

Luke smiled and kicked another pecan. "They'll be okay. It's nothing to worry over. I'll call you later?" She nodded and Luke gave her an innocent kiss on the cheek.

She watched him drive off before heading back inside.

31

INSIDE, JAYNE FOUND herself alone while her mom got ready, Rusty snoring at her feet.

She sat on the couch for a moment listening to the silence of the house, thinking. Her foot was bouncing anxiously, and the familiar piece of hair was twisted around her finger. She was restless and couldn't figure out why. Finally being alone again was giving her the want to just do something, to figure something out. She thought about the files in the kitchen that she still had to go through but felt no pull. She thought again about some of the cupboards and storage spots in the house and again felt no desire.

You have one more place you haven't looked, she heard a voice say. It wasn't Billy and didn't seem entirely her own. It was as if someone had just placed the thought in her mind. She got up and followed her thoughts up the stairs and to the end of the hall.

She stood before the closed door, her ribs flexing with each thump of her heart. She didn't want to go in, but unless she was going to sell the house or board up that section like the Winchester Mystery House, she had to go in there.

Slowly, she reached out and took hold of the time-polished wooden knob. There was a small click when she turned it to the left and then a creak as she slowly opened it. The door swung open when she let go of the handle and a breeze whispered by. She realized her eyes were squeezed shut. The thought of an open window crossed her mind and she worried that the rain may have come inside.

When her eyes focused, everything was still with no windows open. She breathed in deep. The air smelled of cologne, old wood, and dirty laundry. The pungent, sweet-sour undertone that lingered at the end of each breath reminded her of the smell of one's skin after a weekend bender and she felt a wave of nausea creep up from the drinking the night before.

Everything was in the same place as it had been when she was younger: the bed was to the left, with a desk straight ahead with the window above it casting shadows from the clutter on top. The bathroom was to the far right, beside the walk-in closet. She took in the smaller details like the stripped bed, missing mattress, and a glass of evaporated water on the nightstand with a pair of reading glasses and an empty tumbler.

There was a pile of laundry halfway in and out of the bathroom. The hallway bathroom door clicked and Dani called Jayne's name. It was more of a statement than a question.

"I'm in here," she answered. Her eyes caught the pictures on the dresser and she moved to pick one up.

Dani came up behind her, smelling of hibiscus and lime. "That was you when you were about two." She took the frame out of Jayne's hands. "It was hot as hell during the summer, so we set up the sprinkler and you had a blast."

Jayne looked at the photo again. It was of a small girl wearing a polka-dot bikini, half wet with unruly sun-bleached hair and sun-kissed skin the color of Earl Grey tea with milk. She was squinting into the camera, holding a piece of watermelon, happy as could be.

Jayne looked at a few more photos and grabbed one from the back. The frame must have been real silver judging from how tarnished it was. A black-and-white photo of a family of four—husband and wife and two small kids—stood in front of the old house. There were pots of flowers framing the steps and everything looked brand new. Jayne recognized Billy and the woman beside him. She looked closer at Evelyn.

"Wow, it's been a while since I've seen this. It was tucked away in a box. Your dad must have fished it out. You look just like her," Dani said.

"That man, that's Billy, Dad's great-grandfather. He's the one I told you about, from the article. That must be his wife Evelyn and their two boys, Ted and Gerry."

"How do you know that?"

"Oh, I guess just the stuff I've been looking through lately." Jayne put the photo down and walked over to the seat in the window beside the bed.

"Do you remember when you were younger and you had that imaginary friend?" Dani said, straightening the photos.

Jayne blinked twice. "I suppose so."

"Do you still see him?" Dani asked very abruptly.

"What?" Jayne asked, trying to sound surprised.

"Do you still see him?" Dani repeated. "I've heard you talking to someone in your room and your eyes move around the room sometimes when it's just us. There have been a few other times when I've noticed you talking to what seems like yourself." Dani sat beside Jayne in the window seat.

Jayne didn't know what to say. She didn't know if she wanted to admit everything or deny it. She wanted to tell her mom the truth, but what if that made her look like a loony?

"Because I've seen him too," Dani said.

"You've seen him?" Jayne asked.

"Three times. And *her* once. Once when you were first born. I think he was around a lot; I never felt alone with you and one night you were fussing. You must have been about two months old. I got up, extremely tired and only half-awake. The veil between the real world and the spirit must have been thin because you were in the bassinet right here" — Dani pointed to a spot beside the bed — "and he was sat where you are now, in the window. His knees were drawn up to his chest, ankles crossed, arms around his legs — like how he sits on the banister out front. That's the other time I've seen him, just a few days ago. It's only glimpses I see before he disappears, but I got a look at the hat and the suspenders and I know it's him." She nodded to the picture.

Jayne was in shock; she really did see him. "When was the other time? You said there were three times and you've seen Evelyn?"

"Oh, yeah. It was before you were born. I was sick, really sick, some kind of flu. I hadn't been able to get out of bed for days. I could barely stay awake. I couldn't even get up to go see Dr. Marsh; he had to come here. Anyway, it was one of the nights, I'd been in and out of sleep, having fever dreams and sweating through pairs of pajamas. I woke up, soaking wet, and there was this woman standing over me. She was smiling. I wasn't scared at all. In fact, I felt calm. I thought, 'This must be it, she's come for me.' Instead she placed a hand on my forehead and for the first time in days I fell into a deep sleep and woke up feeling more like myself. She looked *just like you* now that I think about it." She placed her cold hand to her forehead.

Jayne looked at her mom for a long time. "That's incredible. I thought I was the only one. What about Dad? He had me going to those doctors when I was little. I know you couldn't tell him you were seeing things too, but how come I still had to go?"

"I have nothing to say except that it was easier that way. I didn't know what I was seeing, I didn't know if I was crazy either. He didn't talk to me like he talked to you; I didn't know his name. And you know your dad. He was hardheaded, stubborn, and only believed in what he could touch with his hands. I didn't like it though. He knew that, but he didn't care. He made it sound like a discussion we were having, but he would have already made the appointment. He just cared about you so much. He was overly cautious that way, always making sure there was nothing wrong. He was a bit of a hypochondriac like that. You only had two appointments before we left. Though, I'm sure he took you when you came to visit without me."

"He did," Jayne said.

"Where is Billy now?" Dani asked, looking around the room.

"I don't know. He's probably out at the old house. He likes it there since that's where he grew up."

"Oh, the old house," Dani said remorsefully. "Have you seen it since last night? It looks pretty damaged."

"I've only seen it from the porch. I don't know if we can fix it."

"We can try." Dani stood and helped Jayne up.

"I don't know if it would be worth it."

Dani gave her a soft smile. "Let's go get a movie. I think we could use it, and Rusty too. You can work on some of your social media stuff or painting too."

"That's a great idea."

They drove into town to the rental box at the convenience store. In the car Jayne turned to Dani and with a soft voice said, "Billy told me about the affair."

Dani took in what she said with a deep breath, but didn't look at her.

"He told me about Melody, and how Anthony heard Dad over the phone."

"Why did he tell you?"

"Why didn't *you* tell me?"

"It wasn't important. Your father was a good man, he cared about *you*, and that's all that matters. I didn't need to taint his reputation or your relationship with a few details."

Jayne rubbed her neck. "I guess Billy just figured I ought to know. Plus I made him tell me. I ran into Melody's son at the bar when I went with Luke. He was saying some things. I asked Billy about them and he confirmed it. He didn't want to, but I made him tell me the whole story so I wouldn't get it confused."

"I see," Dani said. It was raining again. The windshield wipers struggled to keep up. The charcoal clouds were fluffy and gray, making it feel later than it was. "Are you surprised?"

"Not really, I guess," Jayne said. "It's common and I don't see why our family should be immune to it. I *am* sorry it happened to you though." Dani shrugged. "I'm proud of you for leaving. I think our life would have been a lot different if you'd have stayed."

"I think you're right, kid." Dani paused. "I'm proud of you for not staying too."

Jayne smiled but raised her eyebrows in question. "Thank you. I thought you liked Blake, though?"

"I did. But you need to follow your heart. Grandma Reina liked your dad a lot, but when everything happened, she changed."

"I see." Jayne looked out the window.

"You need to be happy for the rest of your life," Dani said. "Not just a few years."

Jayne reached out to squeeze Dani's hand. "Where are you going by the way?" She noticed they were headed to Main Street instead of home.

"I thought we might stop and grab coffee and a muffin."

The Café was very quiet with Liz behind the counter and one customer sitting by the window. The lack of music brought attention to the silence.

"We weren't sure if you would be open or not," Dani said.

Liz turned around from preparing a pot of coffee. "We just . . . Jesus, Joseph . . . Dani." She rubbed her short blond hair. "Joe told me he'd seen you. I was hoping you'd stop by." She rushed around the counter, wiping her hands on her apron.

Dani embraced her tightly. "I'm sorry I haven't seen you sooner. We came by the other day but you weren't here."

Liz waved her hand. "We've all been busy." She looked at Jayne and pulled her in for a hug.

"Luke told me you had some flooding in your laundry room. Is everything okay?"

"Oh yes, nothing that Joe can't handle. I'm more worried about the people on the outskirts, at the bottom of the valley. I heard they have pretty bad flooding. Minimal home damage but their belongings and cars are toast." She crossed her arms. "I'm actually here to take some inventory of what I need to make some muffins and sandwiches to take down to them. Some of the people who had to leave their homes are in the high school gymnasium right now. They won't be able to see how much damage they've had until the rain stops for good."

"Is there anything we can do?" Jayne asked.

"I'm sure we could think of something," Dani said.

"What if we donated some of our older pieces and auctioned off some others to raise money? If the guys are willing, we could throw together some easy tables and chairs—nothing fancy, but we could sell them for the cost of the materials. We can donate time, tools, and scrap materials."

"That's a great idea," Liz and Dani both said.

"Liz, can you get Joe to contact some of the guys and see who's willing to help? When I get home, I'll send out some messages and do some marketing for it. Do you think we could do this by the end of tomorrow or the next day?"

"That's my plan," Liz said.

"Okay, let's talk later then."

Liz smiled. "What can I get y'all?"

They took a couple coffees and muffins to go. The rain was coming down harder and they didn't want to get stuck on the wrong side of the river.

They arrived back at the house just in time for the rain to stop.

"So you're going to stay?" Dani asked, helping Jayne with the coffee.

"I think so. I think I've made up my mind."

"That's exciting," Dani said with a hint of surprise in her voice. "I'm happy for you."

Jayne stopped at the porch. "I'm going to walk around to the old house, assuming I can get there." Dani nodded and went inside. Jayne walked around between the shed and the house. She started noticing things: the frayed hose, chipped blue paint, and unused garden space with plants long gone, only holding onto the ground by the thinnest roots. *These are all things I'm going to have to take care of,* she thought.

The grass squished with each step, pooling water around the soles of her shoes and making a slurping sound every time she took the next step. When she rounded the back of the house, she saw how high the creek was. It had gone down from the night before, contained to its banks, but just barely; it lapped over the sides at the curves. The bridge across had less than an inch of space to let the water pass through underneath. She had two options: make the effort to try and cross, risking some kind of collapse, or she could go back to the big house and call Billy to come there.

She walked around to the other side of the big house where a couple pecan tree limbs were dripping out over an old cement bench; the yellowing leaves could almost touch her head. *Perfect,* she thought. The bench was wet and she started to take her sweater off to dry it, but when the cool air touched her bare arms, she reconsidered and used her hand instead. She closed her eyes and asked for Billy. After a few moments she called again . . . and again. She could hear the birds chirping in the trees, checking on each other, enjoying the pause in the rain. Finally, when she opened her eyes, she saw Billy had crossed the bridge from the old house. He waved and she waved back.

Billy sat in the droplets of water on the bench, his weightlessness leaving each rounded droplet unchanged.

"What's up, Bunny?" he asked. "You okay? How'd your errand go?"

"It was fine," she said. "I actually just really needed to talk to you." Billy looked at her quizzically, like he was about to be in trouble for something he didn't know about. Jayne used her coffee to warm her hands. "I told my mom about you." Billy stared forward. "She believes me. She's seen you. She's seen Evelyn too." Jayne smiled.

He looked back at her then, surprised. "She has? Recently?" His hands became still on his legs and his back went as stiff as a two-by-four during a hard freeze.

"No, no," Jayne said. "Years ago. Before I was born." Billy's shoulders loosened. "Mom said I looked just like her." A water droplet dripped off the leaves above onto her lap. She watched the droplet soak into her jeans, making a small dark circle.

"I guess that makes sense now," Billy said, eyes off to the corner, thinking.

"What makes sense?" Jayne asked.

"Your mom's friend, the kooky one, what's her name? She always had short hair, lots of rings on all her fingers — she would be like a gypsy or fortune-teller in my time."

Jayne laughed. "Suzanne."

"Yes, that's her. I remember she had a name that sounded like it was out of the *Great Gatsby*. Anyway, your mom, I guess, had told her about some encounters with 'ghosts' in the house because she came into the house one day, waving around a big thing of dried leaves they'd lit on fire. They kept walking around the house saying things like, 'Be gone negative energy,' and asking to fill rooms with certain things like happiness and health. It smelled something foul. I had to leave the house for days until the stench was finally gone." Billy scrunched his nose in the memory.

"Sage? They smudged the house?" Jayne laughed. "They were trying to get rid of you. I didn't realize that's how it works. You can smell things?"

"No, normally I can't. I could smell *that* though,

and it smelled like a rotten fish in a pile of garbage left out for months. It was unbearable. I don't know why anyone would want to wave that around their house."

"That's not actually what it smells like," Jayne said. "It's more like . . . like marijuana."

"Oh," Billy chirped. "You've used this?"

"No. Well yes, a few times in the apartment. It's supposed to cleanse the air and get rid of negative energy. You're supposed to do it a few times a month or something. I always forgot though."

"I see. Well, I'm certainly glad your mom didn't do it again."

After a moment, Jayne glanced at him through the corner of her eye and took a slow sip of her coffee. "Billy, what happened to Evelyn?" A gust of wind blew from behind them, tossing some strands of hair around her face. She used her damp hands to smooth them back.

"She died in her sleep," he replied.

"You know what I mean," she said. "After."

"I'm not sure how to explain it. She's gone; she felt a calling and had to go." Billy was being tentative with his words and Jayne could tell.

"A calling? Was she trying to be an actress?" Jayne was trying to be funny but only received a lopsided smirk. "Billy, what do you mean?" she asked again.

"There was a family—a couple—who for a few years had been trying to have a child. It was affecting their life, their marriage, and their happiness. She had the ability to take the form of that child, so to speak; to provide that family with the child they longed for."

The air swirled around them, mixing warm with cold, throwing the sound of rustling trees all around them.

Jayne let her loose hairs swirl around her face, her

hands too heavy to move. Putting two and two together, she asked, "So, Evelyn is me? I'm Evelyn?"

"Something like that. You're still *you*, but Evelyn, as I know her, is your soul, in a way, if that makes any sense." Billy pressed the tips of his fingers to his head.

Jayne thought for a moment. "So what happens when I die? To my soul, I mean. Will it be me or Evelyn?"

"Your soul is just a soul, remembering every life it's taken. Some take many lives, some take one. When you 'die,' you'll become a soul again. I refer to that soul as Evelyn because that's what I knew her as. We're soul mates and have been through many lives together, and some without."

"So, I'm without my soul mate—you—in this physical life?" Jayne said, with hurt in her voice.

Billy smiled to reassure her. "Right now, yes. But a soul mate can take any form, not just a lover. They could be a sister, a cousin, a best friend."

"Will you take on a human form in my lifetime? And would we even be able to find each other?" Jayne's mind was spinning like a merry-go-round, different thoughts hopping on at each turn.

"I told Evelyn I would wait for her. But, I guess I can never say never." He shrugged.

"If you came back in my lifetime, you'd be at least twenty-five years younger than me."

"That's correct. I'd have to be born, so to speak."

Jayne nodded. "Then I would die and my soul would be waiting for you. It would be a vicious cycle. Or would she go on again?"

"That's up to her."

Jayne crossed her arms. "This is all very uncertain." She forced a chuckle. Billy shrugged. "Do you . . . do you love me like you loved her?"

Billy thought. "No. It's different. It's the love you

feel when you've created a child, when you and your spouse have created something that is part of you. You come from my blood line — hers too. But the connection is stronger because she *is* you. I love you like you are *my* child."

Jayne nodded again. "This is so surreal. Is this why I can see you?"

"Perhaps. Or you could just be open to the other side. You know your friend, Luke, he can see me too. Well, he sort of can. It's not the same. He tries not to, but when he has his guard down he catches glimpses of me."

"How do you know?" Jayne barely squeaked out. She felt like her heart was about to flip along with her stomach. She hadn't realized that Billy knew.

"It's just like when someone you haven't seen in a long time suddenly appears in front of you. You double take, half stare, and forget what you were talking about. That happens when he sees me." When Jayne didn't say anything, Billy continued. "I haven't said anything to him. That's why he doesn't know for sure. I don't think he wants to see me."

"He told me he's seen you. It scared him. He's seen things in his house too. He's sensitive to those things. Are there other . . ." Jayne searched for the right word. "Spirits?"

"Sure. I assume so. I haven't seen any. As far as I know, I'm stuck to that house." He pointed to the small house.

"Have you tried to leave?" Jayne asked.

"Once, when your father was going to take you to the doctor after you mentioned seeing me. I tried to get in the car with you. The truck moved and I stayed, sitting in midair like genie."

Jaynie laughed. "Have you tried to walk off the property? Or just appear somewhere else?"

"No, I haven't needed to. But it's also a scary thought. What if I couldn't get back?"

"One day we should try," Jayne said excitedly.

"Jayne?" Dani was calling her name from the back deck. Both Jayne and Billy looked that way.

"Go on, Bunny." He jutted his chin toward the deck. "I'll be here when you want to talk."

"Thank you, Billy." She got up and wiped the cold, damp seat of her pants with her hands. "I'm over here, Mom! I'm coming!" Jayne shouted. When she rounded the corner, Dani was smiling and waiting for her at the top of the steps.

1992

The night was chilly but they couldn't feel it like the living could. They could see it in the bend and flex of the branches when the wind blew. The sound was crisp from the cold, not muted by summer's humidity.

Just like every night, they sat in the rocking chairs on the porch of the old house, talking and laughing about memories from their old lives. They talked about how much they missed their children and grandchildren. Sometimes they would run about the yard, playing tag, or would lie in the grass, looking up at the stars just to get back that old feeling of life. Tonight they were quiet; the conversation was as absent as the daylight.

"I want to speak to you about something, darling," Evelyn said, not looking at Billy.

"Okay," Billy said cautiously.

"Peter and Dani are having fertility issues."

"I know."

"I want to help them," Evelyn said and habitually cleared her throat, waiting for a reply.

"How do you intend to do that?" Billy asked, not taking his eyes off of her.

"I've been doing some thinking, and I believe I can *become* their child." Only now did she look at Billy. He'd stopped rocking and his eyes were wide and staring at her.

"How so?" he asked.

She explained how she could become the energy needed to create a life in Dani. "I've tried it once."

"You've tried?" Billy asked, shocked and annoyed.

"Yes," she replied, talking to her hands resting in her lap. "I did it once. But I got scared and, well, I couldn't leave you without saying anything."

"Well, I'd say so."

"I just know if I can stay in there long enough, I can bond at conception." Neither of them said anything. "But that means I would be gone. Gone from here, gone from you, alive again."

"There are so many what-ifs, though. What happens if she loses the baby again? What would happen to you?"

"Well, I don't—"

"What if it doesn't work altogether? There are so many questions." He closed his eyes and shook his head.

Evelyn pulled on a curl. "But what if it *does* work? They'll have a baby finally and maybe they'll live happily ever after. And the Webber name will go on."

"Unless it's a girl and she gets married," Billy said under his breath.

"Well, yes, but she would still have the blood. And the child would get the land and the houses."

"But, what about me?" he asked softly.

"Oh, darling." Evelyn got up out of her chair and

knelt in front of him, clutching his hands. "I love you so much. I can't bear to leave you, but I've spent over a hundred years with you on this land. I need to do something good, something for our family, before it dwindles out like a candle flame at the end of its wick. Would you please just let me try? I'll come back to you when I leave that body, if you're still here. Or you can come to me," she said excitedly. "You can come as another child and be my sibling." She smiled at him. "We would be the best of friends."

Billy thought hard, breathing deeply. His grip loosened and he placed a hand on her face. "I love you so much, you know that." She nodded. "And one of the things I love most about you, behind your youthful beauty and wits" — she laughed — "is your altruism. You've never just done something for yourself. When will you? Probably never." He chuckled. "I can't deny you this because it would be the greatest gift you could give. But how on this earth — and beyond it — am I to live without you? I'll be bored out of my mind. You know how slowly time passes here." His eyes dropped. She pressed her cheek into his palm. "When will you go?"

"The next time they take to the bedroom, I suppose." She hadn't thought of this. How much time would they have together?

"I was afraid you would say that." He nodded toward the shadows moving, touching, and groping in the master bedroom window.

Evelyn looked up at the big house and back at Billy, her eyes wide, pleading, but soft around the edges. "I love you, Mr. Webber. I won't forget you. I can't."

He kissed her and then helped her to her feet. He wrapped his arms around her, squeezing so tight she wouldn't have been able to breathe if she were in her human body. A tear rolled down Billy's face and when it hit the deck, it made a watermark. They both looked at it; that was the first time either of them had made condensation. She looked at him, took in his sadness, and kissed his cheek.

"Go," he said. "Go now before it's too late and I change my mind." He watched her as she floated backward toward the big house, a look of concern on her face. He forced a smile. She turned and looked to the window and disappeared.

Billy sat back in the rocker and waited. He waited there, in that chair, through twenty-one sunsets and twenty-two sunrises. On the morning of the twenty-second, he heard a scream from the house. He looked up and saw Dani run out to the patio—to Peter, who was drinking his coffee. She was clutching something and when she showed Peter, he jumped up, spilling his coffee on the table, and picked her up to twirl her around. They kissed and hugged again before Peter knelt down and kissed her belly.

Billy watched. He knew he should feel excited, but still selfishly hoped that Evelyn would return to him. For the next nine months, he watched as Dani's belly grew. He wandered around the house and yard, waiting. Waiting until nine months later when he would finally experience a life again. When the child was born, something about that child brought happiness and love straight back into his being like an electric jolt from a bolt of lightning. When he looked down upon her newborn eyes, just barely seeing, he was no longer alone; she was with him again.

32

2017

THE WIND WAS starting to die with the rain. Dani warmed the muffins and grabbed their coffee to take out on the deck. The sweaters and big socks they'd bundled themselves in kept them warm in the chilly air. Rusty sat patiently at Jayne's feet, waiting for some crumbs to be tossed his way.

"So, what are we going to do about the old house?" Dani asked.

Jayne looked out at the half-collapsed house. She sighed. "I don't know. There's really no point in fixing it for another storm to take it down again. If it wasn't for Billy I'd tear it down myself."

"What do you mean?" Dani asked, with a mouth full of muffin.

"That seems to be his home. He goes there when he doesn't hang around the house. He's attached to it."

"Ah, I see."

"Maybe we could tear it down and rebuild it. You could live there," Jayne said.

"Me?"

"Yes, you. " Jayne leaned over and bumped Dani with her shoulder.

"But Grandma . . . she needs me right now; I can't go anywhere."

"Well, if you're open to it, we can just plan for it." There were a few things Jayne didn't feel like talking about right now and the inevitable passing of her grandmother was one of them.

Dani smiled. "Well, kiddo, I think that might be good. If you don't mind having your mother living with you."

"I wouldn't want it any other way. I would actually prefer it to you living far away."

"Me too." Dani grabbed Jayne's plate. "I found another box of documents. Do you want to see something?"

"Heck yeah." Jayne got up.

Dani had already put them on the kitchen table and had taken out a document that was folded into quarters to be the size of a normal sheet of paper. She let Jayne open it up and spread her hands over the weathered paper.

"It's a property survey," Dani said. "Look here at these lines. That's the edge of the property." Dani drew a finger around the dotted lines surrounding the property.

"I always thought the property ended where those trees started. She drew another line a few inches in. This goes at least twenty more feet on every side. At least forty on that back side. How old is this?"

Without looking at the date, Dani replied, "Probably right after this house was built."

Jayne traced her finger around the lines, mapping the property in her mind. "Wait, what's this?" Her finger rested on a small square at the far corner, past what would be considered the property. "It looks like an outbuilding of some kind. Maybe a shed? It's almost as big as the garage but too small for a car. Why would it be at the back of the property, hidden away?"

"I imagine it was probably for the old house. It could be for the water pumps, maybe? No, that's too far away. I didn't even know it was there." Dani said, surprised with all the years she had lived here.

Jayne got up and walked out to the porch. She squinted, trying to see if it was still there.

"I can't see anything out there," Dani said.

"Me neither. I wish we could get across that bridge," Jayne said, disappointed. She thought for a moment. "I'm going to call Luke. He just mowed over there the other day. He may have seen it."

Luke picked up after two rings. "Hey Jayne, what's up?"

"Hey. Um, I had a question. When you were mowing the other day, did you happen to notice a small building, like a shed at the back of the property? Toward the back, past the line of trees, in another little wooded area?"

Luke paused to think. "I can't say I remember for certain. There are a lot of trees back there."

"Hmm, okay. Thanks anyway. Mom and I were looking at the property survey and noticed that there's a small shed-thing noted back in the trees but we can't get back there right now with all the past rain."

"Oh. Well I wish I could remember better. I had my headphones in and wasn't paying attention. Sorry."

"No problem. Thank you anyway."

Jayne went back into the kitchen and relayed the message to Dani. "Wait, there's someone else I can ask. Just a minute."

"Where are you going?" Dani asked as Jayne was making her way to the back porch.

"Billy," she said quickly and softly. She went and

looked at the old house, cast in the gray shadows of the clouds that were just about gone. She asked for Billy to come to her and within a few seconds he appeared next to her.

"What's up?" he said, standing beside her, mimicking her position of crossed arms, leaning on the balcony.

"Mom found a land survey and it shows a small shed-like structure in the back, over there." She pointed to about where the shed would be. "I'm wondering if it's still there and what it's for."

Billy chuckled. "It's still there."

"What's funny?" Jayne asked.

He pointed to the full creek. "Did you ever wonder why this creek here is called Whiskey River? It's hardly a river and has nothing to do with whiskey."

"I didn't realize it had a name," she said, surprised.

"Well, that shed you're asking about, it still stands. It was built in the twenties. Did you learn about what happened in the twenties?"

She thought for a moment. "Prohibition." A shed hidden away in the woods now had a different meaning.

"Bingo. That there was a whiskey shed. It stands empty now, but it held gallons of illegal whiskey made in Glen Rose and distributed throughout the towns from Dallas to Houston."

"Your dad was a runner?" Jayne asked.

"Oh heck no," Billy replied. "He drank too much of the stuff. He couldn't even run to the end of the drive if he wanted to." Billy laughed. "He was smart though. He knew a guy in Glen Rose who was trying to expand his business beyond Dallas and Fort Worth and Dad knew people because of the furniture shop. This guy had people scattered throughout The Hill Country that would store it for him and then either Dad or this guy would provide runners to take it from place to place.

Sometimes they'd store it in the furniture that he was delivering, but that was more risky."

"The whole thing was risky."

"Nothing was sold on this property. Dad was very clear about that; he was living with us at the time and he didn't want to go to jail or implicate us. I don't think he enjoyed working for his guy in Glen Rose. Or maybe he was being blackmailed."

"You're kidding."

"I'm not," Billy replied.

"Why do you think it was blackmail?" Jayne asked.

"Too often Dad would talk about how he wished the guy would just get caught. The guy was a sheriff, you know. He was a sheriff making moonshine and distributing it. Can you imagine?" Billy shook his head. "Dad skimmed off the whiskey store, though. That was his payment and he was happy with that— being an alcoholic and all.

"He tried to keep that business a secret from my brother and me. We knew what was going on, but we didn't know the details because Dad didn't want us to get busted if anything happened."

"What about your mom?" Jayne asked.

"Mom died when we were teenagers. That's one of the reasons Dad took to the drink so easily." Jayne nodded. "One of Dad's best runners was Rafael Martin. He didn't make a lot of money working for the Carters so dad hired him to bootleg. It should have been obvious: this poor Mexican worker with worn clothing, driving a beautiful car with an engine that could match a team of horses."

"Martin? Is he related to Luke?" Habit made her reach out to put a hand on Billy's arm. They both watched it go right through and land on the balcony. She pulled it back and tucked it in the crook of her elbow.

"Now that you mention it, I bet he is," Billy said. He

stood up straight in realization. "In fact, I'm positive he is. You'll have to do some digging on that one."

"So did your dad get caught?"

Billy turned around and leaned on the balcony. "Almost. He had a few close calls with police coming to the house, asking about runners in the area. Usually my brother James and I would speak to them so Dad wouldn't have to get involved. He wasn't a very good liar and being past drunk himself wasn't a good look. Usually we'd intervene and pretend like he had a mental disability. He played along well as long as he kept far enough away they couldn't get a good whiff of him.

"Once, he was caught coming back from the shed. Luckily he didn't have anything on him He was able to tell them that he had just come home from the shop and was tending to the cows. We didn't have cows." Billy laughed. " But no, he didn't get caught. The sheriff did though. He was among thirty-plus people from Glen Rose to Waco who got caught and sentenced in August 1923. Dad's store was never found. He depleted a lot of it himself and gave some of it away as gifts or payment for services until it was gone. No one knew it was there. I forgot about it myself until now."

"I can't believe it," Jayne said. "I need to see it. But in the meantime, I'm not sure what I'm going to do about your house." She furrowed her brow, sympathy showing on her face. "I talked to Mom and we want to rebuild it. For her to live in," she added. "How would you feel about that?"

Billy thought for a moment. Jayne watched his profile, looking for hints. "Well, I don't know, Bunny. I'm honestly not happy about losing my home, but it makes no sense to keep it standing for a ghost. I would say go for it. It would be lovely to have you and your mom back here again."

"What about Evelyn? Will she find her way back?"

"Yes. I am her anchor and she is mine. It doesn't matter where we are."

"Will anything happen to you if we rebuild?" Jayne asked.

"I don't think so. I can stay in this house too, if I wanted to."

"Okay," Jayne replied. "And you will stay? I couldn't imagine living here if you left."

"Yes, I would," Billy said matter-of-factly.

"Okay, good. Well, I should get back inside."

Dani had been waiting, taking up the corner of the sofa, wrapped in blankets with a glass of red wine in one hand and piece of dark chocolate in the other. Jayne saw the chocolate bar on the table and snapped off two pieces. She snuggled next to Rusty on the floor where Dani had set up her canvases, propped on a makeshift easel of books. Rusty turned his body just enough to wedge his small form between her leg and the floor. Dani passed the glass of wine to her.

Jayne shook her head. "I'm good."

Dani didn't push it. She listened to what Jayne had to say while Jayne pushed her brush into the colors on her pallet, mixing and pulling the colors, transferring them onto the canvas. By the time the movie had finished, she had the pecan tree nearly finished. It felt good to paint again.

33

JAYNE WAS WOKEN up by the shrill ring of a landline telephone. She habitually looked at the time, 3:18 a.m. She jumped at the next ring and got out of bed, stumbling to get to a phone. *I don't know where any of the phones are,* she thought. The ringing stopped and she heard her mom speaking to someone. She opened her door and heard Dani say, "We'll be right there."

"What is it?" Jayne asked before her mom had a chance to say anything.

"The window alarm has been set off at the shop. It sounds like maybe someone has smashed it."

"Let's go. I'll try and call Joe." Jayne didn't change out of her sweatpants and oversized university sweatshirt. Instead, both she and Dani threw on some shoes and hurried out of the house.

Joe's car was already there when they arrived, along with two police cruisers. The alarm company had called them too. When Jayne got out of the car she spotted Luke and suddenly became hyperaware of her mess of hair and the random holes in her pajamas. She groaned.

As they got closer, she could see the smashed window and the graffiti across the entire front of the shop; just one big, long streak of spray paint extending from the corner of the building to the store. The glass panel of the front door was broken too, but the door behind it was still locked.

"Ms. Webber?" the male police officer asked.

"Yes, sir."

"Well, it looks like everything done here was superficial. No one actually tried to enter anywhere. Looks like they were just out for some late-night trouble making."

The female police officer approached. "Do you have security cameras?" she asked.

Jayne looked to Joe and he nodded.

They all went inside and stepped into Peter's office. They stood around, shoulder to shoulder, packed like a can of sardines while the computer buzzed and whirred when started up. Luke took Jayne's hand and led her out to the main office.

"I think I know who did this," he said.

"You do? How?"

"It's not the first time. That's the reason we got the cameras in the first place."

"Who then?" Jayne asked.

"Frankie."

"Frankie? Why would he want to vandalize the shop?"

"The first time, I found out through the grapevine. He was pissed because your dad wouldn't give him a job."

"Why this time though?" Jayne was tired but the adrenaline had her wide-awake.

"I don't have a clue." He pulled Jayne in for a hug. It caught her off guard, but she was grateful for it and glad she took the time to brush her teeth. She wrapped her arms around Luke's chest.

They heard some chatter in her dad's office, so they went back in. The grainy black-and-white video showed two men in hoodies running up to the building. One streaked spray paint across the front while the other smashed the windows.

Luke groaned and everyone looked at him. "It's Frankie."

"You know these young men?" the woman police officer asked.

"Unfortunately I do. That's the son of the deceased owner's ex-girlfriend."

The cop scribbled something in her notepad. "And the other?"

Luke shook his head.

"Do you know where we can find them?" the male cop asked.

Joe cleared his throat and scratched his belly. "Frankie lives with his mom down off Lufkin Street. I can give you a relative address but I don't know the apartment number. She works at the hardware store though."

"Do you want to press charges?"

"Yes," Joe answered. "For now. We can drop them if need be, correct?"

"Correct."

"Then go ahead. File the charges."

They finished the paperwork they needed and by the time everyone was ready to go home, it was 5:15 a.m.

Joe returned to his office and started up his computer. "No sense in going home just to come back in an hour. How about you go get us some muffins and coffee from your mom's, kid? She'll just be opening up now." Luke stretched and moved to get up.

"I'll go," Dani said and Luke sat back down.

"Thanks Dani." Joe smiled and squeezed her hand. Joe turned to Luke. "Do we have any spray paint remover left?"

"I can check."

Jayne had been scribbling something on a half-torn envelope from Joe's desk. "Or, if you have some spray paint . . ." She turned the envelope around to show Joe and Luke. It was a just a doodle, but a doodle by an artist. They could see the makings of a mural: a picture depicting the scene from the bed set they'd just sold a few days ago. "We can remove it, *or* I can paint this. It was the last piece you and Dad finished." She looked at Luke and then to Joe.

After a moment, Joe smiled. "Kiddo, you are something else." He laughed and rocked back in his chair, which squeaked and groaned under his weight.

Jayne smiled. "I can get the supplies and start today. We'll just have to get the window fixed. And there's something else I wanted to talk to you about."

Jayne laid out her plan to help the people in the valley gut and rebuild part of their homes. They would need a small crew of men here building generic furniture with whatever wood they could, then a small crew in the valley to help whoever needed it. Liz would make sandwiches for them to take and Dani would be a runner. Jayne would blast out on social media and help wherever she could. She would paint some pieces and add them to the storefront where they would auction them off to raise money and help those affected locally and on the coast. In the meantime, once the sun came up, she would get started on the new mural on the front of the building. It would only take her a couple days, she said.

"What about Frankie?" Luke asked.

"I'm sure we'll hear from Melody soon enough," Joe said.

When the sun came up, Jayne went outside and snapped some pictures of the damage. She mentally traced the strip in which she would paint the scene of longhorns and cows. She thought of the colors she'd need. She was in her element again and buzzing with impatience to get started.

She blasted out a post across social media describing what had happened to the town and what the shop intended to do to help. She said in four days they would be holding the auction for the pieces and paintings. She requested the help of anyone who was willing and able. They could come to the shop and sign up to help in the valley, "No experience needed." She apologized for the inconvenience of the shop being closed for the following days, which would put a delay on any current works in progress.

By noon she had a few people signed up, the posts had been liked and shared over a dozen times, and people all over town were offering to chip in wherever they could. Business owners offered up their services, and restaurants donated time and food—some even offering to drive down to Houston and beyond with their food trucks or catering vans. Jayne could hardly believe it; all people needed was a little organization and direction and they were more than willing to help.

Jayne went to the hardware store to pick up some more paint and brushes. She saw Melody but didn't care to speak to her. She was unable to evade her though. Melody dashed toward her, stopping her midstride.

"I heard about the shop, Jayne. I'm so sorry."

Jayne gazed at her, wondering how much she knew and how much town gossip had spread already. "Well, you should probably talk to your son."

"I did. He admitted to it." Her voice was meek and breathy.

Jayne scoffed and reached for the necklace, pulling it back and forth on the chain.

"I don't have anything to say. But he did tell me that Mr. Manns paid him to do it. He needed the money and . . ." Realizing she was making excuses to the wrong person, she stopped.

Jayne let go of her pendant. "What? Why?"

"We think he wants the house and the shop, Jayne." Melody reached one of her fingers up to her mouth. Her nails were polished, but that didn't stop her from nibbling on it. "That's why he came to us in the first place—he thought it would be easier for us to get the house and he was going to pay us a lot of money. Then when he found out about you and it looked like you were going to stay in town, well, Frankie said he made a comment like, 'Maybe this would stop her.' "

"He thought vandalizing the shop would stop me from moving here?"

Melody shrugged. "Is there anything I or Frankie can do?"

Jayne blinked in surprise. "Yes. You can just stop. I'm not leaving."

"Oh—"

"Then I'll consider dropping the charges."

"Charges?" Melody squeaked.

I guess she didn't know too much, Jayne thought. "Yes, he's been charged. And he can come to the shop by the end of the day to find out how he can help us get this town back on track."

"He'll be there," Melody said.

Jayne walked away without saying anything. She gathered the things she needed and headed back to the shop.

Dani came back from the house and Jayne was grateful for the clothes and toiletries she brought since she'd been in her pajamas all day.

Jayne called Joe and her mom into the office to tell them what Melody told her.

"That doesn't make any sense," Joe said. "Why would doing this make us sell?"

"I think he thought that I wouldn't be able to handle it and would jump at selling."

Dani shook her head. "We need to talk to him."

Joe dug around the desk and pulled out his business card. He passed it to Jayne. She pulled out her phone and dialed the number. It rang twice before he picked up.

"Hi Mr. Manns, this is Jayne Webber. I was wondering if you would be able to come to the shop today. I wanted to discuss the offer you've been making."

Dani and Joe looked at her with matching confused expressions.

Jayne looked at her watch. "Yes, an hour from now is fine. Thank you." She hung up. "He'll be here at two."

"What's going on?" Dani asked.

"I thought he might be more inclined to show up if he was under the impression I was selling."

Dani stood up. "I'm just going to go with Ed to get some lunch for everyone."

"Ed Stalton?" Jayne looked at Joe and smiled.

"What?"

"Nothing." Jayne's smile betrayed her.

Joe pretended to be busy on the computer.

"It's nothing. He just asked if I could help him grab some lunch for the guys."

"Mm-hmm." Jayne smirked. "Coffee and lunch in the same week."

"Anyway, I better get going." She gave Jayne a kiss on the head and left.

Jayne was sitting in her dad's office when Frederick arrived. She was putting together some posts about the auction and the volunteering they were going to be doing. The lights were off and the blinds were half-closed—the only light coming through was from a crack in the blinds and the blue light glowing from the computer screen.

"Knock, knock," he said, standing in the doorway. The light from the hall behind him cast a shadow into the office.

"Mr. Manns, thank you for coming. Please have a seat."

He pulled out the wooden chair across from the desk and inspected it before giving it a quick brush off and seating himself. "What might you have beckoned me here for, Ms. Webber?"

"I understand you would like to purchase some of my father's estate?"

"You would be correct."

"What is your plan with the house and the shop?"

"Well, for the house, I wasn't going to change too much. I wasn't planning on tearing it down, if that was a concern of yours. At worst, I would just move it."

"You're confident you can move a two-story house built almost ninety years ago?"

"I would try my hardest. You've seen the Carter house—I kept it as is."

"I also understand there's more investment to be

had in a property like that, verses an old, middle-class house that hasn't been updated or renovated in over fifty years. Why do you want it?"

"Well, I'm in the process of acquiring the properties on either side of it and it doesn't make any sense to leave out the Webber property."

"I see." Jayne wasn't expecting that. She'd only met her neighbors briefly when they brought over some food and flowers when she first arrived. "And what about the shop?"

"Well, I can't guarantee the same promise with this building. It's prime real estate; it's historic, a gem in the town, and it's a corner lot. I've been trying to purchase this building from your father for years. He was rather stubborn and wouldn't budge." He leaned toward the table, his elbows on his knees, too comfortable for Jayne, but maybe that was the point.

Jayne could smell the coffee on his breath and could see his blond stubble like sand on his face. He jerked his head to toss a piece of hair out of his eyes. "But, I feel like you're a lot smarter than your father and can recognize a good deal when it's offered to you. Plus you don't have the silly attachment your dad did to this place. I'm prepared to offer you a handsome amount for both properties — more than I offered Peter — and he could have lived the rest of his life off that."

Jayne felt uncomfortable with the informality Mr. Manns took when speaking about her father. She also leaned forward, her elbows pressing into the hard, wooden table. "Well, you see, Frederick, my father didn't sell because he wasn't a stupid man, and I'm just as smart as he was. He didn't sell because he's not the only person invested in this company. Every single one of those men in that warehouse are invested in this company, the town, and its history."

"People can be bought, Jayne," he said, recognizing

all formalities were gone. "You've been here, what, a month? Where do you think their loyalties lie?"

Frederick's casual demeanor came across as rude rather than enticing, and Jayne was tired of it. "Not with someone who hires people to do their dirty work, like vandalize a historic town building."

Frederick jerked slightly, like a boxer who'd narrowly missed a jab. "I'm not sure what you're insinuating—"

"It doesn't matter, Mr. Manns." Jayne relaxed in her seat. "This isn't the first time there's been an attack on the shop and I'm sure it won't be the last, but I can assure *you* that this little charade that you put Frankie up to won't put a dent in anything you were trying to achieve. And to answer your question, no, I won't be selling any of my father's properties to you or anyone else. I wanted to bring you here to tell you in person that I won't be leaving. I'd like to work together in the future, if necessary, but if your behavior continues, I don't know how that will turn out—for you."

"I'm sure I will be fine, Ms. Webber." Mr. Manns smirked.

"I'm sure you will—as long as you leave us alone. I may be new here, but my closest friends have been here long enough that *you* are new to them."

"I see." Mr. Manns stood up, smiling and towering over her like a large, skinny oak tree. "I suppose I'm finished here then." Jayne didn't move to get up, so he turned toward the door. "Oh." He turned back to her. "Just in case you change your mind, this is what I was prepared to offer for both properties." He took the pencil out of her hand and wrote a one, then an eight, followed by five zeros. Jayne felt her stomach lurch and she briefly questioned her sanity.

She took the pencil back and said nothing.

"I can see myself out." Frederick nodded to Joe across the hall as he left.

Jayne looked over at Joe, who sat in his bright office. He raised his eyebrows.

She couldn't help but smile.

34

JOE AND JAYNE gathered everyone in the back of the shop while they were eating the sandwiches Dani and Ed brought back. It was chilly, but the walls guarded them from most of crisp wind. Joe's voice commanded the attention of everyone and they stopped talking.

Joe let Jayne explain what they wanted to do for the community.

"We will be closed for a week to help the town rebuild." There were some murmurs throughout the men. "You're still going to get paid. And I know that you are all paid mostly off of the commissioned pieces, but we will supplement that portion of your income for the week. Was anyone here affected by the storms?"

A beat of silence passed and then someone said, "Keith was."

Jayne addressed him. "Okay, Keith, you're welcome to use the week to help your family and do what you need to do, or you can help us. The choice is yours, but please don't feel obligated either way."

Keith nodded and mouthed, "Thank you."

Joe cleared his throat. "I'm sure you've noticed

what happened to the shop overnight. Keeping with complete transparency, as we always have, it was done by Frankie, Melody's son."

There was a chorus of groans from the men and someone said, "Little shit."

"The thing was," Jayne continued, "not that there's any excuse, but he was put up to it by Frederick Manns. Mr. Manns thought he could scare me out of keeping the shop and my dad's house. I'm not going to lie, he's made me a substantial offer." Jayne shook her head. "But, I've decided to stay. I'll need Joe's and all of your help in running this place, and I don't plan on making anything different than what my dad did here—unless there's anything *you* think I need to change. I'd like to spend some time with each of you in the upcoming days to get to know all of you and vice versa."

Jayne and Joe laid out the plan for the next week. Since each of the men had a different set of skills, she set up a sign-up sheet so each of them could help with different things. She was going to spend most of her time in the shop, putting together the auction and taking orders. Joe would lead the team in the village and Luke would run between the two where needed.

Jayne had been working on the mural for most of the day when she decided to take a break and go home to shower and change. Luke offered to give her a ride since Dani had taken the car home to take a nap.

The weight of the day sat heavy on her tired shoulders, and sleep tugged at her. It would have to wait though. She struggled to keep her eyes open in Luke's truck; the smell of his lavender air freshener was like a personal sleep-chariot whisking her off to the sandman.

The bumps and snaps of the rocks in the driveway jostled her more awake. She groaned and sat up straight, arching her back in a stretch. "Thank you for driving me."

"It's no problem. You should take a nap or something. We can take care of things for a bit."

"It's okay, I just need to get clean and grab a coffee. Thank you." She reached for the door handle and felt Luke's warm hand grasp her wrist lightly. She turned to look at him and he laced his fingers around hers.

"I have to . . ." He moved his hand to her arm and guided her closer, feeling no resistance.

Jayne let go of the handle and moved toward him. Her hand found the back of his neck and her lips were brought to his like a magnet. She melted into him and for a moment didn't know if she would ever part, but the car's heater was blowing on her face, making her overheat. She pulled away and smiled, averting her eyes from his.

"I've been wanting to do that for a while."

Jayne was blushing. "I better get going. I'll be back in a bit."

"Okay," Luke said soft enough that Jayne barely heard him.

The house was warm and somehow felt more welcoming than it had before. Dani was sitting at the kitchen table and Billy was sitting with her. He gave Jayne a sympathetic look and nodded toward Dani. Jayne knew something was wrong. She slid into the chair beside her and placed a hand on her back. Dani didn't flinch. She stared at the table, pressing her finger into the little worn dent.

"Is everything okay?"

Dani shook her head. "Grandma Reina is worse. She's mostly unresponsive. Anthony just called me a couple hours ago."

Jayne felt like she'd just taken a soccer ball to the chest. "No," she said in a breathy whisper. "I'm so sorry."

Dani squeezed her hand.

"Why didn't you call me?"

"I didn't want to bother you, and I needed time to process."

Jayne swallowed and nodded. "When are we going back?"

"I'm going to leave tomorrow. You can come within the next week if that works? You're going to have a lot to do here the next couple of days."

Jayne nodded.

"If it's okay, I just need a moment and I'll pull myself together." She gave Jayne a hug and resumed staring at the table.

Jayne gave Billy a concerned look and nodded to the stairs.

Upstairs, she sat on her bed and placed her face in her hands.

"How you doing, Bunny? I'm sorry."

"It's okay," she said. "It's just so surreal. I knew she was sick, but didn't expect her to pass so close to Dad. I'll have to go back with Mom, and that'll give me time to get my stuff from my apartment. Oh gosh . . ." She pitched herself back onto the bed. "I forgot about my apartment with Blake. I wonder if he's thrown all my stuff out yet. I should call him. I can't imagine how that's going to go." She took a deep breath, grabbed a pillow, and pretended to smother herself, groaning. When she looked back at Billy, he gave her an amused smile. "You're right, I should just do it now."

Billy shrugged.

She pulled out her phone and saw the picture of them from Key West. "Right, best change that too." She picked a generic picture of a flower she'd found in the garden of the Carter house and changed it to her screensaver before maneuvering her way to her contacts and dialing Blake. He picked up on the first ring.

"What is it?" he demanded sharply.

Jayne stood up. "Oh, nice to hear from you too. Anyway, I'm coming back soon to get my stuff. Can you try not to throw it all away?"

"Everything is already boxed up by the front door. You have a key; you can come whenever." There was a short silence on his end. "When are you coming?" he demanded.

"I don't know. Grandma Reina is worse, so I'll be there in a few days. Maybe Monday if I can swing it. I'll let you know." Billy eyes darted back and forth as Jayne paced the length of the bedroom, one hand habitually playing with the necklace.

"Sorry to hear that," he said sincerely. "As long as you get everything out sometime in the next couple weeks." With that he hung up.

Jayne looked at the phone screen to see if the call really was ended and tossed it onto her bed.

"That sounded pleasant," Billy said.

"Yeah." Jayne deflated. "You want to hear what we've got going on at the shop?" She told him about Frankie, the mural, and the broken windows. Then she told him about Frederick Manns and that she was going to be staying now.

"Sounds like you've got it handled, Bunny." She nodded. "When is Luke going to come around?"

Jayne shrugged, looked at her watch, and got up. "I need a coffee and from the looks of it, so does Mom. I have to try to get back to the shop if I can. It's going to be a long day."

A few minutes later, Jayne had finished brewing the coffee. Dani wrapped her hands around the warm cup.

"What's going on?"

"Do you want to tell me?" Jayne asked, looking at her, pleading with her eyes. She knew her mom would be resistant to talk about it, but instead Dani sat back and gave her a look of confusion. "About Grandma."

Dani's face softened and her eyes fell. She scratched the back of her neck and rubbed her cheek. "Grandma took a turn for the worse last night. Anthony thought that she would recover, but he got a call this morning from her nurse." She placed the coffee mug back on the table.

"What happened? She was stable when you left." Jayne propped her face up with her arm on the table, squishing her cheek up.

"I don't know," Dani said, shaking her head, trying to prevent the tears from flowing. "I don't know. Maybe she was waiting for me to leave. You know, people say that . . . that when people are dying, they wait until you've left, like they're trying to be polite or something; like they're doing something they shouldn't." A few tears dripped down Dani's cheeks. She scrunched her eyes and pressed her lips firm.

"I'm sorry, Mom." Jayne came around the table and gave her a hug.

Dani squeezed her and sniffled. Jayne let go and looked at her mom; she took in the laugh lines, now stretched in a different direction as the sadness on her face pulled at them. She grabbed her again, giving her a tight squeeze before letting go.

Dani placed her palm down on the table and found a notch with her finger again. She snorted, followed by a sniff.

"What?" Jayne asked.

"This little mark here." She showed Jayne. It was worn down with time and wear but still there. "Your dad and grandfather made this table. You put that little mark in there, by accident. It was my fault for not watching you." Dani rubbed the dent, the edges round and smooth. "I was sitting right there when I found out about your dad and Melody." She nodded to the chair at the head of the table. "I remember talking about this mark. I didn't know what to think when I heard that horrible news. And here it is again, the little ominous dent."

"I did this," Jayne repeated, reaching for the mark with her finger. It wasn't a question of confirmation, but a statement. Dani nodded. "With a kitchen knife. I think I remember."

"That's right."

"I remember. Dad was upset."

"He was. But not at you, he was mad at me for not watching you."

"It wasn't your fault." Jayne shook her head. "I remember waiting for you to look away." Neither of them spoke for a moment, watching the afternoon light refracting through the trees outside, creating a dancing pattern across the table. "I'm going to come back with you," Jayne finally said. "I need to get my stuff from my apartment."

"Okay, darling," Dani said before yawning.

Jayne told her about Frederick and Dani smiled. She was tired and mentally exhausted, but interested in hearing. She interrupted Jayne, "Where'd you get that necklace by the way?"

"Well, technically I stole this from the Carter house." She laughed and held the stone. Dani's mouth opened without words to fill it. Jayne told her the story about Evelyn's mother and what it took to get the necklace out of the house.

"Really? Should I expect the police soon?"

"I don't think so," Jayne said. "I get the impression

they didn't—and still don't—know about that hidey-hole."

Dani nodded. "So, I was thinking that we should have the Martins over before I go back. That way we can put all those casseroles, Bundt cakes, and breads to good use. We could maybe even invite a few more people from the shop."

"That's a great idea," Jayne exclaimed. "When were you thinking?"

"Tomorrow? Since I'll be leaving tomorrow evening," Dani said.

"That's soon, but let me text Luke." Jayne pulled out her phone and after a brief tapping, she set the phone down on the table. Dani got up to top off her mug.

Jayne's phone vibrated soon after. "That was quick. Luke said they would love that and tomorrow works for them."

"Great," Dani said enthusiastically. "I'll go out tomorrow and get some wine and things for everyone. What would you like for dinner tonight?"

"Let's just get takeout." Jayne got up and went to the drawer where she'd seen some pamphlets for local restaurants that delivered. She shuffled through them. "Do you want pizza or Chinese? Or some Mexican place I've never heard of but claims to have the best tacos in Hill Country."

"It's hard to pass up the 'best tacos' anywhere. I say we go with that one."

"Okay, tacos it is. I'm going to change and head back to the shop to work on the mural a bit. I'll shower tonight."

"Okay, kid."

Jayne spent a couple hours at the shop, finishing the outline of the mural. Joe was already in the village with Liz and Luke, helping to hand out food and assess the damage. He'd called her and explained that it wasn't as bad as they imagined, but people would still need help. Most of the damage was just superficial and with the help of the people signed up, they could be done within a couple weeks.

At seven o'clock Jayne's stomach rumbled. She hadn't eaten since the sandwiches her mom and Ed brought. She called in an order from the Mexican place and picked up the tacos on her way home. As she drove by the hardware store, she realized that Frankie hadn't stopped by the shop like Melody said he would.

She and her mom spent the night together, cuddled up on pillows in the middle of the floor, eating tacos, painting on Jayne's spare canvases, and watching a movie. Rusty bounced from pillow to pillow, amused by the obstacle course, while Jayne looked at the chaos that was the house. It needed to be cleaned and organized before everyone came tomorrow, but in that moment, she was just happy to be where she was, with her mom.

35

JAYNE WOKE UP before the sun and Billy wasn't there. She thought that was weird, but didn't think much more of it. She wanted to tell him about a dream she'd had. Instead, she sat up, feeling more refreshed than most days. Rusty stretched, digging his little nails into her leg like an eagle grabbing its prey.

There was a list of things to do in her mind and she stretched her arms up to the ceiling, arching her back, feeling a tingle start in her low spine and spread up through her shoulder blades. *They say when your back tingles like that, someone is walking over your grave,* Jayne thought. The idea of someone stomping on the spot where her body would be buried was unnerving, but also made her think about her dad's grave in the town cemetery. *I need to visit,* she thought. That made her curious where Billy was buried. There was a small plot of graves behind their property, but as far as she knew, it belonged to the neighbors.

When she got downstairs, her mom wasn't yet awake. She started a pot of coffee, turned the small stereo in the living room on to a local radio station, and felt compelled to start cleaning. By the time Dani came downstairs, Jayne had folded and fluffed all the blankets and pillows, cleaned the kitchen, and thrown out all the expired food from the fridge and the pantry. She hadn't started on the floors yet when Dani sat at the table. Jayne poured her a cup of coffee and brought it to her.

"It looks great down here," Dani said, looking around.

"I woke up and felt motivated. I'm going to rearrange some stuff too." Jayne's arms were up to the elbows in rubber gloves and she was wiping the cabinets down with Mr. Clean.

"What are you going to do with your dad's room?"

Jayne stopped mid-scrub. She put the sponge back in the bucket of soapy water and pushed off her knee to standing. "I suppose I'll move into that room eventually. I need to clear it out and then I'll repaint it. I want to get rid of most of the furniture in here too. It's too memorable. And quite frankly, it's just old and generic."

"How much of it?" Dani asked.

"Dad's bed, the living room furniture, the TV armoire, and a lot of the kitchen stuff. But nothing that Dad made. I'll maybe have a garage sale or something."

"That sounds good, darling." Dani yawned and stared through the sliding back door, her eyes unfocused and almost in a trance.

"Did you talk to Uncle Anthony?" Jayne asked, breaking her spell.

"Yes, and there's been no change. I just can't help feeling like I should be there right now."

Jayne pulled her gloves off and wrapped her arms around Dani's neck, burying her face into her dark, curly hair, smelling the floral and citrus lotion Dani had been wearing since Jayne was little. "I'm sorry, Mama," she said. "I don't want you to think I don't care. I do. I guess I've just got so much going on, I've chosen to push it to the back of my mind, like, if I don't think about it, it's not real. I don't want to lose another family member. I just lost one and broke off an engagement in the same month. I can't let my mind go there. Especially Grandma Reina."

"It's not that, darling. I just think I should go back right away. We'll have the Martins over for dinner tonight and then I'll leave. I've booked a flight for midnight. I have a ride to Austin, so don't worry about driving me." Jayne nodded and swallowed. "You stay here though. Get the shop in order and then you can come down."

"Okay. Are you sure? I want to be there for you too."

"I'll be fine for a few days."

"Okay." Jayne hugged Dani again. "I'm going to shower and head out."

"Okay." Dani smiled, but it was easy to see it wasn't sincere.

Jayne let the shower warm while she walked into her room to get a change of clothes. She checked her phone and there was a message from Luke: "Thinking of you. We still on for dinner tonight? Need us to bring anything?"

Jayne smiled and replied: "Same. Don't worry about anything. We have casseroles coming out the wazoo. Just bring whatever you want to drink if you don't want wine. Xo."

Her heart felt warm and big, like it was taking up too much room in her chest. Her body was tingling and she was smiling. When she allowed herself to think about Luke as a boyfriend, she felt giddy, but it was immediately followed by guilt. *I shouldn't be this happy while my grandmother is dying and people are mourning.* She gathered up her clothes and rushed into the steamy bathroom.

As the hot water poured over her body, her mind wandered to the dream she had the night before, recounting every detail and feeling. It'd felt so real.

She was sitting in a rocking chair, looking out at the horizon. The sun was projecting a beautiful shade of yellow over the land in front of her. It must be fall, *she thought. The grass was yellow and she was the perfect temperature, as if her body was part of the air. Her vision focused, like a camera lens being adjusted, finding crisp edges in every detail.*

She was on the patio of the old house and she could see the creek in front of her. It looked different; there was no big house, just bumpy land patched with grass and bushes, and not all of the pecan trees had been planted yet. The rocking chair moved beside her with no one in it. She looked at the view again. So beautiful, *she thought. She wanted to get up and explore but she was stuck, as if her body weighed four hundred pounds. She needed to just stay there a few more minutes, but when she looked back at the chair, her father was sitting in it. She almost didn't recognize him without his ball cap on, but he looked good. His face was full and rosy in all the right places. He wore a plain T-shirt and jeans and his arms looked the perfect shade of oak. He turned to smile. He looked young and happy.*

"Hi, baby girl," he said.

"Daddy?" she asked. He nodded and reached for her hand. "What are you doing here?"

"I could ask you the same thing. You got here on your own. We don't have much time though."

"I miss you, Daddy."

"I miss you too, kiddo."

"I'm sorry I didn't come back sooner. I was naïve and selfish." Her eyes started to well up with tears.

"Don't you do that." He squeezed her hand. "If anyone was selfish, it was me." He looked out over the yard. "I

wasn't in a place for you to be here, around me. And look at you, look how successful in life you are, darling." Jayne couldn't speak. The tears were caught in her throat. Peter continued, "I wanted to see you because I wanted to tell you that I'm sorry. I'm sorry I wasn't there for you like I should have been and I'm sorry to your mother. I put her through more than any mother and wife should deal with. Please tell her." His eyes were pleading with her. She nodded.

"I also want you to know just how much I loved you. I don't think I expressed that . . ."

Jayne shook her head. "You did. I knew. I love you so much. I wish we had just one more visit together, Daddy."

"I know, baby. I'll try and visit when I can." He paused and looked at his watch. Jayne thought this was an odd gesture. "I'm glad you're here. I'm proud of you and I'm happy you've decided to stay. Tell Luke his grandmother says hi." He smiled and looked past her.

She turned to see what he was looking at. "Daddy, when will I – " She turned back but he was gone. Her palm was faceup but empty of his hand. "No," escaped her lips in a whisper. She stood up and paced the porch, looking for her father. She just wanted a hug. She started weeping and startled herself awake with her sobs.

The warm water started to turn cold. *I just wanted a hug,* she thought. The memory made her feel like a jar full of colored gas; empty, yet full. She knew she saw her dad — it *was* him. But he was untouchable and she didn't know when she would be able to see him again.

In her room, Billy sat in his chair. She sat on the bed, facing him, running her fingers through her hair, catching and separating pieces before it dried into the jungle of curls.

"Hi, Bunny."

"Hey, I was thinking of you. You weren't here this morning."

"You were crying. I didn't want you to wake up to me watching you."

"You won't believe the dream I had. It was incredible." She smiled so big she could feel her cheeks squishing up toward her eyes.

"Try me."

"I dreamt of my dad. He was so healthy and happy. He looked so good. We had a talk." She recounted the conversation to Billy. He listened with all his attention. "I just know it was him."

"It was," he said, sitting up taller. She looked at him and drew her eyebrows together, confused. "I call them 'visits.' I did that with my sons after my death also. They were having a very hard time. Evelyn was on her deathbed too. They started to drink more, calling in to work. Ted was on the verge of losing the shop, Gerry on the verge of a divorce. I knew there was a possibility I might not make it back here, but I had to do it. I went to each of them in their dreams. The same night too, so they would know it was real when they compared stories. We sat on the same porch as you and your father and I told them how much I loved them, and to hold on to all the good memories we had together. They had their own families to take care of and I didn't want them to miss out on a single minute."

"Did you ever visit them again?" Jayne asked, the hopefulness reaching out through her voice.

"I didn't need to. I visited them again before they passed over; I wanted them to be more comfortable. Transitioning can be a very scary process: There are so many questions." Jayne's face changed from shear happiness to a dark shade of somber. "What is it, Bunny?"

"My grandmother. She's about to pass. I just feel like I should be there. I shouldn't be here, being so happy;

I should be sad and mourning the loss of my favorite grandmother."

"You can't worry about that. Even if she was lucid and knew what was going on, dying people don't want their relatives to stop their lives to mourn them." Billy shifted in the chair. "Let me tell you story about when I died." Jayne's eyes got wide. "Oh, pardon me. Would you like to hear it?"

"Yes, I would," Jayne said, eager. She pulled herself onto the bed, knees to her chest and back against the wall.

"Well, my transition was rather sudden, and not planned. I'm sure it's not very exciting either. I died from a combination of old age and the flu. It was the fall of 1972. The leaves were finally starting to change and the weather was cooling off. I had been in town a lot at the shop, more than I normally was. I liked to be there with my son, Ted, who was running the shop at the time. We talked about upcoming projects and I just liked to watch them build since my old hands were pretty much useless with the arthritis." Instinctively, Billy examined his hands, turning them, as if looking for the deformities he spoke of. "Sometimes my grandson, Steve, would even bring your dad to the shop."

"You knew my dad?" Jayne interrupted, slightly shocked and excited.

"I knew him until he was eight years old." Billy smiled. "Your grandfather, Steve, was Gerry's son. Gerry had passed a few years earlier of lung cancer. That was incredibly hard and took a toll on Evelyn. But we all pitched in where we could to help with Steve.

"Anyway, I had been at the shop more than normal and there were a few extra cold days that fall. The kids insisted that I sit inside or put on some more layers, but I was stubborn. I was happy in my chair with my blanket. A few days later, I was bedridden with a bad case of the flu. I was eighty-two, so getting the flu was like getting a foreign disease that could kill you. It didn't help that I got a side of pneumonia. That's what got me in the end. The doctors tried antibiotics and fluids. I was hooked up to an IV bag for a week. Everyone thought I was getting better in the last two days. They allowed me to stay in my home so Evelyn could stay with me comfortably. The kids would come every day and visit. It was quite an awful experience." Billy laughed uncomfortably. "They were all miserable, crying and wishing I would get better. They thought I couldn't hear them when I was sleeping, or see their blotchy faces, puffy and streaked with tears. That's why I don't want you to feel guilty about not being with your grandmother. She doesn't need another person being sad for her." Billy waited until Jayne nodded. "One night I was lying in bed and the side lamp was on, casting a yellowish hue over the room, exaggerating shadows. Someone had left the TV on and some rerun of *Gunsmoke* was playing. Evelyn was asleep on the sofa chair beside me. Everyone had gone to sleep so I could finally get some alone time. Gerry came into the room — obviously an apparition since he had transitioned already.

"He came and sat on the edge of my bed and said, 'Hi Dad.'

" 'Hi Gerry,' I said, a little shocked.

" 'We have to go soon.' He placed his hand on mine. I asked where we were going and he said, 'To see Grandpa William and Grandma Cora. They're waiting for us.' Those were my parents. He told me that my body was too sick to keep me anymore. I took his hand and it felt as solid as if he was alive. We walked out of that room and the house together."

"Did you see your parents?"

"I did for a little while, but then just a few days after

my passing Evelyn passed also. I was there to get her and we decided to stay in our home."

"Just a few days?" Jayne was surprised.

"It's not uncommon for people to pass within days or weeks of their soul mates."

"What about Gerry?" Jayne asked.

"He's in another layer of this world with *his* wife and son."

"Can you see people — or spirits — in other 'layers'?" She made air quotes with her fingers.

"Sometimes, but not often. From what I've noticed, there has to be some kind of . . " Billy was snapping his fingers looking for the word. "Some kind of trauma or event that would lead us to each other — like a tear within the layers. That's why I saw your dad last night. When he came to you in your dream, he passed through the old house. I followed him up to your room. He disappeared and I knew he was paying you a visit. That's when I left."

"This is all so weird." Jayne covered her face with her hands.

Billy chuckled. "I agree." He leaned his head against the chair and started rocking.

Jayne grasped her necklace.

"It looks good on you," Billy said, looking at her through one eye. "The ruby looks good against your pale skin."

"You're calling *me* pale? That's the pot calling the kettle black, isn't it?" Billy laughed with her. Jayne massaged her scalp with her fingertips and shook her hair out. The curls separated, still damp at the ends. She looked in the mirror of the armoire and applied some mascara and a tinted lip-gloss. That was all she ever needed.

"Thanks, Billy," she said softly to the mirror. He

didn't have a reflection she could see, but he was still there.

"Sure," he replied.

"See you later?" He nodded and she left the room.

36

JAYNE STOPPED TO get a coffee before she went into the shop. Liz wasn't at The Café and when she asked, they said she had been in the village all morning bringing everyone coffee and food.

At the shop, some men were working on the pieces of furniture for people who may have lost theirs in any flooding. Luke was there, filling his truck with supplies to take to the village.

"How's it going down there?" Jayne asked.

"Great. Everyone is so appreciative of our help and the guys keep saying that this isn't something they would normally volunteer to do but they love it."

"That's great." Jayne smiled. "I would love to go down at some point."

"Sure. Just let me know." Luke strapped down the last of the tools. "Well, I should get going. What are you going to do here today?"

Jayne sipped her coffee and pressed her lips together. "Um, I'm going to work on the mural and see if anyone has responded to our call for volunteers."

"I took a peek earlier and I think you'll be pleasantly surprised."

"Really?" Jayne's eyebrows shot up.

He smiled and winked at her. "Well, I'm going to go."

"You keep saying that."

Luke laughed. "This time for real." He pause and licked his lips, then as if he had just made a split-second decision, he stepped forward and grabbed Jayne's forearm, pulling her in for a kiss. When he pulled away, the smile transferred from his face to hers.

She waved him off and went back inside to get her painting supplies.

She didn't see Frankie at first when she got into the office. He was coming around from the hallway and startled her.

"Sorry, I was just looking to see if anyone was here," he said. Jayne didn't say anything. She instinctively reached for the necklace. Frankie watched her hand. "I . . . um . . . I came to apologize about the shop. I know it's not an excuse, but I know my mom told you Frederick paid me to do it."

"She did."

Frankie dug into his pocket and pulled out a handful of money, half of which fell to the ground in crumpled bits that he fumbled to pick up. Jayne noticed how small and childish he looked in this moment and almost felt sorry for him. "There's not a lot left, but I want to give it to you to do whatever — for the shop or what you're doing for the people in the village."

Jayne reached out tentatively to take it. It was maybe two hundred dollars, scrunched up into three different balls. "Thank you."

"I also wanted to see if you needed any help either here or in the village. I don't have anything going on and I owe it to your dad — and you."

"Oh." Jayne was surprised and jerked as if he had just tugged her hair. "Well, yes, we can. I'm not sure how just yet, but we need as many people as we can get. Can I talk to Joe and get back to you?"

"Sure." He reached over the desk into a drawer as if he'd been in that drawer a dozen times. His breath smelled of a day's old alcohol. He grabbed the notepad and pen to jot down his number. His hand was shaking when he handed it to her. "I'm no specialist in anything, but I'm kind of a jack-of-all-trades."

"That works," Jayne said. *How peculiar this boy is. He's huge and intimidating, but when pressed, he's as soft and meek as a five-year-old.* "Thanks, Frankie."

He turned to walk out. The jingle of the bell chimed when the door opened and he paused. Jayne could feel a rush of cool air push its way through and brush past her.

"Jayne, I know you've heard things about me. I've messed up a lot and I probably won't stop, but I want you to know I did care about your dad. Despite what happened between our moms, he was the only real father figure I had. He was the only good male in my life. He played catch with me, took me to the river to fish — even bailed me out of jail *and* gave me the talking-to that my dad never did."

Jayne listened and felt a pinch of jealousy in her stomach. She reminded herself: It wasn't Frankie's fault that *her* dad played catch with him and not her, but she couldn't help but feel like he took it for granted. *He was just another man to him,* she tried to tell herself. She nodded but could see he wasn't done talking.

He let go of the door and let it close with him still inside. "Your dad was a good man and he tried to do what he could for me, but I'm pretty stubborn." He laughed and Jayne felt calmer. "He talked about you all the time too."

"He did?"

"Oh yeah. When we would be doing things, he always said he wished you were there. Especially when he'd rope me into helping pick pecans from the pecan trees, or when you would be coming to visit, he'd have me help him clean and do yard work. If anyone says anything bad about your dad, don't listen." He cleared his throat and thought about his next words. "You probably don't want to hear it, but he was good to my mom. I believe they loved each other at one point. She sure loved him. I think I did too. But he couldn't let go of what he did to your family and that wrecked their relationship." Frankie opened the door again, his tall frame filling the opening.

"Thank you, Frankie. I really appreciate that. Would you like to get coffee sometime? Nothing special, I'd just like to hear more stories of him from someone that spent so much time with him."

Frankie smiled. "Sure."

Jayne watched him leave. When the door closed, he turned to the building to see what he had done. He dropped his head, pulling his hood over his red hair before turning away. When he got into his truck, Jayne went back to the office to get her paints. It was quiet in the shop, just the random echo of a hammer and saw penetrating the silence.

While Jayne worked on the mural for a few hours, three more people came to volunteer. That made fifteen including the ones that inquired online. Joe called all of them, including Frankie, and would have a full crew by the next day.

Jayne was outside painting, working on the basic outline of the mural, when a woman said, "Making lemonade with lemons I see."

Jayne was startled and smeared the paint into a spot she shouldn't have. "Shit," Jayne muttered before she turned to see the person behind her.

Liz had come back from the village to update her on everything that was going on. She gave her some leftover food from her trip down.

"They're making real progress," Liz said. "Some of them have already put in orders for furniture. This is thanks to you, kid." Liz wrapped her in a hug. "So, dinner at your place tonight? Is about seven okay? I want to make sure the boys have time to get back from the village."

"That's great. I'm looking forward to it."

"Me too. The mural looks amazing, Jayne. I can't believe how far you've gotten already."

They stood, admiring the colors coming together on the front of the brick. "Me too, actually. It's like it's been in my mind, just waiting to come out."

"I can't wait to see when it's finished. You should take a break though. Go home, relax, and we'll see you soon."

"Just a little bit longer. It's only three o'clock; I have plenty of time."

"Okay, kid. We'll see you soon."

Jayne spent the next two hours painting while she met the window repairmen. Once they finished around five thirty, she headed home. She wouldn't be able to shower again, but she could help her mom finish getting everything ready.

Dani had spent the rest of the day tidying the house. She'd taken down old photos that had been up since before Jayne was born, but quickly put them back when she saw how faded the wallpaper was around them. She helped box up some smaller items and take them to the shed for the garage sale and dusted off the bigger items to let Jayne decide what to do with them.

Dani was sitting on the porch when Jayne got home. "How are you doing, Mom?"

"Oh, good." Dani recounted the day with her. "I pulled everything out of the freezer, so we're ready to go."

"Thank you." Jayne smiled at her. Jayne told her about Frankie and what Liz said. Dani gave Jayne's leg a squeeze. "I'm going to go get changed."

"Okay, kid."

37

LUKE RANG THE doorbell while his parents were at the car bickering about Joe's driving.

"Hi," Jayne said, smiling so big it made her lips felt tight.

"Hi." He hesitated then leaned in quickly to give her a peck on the cheek. "How are you?"

"I'm good. You?"

"I'm—"

"He's happy to be here," Liz interjected, pushing her way through. "How are you my dear?" She wrapped an arm around Jayne's neck while Joe made his way up the porch stairs.

"Hey kid," he said. "It looks different in here."

"Yeah, Mom did some cleaning today."

"That's it; it's clean." Joe laughed. The others smiled, waiting in the living room.

"It smells delicious in here," Liz said, loud enough for Dani to hear.

"Mom's in the kitchen putting together a cheese plate, come on in."

"Cheese plate? Y'all got fancy in North Carolina. I like cheese though." Joe rubbed his protruding belly.

"Just some summer sausage and cheddar cheese," Dani said, putting the plate on the table. She reached to embrace Liz. "What can I get y'all to drink?"

Luke lifted up a small cooler bag. "We brought some beer and wine coolers."

Luke and Jayne took to the kitchen while the other adults reminisced. They removed foil from all the casseroles, enchiladas, and pies that had been brought over the past couple weeks. Luke insisted on writing down the names of the people who had given them the meals so they could remember who to thank for what.

After everything was put in the oven and the timers were set, Luke poured Jayne a glass of wine, he grabbed a beer, and they went out on the front porch. The sun was just about set, low in the sky like an orange on the countertop. Ed Stalton arrived and as surprised as Jayne and Luke were, she showed him inside before returning to her spot beside Luke.

"Can we go to the old house?" Luke asked.

"Sure," Jayne said tentatively. "I haven't been over there since the storm actually. It might be good to have you with me." She left her glass on the railing and headed to the stairs leading off the porch. "What kind of shoes are you wearing?" she added urgently.

Luke laughed and lifted up a foot as if to show her. "I don't know, runners?"

"Yes, but do you care if they get dirty or dusty?"

He laughed again. "No, why?"

"No reason."

They walked around the house from the front. The bridge was still intact, just waterlogged. It would dry out and Jayne would check it again then. They marched through the grass, still short from when Luke had cut it, but the rain had accelerated the growth and the weeds surpassed everything else. The light was just starting to make its way down, making it easy to see the bugs and grasshoppers jumping from weed to weed.

When they got to the house, the rockers were toppled over. Jayne righted them with one hand. Luke examined the columns holding up the porch roof, which were now keeling even farther to one side.

"Well, I'm not sure how salvageable this will be, unfortunately," he said, pushing on the column. The whole thing moved and Jayne made a small noise before jumping off the porch. "Don't worry, it's not going to topple. It will eventually though."

Jayne stepped back onto the porch. "I want to rebuild it."

"The house?"

"Yes. My grandmother is dying. I don't know if I told you that." Luke reached out a hand to her and she accepted with her free hand. "I think I'd like to rebuild it for my mom. Just a small house that she can stay in; a porch she can sit on and we can gossip, just like my grandparents."

Luke smiled at her and gave her a hug. "That sounds nice. And I'm here, whatever you need; if you need me to come back with you to North Carolina, I will." Despite the chill in the air, he was warm and comfortable. He felt like a well-worn sweatshirt on a fall day.

"Thank you. I'll need you here while I'm gone though. I'll only be a few days."

"That's what you told Blake when you came here." He laughed.

Jayne gave him a look, followed by a smile. She squeezed his hand.

Luke pulled back to look at her and her blue eyes found his. He placed a soft, warm hand on her cheek and said, "You are an amazingly strong woman, Jayne Webber. You've amazed me every day that you've been here." She smiled and he leaned in to kiss her. His lips felt full and warm on hers. They heard some hooting and hollering from the big house. Jayne was instantly embarrassed and her cheeks burned. She looked back up at Luke and he had a slight color to his tan skin also.

Luke peeked into the house. "I'd like to go in, but I'm not sure of the stability of it all." He knocked on the side of the doorframe.

"Hey, come with me a sec. I want to see if that old shed is there." She grabbed his hand and led him off the porch and around the house. More hooting ensued as they dashed out of sight, the parents probably thinking they were up to no good.

Luke cleared his throat. "You know, I never really asked how you're doing. With everything. I didn't feel like it was my place. I wanted to though."

"Oh." Jayne was surprised. "I'm good. I'm really good. Now." She smiled at him. "When I first came here, I didn't know what to expect. I've never had to deal with a death in the family until now. And I may have lost one person, but I feel like I've gained so many."

"Two," Luke corrected. Jayne looked at him, confused. "You've lost two people. Not to death, but your fiancé. He's gone too."

"Oh." She realized she hadn't really thought about Blake since he left a few days ago. "You know, now that I look back on it, I'm not sure if it wasn't for the best. I liked Blake in the beginning—of course—and then after that our relationship just progressed as it was supposed to. Almost like a business transaction. Then I met you."

"What about me?" Luke asked, without meeting her eyes.

"Don't worry about it," Jayne said, bumping his shoulder with hers. "Let's just say, it made me reevaluate a few things."

Luke tried not to smile as big as he was, but he couldn't help it. Something caught his eye in the forest and he stopped to look. "Did you see that?" They were almost at the corner with the shed.

"What?"

"I thought I saw someone in the trees."

Jayne looked up and down the tree line but didn't see anyone. "Through here," she said. She pushed her way through some branches and caught a spider's web with her arm. Their feet crunched on the leaves and fallen acorns. A few steps in and she saw it. She didn't know how she missed it in the first place. It was well-covered with bushes and branches overhead. The trees blocked out a lot of the light, which would have been useful now.

"Wow. What is this?" Luke asked, stepping toward the building.

It was an oversized shed, similar to the garage beside the house, but the bottom three feet were made and leveled by stones. The walls were made with rough logs, but put together like an intricate puzzle. The roof was made with wooden shingles but she imagined it had been covered in branches. The shed had no windows and only one door to enter. There were spots for poles that would have held up a porch roof, now long gone. He could see where it had torn off. Jayne could picture someone inside, the door open to air out the fumes from the moonshine while they listened for any unwanted visitors.

Jayne motioned for him to open the door. It was just a large piece of thick plywood with a handle. The humidity had warped and expanded it slightly. He pushed it open and the smell hit them like a brick in the face. Time had not removed the smell of alcohol, but also added moisture, mold, and the ammonia smell of rat urine.

"I can see why no one uses this," he said.

"Yes, I can see that now also," Jayne said, blocking her nose with the back of her hand.

Luke turned the flashlight on from his phone and waved it around. Thick shelves stuck out from the walls. "This must be where they stored the barrels or jugs."

"Jugs. Lots of them," a voice said. Luke and Jayne spun around. Luke shone his light through the doorway. He could see the feet that belonged to the voice, but the light from his phone continued out into the trees. He dropped the light to the floor and saw a boy standing in the doorway. He was wearing pants with stirrups, a cream-colored cotton shirt, and a newsboy cap. Jayne touched his arm and he jumped.

"Billy," Jayne said as an acknowledgement but also a question. Luke nodded. "You see him?" she asked and he nodded again.

"He sees me." Billy smiled. "He's looking right at me."

Luke's voice was caught in his chest. He nodded again and tried unsuccessfully to clear his throat. It sounded like a frog or wounded dolphin.

"It's okay. Follow me. I want to tell you a story."

Jayne took Luke's hand in hers and he squeezed hard enough to make Jayne look at him and squeeze back. They started back to the old house, which meant Luke had about eight minutes to get used to the idea he was talking with a dead person. The hair on his arms was standing on end and he felt waves of electricity pulsing over his body. His heart was thumping like a jackhammer and he willed it to slow.

Jayne and Luke sat on the steps leading up to the old house.

Billy sat cross-legged at the edge of the porch. He looked at Luke, who was looking at him, still shocked. Without pause, he began, "Your great-great-granddad worked for my father in that shed." Luke raised his eyebrows. "Yup. He was a good worker too. He also worked for Jayne's . . ." He counted in his head. "Third great-grandfather — my wife's father, at the Carter house."

Luke took in a breath and released it in the form of, "Really?"

Billy nodded. "He made okay money working for the Carters. He was their landscaper and indentured servant. He didn't speak much English because he had just come from Mexico to pick cotton. Over time he learned more and became very fluent. His name was Rafael Martin. He was Dad's best whiskey runner and worked for my dad many years, until prohibition was repealed.

"Certain nights he would come out here, through a back road — long gone now. Lights turned off, he would either be bringing a batch from Glen Rose, or waiting on a fill-up to take to a mutual pickup spot. It was very risky. He had a wife and child at home. We would see him drive up here" — Billy pointed in the direction the car would have come along the house — "and he'd park at the edge of the trees. Once on the property, no one could see him. That's why Dad planted all these trees."

Now that Jayne thought of it, she realized they were the only house on the road with trees surrounding their land. The rest of the houses sat on open land with a smattering of trees throughout.

"He was about my age," Billy said. "But we never spoke. Dad tried to keep the whiskey business separate from us, like a second family. So, I don't know much. He was a very hard worker though, always trying to help. He took good care of his family and was a loving

329

father. From what I know, he was about eighteen when he travelled here from Mexico. He picked cotton on an estate for a while before finding himself at the Carter's house helping with the landscaping, caring for the estate, and then eventually in the whiskey business with my father.

"Mr. Carter didn't know about this second endeavor, otherwise he probably would have been fired — or worse — and father never would have risked that either. My father tried to take care of him and his family as best he could, but once prohibition ended I never ran into him again. Obviously he stayed here," Billy said, motioning to Luke.

Jayne's name was called from the big house. "The food," she exclaimed. She looked at her watch and thirty-five minutes had passed since they left.

They both headed toward the big house. Luke looked back at Billy. "Thank you," he said.

Billy nodded his head and sat in the empty chair.

The sun had set and the chill spread through the air. Dani set the table, the smorgasbord of meals placed throughout. Jayne took a deep breath in, smelling the homey scent of everything from potatoes to piecrusts to cheese. Everyone took a seat, and Jayne took Peter's chair at the head of the table.

No one said anything for a moment as they took in all the dishes on the table.

"Well," Liz said. "If there's one thing you can say about Peter, he was loved. Just look at all these dishes."

Joe chuckled through his nose, thinking of his old friend. "And he loved you, kid," he said, looking at Jayne.

Her eyes welled up and she nodded. A single tear fell and she wiped it with her fingertips. When her hand returned to her lap, Luke reached under the table and took it in his.

"We're glad you're back, Jayne," Liz said. "Will you stay too, Dani?"

"I think I'll be back soon enough," she said, forcing a smile and digging into the casserole in front of her.

"Oh, I almost forgot," Liz said, getting up and going to her purse. "Your dad had started this before he passed. He said he wanted you to have it. He had some dream about old family members and I guess he started on this the next day." Liz shrugged. "Looks like a family tree."

Jayne took it from her and it *was* a family tree. It was a beautiful pecan tree engraved on a pecan-wood cookie. The edges were ornate and smooth. It looked like it had been waxed, but not varnished because it wasn't yet finished. When she looked at the top of the tree, it started with William Sr., and below it was William Jr. *Billy*, Jayne thought. It continued down until it got to her dad and Dani. Below them was Jayne's name and two lines — one to the left, leading to a blank spot, and another straight down for any future children.

"It was meant to be a wedding gift," Joe said, taking a bite of cheesy broccoli.

Jayne tried to say thank you, but instead, raised a napkin to her face and started crying.

"Oh, honey." Dani dropped her fork and got up to give her a hug. "It's beautiful. Thank you, Liz and Joe."

Jayne nodded. "Thank you," she whispered.

"Sure, honey," Liz said, smiling. "He loves you."

38

TWO WEEKS LATER, Jayne was sitting on the back porch. Her thoughts were with Dani, still in North Carolina. She mindlessly pulled on pieces of Rusty's hair, the wiry pieces slipping through her fingers. He would roll from side to side, loving every minute of it. She looked out on the old house, planning the new layout in her mind.

Her phone rang.

"Hey, beautiful. I got word from Dad: We're done."

"You're kidding? That's fantastic! Are the guys packing up the village today?"

"Yup, we'll be back in the office by ten a.m."

"That's the best news I've received all week."

"That's not even why I called. Some small paper from Austin wants to come here and do a piece on the shop, your mural, and how the town helped the village bounce back from this."

"You're joking?"

"I'm not." Luke could barely contain a laugh.

"That's incredible. I can't believe it."

"Believe it. Will you be at the shop soon?"

Jayne looked at her watch: seven a.m. "Yes, I'll be there in about an hour and a half."

"Perfect. I'll have a coffee for you."

"You're amazing. I love you." Jayne said it before the connection between her brain and her mouth stopped her.

She opened her mouth to protest then Luke laughed and said softly, "I love you too. See you soon."

Jayne was overwhelmed with joy. She had to get to the shop and congratulate all the guys. She was bringing three more paintings with her to hang on their new "Featured Artist" wall. Right now, it was just her paintings, but she had a few local artists she was vetting, including a sculptor and a metalworker.

Rusty followed her upstairs. The door to her father's room was open and she was startled. Rusty ran in and she followed. The light was beaming through the windows, lighting the room better than any electricity. She stood in the doorway, taking in the scent again, this time it had faded into the rest of the house.

"I guess starting in the closet would be the most logical place," she said to Rusty.

Jayne's phone rang. It was Dani. Jayne filled her in on the good news and Dani congratulated her. "What are you up to now?"

The smell of sun evaporating the days of rain from the ground flowed through the open windows and Jayne immediately felt better with the fresh air. "Just about to go through a bit of Dad's closet," she said, taking a big gulp of air. She turned on the old radio on the desk. The tape deck clicked and reeled and "When I See You Smile" by Bad English started to play.

"Sometimes I wanna give up, I wanna give in, I wanna quit the fight. And then I see you, baby, And everything's all right. Everything's all right. When I see you smile, I can face the world, oh oh . . ."

Both of them started laughing.

"What are *you* laughing at?" Jayne asked.

"You go first."

"Dad used to sing that to me. He would pick me up and spin me around the room, like we were dancing in a ballroom. Even when I was older and I would come visit, he would put it on and belt it out like he was one of the band members. I was forced to listen to it over and over." Jayne smiled at the memory.

"He used to sing that to me when I was mad at him." Dani laughed harder. "One time, I was mad at him — real mad. I don't remember what for, probably something stupid. He went and got a brown wig I used for a Halloween costume one year and cut up the front, left the back long and teased up the sides like a mullet. He put in the tape and came up the stairs, wearing the wig and singing. I tried not to smile, but ended up in tears, laughing so hard I was out of breath."

Jayne was laughing too. "He was a good singer."

"He was. He always got the biggest round of applause at the pub on karaoke night."

"Well he didn't pass it down."

Dani chuckled. She filled Jayne in on how everyone was doing after the funeral. Jayne helped get all the arrangements in order and was able to say goodbye to her grandmother, but she chose to come back before her grandmother passed. Dani and Jayne said their goodbyes and Jayne started pulling the shirts off the hangers, folding them and placing them in a pile to be boxed up for the garage sale. Rusty jumped on top and started to dig himself a new bed. Jayne tried to shoo him away but instead ended up with Rusty in her arms cuddling. When Billy walked in, Rusty barked once and snuggled closer to Jayne.

"He seems to have gotten used to you a little bit more," Jayne said, patting Rusty on the head.

Billy shrugged. "You sure you want to get rid of all that?" he said, nodding to the boxes around Jayne.

"I don't know what else I would do with them. Except this one," she said, pulling a red-and-green flannel off the hanger. It was faded and frayed on all the edges. She put it on over her long-sleeve T-shirt and rolled up the sleeves. "I always liked this one best of all his flannels." She lifted the collar to her nose and inhaled. "Just like I remember."

She continued adding shirts and pants to the pile as she made her way around the closet. There was a shoebox on the floor, big enough to hold a pair of rain boots. She opened it up and laughed when she saw it was filled with sports caps. "This one reminds me of when I was little." It was a black hat with a red-and-blue logo of a bull on the front. It was so worn, the fabric on the bill was frayed and peeling back.

Billy came over and looked at it. He pointed at another. "This one reminds me of when you were born."

Jayne picked it up. It was a blue hat, half-red in the front with "Oilers" written across it. A small stitched oil rig sat in the bottom corner. The red was so worn that it looked pink, and the blue was a light shade of baby blue.

"He was wearing that when you were born and he kept bending and unbending the brim. He was so nervous. I didn't realize he kept all of these."

"I don't think I'll give these away just yet." Jayne tucked the box back into the closet.

It didn't take her long to get through the closet and through the desk, which was mostly just papers and paperclips. The dresser drawers were half-empty, but contained some underwear and socks that got thrown out. By the time she finished in the room, it was almost eight thirty.

"I suppose I should start getting ready to get to the shop." Jayne got up and dusted off her butt. She had pretty much emptied out the closet, mind some shoes she would donate and other boxes of knickknacks she would have to go through. She pulled one off the shelf to see what was inside. It sounded like it was full of Legos. When she opened it up, it had a mess of dolls, a sand pendant she made Peter buy her from the Houston rodeo one year, some other plastic jewelry she had gotten from dentists, and vending machine toys. "Holy crap," she whispered. She had no idea her dad kept all these trinkets. She placed the box back on the shelf and couldn't help herself from grabbing another. Billy looked in anxiously. This one had things from her preteens when she'd come to visit: a sock, a plastic necklace her junior boyfriend gave her that she forgot about, and a key chain. She picked up a key chain; she had given it to her dad for Father's Day. It had a circular leather piece for the back and a resin-cast pendant floating on top. "Number 1 Dad," it said. She remembered she had picked it out at a grocery store before she flew to Texas. *It looks barely used,* she thought. She forced her mind back to the time she had given it to him.

She'd come to see her dad for her thirteenth birthday. It was a hot and muggy day in August and her dad was on the porch in the back. She grabbed a cold Coke from the fridge — he always stocked up when she came to visit. She hurried out to sit beside him and he put his arm around her, his right hand wrapped around a cold beer. She leaned in to him and he kissed her on the top of her head.

"I missed Father's Day last month," she said.

"That's okay, kid." He patted her arm.

"But I got you something."

"You did?" Peter said, leaning back to look at her, impressed.

She reached into the pocket of her shorts and pulled out the key chain. She handed it to him and turned to see the look on his face.

He slipped the key ring over his finger so the pendant sat in his palm. He studied it, tiny adjustments to his face before he said, "Thanks, kid. I love it," and gave her a hug.

Only looking back now did she realize what those tiny adjustments to his face actually were: It was an overlapping wave of happiness, which, after a brief thought, changed to disappointment, sadness, and then a façade of happiness.

Why was he sad? she wondered. *Was it the gift? No.* Her heart wrenched. *He didn't believe he was the number one dad.* She clutched the key ring. It had been used for a short time. *He tried and couldn't do it,* she thought. She wanted so badly to tell him he was enough and she didn't need anything else from him. But somewhere, inside, she knew with her whole being that he knew. Billy watched her face mold into different emotions. He didn't say anything.

She squeezed the key chain and put it into her pocket before returning the rest of the box to the shelf.

Jayne picked up Rusty and headed to her room to get changed. She couldn't wait to get to the shop.

Epilogue

Three years later

JAYNE GRABBED TWO lemonades and a small cup of water and went outside. She walked down the deck to Luke playing with their son in the baby pool. She folded herself into one of the Adirondack chairs Luke had made and watched him, bent over, examining something with their son. He whispered something into the toddler's ear. The little boy giggled and stood up, looking at Jayne with a face that would give away any poker hand.

"Mama, look," he said, walking toward her with his hands cupped.

"What is it, baby?" She looked at Luke's face and said, "If that's a spider, I swear to god —"

"Not spider," her son said, and released his possession onto her leg. It was a tiny frog. "Mama, frog." The little frog jumped off and was gone before they could see where. "Oh! Oh!" the little boy screeched and chased after it.

Jayne laughed. "Yes, yes it was." She brushed the leftover grass from her leg.

Luke got up and kissed her. "Your mom is on her way over. I think those pecan trees back there have taken really well."

Jayne shaded her eyes and could see her mom making her way over the bridge from the new house built where the old house had once stood. Luke and Joe had rebuilt the house almost exactly as it was a hundred years ago with added necessities like air-conditioning and more efficient plumbing. After they'd finished that, they did some minor work to the big house: the floors, painting, and small repairs. Jayne decided to plant three pecan trees in memory of her dad and grandfathers, which also conveniently provided some shade for the house.

"How's my little Willy?" Dani asked, messing the child's blonde hair.

"Gama," he said, reaching up for her. Dani assessed his level of wetness. She took a towel from the chair, wrapped it around him, and scooped him up.

"How are you, darling?"

"I'm good," Jayne said, shading her eyes to look up at her.

"How are the twins?"

Jayne placed a hand on her small but rounded belly. "They're growing." She reached out a hand to Luke and he helped her out of the chair. "Let me get you some lemonade. I just made it," Jayne said, walking toward the house.

"I'm perfectly capable," Dani said.

"I know, it's too hot out here for me though."

They walked toward the house, Luke's hand not leaving Jayne's lower back. Dani following behind, popping Willy on the nose, making him giggle.

"Have you and Ed talked more about moving in together? It's been almost three years since you moved back out here."

"He's mentioned it a couple times. I love him, but

I'm happy here right now, being so close to you." Dani followed through the sliding glass door. A gush of fresh air conditioning poured out like an icebox door being opened and she pulled the towel up over Willy's shoulders. "Once the twins are a bit older, I'll think about it." She smiled and Jayne nodded.

The family tree plaque sat perfectly on the wall beside the back door. Dani looked at it. "I guess you're going to have to add two more names to this," she said, tapping the spot beside little William's name.

Jayne looked at it. "I guess so." She touched where the straight lines were carved, leading up to William Jr. *I miss you, Billy,* she thought.

It had been two and a half years since she'd seen him, but she felt him every day when she looked into her son's eyes.

The End

Acknowledgements

It took four years to write The Pecan Trees. In those years I raised a baby, had another child and gained a successful career in the wine industry. It wasn't easy trying to find a balance between writing consistently and being able to keep all the other balls in the air. For that, I thank my husband, Adam for reminding me to pick them up and not forget about them.

If it weren't for my sons who brighten the magic in my imagination, the inspiration for Billy, one of my favorite characters and aspects to the whole novel, wouldn't exist. And if it weren't for my family, I wouldn't have had any interest in ancestry at all.

When you're an unpublished author with no personal writing community, it's hard to find the motivation to keep going and willpower to knock any self-doubting thoughts out of your mind. For that, I would like acknowledge the multiple podcasts (too many to name) that reminded me to keep going and not let the universe take my idea back. And to the many random people I would speak to and ask questions. Including my editor, Natalia Leigh with Enchanted Ink Publishing for not sending my manuscript back to me with a big red line across the front. Thank you.

Lastly, thank you to The Oh Hello's for providing a soundtrack to this novel. Their music was the backdrop that brought me right back in to small-town Texas with Jayne and Billy.

Kristina Moore

grew up in Canada before moving to the USA in 2010. She currently lives in Tomball, TX with her husband, two boys and two dogs. When she's not working in the wine industry, she can be found writing or spending time with her family. The Pecan Trees is her first novel.

Made in the USA
Columbia, SC
19 April 2021

36136669R00209